OBSESSION

The noise had finally died. It was midnight, the time the unit finally settled down into a semblance of quiet, though it was never really still, vibrating with the frustrations of the men imprisoned inside like a ship in heavy seas.

Briscoe's eyes were open. He sat upright on his bunk, back flat against the tile wall. Fists tight at his sides. Noise was part of the torture the prison system provided for its inmates. The unceasing sound bounced off the tile walls. amplifying the tread of boots on metal stairs and the sharp clang of barred gates that continuously opened and shut, the irritation of the television set playing full blast almost from the moment they got up to the time they were locked in for the night. Then there were the anguished cries of the psychotics and the ceaseless conversations of the schizophrenics, locked as they were within two prisons, the one outside and the one within. Only a steeled mind could survive. A mind capable of disconnecting itself from its surroundings.

Briscoe forced his thoughts to focus on the portrait he had done of Dr. Alexander. Onto it, he projected the full force of his will and the entire fabric of his desire.

To my wife, Ruth, who challenges and inspires me.

ICE-MAN

RON CUTLER

PINNACLE BOOKS
Kensington Publishing Corp.
http://www.kensingtonbooks.com

PINNACLE BOOKS are published by

Kensington Publishing Corp.
850 Third Avenue
New York, NY 10022

All Kensington Titles, Imprints, and Distributed Lines are available at special quantity discounts for bulk purchases for sales promotions, premiums, fund-raising, and educational or institutional use. Special book excerpts or customized printings can also be created to fit specific needs. For details, write or phone the office of the Kensington special sales manager: Kensington Publishing Corp., 850 Third Avenue, New York, NY 10022, attn: Special Sales Department, Phone: 1-800-221-2647.

Pinnacle and the P logo Reg. U.S. Pat. & TM Off.

First Pinnacle Books Printing: April 2004

10 9 8 7 6 5 4 3 2 1

Printed in the United States of America

PART ONE

1

It was December.

The woods were silent.

Trunks of pine and oak stood stenciled against the snow-covered hillsides, spreading their interlaced branches like a dark shawl across the bleak Pennsylvania landscape.

The land was steep and wild.

Rugged misshapen hills rose abruptly out of the narrow valleys, then fell to twisting gorges through which water sluiced in fierce torrents, channeled through granite chutes and chiseled passageways barren of habitation.

No one lived there now.

The old stone houses that had once clung to the iron-rich hillsides had crumbled long ago. Only an ancient foundry still stood in a deep hollow two miles from the county road. Iron ore had been smelted there once in the dim decades of a forgotten century. Now the structure stood vacant and abandoned.

Rows of narrow windows looked out from the red brick walls staring like socketless eyes across the rushing stream that foamed past its eroded stone foundations. The stream widened half a mile beyond into a frozen pond surrounded by a palisade of thickly growing pine.

It was where they found the woman in the ice.

* * *

Sound exploded in the winter stillness.

Three dark shapes came down the slope, zigzagging back and forth on the glistening powder. They had driven up from the nearby town and left their SUV parked along the rise where the asphalt, two-lane county road met the narrow dirt lane that twisted down to the foundry.

They were after virgin snow and the thrill of conquering new territory. They had left the familiar slopes nearer home and come to a place of danger and the unknown to snowboard down the steep hillsides.

They came over the slope balanced on their boards, bending and shifting as they went over each unknown piece of ground.

The leader wore a red woolen cap. The others followed as if it were a flaming beacon as he led them toward the ice-covered pond just glimpsed between the trees below. They raced in a line, one behind the other, scoring each rise and striking new tracks in the unblemished whiteness.

A line of trunks formed a barrier in front of them. These they skirted, following the steep descent of the ridge as it plunged toward the frozen blue water just ahead.

Reckless now and a little out of control, they followed the red-capped figure as he cut new tracks in the glaze, speeding toward the thin border of trees that shielded them from the pond.

They navigated a sharp rise as it twisted unexpectedly, sending them down through a chute of powder that broke between the narrow trunks and flushed them out onto the thin sheet of crystal covering the pond.

Spreading out, they skidded across the flat surface bent low on their boards, arms flung out like wings, imagining themselves a formation of fighter planes homing in for an attack, swooping out of the clouds onto the unsuspecting enemy squadron below.

The attack never materialized.

The boy on the leader's flank struck something, a piece of

branch perhaps locked in the frozen surface, and spun help-lessly out of control.

He cried out as his feet lost contact with the board, and then he hurled headlong with his hands reaching out and his startled face imprinted with fear.

He was in the air only an instant before his body struck the ice with a booming crack. The momentum shot him missile-like into the center of the pond as his friends turned, skid-ding away in opposite directions.

The downed boy flew onward. The gloved heel of each palm dug in like a brake on the slippery plane, but instead of stopping, his body began to spin. Spray shot back against his face, clouding his vision. His legs were spread wide as the toes of each boot fought for traction on the glassy surface. His com-panions watched as his movement halted and he came to rest in a slow-motion spiral.

He raised his head, and his vision cleared.

And there, right in front of him, was a woman's hand. It jutted above the surface, the skin blue and shimmering in the crystal light.

The fingers were curled, clutching at something unseen, expressing the torment of a final desperate agony.

Floodlights played eerily over the polished surface, sending shimmering daggers of luminescence across the black sur-face of the pond.

It was night now. The road above was jammed. The black sky was illuminated with the flashing lights of state and local police, along with an assortment of other emergency services. A bulldozer had shoveled the dirt road clear, but only a tracked vehicle could navigate the thick strata of mud that lay beneath the snow.

It had taken several hours for the small army to gather. The boys had used a cell phone to make the initial series of calls. A car had been dispatched. It took almost two hours for the two officers to arrive and make their way gingerly down the steeply dropping slope. Plunging through deep snow, they made their way to the edge of the pond where their flashlights confirmed what the boys had discovered.

Local detectives arrived within the hour. An investigating team from the Pennsylvania state police got there shortly after that. By nine-thirty, most of the fire and rescue vehicles had made their way to the ridge, and men in survival gear began assembling the necessary equipment. Cutting tools had been brought across the ice, and by midnight the work was almost complete.

Now, a crane stood on the border of the pond, its tracks slanted unevenly on the bank as the long mechanical arm maneuvered over the gleaming surface. In the center, a small knot of men in black survival gear worked patiently above the ice, silhouetted starkly against the battery of portable strobe lights. Above them, the steel jaws of the crane hung open and waiting.

The operator received the signal over his ear-mike. The small knot of men moved closer as the massive arm was lowered. The men worked quickly as the crane swung upward. Clutched in its jaws was a massive block of ice.

The block rose clear of the surface and what was inside became visible: the body of a woman, perfectly preserved in the final moment of life.

She was naked. Her skin was blue, shining with an iridescent brilliance, as if she were swimming beneath the surface of a pool. Her head had been shaved. The skin of her skull shone with reflected light.

One arm was raised, her hand piercing the block of ice. The other wrist was tied behind her, locked in place by a leather manacle. Two more manacles were fastened around her ankles, connected by a chain to the leather collar encircling her neck. Her eyes were open, staring fixedly at the men on shore.

Only when the cube of ice was near the bank could they see the markings on her skin.

Her right shoulder had been tattooed.

Dark blue ink framed the image of a small black bird, a starling.

Its wings were outstretched in an attempt at flight. But its tiny body was surrounded by the dark strands of a web, imprisoning its helpless form, and from which there was no escape.

2

Years passed from the time the woman's body was taken from the ice. The shock of its discovery had eased, replaced by other and equally chilling images delivered by the local news. The perpetrator of the crime had been arrested, tried and jailed, bringing a measure of comfort and satisfaction to the citizens of Eastern Pennsylvania. In fact, most people, if asked, would have had to scratch their heads and search for a moment before recalling the facts of the case. Then, on a chilly October night almost five years later, the discordant shriek of a pager exploded in the darkness of Holly Alexander's bedroom.

She sat up suddenly, her eyes focused on the glowing numbers of the digital clock. It was half-past one in the morning. She turned on the lamp beside her bed.

"Shit!"

She grasped the phone and brought it to her ear.

It was the on-call service. The message was brief, intoned in a flat dispassionate voice, but what it contained set her teeth on edge and her body into motion. Ten minutes later she was dressed in a gray turtleneck pullover and black slacks. She paused long enough to slip her prison ID over her head and give herself a sharp, if brief, glance in the mirror.

Holly was long boned and slender. She had an athlete's body, with narrow hips and arms that tapered to a pianist's strong, graceful fingers. She kept herself in shape with a strict regimen of speed walking and a steeply reduced intake of calories. This was a small source of pride, though, like so many women, she had a generally negative attitude toward her figure. Too much butt and not enough bust was her usual response to her reflection in the mirror. She tossed her short blond curly hair back and forth to give it some shape, concluding with a disapproving glance at her attractive features. Her face had a kind of off-center prettiness that drew a fair share of stares but had never satisfied her.

Keys in hand, she hurried down the stairs of her three-bedroom condo and flung open the door of the garage, shivering as the chill air struck her face and neck. Within minutes she had left the quiet confines of her brick-and-shingle complex and was speeding toward the turnpike, leaving visible only the twin red lights of her dark blue Volvo station wagon to mark her path in the darkness.

In truth, the phone call had not actually awakened her. Holly had been having trouble sleeping. Her younger sister, Beth, was due to arrive in less than a week after a monthlong stay in a local rehab. Beth was addicted to alcohol and had been in and out of various treatment centers for almost as long as Holly could remember. There had been other addictions as well—cocaine, heroin, and crystal meth. She had survived each encounter with Holly's help, though her thanks were grudging. Beth accepted her sister's help as if it was due her as a matter of right, but that did not prevent her from resenting her sister for providing it. They were only a few years apart, but they had never been close. Holly had been the perfect student and high-level achiever, while Beth had gone in the opposite direction. Still, Beth was virtually the only family Holly had, and after their parents' accidental deaths while the girls were still in their early teens, the sisters had remained together, bonded by blood and the painful memories of their early grief and dislocation as they were handed off to various relatives. Holly was there whenever Beth needed her, no matter what difficult or inconvenient situation her sister put her in. Was it a form of martyrdom or guilt for her own ability to successfully survive? Holly often wondered. But whatever it was, her door remained open to her sister no matter how painful that experience was bound to become.

The crime site was on the back end of a desiccated asphalt road somewhere off Route 9, riddled with potholes and slimy water-filled ditches. Holly steered carefully around the obstacles as she approached the series of flashing lights on top of the police cruisers. She gritted her teeth and braced herself for the inevitable agony to come.

The house itself was a disheveled asphalt shingled affair in desperate need of paint and tenderness. The yellow police ribbon sealing off the scene was the only bright note in the drabness of the landscape, littered as it was with the rusting hulks of ancient cars and assorted rural trash.

Holly slowed as she approached the scene. Police vehicles were scattered on either side of the house, their red lights flashing. A boxy white truck indicated that there was a forensic team on site, along with the medical examiner's familiar black van. A few neighbors stood huddled in the October chill, eyeing the police with sullen eyes.

Holly eased toward the officer whose bulk loomed up suddenly at her window. She rolled it down and held up her ID.

He scanned the plastic envelope.

Holly Alexander. Staff Psychologist. Brandywine Special Treatment Center.

"You're up at the prison, right?" he asked.

"That's right. I'm Ulman's therapist, or was."

He handed it back. "Just a moment." He stepped away as he spoke into the mike on his shoulder. A moment later, Holly was waved to a narrow parking space between two patrol cars.

Holly clipped her ID to the lapel of her dark blue peacoat,

stepped out of the car, and headed toward the open door of the house.

Her step faltered slightly as she approached the doorway, her lips tight as her eyes filled with the darkening knowledge of what awaited her inside.

The heat was stifling. The house smelled of cigarettes and stale beer and the sweet sickening odor of something else.

Blood.

The entry was decorated with a Confederate flag and the stuffed head of a fearsome gray wolf, glass eyes bulging over protruding yellow fangs. Holly quickly turned away, but the glass eyes seemed to follow her as she made her way inside.

A uniformed officer blocked her way, his eyes locking on her ID.

"Yeah?" he questioned.

"I'd like to see the investigating officer, please," Holly said in a crisp tone, as his eyes raised to take her in with an appreciative glance that traveled down along her body.

"If it's not too much trouble," she added.

He grinned and made a follow-me gesture.

They stepped into the living room and the officer moved aside, allowing her a view inside.

Ulman was sprawled on the couch in front of the TV, his face covered with a towel. His legs were spread apart lifelessly. A shotgun was propped between his thighs. His head was thrown back, and his long dank hair was spread fanlike across the cushions.

Holly felt a wave of nausea, but she dug her nails into her palms and fought it down.

"So you're the perp's shrink?" A sardonic voice intoned. She turned to face the hardened features of a detective, his badge clipped to the collar of his zippered jacket.

"I was his therapist. I just got the call. What happened?"

The detective's lips curled into a grin. "Cut up the wife, then killed himself. Seems your client didn't believe the little fellow she was carrying was of the Caucasian persuasion. So he went in for a look-see."

He half turned, offering Holly a view into the bathroom. Through the door Holly could see an ancient clawfoot tub and the woman lying inside it. Her face was uncovered, but someone had closed her eyes. Her thin blood-streaked legs hung over each side of the tub. Her toenails were painted a bright garish pink.

"Nice job. They should give you guys a Golden Globe," the detective said.

"We do our best," Holly replied. "We don't give guarantees."

"Tell that to her."

Holly turned. Facing her was a pretty two-year-old girl in the arms of a female officer. The child met Holly's eyes with a silent, uncomprehending gaze. The officer turned and the child was carried out, her eyes still locked with Holly's until the door shut behind them.

"Hey, Shepard," the detective wisecracked. "Ulman's shrink is here. Maybe you want to make an appointment."

Holly looked up, as the man he addressed turned to face her. He was about 40, she estimated, long limbed and solid, with the kind of athletic body that could effectively swing an ax or a bat. His eyes were fixed on her with the wary gaze of a veteran, but there was nothing cynical in his expression. Instead she recognized something responsive in his eyes, a look of sympathy and perhaps even of pain.

"You treated him?" he asked.

"At the Brandywine Center."

"Then you okayed his early release?"

"Actually, I vetoed it."

"You were overruled?"

"Something like that. We were overcrowded, so he got early release. I would have put a boot on Ulman's leg."

Something crossed his face, possibly a look of bemusement, but she could not really tell.

"I'm sorry. I didn't get your name."

"Holly Alexander."

"Dan Shepard. I'm in charge of the investigation. Can you give us some kind of explanation for what he did?"

"I could give you a dozen, and they'd all be wrong."

"Then what is it you people do over there?"

"We pray a lot," Holly said.

"He was a sex offender, but he never registered with us."

"I didn't think he would."

"Why did you come out? None of you guys ever did before."

"He was my patient."

He nodded, chewing on the thought.

"What's going to happen to the little girl?"

"County welfare services will take care of her."

"Sure they will," she said. "Just like they took care of her father."

Holly turned and headed for the door as Shepard looked at her. His eyes narrowed, but not with total displeasure.

3

Rain.

Incessant and demanding, it filled the roadside ditches, overflowed the gutters, and latticed the branches with a fine filigree of mist. Through them, the prison rose like a medieval fortress, bastioned by concrete towers and crenellations of curling razor wire.

Visitors always came upon it unexpectedly as the road ribboned over a hilly rise covered with aspens and maples, then dropped steeply into the narrow valley where the institution sprawled over its dozens of denuded acres, made even more oppressive by the dark hills that surrounded it.

It was to this place that the black Department of Prisons van made its way through the pounding downpour.

The van passed through the main gate, where it made an immediate right-hand turn onto a road that skirted the prison itself and continued to a small complex of buildings located just inside the outer perimeter. It was fronted with a black plastic sign framing small white letters: The Brandywine Special Treatment Center.

The van drew up to reception. Several corrections officers in yellow slickers came out to meet it as the transport officers unloaded their cargo.

It consisted of a single prisoner.

He wore handcuffs connected to a chain that was secured by a belt around his waist and continued to double leg irons hobbling his ankles.

The inmate was in his late thirties, tall and well built. His hair was jet black but twin wings of gray looped rakishly over his ears. His handsome face betrayed no emotion as the rain swept down, drenching his dark blue prison denims and plastering hair across his face. He stared straight ahead, seemingly oblivious of his new surroundings. He was immobile in his solitude, still as a statue. Indifferent and untouchable.

The officers were in no hurry as they handled the papers processing him.

The transport officer smiled as he handed over his manifest.

"You got yourselves a celebrity, gents. Inmate 29780. Alias the Ice-Man."

Two hours later the rain abated. The double lanes of traffic eased, permitting Holly to exit the horrific congestion of the turnpike, pass through the tollgate, and speed toward her destination.

It took ten minutes for her to round the narrow line of protective hills, their camelback humps shrouded in an eerie mist, and drive down into the valley where she made the first turnoff onto the service road that surrounded the prison. Facing her was the curved arm of the security sensor. Holly slipped her plastic card into the slot. She waited an instant until the gate swung open and she was passed through onto the grounds of the prison proper.

She drove along the outer ring, past the double row of gleaming razor wire that circled the perimeter, and pulled into her parking spot in back of the single story red brick structure that served the treatment center as an administration building, and which Holly and her coworkers called The Bunker.

Holly started inside carrying a briefcase and an armload of manila envelopes. She was buzzed through the double steel doors into the main vestibule, nodding a warm smile to the two officers staffing the glass-enclosed control booth.

They smiled back and opened the set of double-barred gates guarding the interior, permitting Holly to step into the passage leading inside. One of the gates slid shut behind her with a chilling clang of finality that always sent a strange shiver along her spine. The closing gate made her feel that she would be locked inside forever.

She was now within the inmate area.

A second gate clanged shut. Though she had worked at the prison for almost four years, she had never gotten used to its sound. She tried to act as if this were just another one of the series of clinics she had worked in, but the feeling was different. Alien. Accompanied by the claustrophobic sensation of being incarcerated, a feeling she had never quite gotten used to.

The interior of the building was sterile and modern. It had the feel of a way station in outer space. There were no windows. Light fixtures were set into the ceiling, spooling long ribbons of harsh fluorescents along the stark pale green corridors.

Another gate slid open and Holly passed through into reception, a wide area fitted with benches on either side where inmates waited for both psychiatric and medical services.

Eyes immediately turned toward her, fixing on the movements of her legs, seeking the contour of her body beneath her coat. They recorded the shape of her lips and the shimmer of her hair. They searched out her breasts and the narrow angle of her hips and the way the material shadowed where her legs came together.

Holly passed through this gauntlet each morning. She did not hurry, nor did she increase her pace. Her eyes were level, refusing to meet the gaze of the inmates staring at her. Her face betrayed no emotion.

She had almost reached her division when a door opened and an inmate stepped out, blocking her way. He was in his mid-twenties, with close-cropped hair and narrow lips set in a bland face. His glazed eyes fixed on her magnetically, as his mouth opened in a lascivious grin.

"Love the way you look, doc," he uttered softly. "You are one foxy bitch."

"And you are inappropriate. Please get out of my way."

He stepped closer, his eyes filling with a plea as his voice dropped to a whisper.

"I want to lap your pussy, doc. I want to suck up all the juices in your luscious cunt."

"Move, Kevin," she said sharply. "Before I have to report you."

"You ain't wearing nothing underneath, are you, doc?" he asked, eyeing her hungrily.

"Just the usual," she said, keeping her eyes level with his. "Two layers of chain mail and a chastity belt. The key is in my safety deposit box."

"Fuck, doc. That's bullshit."

"That's reality, Kevin. And you better start facing it. Now, move!"

His eyes met hers in a small show of defiance, then wavered and fell. His face turned away as he stepped aside. A nurse in a flowered uniform stepped out of the door behind him.

"Kevin having some problems with his meds this morning, Ann?"

"You noticed?" The nurse grinned knowingly as she drew Kevin out of the way.

"See you in my dreams, doc," he whispered as she started past. "I'll keep it hard for you."

Holly continued toward the door at the end of the hall. She opened it and stepped inside.

Clara Bennet, the department secretary, looked up as she entered. Clara was in her midfifties. She wore horn-rimmed glasses and was smartly dressed, as usual, in a light blue sweater outfit that accented her slender figure. Her keen eyes missed little and remembered much.

"I know, I know," Holly said as she hurried past Clara's desk into her office. "The rain. The traffic was miserable."

"Better hustle You've got Pierson's P-G at nine-thirty. And the staff meeting's been moved up to ten. Oh. And Ted wants you to write up a report on the Ulman killing. I assume you heard."

Holly turned, opened her briefcase and handed Clara three neatly typed pages. "I was there last night."

"You were there?"

"You don't want to know," Holly said.

She started into her office, then paused to face the older woman. "By the way, did Beth's rehab call?"

Clara made a face. It was the grimace she always made whenever Holly mentioned her younger sister.

"Problem?"

"I hope not," Holly answered. "I wanted to pick her up. She's going to stay with me for a while."

"Here we go again."

"She's all the family I've got, Clara."

The older woman looked at her with admonishing eyes. "Sure. Only how many times have you bailed her out?"

"She needs someone."

"Sure. But why you all the time?"

"She's my only sister."

"She's also an addict."

"She's an alcoholic."

"Come on, Holly. Alcoholism is an addiction. And how many alkies have you worked with? It's a dead end. You've got to let them crash and burn before they'll even think of recognizing the problem, let alone stop drinking."

"She's the only family I've got, Clara," Holly said again.

"I know. But you can't live her life for her. I'm your friend, Holly. And I'm telling you as a friend. It's time to cut the cord."

Holly bit back a response, turned, and headed inside. She paused at her desk and allowed the rising emotion to settle. She had no reason to blame Clara for what she had just expressed. She knew it was said in her best interest.

Clara was more than a coworker. She was also Holly's sole ally. Clara's political contacts not only guaranteed Holly's job, but gave Holly more influence than her position normally warranted. From the beginning, Clara had been both friend and mentor to Holly. The two women had traded confidences, but there were certain painful, deeply hidden things Holly had never told her about her relationship with Beth.

And perhaps never would.

Briscoe stood naked in the center of the gleaming white room, his hands at his sides. His toes touched the red marker painted on the floor.

The large chamber was unheated. He had been standing alone on the freezing tiles for almost an hour. He was used to the usual forms of sadism prisons generally offered. This one would be no different. He would give them no satisfaction. His face remained composed and impassive. His eyes were fixed somewhere distant. They would discover that he could wait far longer than they could imagine. He possessed the patience of a hunter awaiting his prey.

Officers observed him from the glass-walled control room, watching to see that he had not moved or shifted position. Finally, the door opened, and two officers stepped inside.

Briscoe did not react as they took up positions behind him. He knew what to expect. One pulled on a pair of latex gloves.

"On the wall," came the command.

Briscoe leaned forward, placing his palms against the cold tiles of the wall in front of him.

"Spread."

He shifted his legs as the officer with the gloves stepped forward, a malicious grin on his florid face. The other officer proffered a small tube of lubricant, but the first officer shook his head.

"So, how's it feel to be famous?" he asked as he jammed his finger into the prisoner's flesh.

Briscoe's body tightened as the first shock of pain speared through him, but he betrayed no outward emotion. His eyes were unflinching. His face was a frozen mask. He had known pain far greater than this . . .

He was a boy again, cowering inside the terrifying darkness of the hayloft, crouched in a corner, afraid to breathe, afraid his movements would alert the old man rummaging in the barn below. He heard his grandfather cursing under his breath. A minute earlier he had been calling for him. Shouting his name. But the boy had been quick and slipped away before the older man could locate him.

The boy gripped the board in front of him, picturing the crazed violence in the old man's eyes. He squeezed his eyes shut. Praying he would not come up, not find him this time. Even as he knew it was futile, even as he knew that the old man would eventually discover where he was.

Terror froze in his chest as he heard the heavy boot on the step of the ladder. His heart was pounding. The sound filled the boy's ears and throbbed within the rotting shell of the old structure.

Step by step, he heard the old man ascending the creaking ladder. He prayed that it would break, that the old man would fall to his death on the hard ground below. But that did not happen. The ladder held. He could hear his grandfather's wheezing breathing as he clambered up the final step.

"You little bitch. I'll find you."

The boy was shaking now. Huddled deeper in the corner. His bowels loosened as he anticipated what was to come. The boots turned toward him. Coming closer. He could smell the stale odor of the old man's coveralls. The stink of pig shit and urine on his shoes.

"Little bastard!" the cracked voice cried. The old man's hand thrust through the darkness and his hand grabbed the

*nape of the boy's neck, drawing him up, pressing him tight
against his wiry frame. His hot breath seared the boy's cheek.*

"You can hide. But I'll always find you."

*The old man dragged him out of his hiding place and thrust
him down against the dirty straw. He heard muffled movements
as the old man unfastened his belt.*

"Wet the bed again, you little bastard. I'll fix you."

*He reached under the boy, unbuttoning his jeans and
drawing them down to expose the boy's lean white thighs.*

*The old man leaned forward and his weight pressed down
heavily on the boy's young body. His breath was sour, hot,
and thick. The boy clenched his fists, squeezing his eyes shut
as the old man moved against him. He felt the old man's hardness pressing against the cleft of his buttocks, the long thick
club of turgid flesh that would rend him like a weapon. His
limbs went limp, as he opened himself to the pressure, praying that this time there would be no pain.*

*He thought of the little starlings he had found in the nest
under the eaves that morning. He hated their smallness and
their helplessness. He had placed them in an old hairnet of
his grandmother's so he could watch them while they struggled, while he squeezed the netting tighter and tighter around
their small, almost featherless bodies, squeezed until there
was no longer any movement, just the final twitching of their
tiny wings.*

4

The staff conference room was crowded. Six therapists sat around the long table, along with Holly and Ted Avery, her boss.

Avery was tall, balding, and in his mid-forties. He was a rumpled figure with a long, mournful face and clear-rimmed glasses through which he squinted at each person who spoke as if seeing them for the first time.

"And now the bad news," he intoned, after the rest of the agenda was finally exhausted.

Holly was exhausted too. Besides having stayed up half the night writing up the Ulman report which Ted had insisted on reading to the group, the previous hour and a half had been spent going through each of the six therapists' case loads, a laborious process Holly had little patience for. The prognosis for sex offenders was bad enough without having to recount the unit's entire litany of failure.

Not that Holly was pessimistic. Quite the opposite. She believed the various therapies and programs they were experimenting with might actually work. The problem was that she was the only one of her colleagues who did.

Holly had little patience for their cynicism. It was the reason everyone sighed and fidgeted whenever she spoke. Her ardor sometimes wore them out. Her passion was something none of them could match, and because of it, she became the butt of jokes and wisecracks.

Not that Holly was humorless. She had an excellent sense of humor, but not when it came to the impending release of rapists and child molesters who might be sent back into the community. What Ted was now recounting caused her to feel even more on edge.

"It looks very much like next year's budget will be cut another ten percent," Ted said.

There was a general groan.

"So tighten your belts, or get over to Kinko's and start photocopying your résumés." He concluded with a smile and the words that signaled the end of each meeting. "Be happy in your work."

Chairs were scraped back. Cigarettes were lit to the accompaniment of yawns and the embittered laughter that comes from sour jokes. The meeting broke up quickly as each therapist headed off to his or her separate schedule. Only Holly remained seated, her eyes burning as she watched Ted assemble his notes into a worn leather binder.

"So, we just lie down and let those assholes in Harrisburg roll right over us?" she said.

Ted looked at her and smiled his usual condescending smile. "Nice outfit, Holly."

"Why don't you talk about my tits, Ted? Or my ass, so I can really get a lawsuit going."

Ted stared at her, unsure if she was serious or not. "I'd love to. Shut the door."

Holly jumped to her feet, her jaw set. "This is bullshit, and you know it."

"We're lucky it's only ten percent." Ted said wearily. "These are sex offenders, Holly. Not members of the Olympic team."

"Maybe we should send them a thank-you card. How the hell are we going to run this place on more cuts?"

Ted smiled a little vicious smile. "Like we always do. Improvise."

In a moment he was through the door, striding down the corridor toward his office. Holly was ready and scooted after him. She stood a head shorter but was just as quick on her feet—a bulldog in pursuit of a tractor.

"You're not going to fight this, are you, Ted?" she barked at his ear.

"Fight? Christ, Holly. We're lucky to have this program in the first place. Most legislators hear the words sex offender and vote for another lethal injection."

"They have to know we're showing results."

"Like Ulman. What kind of result was that?"

"He killed his wife, not a new victim. He was out almost fourteen months and he didn't repeat."

"Give me a break, Holly. Show them something they can believe."

Holly whipped out a yellow printout and flung it in front of his eyes. "Show them Pierson's P-G. He's making fantastic progress."

Ted stopped and flung away the offensive piece of paper. "Pierson? We're talking about a child molester."

"Attempted. He never carried it out. He never hurt anyone. Any molesting he did was strictly over the Internet."

"Do me a favor, Holly. Try not to get any more over-involved than you already are, okay? Pierson's going nowhere."

"He's proving that what we're doing here actually works." She waved the printout in front of him. "Will you at least look at it?"

"Whether he acted out or not, as far as the system is concerned, Pierson is a sex offender. We don't cure sex offenders. We warehouse them until the state sees fit to release them."

"Knowing they'll offend again. And again. And again. Until somebody has the balls to set up a program like this one that will intervene to break the cycle."

"So far we haven't proven that we can do it."

"Then why do you have me giving him therapy eight times a week?"

Ted looked at her. "Because it's your job."

"Fuck you," she said, her eyes flaming.

"Holly. When are you going to learn that you're not personally responsible for every inmate in here?"

She leaned into his face. "When you tell me who the hell is."

She turned away sharply, but his voice stopped her movement.

"Just one minute!"

Holly spun around and waited.

"I'm giving you the Briscoe file."

Holly glared at him. "What the hell is the Briscoe file?"

"The Ice-Man. Remember?"

She looked at him, still uncomprehending.

"About five years ago, remember? A young woman found in a block of ice. Briscoe claimed it was consensual sex that got out of hand. The jury decided otherwise. They gave him seven to fourteen on Murder One. He's up for early release, and the parole board needs an evaluation."

"Murder One is not a sex offense."

"Technically, no. But because of the nature of the crime, the board placed him in that category."

"More bullshit. And you just let it roll over you."

"Come on, Holly. I don't make the rules. It's my job, for Christ's sake."

Holly threw up her hands.

"Another early release? Why don't we just turn this place over to the fucking Marriott?"

"This is a oner. He won't get another chance, and I doubt if they'll parole him anyway. The case was too big. Too much publicity."

"And?"

"He still claims he's innocent. He's tough. But you're tougher," Ted said, grinning. "He's also considered extremely dangerous. I know that turns you on." Ted's grin widened lasciviously.

"It's wonderful to be appreciated."

"When you're the best," he said and extended the file for

her to take. His smile was enough to make her retch. But she snatched the folder out of his hands and strode away.

He shook his head as he watched her go. She could never say he didn't give her the more interesting cases.

Two officers escorted Briscoe from reception to the housing module.

The module resembled the spokes in a wheel radiating out from a two-story central hub. The hub contained elevators, stairs and the glass-enclosed control booth from which the correction officers could monitor the activity within each individual unit.

Each living module had twenty rooms divided equally on two tiers and could hold up to forty inmates at a time. The rooms were thirty by fifteen and were fronted by a wooden door inset with a pane of unbreakable glass.

The main level contained the central living area, which had Formica-topped tables for dining and recreation. There was no separate mess hall. All meals were delivered by truck from the prison's central kitchen and were wheeled in on large metal carts. Each meal came on an individual tray, like those served on airplanes. There was a lounge area, where several couches were ranged around a large television set. Smaller tables could be used for board games.

Inmates spent little time in the recreation area. Their time at the center was filled with a series of therapies, both individual and collective. Keeping them segregated from the rest of the prison population also served to keep many of them alive. Sex offenders, especially child molestors, were often dealt with summarily by members of the general prison population.

Briscoe was admitted to Unit A and housed in a room on the second tier, a room that he would not have to share because of the special nature of his evaluation. His eyes were fixed straight ahead as he was led through the unit, but he was aware of the other inmates in the lower area whose eyes followed him with interest as he climbed the stairs behind the corrections officer. Word of who he was had already spread through the prison grapevine. Being a celebrity was not something that most inmates wanted. It attracted malice and the peculiar envy that often consumes men in confinement, an envy that often leads to bloodshed.

The officer stopped outside an open door. Briscoe stepped inside the gleaming beige-walled space. Like the area outside, the room was tiled from floor to ceiling and was as warm and welcoming as the corridors of a hospital.

His belongings were waiting for him in a cardboard box set on the bed. There was a small metal table fixed to one wall adjacent to the metal toilet. Beside the toilet was a matching metal sink, and above it, a metal mirror set into the wall. There was no window; a series of opaque glass blocks set high in the wall admitted outside light, but the main illumination came from the fluorescent fixture set flush against the ceiling.

Briscoe stepped over to the bed and opened the box, giving the contents a cursory glance. There were few items inside—some toiletries and little else, nothing he would feel the loss of should it be stolen. Nothing anyone could take that might give them a hold over him. He turned toward the table. On it was a large manila envelope lettered with the words Therapeutic Programs. He opened it. Inside was a small stack of printed materials. Briscoe glanced at them with a look of contempt, then put them back in the envelope. He sensed a presence behind him and turned around to face the inmate standing in the doorway.

The inmate was slightly built and looked to be in his late twenties. He had thinning sandy-colored hair, light blue eyes, and regular, almost boyish features. He was wheeling a metal handcart filled with books and magazines. His eyes regarded Briscoe with fascination.

Briscoe met his gaze, and his eyes narrowed with distrust. "What do you want?" He questioned.

"Library services," the young man responded. "My name is Pierson." He lowered his voice. "You're getting Dr. Alexander. She's the best shrink in here. She's my shrink, too. So if you want to compare notes, just give me a holler."

He started out, then turned back. "Word is you're getting special treatment. Some of these freaks are pretty dangerous, so watch your back."

"Thanks," Briscoe said, meeting the young man's glance. His look was dark and probing, staring into the young man's eyes as if he were able to read his soul. He abruptly turned away. His glance was dismissive, as if he had confirmed what he already knew from the other's watery gaze.

Flustered, Pierson pushed the cart away as Briscoe closed the door and went to the sink. He put his hands on the wall on each side of the metal mirror and intensely studied the distorted image reflected back to him.

His eyes were dark, cold, unreadable. But there was also a glint of calculation. Perhaps he had just been given a key, a way through the maze of his next ordeal.

5

The spotlights were already on, illuminating the area around the prison, when Holly left for the day. Pools of warm yellow light bathed the walls and towers as she drove past them. She had stayed late to finish up several reports, the last of which still bothered her. She had given Calvin Washington, one of her inmates, a negative recommendation on his application for early release. He was a violent sex offender who had seriously injured his wife after a long history of domestic battering. Though he was making progress in controlling his impulses, Holly did not think he was ready for the outside. These were always the most difficult decisions, especially when she and the inmate were in close personal contact. She would have to deal with him and explain the reasons for her decision, never a pleasant task when the inmate had expectations of being released. It was just something she would have to deal with, as she would have to deal with her sister when she finally arrived.

Holly made two stops before returning to her condo: one at the cleaner's, the other at the convenience store for several items she knew Beth liked. Her sister was a chocoholic. Holly had stocked the pantry with cookies and other goodies, but when it came to Beth she always felt as if she had not done enough. Holly knew that no matter what she did, Beth would be disapproving. It had always been this way. They were just so different, she and her sister. Holly had been the achiever, respectful of her parents' desires and expectations, a driving engine of responsibility and success. Beth had never done what her parents wanted her to. And when their parents had died in the accident when Holly was fourteen and Beth was twelve, they had gone to live with their mother's sister and her husband, who had no children of their own. From the beginning, Beth stubbornly refused even the most reasonable requests made of her. She balked at doing chores, dreamt her way through school, and drifted into one bad relationship after the other, first with girls her own age who were considered difficult, then with a whole string of boys, none of whom ever seemed to make her anything but miserable. Happiness was something Beth never seemed to achieve. She had two abortions before her senior year, graduated from pot to alcohol, and had been in and out of rehab over half a dozen times since.

Holly had felt abandoned by her parents' death, but Beth did not seem as affected. The terrible grief and longing Holly felt for so long was absent in her sister. Strangely, her aunt and uncle attributed Beth's behavior to her parents' demise, when that was never the reason. Beth had been the way she was before her parents died. Their sudden departure only amplified the tendencies that had been there all along. While Holly struggled for normalcy, trying to maintain her grades as well as aiding her aunt with the housework, Beth drifted further and further into her own particular world of negligence and irresponsibility.

In spite of what looked like impending rain, Holly left her car in the driveway and hurried inside. The neat lines of the town houses were obscured by mist. They were brick-faced imitations of old-style colonials, and their regular suburban features only irritated her sister, who preferred the funky dilapidation of run-down hamlets where she usually looked for an apartment. Beth would just have to put up with it.

Holly laid her packages on the counter, then stripped off her raincoat. There were a few thing to straighten up, but on the whole the house looked presentable. Not that Beth would notice. She cared little for domestic order and threw her things anywhere. She lived in mess and clutter.

As she put away her purchases, Holly fought to dismiss these thoughts from her mind. Being negative was the last thing she needed right now. It would poison the atmosphere and get them off on the wrong foot. But she could not fight off the dark cloud that had been hanging over her ever since the meeting with Ted that morning. She knew Ted and the others thought she was naïve, and perhaps she was, but she could not help feeling the way she did about the program. She was a fighter. She had always found a cause to struggle for, starting when she was in high school and had organized the battle to keep an instructor from being fired for assigning books the school board had banned. She had an obsessive, driving nature, an analysis she had made of herself while still an undergraduate. Once she fastened on to something, she was like a terrier and would not let go. She had a single-mindedness about her work, a passion to put together shattered lives in a way that others thought impossible.

Her work was more than merely a vocation. There was another reason, a secret reason that Holly had never revealed to Ted or to anyone else, the reason she had gone to work in the prison in the first place. It was something she had discovered only after she had completed graduate school and was interning at a clinic in Philadelphia, where her father had been an Assistant District Attorney with an enviable trial record and had built his reputation as a forceful prosecutor. That was something she had always been proud of, even enrolling in law school to imitate him, until one of her graduate professors took her out for coffee and casually mentioned that he had known her father. Over the years, the professor had been an expert witness for several leading law firms. He specialized in analyzing sexual offenders, several of whom her father had prosecuted. In fact, he continued, her father had made something of a specialty, within the DA's office, of prosecuting sex offenders, and was quite successful at it. The problem, the professor said, staring at her through the half lenses of his peculiar horn-rimmed glasses, was that several of the men her father had convicted were actually innocent and had been serving time for crimes they did not commit. Many had been subsequently released when new DNA evidence techniques had proven they had not committed the crime they had been accused of.

This news came as a shock to Holly. At first, she protected herself by crawling into a comfortable shell of denial. But when she researched it, she discovered that what the professor had said was true. In his zeal to prosecute, her father had played fast and loose with the law. All the releases had come after his death, so he never had to deal with the outcome of his actions. But innocent men had spent years behind bars because of what he had done.

In a strange way, Holly was atoning for his actions. She knew it was not her responsibility to correct the mistakes her father had made. The sins of the father did not get passed on to his daughters, but somehow that was what happened. There had to be a reason why she was so drawn to this kind of work. It had not happened overnight. Holly had worked in several clinics and even tried private practice, but when the job at Brandywine opened up, she found herself applying for it over the objections of her friends and colleagues who thought the work was too dangerous and inevitably unrewarding. With a sigh, Holly wondered if they had been right all along. It *was* dangerous and unrewarding, and in actuality, she had gotten precious little out of it. Yet, somehow she was still here, still fighting battles she knew were futile and unwinnable, but she could not help herself. It seemed a destiny she had to fulfill.

It was going to be one of those killer weeks.

Holly should have suspected it when Ted gave her the file

on this Briscoe character. She had not had time to glance at it since her conversation with him several days before, and now she was running late for her group therapy session.

That turned into an immediate disaster.

Perhaps it was the rain. A change in the weather always had an effect on the inmates. But she could feel the tension as soon as she entered the room.

It was a given that sex offenders were the victims of some kind of abuse, whether physical, sexual, or psychological. The aim of each session was for each inmate to uncover the abuse in his past and be willing to share it with the other men in the group, who then would feel free to uncover their own damaged psyches and support each other in a mutual exploration of each others' pain. And, in theory anyway, to feel the pain of their victims.

That was the theory.

In practice, her sessions could be anything but. She had learned through bitter experience that the inmates' revelations could lead to disturbing and unpredictable results.

The session began with one of her more recent arrivals, a wiry first offender named Kroll with white supremacist delusions, who had been goaded into confessing some of the feelings he experienced during his rape of a young Hispanic female. Kroll had attended only two previous sessions. He had been silent, reluctant to speak at first, but the other members now focused in on him and their comments egged him on.

"Come on man. Give it up. Tell us how you did the ho."

Normally words like whore and bitch were forbidden. The group had agreed not to use them, as they denigrated women and turned their victims into objects. This time, however, Holly resisted interfering, allowing the group dynamic to work, aware that the other inmates were lulling the new arrival into a sense of false security, waiting until they pounced.

When he finally responded to the goading, it was with the usual cocky boastfulness.

"Man, I did the little puta good. I fucked her hard. I had

to cut her a little, but I had to fuck this bitch. I was on Meth. But, man, I needed to fuck her. I had to spread those legs and get me a piece of that pussy."

The group was led by a wily, heavyset inmate named Reyes, who eyed the newcomer with jaded eyes.

"Bullshit. It had nothing to do with her pussy. It was all about you getting even, man."

"What the fuck do you know about it? Me, get even with some bitch?"

"Not the bitch. I mean, getting even with whoever it was who fucked you."

"Nobody ever fucked me, man! I ain't no punk faggot."

"Of course, you're a punk faggot. To the motherfucker who did you, you were a punk faggot. And in your mind you're still a punk faggot, motherfucker."

"Fuck you! You don't know shit!"

"What I do know is that you needed do a power trip on that little bitch to prove no one was still fucking you."

"Fuck you, asshole! I don't got to hear this shit!"

"No, fuck you. You're the one's being fucked in the mind and up the ass. Only you still don't know it. Every time you took some pussy by force, you were just playing back the time someone did it to you. You became the pussy you were doing—dig?"

The young inmate flew out of his seat. His eyes were on fire. His hand reached down into his boot, and when it rose, it held a blade made from the shank of a screwdriver.

The others were ready for him, and he was subdued quickly, spread-eagled on the floor and held down by six pairs of aggressive hands. But the rules demanded that Holly ring for help, a rule she knew she had to enforce, and that ended the session. Plus she had to fill out an incident report, further throwing off her day.

Holly struggled with her irritation as she continued down the corridor toward her office.

She burst inside, saying, "Clara, I need these copied."

Clara's desk was vacant. She was probably on her break.

"Hell, I'll do it myself." She said aloud, continuing toward the copying room.

She went through the inner door to a dimly lit service corridor at the rear of the suite that offered access to a supply closet and the small windowless copying room.

A floor polisher stood unattended in the center of the corridor. Its motor had been left running. It was circling aimlessly across the dull green linoleum.

"Hello, somebody." Holly called. "You left your machine on."

Holly edged around it, went through the doorway, and started toward the copier. She placed her folder on the beige surface and started to check the settings when the door slammed shut behind her.

A powerful hand locked around her throat, jerking her off balance and cutting off her breathing. She felt something sharp dig into the skin at the base of her chin.

"Scream, bitch, and I'll cut your throat!"

Her head swam as the words rushed hot against her ear. She could smell the acid reek of her attacker's sweat.

She lost focus for an instant.

"Look at me, bitch!"

Her vision cleared. She was staring into the frenzied eyes of a massively built African-American man wearing a stained T-shirt and prison jeans.

"Calvin." That was all she could utter before he shook her hard and slammed her back against the wall.

His voice hissed venomously. "You fucked my release, bitch. Now, I'm gonna fuck you."

Holly reached for the beeper in her belt. But his hand closed over her wrist, smashing the beeper against the wall.

He twisted her arm, swinging her body toward him and locking his knee between her thighs.

"I'm gonna do you good, bitch, then I'm gonna make you bleed."

He forced her back, easing the grip on her throat as his hand covered her breast, gripping it painfully in his powerful fingers.

"Cutting me won't get you out of here," she cried through her constricted throat. "It won't make the pain go away."

"Shut up, bitch, or I'll cut out your motherfucking tongue."

His eyes were bulging as he brought the knife back up hard against her throat.

She knew she had only an instant before he cut her. Her words exploded in a sharp staccato rush.

"Like they cut you when you were seven and those men took you up on the roof? Is that what you want to do to me?"

Something passed through his eyes. "Shut the fuck up!" he shouted hoarsely.

"Do you want me in your nightmares, Calvin? Like those other women you hurt? The faces you see when you close your eyes?"

He was silent. His chest was heaving. His eyes were wild. The blade against her neck dug deeper.

"I'm warning you, bitch."

Her voice was a hoarse whisper. "This isn't what you want, Calvin. I know this isn't what you want."

Fear clawed at her, but she knew she had to keep talking, no matter what. It was the only chance she had.

"Look at what you're doing, Cal," she gasped. "Ask yourself, are you ready for the outside? Tell me you're ready, and I'll change my report. I'll give you early release."

"Lying bitch." He gasped. "Fucking lying bitch."

"It's not a lie, Calvin." Her voice was a barely audible rasp. "I've never lied to you. You're angry. I can understand that. It's okay. Be angry. But you don't have to hurt me. Or yourself. You can regain control. Just put down the knife and walk away. You've done it before. You can do it now. Please, Calvin. I know you can do it. I believe in you, Calvin. I've always believed in you."

She watched his eyes as they flicked back and forth, sensed

the struggle going on inside him. Sweat beaded along his forehead. She could smell the acid reek of his breath.

"I'm on your side, Cal," she whispered. "I'm not your enemy. I won't hurt you. Just put down the knife and walk away."

He looked down at the blade pressed against her neck as if seeing it for the first time. Tiny beads of blood marked her skin.

"Just let it go. You can do it, Cal. Take control. Put down the knife."

His hand began shaking. His eyes closed for an instant. His body seemed to convulse. He opened his hand and the knife dropped from his fingers and clattered across the floor.

"Fucking shit." He gasped and turned away, his body hunching as he struck the wall with his head.

The door burst open. Officers rushed inside and seized him, pulling him out of the room.

Clara hurried in, followed by Ted.

"I knew something was wrong when I found the door locked," Clara said. "Are you all right?"

Holly nodded. "I'm okay."

"Jesus Christ, Holly," Ted exploded. "Why didn't you use your beeper?"

Clara picked the broken pieces of the beeper off the floor and held them out to Ted.

He clenched, tightening his lips. "I'll take care of that son of a bitch. He won't go near you again."

"He's my patient," Holly snapped. "I'll make that decision, thank you."

Ted regarded the fierceness in her eyes.

"Okay, Holly. Whatever you say. But take some time off, huh?"

"I said I'm okay!"

"Holly, go home." Clara urged softly.

"If I do, I won't come back." Holly answered sharply.

She turned and walked out of the copying room, trying

not to let them see the wobble in her legs. She returned to the office and crossed hurriedly to the bathroom, swiftly locking the door behind her.

Inside, she faced the mirror, her hands gripping the sides of the sink. She retched hard; the acrid bile rose in her throat. Finished, she ran the tap, then glanced up at her face reflected in the mirror. Her eyes were wide, and her skin was ashen.

"Nice work, babe," she whispered. "You almost got yourself killed in there."

She turned off the tap and sat down on the closed toilet. She bent forward, wrapping her arms around her knees. It was the only way she could stop herself from shaking.

6

It was late when Holly pulled out of the parking lot and drove away from the prison. The night sky was clear. Stars filled the void above the trees as she drove along the winding stretch of rural highway. She kept her eyes on the stars as she drove, allowing a certain peacefulness to calm her.

The peaceful rural stretch came to an abrupt end. Strip malls lit the night sky, advertising a XXX video store, a top-less bar, and an adult motel. As she passed them, Holly's mind shifted to the tormented psyches of the inmates she treated.

Holly did not believe in evil. What she did believe was that something specific in the past had formed the dark impulses of an inmate's personality and could, with immense effort, be reformed in a positive direction. This approach caused some of her colleagues to criticize her. But it was the only way Holly could maintain her optimism in the face of what sometimes seemed to be the overwhelming forces ranged against her.

Perhaps it was her aunt Katie who had planted that seed. She was a gentle woman with an inner strength most people failed to understand. Katie could never find evil in anything or anyone, only behavior she attributed to hurt and misguidance. She believed in the inherent goodness of people, a belief she deeply inculcated in her niece. Holly had looked to her for the solace and comfort that she never got from her strict, conservative father and her distant mother, whose main preoccupation was social advancement.

Holly felt a sharp pang of guilt whenever she thought of her aunt and how much she had loved her. If it had not been for the horror of her parents' tragic accident, she would never have known that kind of love or have been introduced to her aunt's generous depth of understanding.

Holly had had long and bitter arguments with some of her professors during the period of her training when she was assigned clients to work with. She faced her teachers' cynical expressions as they dismissed whole categories of mental disturbances as incurable, scoffing at her eager enthusiasm to take on the world and all its problems. In some ways they were right. Many of her clients were incapable of change, but that did not mean they suffered less. Holly had inherited her aunt's gift for understanding their pain, which many of her classmates and teachers failed to understand.

Many of her classmates had been drawn to their profession by the lure of quick money in a lucrative suburban practice, where they could listen patiently to the complaints of the mildly neurotic in prettily decorated offices whose doors were stenciled with the letters of their prestigious degrees. It was Holly who always took on the more difficult cases—patients classified as borderline and who most practitioners found impossible to tolerate, their narcissism being too deep to be modified. But their pain was real, nevertheless. Just as she found the kernel of agony beneath the layers of indifference and denial in the men she treated—men whom both the state and her colleagues believed to be incurable.

Psychology had not been her first occupation. She had graduated from college with a degree in political science and gone directly into law school at the University of Pennsylvania. Her first job had been as an Assistant District Attorney in her father's old office in Philadelphia. It had given her an education in despair and an insight into the dark side of human existence. She had learned a great deal. You either learned, or you went under, as many of her coworkers had, lost in the rapids of the criminal justice system with no hand outstretched to pull them to safety. Holly had survived. But four years had been enough.

She had burned out handling a huge caseload. Through her hands passed hundreds of lower-echelon criminals who went in and out of the system like kids through the revolving door of an amusement park. Addicts, thieves, shoplifters, low-level pushers, pickpockets, muggers and assorted street rats were her stock in trade. It was a world of dirt, disgust, and depression. It was also work that went nowhere, which was why she switched to a profession that offered the possibility of helping other human beings, rather than sending them to rot in one of the state's many prisons.

It was not the profession her father would have chosen for her, or have even respected. He had no belief in the subconscious functions of the mind, only in the actions of the body. She had chosen the law to follow in his footsteps and complete the career that had been cut short by his early death. But she was not able to fulfill that ambition. Something inside her rebelled. It had taken her a long time to overcome the sense of guilt she felt over it. A good therapist had helped, but she still felt pangs of betrayal every time she thought of her parents and their dreams, dreams that had evaporated long ago but that she still carried for them somewhere deep inside herself.

Holly turned off the highway and pulled into a spot in front of Charley's.

The tavern was half filled and cheerfully lit. The young maitre d' smiled at Holly familiarly as she went inside and gave her a flirtatious look. Charley's was where her coworkers went to unwind, and their boisterous voices resounded from the bar.

They were already several drinks ahead when she made her appearance, and they applauded her vigorously. Holly made a mock bow as she stepped over to the bar where Henry Adams, a heavyset African-American psychologist, handed her a martini.

"Been keeping this chilled for you," he said with a broad smile. "You've had one hell of a day."

Holly stared at the drink in shock. "Henry's buying?" she gasped. "My god, what does this mean?"

Laughter burst around her as Henry leaned close to her. "You know what it means, woman," he growled seductively in deep bass tones.

"Whoa. Better make it a double," Holly responded. "I'm not sure I can handle it."

"You could handle it," someone shouted as Henry raised his arms proudly and did a bump and grind to the pleasure of the onlookers.

Holly pretended a mock faint, as the others whistled and hooted.

"Somebody's got to rescue her," Clara said, taking Holly by the hand and leading her to a nearby booth that Clara had staked out for them. Holly vamped playfully for Henry as she sidled in beside Clara. She toasted him, then took a long sip of the chilled martini.

"I needed that," she said, meeting Clara's gaze.

"You should go home," Clara urged. "After what you've been through today."

"On my last night of freedom? Forget it. Beth is arriving tomorrow."

"You won't listen, will you?" Clara said impatiently. "You've got to cut her loose."

"I can't. I can't just walk away from her."

"Why can't you?"

"Because that's what my parents did. They walked away from the two of us.'

"They were killed in a car crash."

"That's not what I mean. They walked away from us long before then." Holly looked up at Clara. "They were indifferent to our needs. They cared only for their own. It sounds terrible, but it's the truth. My father was an ambitious lawyer who went into politics to advance his career, not to protect the innocent. He sent men away who were later proven to be innocent. Many of them were sex offenders, like the people we're treating. He made a specialty out of it. It was his ticket in, how he was going to build his base of public support. He died before he could get things going."

"I'm sorry. I didn't know."

"Neither did I. Not until one of my professors enlightened me. My aunt and uncle never said anything, but when I confronted them with it, they never denied it. That's a heavy trip, considering the kind of work I do."

"How did all that affect Beth?"

Holly was silent for a moment as she twisted the stem of the martini glass in her fingers. Her eyes rose to meet Clara's.

"I don't think Beth ever really had a chance. Not when it came to my parents. She wasn't pretty enough for my mother to show off to anyone. She wasn't smart enough for my father to boast about to his influential cronies."

"She is pretty," Clara insisted.

"Now. But my parents didn't see it. Not then. And what mattered most to them was appearances."

"But you've always said your aunt and uncle were different."

"They were. But by the time we went to live with them it was too late. Beth was already who she was. The little reject who never got the prizes. Only I did." Holly finished with deepening regret.

"I was their little all-star. I got the blue ribbons. I excelled. I was the one they boasted about. Beth got the crumbs. Even her birthdays were afterthoughts. She never really got what she wanted. My mother never paid enough attention to her to find out what that was."

"Lots of kids grow up that way."

"And lots of kids are in lots of pain because of it. I know. I've treated enough of them."

"You can't spend your life blaming your parents for everything."

"No. Beth never blamed them. She just went off into her own little world."

"The flawed little rabbit who found her own hole," Clara said. "Let's be real. She's a number-one flake. Check all of the following. Ditzy. Disorganized. And disconnected."

"She's still my sister."

"I wish she'd give you the same consideration. You're her dumping ground. Every time she goes off on one of her little binges, you're the one who has to pick up the pieces."

"There is no one else."

"It's called the tyranny of the weak."

"I don't see it that way."

"Then let's call it mutual dependency. Isn't that the technical term? You're afraid to tell her the truth because you're afraid that if she hears it she won't love you anymore."

"Maybe."

"So you admit I'm right. You know, sooner or later you're going to have to cut the cord."

Holly nodded. "I'm sorry I dumped this on you."

"Hey. What are friends for?" Clara shot back. "I have no secrets from you, do I?"

Holly smiled. Clara's past was a complication of marriages, children, grandchildren, and several current involvements. Just keeping up with the daily mayhem took an effort. But Holly prized their friendship. Clara was honest, forthright, and kind.

"What you need is a man," Clara said forcefully.

"Oh, oh. Who is it this time? Did one of your cousins just get divorced or is it someone you met on the checkout line?"

"You're so funny, you should be on Letterman," Clara retorted. "Don't worry. I've given up on you."

Holly reached across and placed her hand over Clara's.

"Don't give up on me. I've just been running on empty for awhile."

Clara turned to her. Her expression was suddenly serious. "I've known you a long time, Holly. You want people to think you're tough, but you're not. Your divorce hit you a lot harder than you want to admit. You're a lot more vulnerable than you think."

Holly looked at Clara, touched by her show of passion. She raised her glass and clinked it against Clara's. "Thanks for being there for me," she said softly.

"Any time, kid."

Holly smiled. "Be right back. Got to tinkle." She rose and crossed the room, skirting the bar. When she came out of the ladies' room, someone at the bar stepped in front of her.

"Dr. Alexander," he said, smiling. "I don't know if you remember me. Dan Shepard, from the CID unit investigating the Ulman case."

Holly started. It was the tall detective she had spoken to at Ulman's house the night he killed his wife and then himself.

"Yes. I remember you," she said cautiously. "Is this a coincidence, or am I under arrest?"

"Actually, I called the prison. They told me you had just left and might be here. I wanted to clear up some loose ends."

"I submitted a report. I could fax you a copy."

"Actually, I was hoping we could discuss it over dinner."

"I'm with friends now."

"Some other time, then. How about Friday?"

Holly looked at him. What she read in his eyes indicated that his interest was not necessarily business. For a moment, she wavered. He was attractive, and his manner had not been unpleasant. So why not? Clara's words echoed in her mind. But something tightened inside.

"I'm sorry. I'd like to, but my sister is arriving for a visit tomorrow, and I'll be pretty busy for the next few weeks."

"That's too bad," he shrugged. "I think you would have enjoyed it."

"I can fax you a copy of my report. Do you have a card?"

He fished one out of his jacket pocket and handed it to her with a smile. Their eyes met. There was something pleasing in his gaze, and Holly found it difficult to look away.

"Well, good-bye," she said finally.

"Good-bye," he answered, his eyes still fixed on her.

She turned away and continued, wondering if she had been stupid to refuse his invitation. Clara, of course, would kill her. But the thought of Beth's arrival clouded her consciousness. She continued back toward the booth where Clara was waiting.

"Who was that?" Clara asked when Holly had sidled back into her seat.

"Oh. Just some cop who was investigating the Ulman case. He wanted to clear up a couple of loose ends."

"I hope one of them was you. He's cute."

"Don't be silly. It's just business."

Clara was staring at her dubiously. "It didn't look that way to me."

"I have an idea," Holly said brightly. "Why don't you buy me another drink?"

The hands on the clock in the control booth indicated that it was just before seven. The area in front of the TV was deserted. Most of the inmates were crowded around the tables in the dining area finishing their dinners. Only a single inmate sat on the couch in front of the set, watching the flickering images on the small black and white screen.

The inmate was Briscoe.

This was the first time he had left his cell and made his way down to the first tier. He had waited until the area cleared out before he started down. Since arriving, he had remained in his cell avoiding contact with the other inmates. One or two of them had made comments or catcalls in his direction, but he had ignored them. He had requested his meals in his cell, which had been granted because of his temporary status. Normally, he would have been housed in a special unit reserved for prisoners being evaluated, but that unit was overcrowded.

He glanced up at the clock, aware that the area would begin to fill as soon as the inmates had finished their evening meal and had been released to return to their cells. Briscoe was watching the news on the local public affairs channel, something the other inmates rarely did. They preferred cartoons or action movies on one of the two cable channels they were permitted to watch.

The commentator was talking about Briscoe's case and the evaluation he was undergoing. Briscoe had been alerted to the program the night before by Pierson, the inmate who wheeled the library cart. Now, he watched as the former prosecutor of his case gave his opinion that Briscoe was a dangerous killer who should never be allowed out on early release. The prosecutor was blond, pudgy, and balding, his neck stiff in a starched white shirt with a metal crossbar beneath the tie. His pompous features were puffed up with self-righteousness as he recounted the evidence against Briscoe. The commentator was about to turn to Briscoe's defense attorney for his opinion, when a pair of boots crashed onto the table in front of Briscoe and a hand grasped the remote, instantly switching to a dubbed Japanese action cartoon.

"Fuck, man! We don't want to hear that shit, do we?" the inmate said.

Briscoe faced a stocky inmate with a red face and a closely shaven skull. His shirt was cut off at the shoulders, revealing muscular arms covered with green and blue tattoos.

"Not a fucking chance. Right, punk?"

A second inmate had dropped onto the couch beside Briscoe. He was shorter than the inmate holding the remote, but equally stocky. His face was swarthy and acne scarred, and one of his front teeth was missing. He grinned at Briscoe and winked.

"What's the matter. Ice-Man? Don't you wanna break the ice?"

Briscoe smiled. He nodded pleasantly as he leaned over, which caused the other two to exchange looks of self-satisfaction.

In that instant, Briscoe rose from the couch in a movement so sudden it took both men by surprise. His elbow struck the man beside him in the temple as he flipped the small table up into the other inmate's face. The inmate tried to react as the table came toward him, lifting his arm to ward off the piece of furniture. But his actions were too slow. The table struck him in the forehead, propelled by Briscoe's foot, which jammed the table hard against the inmate's face.

The inmate fell backward off his chair as Briscoe lunged. The heavy sole of his boot caught the fallen inmate under the chin, as his hand grasped for the remote, which flew out of the man's hand. Briscoe turned with a single precise movement and lunged—thrusting the remote deep into the second man's open mouth, dislodging his remaining front tooth, and spraying blood across the front of the screen.

Both men lay writhing on the floor, moaning in agony as blood dripped down their still-startled faces.

Briscoe leaned over and turned off the set. He stepped past the two wounded inmates and continued through the lounge and up the stairs to his tier before the guard in the observation deck had even turned in his direction.

Holly was on her way home.

The night had turned chilly, but she had not turned on the heater. She was still feeling the warmth from the two martinis. Lights flashed, warning her to turn off her brights, but she failed to notice. The meeting with Shepard had left a warm spot in her psyche that had not quite lost its heat. Nor had Clara's remarks.

It had been two years, but the pain of the divorce and

Philip's betrayal still haunted her. It had left a wound that was not yet healed. Sometimes she wondered if it ever would.

The facts were common enough; in fact, they were almost banal.

A few months before their tenth anniversary, she had discovered that her husband was having an affair.

She had been wrapped up in her work, and he had found someone else to provide the adoration he so ardently craved. Holly found it difficult to admit, but perhaps she had just grown tired of providing it.

Holly had needed some adoration herself, which Philip had failed to provide. Philip took, but he didn't know how to give her the kind of affection and attention she desired.

Perhaps she had loved him too deeply and that had been her undoing. He was too good looking and self-centered, too narcissistic to consider others. She had been warned and had ignored the warnings. But she continued to provide sustenance long after she knew a vital part of their marriage had grown stale and predictable.

Philip was a talented architect whose work had been steadily gaining international attention. They had married right after she had gotten her master's, both of them launching their careers at the same time. Holly felt protected by his love and his appreciation for the kind of work she was doing, unlike other men who felt threatened by the thought of their wife's career. Within a period of two years they had moved from a small one-bedroom apartment in Germantown to a large modern home of his design in a prestigious Philadelphia suburb, primarily due to Philip's lucrative commissions. His rise was swift. He had partnered with two other young visionaries, and their work was being sought both in the States and abroad. So Philip began traveling.

His work required that he remain away for long periods. At first, Holly had been understanding. She knew the kind of patience it took to launch a career. Besides, she had her own work to do, patients to see, a practice that was taking long hours to build. Her sympathetic nature and quick understanding was drawing a large client base, while others who had graduated with her were still struggling.

At the same time, Holly began training in clinical work, making time to see patients who could not pay and whom the county considered untreatable. These were the most difficult cases of schizophrenia and bipolar disorder, patients who went in and out of hospitals continually and whose lives were as unstable as fault lines in an earthquake zone. It was the kind of work she was drawn to, and she often found herself thinking of these patients while in session with her more normal clients, whose complaints seemed almost trivial in comparison.

Everything seemed to be working out for them as a couple, except for the loneliness that could not be erased by a half-hour phone call. Then there was the still unresolved question of children. When either of them brought up the subject, it was usually in regard to someone else's child. Between them, it was silently understood that children would come in due time, when Philip had successfully launched his career and Holly had hers. But the idea of children warmed her and made it less difficult when Philip was away.

She conjured up a fantasy family: two boys and a girl, or two girls and a boy, she could never decide which she preferred. It was not an easy fantasy for her. The idea of motherhood was a little frightening. Perhaps it had to do with her parents and the distance they preferred. But she knew in her heart that she could make the connection. Unlike her mother, she knew she had the ability to love. It was a lovely dream, and just as she was ready to claim it as a reality, the roof caved in. Philip's calls became less frequent. His absences seemed to multiply. That was when she discovered the truth.

She had been a fool. Those were the facts. It was all there for her to see, but she had preferred to remain unseeing.

Strangely enough, Philip did not want a divorce. He was quite content with the way things were. He professed that he loved her and that none of his affairs had meant anything. He was willing to give them up, even to have the children she wanted. Hurt and angry as she was, Holly almost believed him. She still loved him, but something inside rebelled, as it had with her decision to pursue her father's career. She could not live with the betrayal. The same thing had happened to millions of other women. The reasons were identical. They had suffered and moved on. So why was she still grieving? Why was a vital part of her unable to give up the pain and allow her to continue with her life? The question provided its own agony.

She knew she had to find something to replace the emptiness. But each time something or someone presented itself she turned away, just as she had done tonight.

Clara was right. She couldn't keep using Beth as an excuse. She came running each time Beth called, even though she knew she might be doing Beth a disservice by coming to her rescue and depriving her of the self-reliance she needed to direct her own life. But Holly was unable to prevent herself. Just as she had been unable to say yes to the invitation in the tall detective's eyes. She was like one of those shrink jokes, where the shrink cures everyone's kids but his own.

She shook the thought away. She had to focus on something else. She had to examine the Briscoe file before she went to sleep. She was scheduled to begin his evaluation the following morning.

7

Briscoe stood inside the bare green-walled interview room, still and unmoving. His face was immobile, an emotionless mask. Holly had seen the look before. It was formed by the dead, disconnected void of incarceration.

The escorting officer awaited a nod from Holly before shutting the door and leaving them alone.

Briscoe stood facing her. Flat metallic light came from the fluorescents in the ceiling, sharpening his features and shadowing deep pockets under his eyes while emphasizing his lean good looks. There was something disquieting about him, an animal-like energy that filled the room from the instant he entered. His angular face, black straight hair, and gray eyes reminded her of a wolf. His arms hung straight at his sides. His fists were clenched. His body was under tight physical control, but she sensed the tension of suppressed rage. His file was in front of her, along with a small tape recorder, which she turned on as her eyes rose to meet his pointed gaze.

"Take a seat, please," she said in an impersonal tone.

He remained motionless. His eyes were fixed on her, measuring her with an almost piercing directness. She felt a sudden stab of tension and had the uneasy feeling that he could somehow see under her skin.

"Is there a problem?"

"I didn't expect a woman."

"You'll get over it. Sit down."

He did not move. His eyes remained fixed on her. She felt something fierce radiating from them.

Ted's words returned to haunt her. *This man is dangerous.* Still, she faced him doggedly, refusing to surrender to the power she felt emanating from him.

"I said, sit down," she commanded.

The look in his eyes changed, as if he were deciding something. He took the chair opposite. He sat slightly forward, keeping his hands out of sight beneath the table. But his eyes were still measuring her.

Holly returned her gaze to him. These first moments were always critical in setting the tone and determining what was to follow. If any of it was to work, she must remain dominant.

"Did you read any of the material I left for you?" she asked in the same flat tone.

He did not answer. His eyes never left hers. There was an electric tension between them. Holly felt her diaphragm tighten. The moment lengthened uncomfortably.

"I suggest you read it," she said finally.

He remained unmoving, and Holly felt a twinge of discomfort. She had not expected him to be so off-putting or impersonal. Most sex offenders were masters of manipulation. They were usually ingratiating at first, sizing her up as they looked for an opening in which to work a con, especially those who had been long incarcerated. This inmate was different. He seemed to be actively trying to antagonize her.

"Did you read any of the material I left for you?" he asked.

"If you mean your case file—"

"Not my case file. That's bullshit. The transcript of my trial."

"Yes. I read the transcript. You were indicted for murder."

"Murder requires the intent to kill," he said. "There was no intent."

"There was one count of forcible rape."

"Rape requires an act of sexual aggression against the will of another. Neither charge applied to me."

"A jury believed they did."

"On evidence rigged by a scumbag prosecutor who decided to jump-start his career by making me his fairy godmother. I was guilty before I was even arrested."

"Then what did they prove?"

"That I broke their moral code. For that I was punished. Nothing else."

"So, you're innocent?"

"You read the transcript. You tell me."

"Why don't you tell me?"

Their eyes met and held. There was a silence. The room seemed sucked of its oxygen by a seesawing struggle of wills. Holly's stomach was taut.

"Why don't you save us both a lot of trouble and just have me castrated?" he said finally. "Isn't that what you people really want?"

"Is that what *you* really want?" Holly rejoined. "You wouldn't be the first to ask for it."

"Do you bronze their balls afterwards?" he asked pointedly. "Is that how you decorate your office?"

"We've never done the procedure," Holly replied.

He remained unsmiling. His lips formed a taut, humorless line.

"You do know why you're here?"

"I've been through this evaluation crap three different times with three different shrinks. They wanted to stick electrodes on my dick, show me dirty pictures, and watch me drool. Is that how you get your jollies, doctor?"

"Sorry. No electrodes. No porn. No drool. Just you, me, and the tape recorder."

"So, I get to sit here while you play Oprah. No thanks."

"My job is to evaluate you. The only way I can do that is if I ask the questions and you answer them. That's simple enough, isn't it?"

"Maybe for you."

His eyes never left hers. She was beginning to feel the strain. Her back and shoulders were aching.

"You're being offered the possibility of early release. Doesn't that interest you?"

"I'm not that stupid."

"You don't believe it's possible?"

"What do you believe, doctor?"

"Early release is a reality we deal with every day."

"Not for sex offenders."

"You're wrong. I wouldn't be doing this if it weren't possible. I don't like wasting my time."

"I'm up for release in 24 months."

"Not if we send the parole board a negative evaluation."

"You think they would release me, anyway? I'm the Ice-Man, remember? That's worth a headline, isn't it? Which is why they'll never release me."

"Will you allow me to evaluate you, or won't you?"

"Do whatever you want."

Holly's gaze was unwavering.

"All right. I'll save both of us a lot of trouble. Let's make this voluntary. Come or don't come. It's your call."

"And if I don't? What then? Isolation?"

"I don't believe in isolation. If you don't come, you get yourself a three week vacation in here, on me. All expenses paid before they return you to maximum security. But if you do decide to come, my name is *Doctor* Alexander. And you *will* answer the questions I put to you."

His expression did not change. Holly pressed the buzzer under the table. Their eyes were still locked when the guard opened the door several moments later.

Briscoe rose. His gaze was still fixed on her, but his expression was quizzical, almost bemused.

"Nice meeting you, *Doctor* Alexander," he said, emphasizing the word sarcastically.

He stepped outside and the door closed.

Holly unclasped her hands, leaned back in her seat and exhaled. "Not too cool, Doctor Alexander," she said aloud. She had no right to make the evaluation voluntary. Nowhere in the regulations did it say that. What they did say was that if an inmate refused to cooperate he could be sent to isolation or immediately returned to maximum security. She was sticking out her neck on this one. The question was why. Perhaps she had wanted to pierce the smugness of his expectations or to offer him something no one else had. Hope, perhaps? But what right did she have to offer that to any inmate? The system refused hope. It existed to punish, not to forgive or rehabilitate.

There was one thing she could not avoid. What he had said about the case file had been true. It was an often ambiguous hodgepodge of differing opinions. She usually discounted its conclusions. The transcript of his trial had also been ambiguous. What exactly had been proved? That he was a sexual adventurer who had outraged the community on several occasions? That he and the victim engaged in dangerous sex practices? But the contention of the prosecution that what he had done was deliberate and premeditated was a difficult conclusion for her to draw, especially on the evidence that had been presented. She was supposed to evaluate him on the basis of his being a sex offender. But what he had done was not a sex offense at all, not in the traditional meaning of the statute, which covered rape, sodomy, molestation, and pedophilia. Of course, it also mentioned unnatural acts. Was what he had done an unnatural act? The community certainly thought it was. And the community standard was what governed.

So what, then, was the evidence against him? There were drawings of the devices he had built, showing their dangerous nature and attesting to the fact that he had full knowledge that they might cause his partner's death. They had also discovered literature in his possession relating to suffocation and sex. The prosecutor claimed it was an obsession. And that the literature proved intent. Most damaging were the testimony of several witnesses relating conversations with the accused in which he had expressed his understanding and even his desire to push the envelope, even if it meant playing with the inevitable.

The defense's contention that the victim had purposely lured him into a situation in which she had desired death as an outcome had been largely neutralized by conflicting expert testimony. It would have been hard to prove in any case. The victim's therapist had testified to her client's unstable mental state, but much of her testimony had been stricken from the record and her case notes had been ruled inadmissible. Holly wondered if there was anything in them that might prove his contention.

She stretched out her hands. She had been clasping them so tightly that her joints felt on fire. She turned off the tape recorder, torn between wanting him to accept what she had offered and the elusive hope that he would decide not to return.

8

The rehab was a drab two-story frame complex set back behind an untrimmed box hedge that towered almost ten feet above the sidewalk. Holly parked in front and headed inside, where she paused at the reception desk. It was staffed by a small woman in her early sixties whose features had the ravaged look of a chronic alcoholic.

"Hi. My name is Holly Alexander. I'm here to pick up my sister, Beth."

The receptionist regarded her with weary eyes. "Just a minute. I'll get Dr. Kahn."

Holly thanked her and stepped into the small waiting area off the main lobby. The management had changed recently and attempts had been made to create a homey atmosphere. Plants clustered on the dark black and white checkered linoleum, and several new-looking couches, upholstered in bright yellow and brown tweed, stood against the walls. But it would take more than decor to erase the reek of failure and futility that clung to the building.

Holly heard a door open and turned to face Dr. Kahn as she exited her office and offered Holly a welcoming smile. The two women had attended several seminars together and shared several lunches.

"I'm sorry. My meeting ran late," Holly said.

"That's all right." The other woman smiled and made a dismissive gesture. "Beth's waiting in the lounge. She's packed and ready."

"How is she?" Holly asked.

The doctor's face changed expression.

"Still very vulnerable, I'm afraid. In a way, I'm sorry she's leaving. I hope she continues as an outpatient."

"We can hope," Holly said, her brow lining with the forlorn look of someone who has been through it many times before.

"She's promised to attend AA. And that's a positive. But it won't be easy."

"It never is," Holly said with a smile. "Thanks for all you've done.

"How are things at the center?" The doctor asked.

"Possible ten percent cut across the board. And lots more inmates."

The doctor made a sympathetic face. "That seems to be the story everywhere. Sorry, I can't walk you out. I've got a meeting."

"I know the way." Holly said with a smile, as they hugged and parted.

Holly turned and continued down the corridor, which had been painted bright earth tones in a further effort at cheerfulness, but the smell of disinfectant erased the effort. She paused in the doorway of the lounge. Several shabby vinyl couches faced a big-screen TV. Beth was seated on one of them, leaning back against the couch; otherwise, the room was empty. Her hands were clasped in her lap, and her eyes were closed.

A stranger entering the room would have immediately picked them out as sisters, though Beth was younger and less pretty. Her hair had been dyed black, and with her lack of makeup, this gave her an artificially severe expression. Her skin was pale, almost wan, and the skin under her eyes was puffy. She wore the shearling coat Holly had bought for her two years before, and tight leather boots with extremely high heels. Her thighs were bare to the edge of her miniskirt. To Holly she resembled someone trying to give the illusion of a toughness she did not possess.

Beth opened her eyes as Holly stepped toward her.

"Hi," Holly said, suppressing her desire to smile. She had learned not to offer Beth too much in the way of greeting.

Beth remained expressionless.

"Ready?" Holly asked. Beth rose wearily and picked up one bag. Holly already had the other. Together they left the room and shouldered their way silently down the bright yellow corridor.

It was already dark when they reached Holly's town house in a complex of identical brick structures on the outer edge of a large suburban shopping mall. The area had been recently developed out of farm land and was criss-crossed by several county highways making it convenient to nearby shopping and to Philadelphia further to the south. It looked like a hundred other suburbs and Holly had moved there exactly for that reason. The roads were lined with chain stores and the usual conveniences, from Kentucky Fried Chicken to Burger King, all of it predictable and familiar and thus a cause of irritation to her sister who desired something unique. Beth wanted to live somewhere like Woodstock, or one of the historic towns in Bucks County filled with stone buildings that dated from the Revolution. Beth called Holly's locale 'nowheresville'.

Holly had offered dinner out somewhere, but Beth shook her head. She smoked a cigarette with the windows wide open and said almost nothing as they drove. When they pulled up in front of Holly's place, Holly got the bags out of the trunk as Beth headed for the door, her eyes fixed straight ahead. Holly knew Beth had an aversion to meeting the neighbors.

She unlocked the door and they stepped inside. Holly had left the lights on in an effort at welcome, but Beth seemed indifferent to her surroundings.

"Tired?" Holly asked.

Beth merely shrugged. "Don't worry," she said off-handedly. "I'll be looking for a place as soon as I get a job."

"Sure. But you know you can stay with me as long as you like."

"Like forever, maybe?" Beth turned toward Holly with a darkening glance.

Holly refused to take the bait. "You know where everything is," she said, concealing the hurt Beth's words were meant to convey. "I've got a big day tomorrow."

Holly started toward the stairs.

"Nighty, night," Beth said, continuing in her sarcastic tone.

Holly turned to her sister and their eyes met. "Do you think we could start again?" she said evenly. "Welcome home, sis."

"It's not my home." Beth's smile was chilling.

"What do I have to do, Beth? Get down on my knees?"

Beth looked at her and her eyes softened. "You could make me a malted."

Beth remained silent as Holly got out the familiar ingredients and poured them into the aluminum container, then placed it on the base of the blender and hit the frappe button. The machine whirred as they stood on opposite sides of the workstation set in the center of the kitchen.

Holly's glance traveled down to the small aquamarine birthstone on Beth's finger.

"You still have the ring I bought you."

Beth actually smiled. "First present I got I ever really liked. I always wanted what you got. Maybe that's my problem."

Their eyes met, radiating warmth, then distance, in the familiar pattern that had always existed between them in spite of all of Holly's efforts to break through to something else.

The machine stopped. Holly poured the thick liquid into

two glasses. Each drank a portion, then Holly put down her glass and looked up at Beth. "Why is there always some kind of bullshit between us?" she asked.

"Because you're always trying to be my shrink. Maybe you should try to be my sister."

"I've always been your sister."

"I'm not a kid anymore, Holly."

"I know that."

"Then why can't you just let go once in a while? Try trusting me for a change."

"I do trust you." Holly said. "I want you to go out and meet people. Have friends. Find someone and get married or live together or do whatever the hell you want. I just want you to be happy."

"Are you happy?"

Holly looked away. "I manage," she said quietly.

"Men?"

Holly smiled. "A few. It's been hard. I guess I'm still grieving the divorce. So it looks like we're both in recovery."

"Maybe you just need a good fuck," Beth said.

Holly looked at her, and they both burst into laughter.

"Maybe I do."

"I know I do," Beth said as she turned away. "I'm gonna get some sleep."

Beth took the glass and started inside, but when she was at the door she turned back impulsively. Holly stiffened in surprise as her sister's arms went around her.

"Thanks for being there," Beth whispered.

"Wait!" Holly whispered.

Holly put her arms around her sister, feeling a sudden upsurge of emotion.

"See you in the morning," Beth said as she broke off the embrace and started back out of the kitchen.

"Beth." Holly called out. "You know I'll always be there for you."

"That's what I'm afraid of," Beth said, smiling. She picked up her bags and headed upstairs.

Holly picked up her attaché case and carried it into the den. The answering machine was blinking. She had one message. Holly turned it on, and Clara's voice crackled in the air.

"Hi, doll. Just thought you'd like to know. Your reluctant inmate has decided to cooperate. I set up an appointment for ten sharp tomorrow."

The tape clicked to a stop. Holly paused, unsure of how to take the news. It did not make her happy. She sighed, unzipped her briefcase, and took out the file inside. She had decided to read it again in the off chance that she had missed something of importance.

She paused a moment, as if she were reluctant to open it. It took an effort of will, but she flipped open the cover.

Immediately, her expression changed.

Facing her was a photograph.

It was the woman in the ice. Her face was eerily serene, more like the effect created by a wax museum than a human face. But that was because of the long period of preservation in the cold.

And tomorrow Holly would again interview that woman's killer.

9

Holly was already seated when they led Briscoe inside. It was a dreary morning. The sky was gray and cloudy and lent the chamber a bleak suffocating atmosphere.

The manila file was set squarely on the table in front of her beside her closed attaché case. A tape recorder sat alongside the file.

Briscoe took the chair on the other side of the table.

The two chairs and the metal-edged table were the only pieces of furniture in the stark cheerless chamber.

She looked up when he had taken his seat. His eyes were impassive but remained fastened on her. She felt the same surge of energy, the sense that the air in the room was charged.

"So, you decided to come?" Holly began.

"It seemed better than the usual boredom."

"I'm glad we're able to entertain you."

His lips formed a smile. "Can I smoke?"

"If you want to."

He took a pack out of his pocket and placed a cigarette in his mouth. His eyes rose to meet hers, and Holly felt a tightness in the pit of her stomach.

"They don't let us handle matches."

Holly nodded and opened her attaché case. She placed a pack of matches on the table between them as well as a small metal ashtray. He picked them both up and turned them over in his hands without removing his gaze from hers.

Holly did not look away as his eyes danced with hers. His manner was a provocation. For the first time, Holly realized the ashtray could be used as a weapon.

She turned on the tape recorder.

"Tell me about the woman in the ice."

"Her name was Carolyn."

"I know her name."

"Okay. What do you want to know?"

"Everything the jury didn't want to believe."

"Everything?" He smiled and Holly tightened.

"Everything."

There was no avoiding the current of tension between them. It left her slightly unbalanced, a balance she knew she must restore at all costs if she was to remain in control.

His eyes probed hers as if he were trying to read her thoughts. He smiled to himself as he flicked open the cover and struck a single match. She watched as he let it burn without bringing it to the cigarette dangling from his lips.

"They believed she was the victim," he said quietly as the matched burned on.

"That isn't true?"

"She was nobody's victim but her own."

Just as the flame reached the tips of his fingers, he shook his hand and it flickered out.

"What was she, then?"

"That depends who's telling the story. Me or the prosecution."

"What did the prosecution want them to believe?"

"That Carolyn was open. Generous. Warm. And forgiving."

"What did *you* want them to believe?"

"I wanted them to see the other side of her. The real side."

"Which was?

"Neurotic. Possessive. Paranoid. Demanding. Especially if she didn't get what she wanted."

"Which was?"

"Fucking, usually."

His eyes met hers.

"Explain."

He shrugged. "Any way. Anywhere. Any time. All the time."

He struck another match, stared at the flame, then blew it out.

"Was that a problem for you?"

"I don't need Viagra. Not yet, anyway."

"I didn't mean that."

His smile widened. "Not at first. You see, she was beautiful, and I was obsessed."

"With her or the sex?"

"Both."

"What kind of sex?"

His eyes fixed on hers questioningly, seeking something she would not offer. Holly's face was impassive, a neutral mask.

"Magical sex," he said finally.

"Explain that, please."

His voice dropped almost to a whisper. "Sometimes just looking at each other made it happen. Just her eyes on mine could make us come. Ever done that, doctor? Sat across from someone and reached orgasm just by looking at them? Try it some time. It's quite a trip."

"I'll take your word for it," Holly said calmly. "But you did more than look at each other."

"It's all in the transcript. Or didn't you bother reading it?"

"I want you to tell me."

"The gory details?"

"All of them."

He was silent, watching her. Bent forward slightly, the unlit cigarette still between his fingers, the matches in his other hand.

"She liked to experiment."

"Go on."

"The more way out it was, the more she liked it."

"Didn't you?"

"We didn't do anything we both didn't like."

"Be specific."

"This turning you on, doctor?"

"Just answer the question," she said sharply.

His eyes filled with amusement. "Are you always this tough?"

"Continue or I'll end the session," she said flatly, meeting his gaze. They locked glances as the pause lengthened.

"I guess you are."

"Do you want me to repeat the question?"

"Not unless you want to."

He bent a match with his thumb and struck it. His eyes never left hers as he brought the match to the tip of his cigarette, but he did not ignite it.

"She liked it when I tied her up. She called it going into free fall."

"Tied up how?"

"With her wrists and ankles bound together and connected to a chain behind her. She would be blindfolded and naked. She liked being naked. She had a beautiful body and liked showing it off. But I guess you've seen the pictures."

"Go on."

He leaned forward and touched the manila folder. "Are they in there?"

Holly remained unmoving. "Go on, please," she repeated.

"What else do you want to know?"

"What you both did together. How you interacted."

"Interacted?" he said as his lips curved into a smile. "We didn't interact. We fucked."

"Yes."

"You want me to tell you how?"

"Are you afraid you'll embarrass me?"

"Is that possible?"

Holly remained silent.

He leaned forward, his eyes fixed on hers. A wolf's eyes, fierce and hungry.

"She wanted me to penetrate her while she was suspended from a hook screwed into the ceiling. She wanted me to put my hand around her throat, just tight enough to let a little air through. Then tighter as she began to come."

Her naked body was beneath him. Her eyes were locked with his, confident, almost arrogant of her power over him. His fingers rose just below her throat, covering the soft whiteness of her skin.

His eyes were locked on Holly's, glittering brilliantly in the half-light.

"She'd whisper, tighter. And I'd squeeze. Gently at first, just there."

His finger rose, and his arm crossed the distance between them, stopping an inch from Holly's throat, but he did not touch her. She remained unmoving. Her eyes were still glued to his.

His fingers tightened. Her lids closed. Her breathing became more rapid. His eyes fixed on the swollen tips of her breasts, then rose to the moistness of her lips. Her pupils rolled back, revealing the opaque white of each eye.

"I'd increase the pressure as she went into her spasm. She wanted to feel the restraints as she began to lose control. That was the kick. Being controlled and losing control at the same time."

"That was when you cut off her breathing completely?"

He nodded. "Just for a few seconds. Just so she could get to the edge of blacking out the instant before she came."

"You knew the danger?"

"That was what she wanted. The danger. She liked going over the edge. She thought the payoff was worth it."

"Quite a risk, just for an orgasm."

He smiled, his eyes dancing slightly. "Some people would kill for one. Especially one like that. Wouldn't you?"

"The question is, did you?" Holly asked pointedly.

"What do you think?"

He looked at her. Silent. Motionless. The moment lengthened as their eyes continued the duel.

The buzzer finally sounded.

"Our time is up," Holly said.

"How did I do, doctor?" He questioned.

"We don't give report cards."

"Maybe you should." He grinned. "I'd give you an A."

The door opened, revealing the officer waiting outside.

"Hope you enjoyed the session as much as I did, doctor," Briscoe said, snapping the cigarette in his fingers.

He rose and stepped out, and the door closed behind him.

Holly turned off the tape recorder. She remained motionless, her eyes fixed on the cigarette broken in the ashtray in front of her.

Night came early now but the night brought no peace, only the anticipation of danger.

Briscoe lay on his bunk. His eyes were fixed on the area outside the open door of his cell.

The tier was quiet.

Inmates were still out on their assignments. Ever since the incident in the TV area, he had remained inside except for his interview. So far there had been no repercussions, not from the staff, anyway. The inmates were another matter. He expected some kind of retaliation, if not from the two inmates involved, then from their crew, if they had one. Five years inside had taught him to strike quickly and strike first. And deal with the fallout when it came.

He heard footsteps on the tier. He tensed, rising to face the open door. He had no weapons. Whatever he did, he would have to rely on speed and his ability to outthink his opponents on his feet.

An inmate halted before his cell.

Briscoe recognized him, and his shoulders relaxed. It was Pierson, the inmate who wheeled the library cart. He held several magazines in his hand.

"Thought you might like these. They just came in." He held out the magazines.

"Put them down."

Pierson took a hesitant step inside and laid the magazines on the bed.

"Did you get to see the show I told you about?"

"Not all of it. I had a little problem with the reception."

"So I hear," Pierson said. "I also hear that you took care of it."

Briscoe shrugged indifferently.

"Must have been quite a performance. They both had to go to medical. They both said they slipped and fell downstairs."

"Maybe they did. Should I worry?"

"Norris is dangerous. Binns is his stooge. He does whatever Norris wants. They're both in for multiple rape. They worked as a team."

"What are you in for?"

Pierson was silent.

"I'm not anyone's judge or jury," Briscoe said.

"I was into kiddie porn on the Net. But I never touched anyone. No kids, nobody. I just watched."

"Watching's not a crime," Briscoe said flatly. "Not if I made the law."

Pierson took a half step inside the doorway.

"How'd it go with Dr. Alexander?"

"Okay. You said she was your shrink?"

Pierson nodded. "For three years. Almost since she got here."

"What do you know about her?"

Pierson shrugged. "I hear things."

He looked up. Briscoe's eyes were fixed on him.

"Step inside."

Hesitantly, Pierson took another step inside. He looked up as Briscoe's eyes fixed on him. They caused him to tremble.

Briscoe took a step toward him. His eyes glittered in the half-light.

"Are you afraid?"

Pierson shook his head.

"Then come closer."

Pierson shuffled toward him until they were separated only by inches, until his vision filled with nothing but the intensity in the other man's eyes.

"Now tell me everything you know."

It was late when Holly returned to her townhouse.

A blanket lay across the couch. A half-finished glass of milk stood on the coffee table, together with a plate of chocolate chip cookies.

Instead of feeling irritation at the mess, Holly felt a warming sense of comfort in knowing Beth was there and that she was not entirely alone. The thought arrested her. She had not actually felt alone before. The incessant drumbeat of work had always helped ease her feelings of loneliness. Strange, that these thoughts should come now that Beth was staying with her.

Holly continued upstairs. She stepped over to Beth's door and peeked inside.

Beth was asleep, half-covered by the quilt. Her black hair lay like a raven's wing on the snowy whiteness of the pillow, setting off the pale innocence of her features.

Holly gently closed the door and went into her room. She shut the door, slipped off her coat, and began undressing. Only when she was under the shower and felt the needles of hot water massaging her skin did the tension begin to ebb. Only now could she free herself from the imprisonment of Briscoe's haunting gaze and allow herself to sleep. But sleep did not come readily.

Images floated through her mind, images of Briscoe and the woman he was accused of killing. Of their naked bodies coupling. She tried to erase them, but they persisted. Her skin felt hot. Her belly was taut, her thighs were restless. Her hand lay between her legs, but she resisted touching herself. Beth's words echoed in her head.

What you need is a good fuck.

She'd forgotten when she'd had sex last. She had erased that need just as she had erased the feelings of loneliness, masking them by absorbing herself in her work, pretending that work was everything. But she was lonely. And she needed sex. She had pretended that her need did not exist. Touching herself gave only temporary relief. She needed the feel of male hands on her breasts, the feel of someone handling her. She need to open herself and experience the sensation of being penetrated. The satiation of being completely filled. She needed to hold a penis in her hands, feel it throb, pulse, and eject its essence. She wanted a male body on top of her, overpowering her—feeling its strength as she clasped it tight between her legs.

She knew that her primness was often mistaken for frigidity, when exactly the opposite was true. She had been responsive from the beginning, when she had lost her virginity in her first year of college to an deceptively nerdy young man whose main expertise was sex. She had been lucky with Karl. He was an expert teacher, which was what he was later to become. He had no reservations, and he quickly eased her into a regular routine of sexual experimentation. There was no position in the Kama Sutra that they did not try, even the more comical ones. He brought her to orgasm with surprising ease. The succession of boyfriends that followed had no complaints. She often surprised them with her expertise and delighted in the amazed looks on their faces when she lowered her head to their laps with a mischievous smile, asking if this was something they liked.

Philip had known how to take her. He surprised her with his passion, taking her spontaneously, or forcing her to have sex in some outrageous place just before they were to have dinner with some important client. Or sometimes in public—somewhere they might be imminently discovered by anyone walking past. She loved the sensation of risk and of daring. Risks she would never have taken herself, but with him, she was always game. Hot and wet and ready, he called her. And she was proud of it, proud of that hidden side of herself, a side she secretly wanted the world to know.

But all that was now gone. Perhaps it was what she missed most of all about her marriage. Not Philip, not missing him exactly, but missing what he brought out in her. Missing a part of herself that she was too frightened or repressed to ignite herself. An incompleteness that she did not know how to resolve.

10

Rain pelted down in dull metal sheets, softening the stark contours of the prison buildings and glistening on the razor wire like festoons of twinkling holiday lights. It poured off the buildings in sheets and filled the runoffs with brackish foam.

The interview room she was assigned was not the one Holly usually used. This one had a series of windows along the ceiling, the glass panes embedded with wire mesh. Rivulets of pelting rain ran down them like tiny intersecting streams. She preferred windowless chambers that afforded little distraction and concentrated the mind.

She waited a moment before she entered, seeking her usual composure before she stepped inside, but she found that impossible. Her pulse was already racing in anticipation. She felt slightly out of control in this man's presence, as if she were holding the reins of a horse that was too strong for her to manage.

The room was in semidarkness. Briscoe was already seated behind the table, his figure half-shadowed in the gloom.

He held an unlit cigarette between his fingers. She felt his eyes fix on her as soon as she entered and took her place. His look was almost palpable. She felt enclosed, as if a huge hand had closed its fingers around her. She reached over to turn on the light switch when he spoke.

"Do you mind if we leave it off?"

She hesitated, then nodded her assent. She opened the file, then raised her eyes to meet his.

The look in them was different. The hostility of the other sessions was gone, replaced by an expression she could not quite fathom.

"Tell me what your mother was like," she began.

"My mother?" he echoed with surprise. "That's a good one."

"Why?"

"Because I never knew my mother. She had me when she was sixteen, then split for parts unknown. My grandparents raised me."

"What were they like?"

He made a noncommittal gesture. "Old."

"Kind? Cruel? Understanding? What?" Holly questioned.

He did not answer for a moment, gathering memory from somewhere in his consciousness.

"They didn't get in the way, like other kids' parents did. They let me do what I wanted."

"There was some mention in the transcript about your grandfather beating you when you were a boy."

He shook his head negatively. "That was just a lot of crap my lawyer cooked up. Trying to get some jury sympathy. He hit me, sure. But I usually deserved it. It was no big deal."

"He never abused you sexually?"

"That's usually question number one."

"You don't want to answer it?"

"The answer is no."

"Do you have any desire to find your birth mother?"

"What for?" he questioned blankly. "She never came to find me."

"Some children do." Holly told him. "They have a need to know their real parents."

"That sounds like a waste of time and energy, trying to get something you probably don't want anyway."

"Tell me about the tattoo. The bird in the web. What did that mean?"

He smiled as his eyes narrowed questioningly. "I don't know. Maybe you could tell me."

"It wasn't your idea?"

He shook his head. "It was all in her head."

"I thought you were the one in control?"

"Control was never the issue."

"What was?"

"Trust."

Holly stared at him. The word touched a nerve. Trust had been her issue with Philip. The bar that pried them apart.

"Explain that," she demanded, embarrassed by the sharpness of her tone.

"Why?" he asked. "Haven't you ever trusted anyone?"

His look was probing, intense, and his eyes seemed like tiny scalpels searching for her vulnerability. Her skin felt hot. She felt as if she were being suffocated like the woman whose murder she was investigating.

"We're not here to discuss me."

His smile widened. "Maybe we should. I think you and I are more alike than you want to believe, doctor."

She glanced away but his eyes refused to leave hers. She shifted edgily in her chair. Her lips felt dry and she moistened them with the tip of her tongue. She crossed her legs under the desk and felt each of her movements recorded in his eyes.

"Tell me what the word *trust* means to you," she asked, seeking to regain an acceptable distance between them.

"Carolyn put her life in my hands. Hard to trust more than that."

"And she paid the price."

"What price?"

"You killed her."

He shook his head. "No. I didn't kill her. What happened was an accident. It never should have happened."

"But it did happen. You knew it could happen."

"So did she. Whatever we did, we did it together. We both took the same risk. That's what two people do when they love each other. Or haven't you ever experienced that emotion, doctor?"

Holly's face flamed. Her skin was burning.

"Only you're alive and she's dead," she said evenly.

"You're wrong," he said softly. "I'm in here. That's not being alive."

"But Carolyn doesn't have that choice."

"We never played it safe, the way you and I are doing."

"Is that what you think we're doing?"

"You know it, and I know it."

"Know what?"

"You want me to trust you, but you have no intention of ever trusting me. You've already closed the door on me."

"Trust is something you earn."

"That works both ways, doesn't it, doctor?" His eyes framed a challenge.

"You want me to trust you?"

"I don't think you can." He looked at her knowingly. "I don't think you've ever trusted anyone."

The buzzer rang, signaling the end of the session. He snapped the cigarette in half and dropped it in the ashtray. He rose slowly, but his gaze never left her as he stepped over to the door and exited the chamber.

A shiver passed through her. The door was closed and she was alone in the room, but she still felt his eyes fixed on her like icy metallic dots.

She had been in the presence of inmates with powerful charismatic personalities. She knew how to defend herself against their attempts to seduce her both physically and mentally. Mind fucks were one of the first things you learned to defend against, or you quickly went under. Holly thought she knew most of the tricks. But this was different, and she did not know how to categorize it. But there one thing she did recognize. She was less certain of his guilt than she had been earlier that morning. Why that should be she didn't have a clue. But the feeling was there.

Clara picked up on her mood as she entered the office. "Tough session?" she asked.

"You could say that."

"This guy's not getting to you, is he?"

"Nothing I can't handle."

"Said Little Red Riding Hood when she saw the wolf. And he's got eyes like a wolf, or haven't you noticed?"

Holly forced a laugh. "Don't worry so much."

"When it comes to you, I always worry."

Clara offered her a printout. "Pierson's P-G. He got an A plus."

Holly looked at it and immediately brightened.

An hour later, Holly was sitting opposite Pierson's slight, almost delicate figure in a green-walled interview room two doors down the corridor from her office.

Pierson was her prize pupil, the one inmate she was sure had truly benefited from the treatment the center had to offer. Holly knew success was a fragile thing here and she chose carefully among the inmate population for those who had even the slightest possibility of being transformed. It was not an easy task. She was often frustrated and disappointed when one of her prize candidates went south. But Pierson was different. He had not actually acted out on his impulses. He had been arrested for possession of child pornography from the Internet. He was also one of the first to be prosecuted under the child molestation laws recently enacted by the state legislature.

Unlike many of the inmates at Brandywine, who were often in total denial, Pierson was actively engaged in his treatment, and that had given her hope. She felt that together they could find a solution that would allow him to reenter the outside world as someone society need not fear.

His latest P-G proved it.

The plethysmograph, or P-G, was the latest weapon in her limited arsenal. The machine worked like a lie detector. Electrodes attached to the inmate's genitals monitored his sexual responses to various stimuli projected on a screen.

In theory, the greater the inmate's arousal, the less effective he would be in controlling his impulses. The P-G gave an accurate depiction of the inmate's general level of arousal and allowed the team of psychologists to adjust their treatment plan accordingly. However, the success of his latest P-G was not the subject now obsessing Pierson's thoughts.

"What's going on? You look different," Holly said when they were seated together.

Pierson reddened and shook his head.

"Is there something you want to tell me?"

His eyes rose to meet hers. They were filled with feeling. "I think I've fallen in love."

"That's wonderful. Do you want to tell me about it?"

"I knew when I first saw him that I was going to have feelings for him," Pierson said.

His words surprised Holly, as did the passion in their tone. He continued. "There's something magical about him, don't you think? Something different."

"Who are you talking about, Mark?" she asked softly.

He looked at her, and his eyes were glowing.

"He's one of your patients."

"My patients?"

"Not a patient, exactly. You're evaluating him for early release."

"Do you mean Briscoe?"

"Yes. I think I'm in love with him."

Holly sat back, experiencing a series of darkening emotions she fought hard to quell.

"I know he's not gay or anything, but he's the first man, the first really adult male, I ever felt anything for. That's progress, isn't it?"

His eyes were pleading as they fastened on hers. In them she read hope and the desire for her approval.

"Yes," she said quietly. "That is progress."

They had decided to take Briscoe out when he entered the second-tier balcony.

They had discovered a blind spot.

When one of the officers went outside to check on something in the main area, only one was left inside to staff the entire control booth. That was the shortcoming of having the observation post in the center of the module. It took two officers to observe the entire area.

They would do it just before the evening meal, when there was enough movement in the unit to distract the guards and cover their action. One assailant would act as a block, and the other would shoulder him over the railing. They were expert at the move. They had done it several times before, acting as a team. The other times had been contract hits, or payback for various inmate-to-inmate violations. This would be different. This would be purely for pleasure. And for payback for one of their own.

So they waited, the two of them, each in his separate cell, observing carefully as inmates came and went throughout the day.

Briscoe had been scheduled to return to the module just before five. He had been escorted to psych services, where he had been installed in a small windowless cubicle and had undergone a series of tests under the watchful eye of a heavyset female technician in a starched white coat.

He returned from the exam along the main corridor, walking a yard ahead of the officer escorting him. There was a marked difference between being incarcerated in a treatment center like Brandywine and the maximum security prison he

had been sent to. In maximum, any excursion outside an inmate's cell was a walk into terror. Men were killed, maimed,
and blinded for daring to stare at another inmate too long, or
for any number of perceived slights, along with becoming a
casualty of the ongoing gang feuds and warring cliques.

Brandywine was a kind of paradise, free from the usual
dangers, except for the dangers he had brought upon himself.

Most of the inmates now seemed indifferent to his presence, but in spite of all the noise and casual activity in the
main area, Briscoe remained constantly on alert. He spoke to
no one other than the library clerk. He stayed inside his cell
and took his meals alone.

At two minutes past five, Briscoe was returned to the
housing module and checked inside by the escorting officer.
Briscoe waited for the okay, then stepped through the arch of
the metal detector, allowing the officer on duty to scrutinize
his upheld palms and peer into his open mouth.

The officer nodded, and Briscoe started inside. He began
moving along the railing on the second tier, past the first row
of cells, when an inmate stepped out of a doorway and came
directly toward him.

He was a big man, red faced and heavily muscled, his cheeks
deeply ravaged by acne scars and a recent facial wound. The
same man whose face Briscoe had embossed with a small piece
of furniture. As he moved toward Briscoe, his face broke
into a broad welcoming grin.

"Whaddaya say, Mr. Ice-Man?" he called out.

Briscoe returned the smile.

The next few seconds became a chaotic blur. The smiling
inmate was unaware of just how Briscoe managed to get behind him, but before he could react he was in agony, lying
face down on the tile floor, hearing two of his fingers snap
within the viselike grip of the man standing over him.

At that instant, the second inmate stepped out of a doorway and lunged—the man into whose open mouth Briscoe
had wedged a TV remote. Whatever his action was meant to

accomplish, he never completed it. Briscoe sidestepped, and the force of his attacker's motion carried him over the railing, eyes wide with terror, mouth contorted in a horrified scream.

When the first inmate tried to rise, Briscoe's knee crashed into his chest and his hand clamped around his windpipe.

The inmate cried out in pain as he fought for breath. His eyes were wide, fixed on the eyes of his assailant now staring directly into his own.

Eyes that glittered unnaturally, burning deep into his psyche.

Spelling his death.

Holly and the tall man were dancing.

She looked up at him adoringly as he held her in his arms. She drew closer, encased in his warmth. She lifted her lips to his, kissing him softly at first, and then more passionately. The kiss went on and on, pleasing her deeply as she had not been pleased for a long, long time.

His hands moved over her, slowly and possessively. She felt herself relax and the tension begin to build, rising from between her thighs and the depth of her belly. His hands covered her breasts, manipulating them gently as he took each nipple in his strong fingers. She moaned as the pressure came. His hands slid over her buttocks, separating her thighs. She drew up her gown as his hand slid lower. She wanted him to enter her with his fingers, and as he slid them inside her, she sucked greedily at his lips and tongue, reaching down for him with hunger.

Her mouth descended to take him, tasting the softness of his skin and the easy way his thickness fitted between her lips. She sucked the crown and licked along its length, then leaned back, gripping him tightly as she opened her thighs, drawing him into her with the tips of her fingers.

Drawing him deep within her body.

She opened her eyes and looked up at him. His eyes locked

with hers, twin pools of light in the darkness, glittering un-
naturally like the sheen of opals.

For the first time she recognized his face. She drew back.
Terrified.

The man in her arms was Briscoe.

Holly sat up abruptly.

Her heart was hammering. Her nightgown was wet with
sweat. It trickled down between her breasts and formed a wet
spot on her belly.

The effect of the dream lasted for another instant until
she shook free of its compelling image.

She sat up and threw off the covers. The room was in total
darkness except for the digital clock, which read 2:45. She
left the light off in the bathroom as she filled a glass and drank
greedily. Her throat felt dry and constricted. Her hand was
shaking.

She replaced the glass on its holder and stepped out of the
room.

Beth's door was slightly ajar. Holly stepped toward it, feeling a sudden need for reassurance. But waking Beth would
be unwise. Beth had just started working at a diner on route
9 and would be exhausted. Holly started past the open door
when something caught her eye. She stepped back and glanced
inside.

The room was a mess. Clothes were strewn everywhere.
The bed was unmade.

Holly pushed the door open, her eyes widening in surprise.

Beth's room was empty.

11

More rain slicked the roadways as Holly eyed the speedometer. Would it never cease? The thought of it falling day after day became maddening. She was doing 70 when she should have been doing 35. Her tires plowed through gray troughs of water as she turned off the main road toward the prison, which was almost invisible in the downpour.

She was going to be late, and she hated being late. She was scheduled to see Briscoe at nine. Her interview with him would be cut short, just when she needed more time to resolve the strange feeling of doubt that now pervaded her system.

What if he really were innocent?

The question gnawed at her as she drove, mixing with the images of the scene between her and Beth that had happened half an hour earlier.

Holly had not intended to make the detour, but something had impelled her, and she found herself pulling into a spot in front of the crowed diner. She made her way inside and took a seat at the counter where Francine, a veteran waitress, was cleaning the toaster.

"If you're looking for your sister, she's working the window section," Francine said as she placed a cup of coffee in front of Holly.

To Holly's relief, Beth appeared an instant later. She came through the kitchen doors, dressed in her yellow waitress uniform, holding a glass coffee urn. She was smiling. Her expression was radiant as she turned to speak to the young Latino cook behind her. It was obvious to Holly that there was an intimate connection between them. Beth's smile faded when she spotted Holly.

"Hi," Holly said with as much brightness as she could muster.

"Checking up on me?" Beth snapped.

"I was a little worried. You didn't come home last night. You didn't tell me you'd be out."

Beth's expression hardened. "Isn't that what you wanted? Make new friends and be happy."

"I just thought it might be a good idea to establish some ground rules. Like calling when you're not coming home."

"You don't have to worry, sis. I won't be around that long."

Beth stepped away to wait on a customer, leaving Holly feeling as if she had just been slapped.

Francine turned away from the toaster and stepped in front of her, leaning close as she spoke.

"I've got two kids at home, and it's the same deal. Damned if you do, damned if you don't. Just don't let it get to you. More coffee?"

Holly shook her head. She put down enough to pay for the coffee, added a generous tip, then hurried out.

Her glance in Beth's direction went unanswered. Beth had turned her back.

Razor wire gleamed with beads of liquid, giving the perimeter fencing a strange ethereal quality as if she were approaching the gates of some magical kingdom instead of a stultifying arena of incarceration. For the first time in ages,

Holly felt like turning around and returning home. She could call in sick on her cell phone and speed away without anyone seeing her. No one would be looking out, especially not in this weather. But in spite of these reservations, she did what was expected of her—gathered her bag and envelopes, grabbed her umbrella, and dodged between the puddles toward the main entrance.

Clara's eyes recorded her transgression as she barged through the door, her raincoat still slippery with water.

"I know," Holly shouted, heading for her office. "There was a jam-up on the interstate."

"Slow down," Clara said calmly. "Your nine o'clock's in the disciplinary office."

"What happened?"

"He had a little accident."

"Is he hurt?"

Clara eyed her with a knowing expression.

"He'll live. The question is, will you?"

Holly looked at her as a knot formed in her stomach. "What is that supposed to mean?"

"Just watch yourself, that's all. This guy could be dangerous to your health."

Holly turned away. She tore off her raincoat and started out of the office as Clara watched her with a narrowed gaze of concern.

In her office, Holly closed the door and sat behind her desk. *What was happening to her?* The dream had thrown her. Its meaning was obvious: The attraction she had been feeling was real. Briscoe was having an effect on her emotionally, something she could not allow to happen. She was determined to put a clamp on her feelings. When a patient transferred his feelings to his analyst, it was called transference. But the opposite could also happen, even to the best-trained and most experienced practitioner. It was called cross-transference and was a common difficulty in her profession.

It was nothing to be ashamed of. She had caught it in time and could summon the strength to do something about it. But she was in the middle of his evaluation. She had to base her report on logic and professionalism, not on instinct. Yet it was these very instincts that were telling her Briscoe might be innocent; and the worst part about it was that these were her professional instincts, not her personal ones. Or could she still separate the two? Her father had sent men to prison, men who were later found to be innocent. He had committed a miscarriage of justice.

She could not allow another one.

Half an hour later, Holly was striding down the corridor toward her first group meeting of the day when Ted stepped out of his office and turned toward her.

"Heard what happened to your client?"

"Not really."

"He crushed one inmate's thorax. It took three guards to pull him off. The second inmate went over the railing. Concussion, two broken arms, and a compound fracture of the patella. I told you the son of a bitch was dangerous."

"Was it self-defense?"

"I don't give a shit if it was justifiable homicide. You know the rules. Any involvement in a violent situation, and we send them right back."

"You're not sending him back. I'll take full responsibility."

Ted looked at her sharply. "Is this going to be one of your crusades?"

"You asked me to evaluate him. That's what I'm doing."

"And how's it going to come out? Good or bad?"

"I don't know yet."

Ted shook his head. "He's not going anywhere, no matter what you find. They'll never give him early release."

"Then why did you give me the case?"

"Why, because it's political. And you're the only one around here I can count on to make us look good."

"And that's all that counts. Looking good. Not his guilt or innocence?"

Ted's eye brows rose incredulously. "Come on, Holly. Now you think he's *innocent?*"

"I didn't say that. I just don't know. I do know he deserves the same chance as everyone else."

Ted eyed her dubiously. "Do you know what you're doing?"

Holly met his eyes, then stared past him, perhaps not as sure as she needed Ted to believe she was.

Briscoe was seated at the small shelf in his cell that he used as a desk as the sound of the library cart came closer.

He was drawing something on a sheet of paper. He did not turn his head as Pierson pulled the cart to a halt just outside his door.

Briscoe put his pencil down and turned, looking up into Pierson's adoring gaze. Briscoe did not avoid the other man's eyes, but rather seemed to accept the homage.

"Got something for me?" he asked in a flat tone.

Pierson nodded and took a hesitant step inside, holding a stack of magazines.

"You got lucky," he said in a low tone. "They were going to send you back to maximum, but Dr. Alexander intervened. She put herself on the line for you."

Briscoe nodded almost as if he had expected it. He did not question the information. Trustees like Pierson usually knew everything. They had ears everywhere, even in the administration offices. He turned back to his desk and picked up his pencil.

Pierson waited a moment, watching Briscoe as he continued his drawing, wanting to speak but not having the nerve to interrupt.

"Something else?"

"No," Pierson answered. "Not really. Is there anything else I can get for you?"

"I'll let you know." Briscoe did not turn his head.

Pierson waited another moment, then stepped back outside and wheeled the cart away.

Briscoe paused and looked down at his work. Satisfied, he took a wad of gum he found under the desk and stuck it to the paper, then smashed the picture against the wall in front of him.

It was an extremely good likeness of a woman's face.

The woman was Dr. Holly Alexander.

Holly was already seated behind the desk of the interview room when Briscoe was ushered inside.

His face was bruised. A black and blue mark covered one cheek and he wore a bandage over one eye.

"Good morning, doctor," he said coyly, as he dropped into the chair opposite.

"I'd like you to tell me what happened."

"Worried about me?" A smile played around his lips.

Holly steeled herself. She had been thrown off balance by news of his altercation.

"Tell me what happened," she repeated.

"What's the difference?"

"You are my patient."

"Am I? I thought I was strictly a guinea pig."

He leaned forward, bringing his eyes to meet hers. "Who worries about you, doctor?"

Holly was silent for a moment, then she reached over and turned on the tape recorder.

"At the trial you claimed Carolyn's death was an accident. Why didn't you report it immediately?"

He did not answer. Something dark clouded his features.

"Why did you put her body in the pond if it was an accident?" Holly continued. "Didn't you realize how that would look?"

"They didn't want the truth," he said harshly. "They wanted a crucifixion. I didn't give a fuck how it looked."

"Then why did you do it?"

His eyes clouded. His fists clenched. He seemed to be struggling with something buried inside himself. He looked up at her abruptly and their eyes met. She read agony in his gaze.

"Why? Simple. I couldn't let her go."

"Explain that."

He sat erect suddenly, his back straight against the chair. His eyes were fixed directly ahead, looking not at her but through her to somewhere distant.

"I was holding her." He began in a strangled tone that rose from some place deep within him, expressing an emotion she had not seen before.

"I held her in my arms. It must have been hours. Days. I don't know. I lost track of time. I was lost somewhere inside myself. When I came around it was night. I was still holding her. She was so beautiful, even like that. Even dead. Cold. So I put her body in the water. I wanted it to freeze. To stay that way. Preserved. So I wouldn't have to put her in the ground. So I wouldn't have to lose her forever."

His eyes returned, focusing on her. "Does that get me a chapter in the crazy book?"

"I'm not here to judge you."

"You're my judge and my jury," he said suddenly. "You're the only chance I've got."

His eyes held hers magnetically. His gray wolf's eyes. She could not look away. His gaze seemed to imprison her.

"She was in therapy, wasn't she?" Holly asked, forcing herself to look away and glancing down at his file.

"That was before I met her. What about it?"

"Your lawyer tried to get the therapist's notes admitted into evidence, but the judge ruled them inadmissible."

"So?"

"They might have shown that Carolyn purposely put herself at risk."

"Bullshit!" His eyes were suddenly hostile. "I told you. She was nobody's victim. Neither was I."

"If those notes had been admissible and had shown her to be mentally unstable, you might be free."

He shook his head. "Not free. Don't you understand? Just out of here."

He was silent. His eyes were still fixed on her.

"We knew what we were doing. You've got to understand that. Maybe I should have stopped it. Maybe I should have said no even if it meant losing her. Maybe I never should have gone near her in the first place. That was my mistake. That's the price I've had to pay for what's happened. That's the agony I live with. Every hour of every day."

He paused and looked up. His eyes were wet. His voice had become a strangled cry.

"I loved her. Can't you understand that? She was my whole fucking life. My entire existence was wrapped up in her. Christ. Why did she have to die? Why did I let it happen?"

He sat forward and his shoulders hunched. His hands slammed onto the table. His fingers were clenched. The knuckles were white.

"She was the only thing that ever mattered to me, and I killed her."

His eyes were fixed on hers. Tormented eyes filled with pain.

"I killed her." He repeated slowly, then he lapsed into silence.

Holly watched him without moving. The silence grew longer. There seemed to be no air in the chamber. She felt as if the walls were under pressure and would come together, crushing them both.

He looked up suddenly, reached over, and shut off the tape recorder.

"What are you doing?"

"I want to know why you won't let anyone in. Why won't you let anyone see what's behind all that armor you're wearing?"

"We're not here to discuss me," Holly managed through her constricted throat.

"What are you so afraid of?" His voice had become a plea. "Not me. You can't be afraid of me. I'm locked up in here. I can't hurt you."

She remained silent as his eyes probed hers. She was trembling. She felt naked suddenly, as if he could see into her, into the deepest part of her being.

"I'm not a murderer, Holly." He continued in the same agonized tone. "What I've told you is the truth. I loved Carolyn. I would never have hurt her. I know how hard it is for you to believe that. I know you've been burned. I know you've got a scar somewhere deep inside you, just like mine. I know because I can feel it."

He unclenched his fists and placed his hands on the table.

"Why is this so hard?" he asked, looking down. "Why does it hurt so fucking bad?"

He raised his head and his eyes locked with hers.

"I need someone, Holly. Someone who'll believe in me. Some who'll help me through this. Someone who understands the pain. Who understands that I'm human. I need you, Holly. I need you very badly."

Holly remained silent. His words resonated. His eyes were magnets. She was unable to draw hers away.

"I can't do any more of this," he said in an almost inaudible voice. "No more questions. No more answers. You want to send me back to maximum, fine. I'll go back. But that's it. No more. Help me or don't help me. It's up to you. But I'm done."

He broke off his gaze and rose suddenly. His movement startled her. He turned and went to the door, banging on it with his fist. The door opened, and he stepped outside without looking back.

Holly remained in her chair, her eyes fixed straight ahead. The pressure she felt earlier had vanished, but the room still resonated with the dark timbre of his voice.

I need you, Holly. I need you very badly.

*   *   *

His file totally absorbed her.

It seemed to have a life of its own, a special vibration that made her open it and read it again and again.

The prosecution: You knew that what you were doing could lead to Carolyn's death.

The witness: I knew we were taking a risk.

The prosecution: No. You knew you were walking a deadly line . . . a line from which there might be no return.

The witness: We both knew it.

The prosecution: And yet you still went ahead, regardless of the consequences.

The witness: We both knew the consequences. We were willing to take the risk.

The prosecution: Why?

The witness: Because we loved each other. What's the matter? Haven't you ever been in love?

Love. Yes. But that didn't satisfy Holly. It was evident that there was something missing, something left untold. It was the girl. She was the mystery that had to be unraveled. Discovered. Deciphered.

We have to consider the victim. Her life was cut short by the deliberate intent of the accused. Cut short in the prime of her life. A girl who was loved and admired by this community . . .

The victim was a calculating, desperately sick young woman who planned her own destruction and lured the defendant into a scheme whereby he would be the accomplice in her own murder . . .

What was the truth?

Holly lost track of time. When she finally looked up she realized that it had grown dark outside.

Clara was standing in the doorway with a knowing look.

"Problems?"

"I guess so."

"You're thinking he might not be guilty, aren't you?" she asked.

"I'm not sure."

Clara took a step into the room. "What is it? Have you got a thing for this guy?"

Holly stared at her, feeling suddenly vulnerable.

"Come on, Clara," she said emphatically. "He's an inmate. And I'm a psychologist doing an evaluation."

Clara's sharp look revealed that she wasn't buying it.

"You're also a woman. And it's been a long time since you were with a man. Add that to your evaluation."

Clara shot her a parting glance, then turned on her heel and left the room, leaving Holly unable to frame a response.

Her bones ached and she knew she should sleep, but sleep would not come.

Holly got out of bed and went to her desk, where she opened her canvas bag and extracted Briscoe's file.

Clara's words still resonated in her mind. They were like a slap of cold water. What Clara had suggested about Holly having fallen under Briscoe's spell could not be true. Holly struggled against the idea. She had dismissed the idea of cross-transference. That had not happened. It would have been a breach of Holly's professionalism and her well-guarded sense of self. But she was also aware of her own vulnerability and how easily emotions slipped beneath the radar screen. Holly knew that in the past, intimate contacts had occurred between inmates and female counselors, contacts that were both emotional and sexual.

There had been talk of one such affair during one of her training stints before she had come to Brandywine. But that had been before Ted took control. The rules were more permissive then and the counselors not so well trained or so well screened. Nothing of a similar nature had taken place since then. Not that she knew of, anyway.

Holly did not consider herself invulnerable to that kind of situation. It was only human to allow feelings to grow between herself and certain of the inmates. Pierson, for example. She felt a great deal of empathy for him, empathy that bordered on affection. But she was careful.

Difficult as it was to admit, she didn't know how she felt. What she did feel was confused and shaky.

The vividness of the dream returned. She had recognized its significance, but had dismissed it as a natural consequence of her loneliness. Was it? Or had she been closed off so long that she could not recognize the power of her own emotions, and was she more deeply involved than she could afford to admit?

The questions pounded. She could not deny the weight of feeling that drew her to believe in the possibility of his innocence. Did she need that reassurance before she would allow herself to feel anything else?

And should she feel anything else?

He was an inmate, a convicted felon. A murderer, possibly. In any case, he was a patient. The ethics of her profession forbade her from having these feelings, and certainly from acting upon them. Then what was the proper course of action?

These thoughts were unsettling to the image of herself as an impartial professional. Yet she owed it to that very professionalism to follow through on what her instincts told her about his guilt or innocence.

She had to know.

She heard a car approach and glanced at the clock. It was a little after two AM. She rose and went downstairs as the door opened and Beth entered. She was wearing her uniform under her coat.

"Waiting up?" Beth questioned in a mocking tone.

"No. I had some reading to do."

"Well, I got the breakfast shift, so nighty-night."

Holly stepped back as Beth passed her.

"Beth."

Her sister paused and looked at her questioningly.

"I could use a hug."

Beth smiled and quickly embraced her.

"Anything you want to talk about?" Holly said, releasing her.

Beth shook her head. "You?"

Holly hesitated. The rules of confidentiality prevented her discussing a case with anyone not in a professional capacity. Holly had always been scrupulous when it came to confidentiality.

"Just work stuff."

"Sure."

"Look, about the other night. I was just worried, that's all. Not making any judgments on what you do or who you go out with."

"No problem."

Beth made a weary gesture, then struggled up the stairs. Holly went back to her desk.

She stared down at the horrific pictures of the naked young woman imprisoned in the ice, and the mystery of her enigmatic tattoo.

Her eyes darkened as she picked up a pencil and began to write, forcing herself to make a decision that could put her entire professional career in jeopardy.

The noise had finally died. It was midnight, the time the unit finally settled down into a semblance of quiet, though it was never really still, vibrating with the frustrations of the men imprisoned inside like a ship in heavy seas.

Briscoe's eyes were open. Light from outside was reflected in their twin gray irises.

He sat upright on his bunk, back flat against the tile wall.

Fists tight at his sides. Noise was part of the torture the prison system provided for its inmates. The unceasing sound bounced off the tile walls, amplifying the tread of boots on metal stairs and the sharp clang of barred gates that continuously opened and shut. Added to the incessant cries of the other inmates was the unceasing irritation of the television set playing full blast almost from the moment they got up to the time they were locked in for the night. Then there were the anguished cries of the insane: the delusions of the psychotics and the ceaseless conversations of the schizophrenics, locked as they were within two prisons, the one outside and the one within. Only a steeled mind could survive and keep from going insane. A mind capable of disconnecting itself from its surroundings and focusing its thoughts deep inside.

Briscoe possessed such a mind.

It had helped him survive his childhood and five years of maximum security. Five years of a virtual lockdown, where the majority of inmates were kept imprisoned in their cells for twenty-four hours every day, seven days a week, serviced by a small group of trustees who did their laundry and served them meals in their cells from huge rolling carts that came by three times a day on screeching wheels. The noise level was beyond comprehension, a never-ending barrage of screams and insults. Prisoners chattered and screeched like chimps. Exploding in frustration, they destroyed everything they owned, pissing through the bars and flinging excrement at the guards watching on the tiers opposite, or into the cages of other inmates.

To concentrate so deeply that your mind could erase the noise and the stench was the sole path to remaining whole. It required the skill of a Zen master and the patience of a samurai.

They were both arts Briscoe had mastered.

Now, in the comforting silence, he forced his thoughts to focus on the picture he had drawn earlier and stuck to the wall opposite. The portrait he had done of Dr. Alexander.

Onto it, he projected the full force of his will and the entire fabric of his desire. Bound and caged, he was still the hunter, still able to bait his trap and procure his prey.

All he had to do was wait.

12

Ted burst into Holly's office at nine-thirty the following morning.

"So what's the diagnosis on Briscoe? We've got a deadline."

"I know. It's still pending."

Ted looked at her curiously. "What the hell does that mean?"

"That I haven't come to a decision."

"You're still evaluating him, right?"

"Yes, but he won't come anymore. He's said all he's going to."

Ted stared at her, "Doesn't he know we can send him back to maximum?"

"He knows."

"Then write the order."

"I'm not sending him back."

"So where the hell does that leave us?"

Holly looked up at him. "I don't know."

"Oh shit." Ted exclaimed. "I know that look. No! No! No!"

Holly turned the file toward him.

"Judge for yourself. The case just doesn't add up. You asked me for an evaluation. I'm doing my best."

A look of pain crossed Ted's face. "Oh, Christ. Okay. What?"

"It was a small town. There was a lot of strict religious sentiment. Briscoe and the murder victim flaunted their disregard for the local mores. I think Briscoe may have been railroaded by an opportunistic prosecutor who played right into the deepest fears and prejudices of the jury."

"You're saying he didn't kill her?"

"No. He killed her. That was never an issue. Only the act wasn't premeditated. It could have been an accident, just the way he claimed. That would have been manslaughter, not murder. And certainly not sexual assault."

"Holly," he said impatiently, "grounds for early release are based on his chances of recidivism. The state doesn't give a shit if he's innocent or not. His guilt is a given. The system is only interested in the possibility of his doing it again."

"I know. That's exactly what my report is based upon. If he didn't do it in the first place, then it wasn't a sex crime, and his eligibility for early release wouldn't even be in question."

"You're wearing me out, do you know that?"

"I'm sorry," she said sharply.

"Okay. Then what about the woman in the ice?"

"I put together my own intake assessment. I think she was a borderline personality who inveigled him into playing a sadistically sexual role that got out of hand, just the way he said it did."

"And just what are you using for corroboration?"

"I'd need her therapist's notes."

Ted looked at her thoughtfully. "Then get 'em. We can't afford another Ulman."

Dr. Alter was a matronly woman in her early fifties who wore her hair in a Victorian topknot and dressed in Laura Ashley. Her office was on the second floor of a small office building located in a corner shopping mall.

The woman in the ice would have had to drive almost thirty miles to see her, but in two years she apparently had never missed a session.

Dr. Alter had reluctantly agreed to see Holly, but only after two pleading phone calls in which Holly had been her most persuasive. Now they sat opposite each other in the pleasantly decorated office, Dr. Alter in her large leather armchair and Holly on the couch opposite.

"You know what you're asking is impossible," Dr. Alter began. "Carolyn's records are confidential."

"Carolyn is dead," Holly said. "I understand your concern, but reading them can't hurt her or her family. I'm asking to see them in strictest confidence."

Dr. Alter's brows furrowed. "I'm sorry, but I just can't. Besides, they were ruled inadmissible at the trial."

"What if the judge was wrong?" Holly asked, leaning forward. "Only a jury could decide his guilt or innocence. They should have been allowed to hear all the evidence."

"Do you believe he is innocent?"

"I don't know yet. I do know that the trial was seriously flawed. I think you know that too."

Dr. Alter looked away. "I have to protect my client's memory."

"Yes, but not at the expense of justice. I think we both know just how disturbed Carolyn really was."

"What if he actually is guilty and he goes free because of my notes?"

Holly shook her head. "I can't set him free. All I can do is recommend his release. I won't do that if I don't think the evidence warrants it. But we have to know, don't we? A man's future is at stake."

The doctor stared at her visitor, balancing her misgivings against the intensity in Holly's eyes.

It took almost a full day to read through all of Dr. Alter's material.

Holly kept at it, staying away from the prison and working in her office at home. By evening she was both exhausted and exhilarated. But she had her answer.

By the time Beth entered the house just before ten, Holly was hunched over her laptop working on her report. Beth looked in at her then went into the kitchen to make tea.

"Hey, make me one too, huh?" Holly called out. She put down the computer and rose, stretching her tired muscles as she went into the kitchen.

"You don't have to worry about me anymore, sis," Beth said, handing her a steaming cup. "I got a job over near Lancaster and I put a rental deposit on a cute little house."

Holly saw the look of triumph in her sister's eyes. She felt a deep stab of misgiving and the sinking feeling of loss.

"Lancaster," Holly repeated, struggling for a smile. "That's great. Are you sure? I mean, they said you were doing so well over at the rehab."

"I have to, Holly. I have to live my own life. I'm six months sober. I can do it."

"Aren't you seeing someone at the diner?" she ventured.

"Oh, Carlos? That wasn't serious. Just a little fling." Beth was staring at her. "Aren't you going to say anything positive?"

"Oh baby. I'm just going to miss you, that's all."

Holly put down the cup and took Beth in her arms. Holly felt her eyes filling with tears.

"Shit," Beth said. "I'm sorry. I didn't want you to cry."

"It's because I'm happy for you," Holly said, wiping her tears. "Really happy for you."

Beth looked at her sister, and a tear rolled down her own face. She brushed it away quickly.

"Hey. You're supposed to be the tough one," Beth exclaimed. Then they were hugging each other, both of them laughing and crying at the same time.

* * *

Holly entered Ted's office at nine-fifteen the following morning.

Her eyes were clear and the puckers of worry she had worn for the last several weeks no longer marred her features. She laid the report on his desk with a resounding slap.

"I'm recommending Briscoe for probationary release," she said crisply.

Ted's expression assumed the usual bureaucratic uncertainty.

"Be sure. We can't have this backfiring on us."

"I'm sure," she said firmly. "Dr. Alter's notes confirmed my diagnosis."

"Which is?"

"That Carolyn instigated the kind of dangerous sex they were having out of a deep need for self-punishment. She pushed it further and further, knowing the kind of danger it represented. Sex was a kind of ritual in which she received both pleasure and the pain she needed to assuage her feelings of guilt. It was all there in the notes."

"What about Briscoe? Where did he fit in?"

"He was her accomplice. She recruited him."

"He had nothing to do with it?"

"I didn't say that. He fell in love with her and went along with the program she set up. Look, she was a beautiful girl. Most men would have gone along with what she wanted."

"Beautiful or not, do you actually believe most men would enjoy strangling the woman they were making love to?"

"All right. Not most. Some. But I believe he was the real victim, not the other way around."

"He killed her. You said so yourself. How does that make him a victim?"

"Yes, he killed her. But without premeditation. Without the intent to kill, it isn't murder. It's manslaughter, for which he's already served five years."

"Right, Sherlock. I'm still waiting for the victim part."

"He loved her. He was so passionately involved that he

put her body in the ice so he could keep it with him as long as possible. That's how deeply he adored her. That's why what happened made him the victim, too."

"Come on, Holly. You know perps like to keep their victim's corpses nearby and get off on them. Again, I'm not buying."

"Then you take over the evaluation. Mine says there was no sex crime."

Ted looked at her. His eyes were still uncertain, but she saw that she had convinced him.

"Okay. Then file it."

Holly smiled. There was no longer a shade of doubt clouding her heart.

The wheels of the library cart rumbled along the tier, stopping at the door to each cell. Briscoe counted each stop. He remained seated on his bunk in front of the shelf he was using as a desk, sketching a design for a new floor plan on his drawing pad. He had been working on the plan for several weeks. A real estate magazine lay open on the blanket beside him. It showed pictures of a lovely farmhouse that would make a spectacular country inn. It was a property he coveted, one he knew he would have possession of very soon. He would write to his lawyer instructing him to make a suitable bid.

The cart squealed to a stop outside the open door of his cell.

Briscoe put down his pencil, closed his pad, and rose to face Pierson, who had taken a step inside.

Pierson's face was alight. His eyes were glittering unnaturally.

"What's going on?" Briscoe asked quietly.

Pierson's words came in a rush.

"Doctor Alexander. She's recommended you for early release."

Briscoe was still for a moment. His eyes became unfocused. A smile played across his lips.

"I just heard it from one of the guys who cleans the office."

Briscoe nodded. "That's good news. Thank you."

"We should celebrate," Pierson said excitedly.

Briscoe looked at him. His eyes were calm. "I already have."

13

Holly stood beside the slide projector in the rear of the classroom.

It was the second week of the abnormal psych course she taught two nights a week at the local community college. She shared the thirteen-week course with three other psychologists, each of them taking a three-week portion, then doing a combined session for the final week. The schedule allowed her to offer the students a look into the realities of her world without tying her down to an entire semester's work.

The faces she looked out over were young, a cross section of the suburban county that had once built red-roofed barns and towering silos, and now sprouted malls and subdivisions and the complexity of life that went along with them.

"The men you are looking at are all convicted sexual predators," she began. "They are from all races and economic classes. All ages and professions. They are everything from teachers to construction workers, computer hackers to day laborers. The question we as a society have to ask is, can they be treated? And if not, how is society to deal with them once they have served their sentences and are sent back to live among the rest of us?"

Expressions changed as Holly paused to allow the question to sink in. A few hands shot up.

"There are no real cures for these offenders, are there?" The question was asked by a skeptical young man in worn jeans and a loose-fitting motorcycle jacket.

"We haven't found one for AIDS," Holly responded. "Should we stop looking?"

"I see what you're saying." He continued, "But from the point of view of the victims—"

"Which victims?" Holly interrupted. "Most sex offenders are also the victims of someone else's abuse."

"Right. But that's no excuse, is it? I mean, for committing the offense?"

"Agreed. But we have to see it in context. If you caught a disease from someone else, should you be punished for spreading it?"

"No," he said. "But there is a thing called personal responsibility. Otherwise no one would be responsible for anything."

"That's true," Holly admitted. "I'm not advocating that we abrogate personal responsibility. The criminal should be punished for his crime. What I am advocating is societal responsibility for treating the criminal once the crime has been committed. Especially when we know the sentence will come to an end and the criminal will, I repeat, will, commit the crime again. Divida. It is Divida, correct?"

A dark-skinned young woman nodded as she rose.

"You say we know the criminal, the sex offender, is certain to commit a crime again. Then why is he being released?"

"We have determinate sentencing in this country, meaning that each crime has a specific punishment. Once the criminal has finished his sentence, he is generally released, except in the case of sex offenders. Many jurisdictions, including this one, retain the offender after he has served his time. In other words, he is being detained by the state in the expectation that he will commit his crime again. This is the only category of crime where this happens. I ask you. Is that fair?"

The class was silent. A hand rose in the back.

"Otto."

A boyish-looking young man in a tweed jacket half rose from his seat.

"Do you think it's fair?"

Holly turned to face him. "No."

"Then are you advocating we set him free?"

Holly was silent. "I don't know the answer to that question."

Another hand rose.

"Alicia."

The young woman she called on rose from her seat, her brow furrowed with curiosity. "Why do you want to work with offenders rather than their victims?"

"To prevent more victims," Holly answered. "I worked with victims for several years, until I realized we had to break the cycle somewhere. That's why I decided to work at the center."

The young man in the motorcycle jacket leaned forward. "Yeah. But what would you do if one of the guys you were working with got out and molested your own kid?"

She looked at him squarely in the eye. "I'd probably want to kill him. Wouldn't you?"

There was a sober silence.

"I didn't say this was going to be easy, did I? And by the way, that is the subject of your next paper," she said, picking up a piece of chalk and writing on the board: *Should sex offenders be released after serving their sentence?* She used the remote to turn off the slide projector and turn the lights back on. "Don't forget to put last week's assignment on my desk when you leave."

Students rose and filed down the aisle to hand in their papers. Holly came forward to collect them and to face the small pool of students who now stood beside her desk, each of them eager for her to solve all the problems of the world.

* * *

Fifteen minutes later, Holly was seated alone at a table in the faculty cafeteria sipping a cup of coffee and going over the stack of student assignments. She had just taken a bite of the bear claw on the dish beside her when a voice boomed.

"Doctor Alexander."

Holly looked up warily. A man of forty-five or so stood on the other side of the table holding a tray. He wore a beard sprinkled with gray, and a broad smile. He was a professor in her department. She recognized him from one of the wearisome meetings she was forced to attend before the semester began.

"The term is flying by and we haven't had a chance to talk," he said, widening his grin.

"I'm sorry. I've just been so busy." She tried to sound affable, but there was an impatient edge to her voice.

"Papers to grade. We all have them," he continued.

"Actually, this is an evaluation for one of my patients at the prison. It's due tomorrow."

The smile faded. "Of course. Sorry. I didn't mean to intrude."

He turned and started away.

Holly was immediately regretful. What was the matter with her? Okay, so she was tired and a little on edge, but she didn't have to be so abrupt. She exhaled, feeling an immediate disgust with herself.

It had been over a month since she handed in her report on Briscoe. She was impatient for a result and hated the waiting. Was that the problem, or was it something else?

She had been preoccupied with work as usual and with moving Beth to the new house she had rented in a small town outside Lancaster. Beth had refused her offer to help redecorate. She insisted on doing everything herself. Perhaps that was a good thing. Beth needed to feel independent and successful. That was basic. Holly would have prescribed it for any of her patients. But with Beth it was always different.

That Beth was maintaining herself successfully on her own should have been a source of joy, and Holly had to force herself not to call more than once a week. But she did not feel any joy. The truth was she missed being depended on, being the grown-up sister who always shouldered her weak sister's burdens. It was immature and stupid, and she should have grown out of it.

Holly took a sip of the still-warm coffee, discreetly eyeing the professor who had found a place at a table with two other teachers, both of them women. They were all chatting away, which only increased her irritation.

She knew the professor had only wanted to flirt, and most probably ask her out. Why had she been so curt? She had heard him lecture. He was amusing and personable. They had even exchanged glances. What was the matter with her? He was the second attractive man she had snubbed in as many months.

The image of Dan Shepard suddenly blitzed through her mind. He was certainly attractive and not the usual insensitive breed of cop. There had even been something soulful about him. So why had she refused his offer of dinner?

She could no longer blame it all on Philip and the traumatic effects of her divorce. She had made up her mind to move on. Why hadn't she?

For an instant, she pictured herself back in the interview room, facing Briscoe, staring into his gray wolf's eyes. Her stomach tightened at the memory. She was sweating slightly and her pulse was racing.

His passionate gaze filled her mind, along with the deliberate way he had of slicing through her defenses. Thinking about him brought further confusion, and she struggled to dismiss his image. Having anything to do with him was an impossibility even if he were to be set free tomorrow.

She had not seen him since their last encounter, though he was still incarcerated in the unit pending his final review by the parole board. She convinced herself that thinking about him was only natural. After all, he was one of her patients.

Was it the knowledge that an innocent man had been imprisoned that brought on these thoughts? Or did she feel that he had been punished enough for what had happened? Did his continued incarceration disturb her innate sense of justice? Or was it something else?

Was it the woman under the ice? Her face pressed to the transparent surface. Her eyes open. Staring upwards. Trying to speak.

Holly shook herself free of these thoughts. She picked up the stack of themes and deposited them in her briefcase, then rose and slipped out of the cafeteria, careful not to allow the professor to see that she was leaving.

The plethysmograph room was dark.

Images of young boys flashed across the screen. Some were clothed, others were naked. Some lay on couches or sat in chairs, other stood in provocative poses. Many of the images were of commercial models, while others were almost pornographic.

Pierson was seated in the chair facing the screen. His chest and arms were wired with electrodes connected to the P-G machine itself. Wires snaked down along his thighs and were fastened to the soft skin at the tip of his penis.

Holly sat in the room next door watching Pierson through the one way glass. The technician was heavyset and dour. He sat beside Holly, monitoring the graph as it fed through the machine. His hair was thinning and he had a paunch. He emanated a sour odor of distaste.

Holly could observe Pierson's reactions through the window. He blinked as each image changed, but otherwise his face remained placid, almost emotionless. However, his facial reactions were not what counted. She respected his privacy too much to look for an erection.

The screen went to white as the technician turned off the feed.

"What do you think?" Holly asked with mounting impatience as the paper fed through the final spool.

The technician was unhurried as he looked over the length of paper passing though his pudgy hands. He was the individual Holly liked least of all the people she worked with. He seemed to enjoy prolonging her suspense. Whether to increase his own self-importance or just to annoy her, she had never quite figured out, but he was an officious, irritating bastard.

When he finally turned to her it was with a malicious grin, and her heart fell.

"Well, I'll tell you, doctor. I've seen straight-ahead heteros who spiked over these pictures. This graph is as flat as Florida. And the peter-meter never lies."

Twenty-minutes later, Holly strode into Ted's office. She placed Pierson's P-G on his desk with a flourish.

"Take a look," she said with a smile of satisfaction.

Ted perused the graph and looked up. "Not bad."

"Then you'll support his parole." It was not a question.

Ted offered a lukewarm nod. Holly brightened.

"Ted, you're an ace."

Holly picked up the P-G and was about to exit when Ted's voice called her back.

"By the way, Holly, looks like you're on a roll. Briscoe was just granted probationary release. So, congratulations."

Holly stared at him as the effect of his words sank in.

"He's being released," she stated simply.

"As soon as possible. They'll return him to maximum security and process him out from there. Hope you're happy."

"Thanks." She turned and started out.

Strangely, there was no elation in her step.

* * *

"You don't look happy," Clara said when she stepped into her office a few minutes later.

"No. I'm fine. Pierson passed his P-G."

"That's good news. I also heard about Brisoce getting a provisional release. So why aren't you smiling?"

"I don't know."

Clara looked at her. "I think I do. But maybe it's something you don't want to hear."

Holly hesitated, then raised her eyes to meet Clara's. "No. Go ahead."

"I think you have feelings for this guy you don't want to admit. And now that he's leaving, you're feeling a sense of loss."

Holly waited a moment before speaking, allowing the words to register.

"You're on the wrong side of the desk, Clara. You should have my job."

"So I'm right for a change?"

"You're always right," Holly said. "I've been trying to deny it. But to tell you the truth, its been a pretty confusing ride."

"Look, it happens to the best of us. The situation was pretty intense. You were the only one who went to bat for him. And he is a damned attractive guy. Plus all the stuff with your father and the idea of allowing a possibly innocent guy to get railroaded by the system. Your emotions were bound to get involved, one way or the other. The good thing is you didn't act on it. So, nothing really happened, except in your mind. It'll pass, you'll see. In the meantime, isn't there anyone you could spend some time with? Of the male persuasion, I mean."

"I've been pretty stupid in that department lately," Holly said quietly.

"There is no such thing as stupid when it comes to men. You've got nothing to lose. Make a call. Say, 'Hi, let's get together and catch up.' It's easier than you think."

"You're a beautiful woman, do you know that, Clara?" Holly said, brightening.

Clara returned the smile. "So are you, doll. Just have a little faith."

Holly nodded. Perhaps that was just what she needed.

14

The release process was a slow-motion ordeal for someone with the taste of freedom on his lips. But the slowly grinding gears of the bureaucracy had to be satisfied. Briscoe was scheduled to be released from the Brandywine Center and returned to his maximum security prison for final processing.

He was taken down from his cell by three correction officers in helmets and body armor, prepared for any possible attack that might occur before he could leave the unit, but fortunately nothing transpired. Inmates were ordered inside their cells during the exit procedure. They stood behind their shatterproof glass doors watching in silence as he passed. Several sets of vengeful eyes were fixed on him as he walked down from the tier to the entrance. He met each gaze with a steely look of contempt.

He was passed through the twin-barred gates at the entrance to the unit and picked up by two corrections officers waiting in the corridor outside. They escorted him from the unit to reception, where he was told to strip and spread as an officer examined him for possible weapons. He was ordered to dress, placed in handcuffs, and shackled to a belt with a connecting chain to irons around each ankle. He received an inventory of his belongings and signed them out.

He checked the list against the items in the cardboard box in a slow and purposeful manner, while the escorting officers waited impatiently for him to finish. When he finally scrawled his signature across the bottom of the pink form and slid it back over the counter, it was Pierson who picked them up.

"You do all the work around here?" Briscoe asked.

"No. I just wanted to be here when you left."

Briscoe looked at him. Pierson reddened under the other's direct gaze.

"Good luck," Pierson said quietly.

"Thanks," Briscoe responded. He looked up and their eyes met.

"I'm getting paroled," Pierson continued softly. "So if you ever need a place to stay, this is the number where I can be reached. It's my brother, so he'll always know where I am. I'll put it in the box, if that's okay."

Briscoe regarded him curiously as a smile played across his lips.

"Sure," he said. "You never know."

"Let's move it," the guard's voice commanded.

Pierson dropped the slip of paper inside. Briscoe nodded a farewell and turned to go as the officers fell in behind him. Pierson stared after them, watching until the heavy steel door shut with a hardened clang.

Cold slapped Briscoe's face as he was led outside. He inhaled the crisp fall air as the escort hustled him over to the Department of Corrections van parked in the courtyard, its windows grated with steel mesh. His eyes swept the area. A pale sun focused shadows across the yard. The sky was blue with wisps of cloud.

Just before he stepped inside, Briscoe turned and looked up.

A woman was silhouetted in the window above, looking down into the courtyard.

The woman was Holly.

His eyes met hers for a magnetic instant before she stepped away, leaving only a darkened rectangle.

Briscoe's lips formed a knowing smile. His gaze remained fixed on the empty window for a moment before an officer placed a hand on his shoulder.

Briscoe ducked inside the van.

The doors closed. The bus started up and pulled out of the courtyard, continuing along the peripheral road beside the double line of razor wire until it reached the main gate. A few minutes later it was on the road leading out of the valley, a moving dot driving toward the horizon.

Holly walked back to her office. Her face was still hot. Going to the window was decidedly unprofessional. Yet, there was no rule that said she had to stifle all normal human response. She was responsible for Briscoe's release so it was natural that she should see him off.

Then why had she not gone down to reception and faced him, proffering her hand in a gesture of friendship and good luck? It was a question she could not answer.

She stepped into the psych office as Clara turned to face her with a knowing look.

"So, he's gone?"

Holly nodded, starting into her office.

"You saw him off?"

"No. I did not see him off," Holly said firmly. "I merely watched him go."

"He left this for you."

Clara extended her arm, offering an 8x10 manila envelope. Holly took it from her as Clara grinned. "Maybe it's a love note."

Holly ignored the taunt and stepped into her office, knowing Clara would be burning with curiosity. She closed the door, went to her desk, and uncurled the string fastener. She reached inside and drew out a page torn from a drawing pad.

It was a charcoal rendering of a woman.

It took Holly a moment to realize that she was looking at an image of herself. The drawing was impressive. The artist had considerable talent. He had captured something of his subject. Her eyes stared boldly, straight at the viewer. Her lips were composed in an enigmatic smile, reflecting some secret inner thought. Around her shoulders and hair were the lacy lines of what she first thought was a shawl. But it was not a shawl.

It took her a moment to realize that it was a web just like the one in the tattoo on the woman in the ice.

Beth's rented house was a small, simple white-frame dwelling on a tree-lined street filled with similar homes once lived in by workers of the last century, a memory of the smoke-belching factories that once dotted the area and no longer existed. The exterior was charming. The interior was a mess.

Although Beth had refused Holly's decorating help at first, she had finally given in. Now, Holly was spending the weekend, happily standing on a ladder, paint brush in hand.

"Better be careful," Beth called to her from the other side of the archway that led from the narrow hall into the living room. "Think any deeper and you'll fall into the can."

Holly lifted her head, surprised at her own reverie. "Just a passing thought," she answered. "Nothing important."

She had been thinking of the drawing Briscoe had given her. Its image had been haunting her ever since she opened the envelope and held it in her hands.

"Looked like a big one. Who or what is on your mind, sis?"

"Nothing. No one. Just work."

"No one?" Beth asked. "Come on."

"Well, I did meet someone. A while ago."

"No kidding? Who is he?"

"A cop, actually."

"Oh, oh. Maybe I better not know."

"Tell me about these new friends of yours."

Beth smiled, happy to describe them. "There's Helen. She's my sponsor at AA. She's introduced me to a couple of her friends. We all went out together a few times. I really like them. Some are in recovery, just like me."

"Any men?"

"At AA? You've got to be kidding."

"I thought it was the hot place to meet guys."

"Give me a break. I'm a recovering waitress. Men. Who needs 'em! Well. There is one thing I do need now and then . . ."

Beth lifted her brush and painted an enormous penis on the wall. She put a bow on it, then she quickly painted it over as they both began to laugh, the sound of their laughter echoing throughout the tiny house.

Pierson stood alone in front of the two-story red brick administration building located just outside the perimeter of the prison. He was dressed in tan slacks and a blue zippered jacket, his collar up against the chilling wind that swept through the valley with razor sharpness. A suitcase rested on the ground beside him.

Holly left the building wearing a raincoat against the occasional drizzle that had punctuated the dismal November morning.

"I just spoke to your brother," she told him. "He's coming to pick you up. They rented a nice place for you. It's what you wanted. I think you're really going to like it." She stopped and looked at him. "Are you all right?"

"I'm scared shitless," he said through chattering teeth. "I don't think I can do this."

"It's only natural that you're scared. I know you can do this or I never would have recommended you for parole. Now, make me feel better and tell me you're going to be okay. Because I know you are."

"I'll be okay." He spoke firmly, then his voice changed. "You'll still be seeing me?"

"Once a week. Like a bad clock. You're going to hate seeing my face."

"I'd never do that," he said. "You're all I've got."

Holly smiled and he forced a grin, but she could see just how frightened he really was. And in a very real way, she was every bit as scared.

The ringing phone tumbled her out of sleep.

Darkness shrouded the room except for the light from the green shaded banker's lamp. It was only nine-thirty, but Holly had nodded off at her desk.

She reached for the receiver and brought it to her ear as the voice on the other end brought her to clarity.

"Yes?" she answered abruptly.

"Hello."

The voice was male, low, and distant. The tone was familiar, but she couldn't quite place it.

"Who is this?"

"I was hoping you'd remember."

"I'm sorry. It's late and I'm tired. So just tell me who you are."

"I'm sorry. I know it's late, but I just wanted to say thanks. I can call back if you'd like."

Recognition suddenly dawned.

Briscoe.

She was instantly awake, fingers of ice gripping her belly.

"That's okay."

"I'd like to do something else beside just saying thank you," he said softly. "I'd like to take you to dinner."

"That's not possible."

"Why not?"

"It wouldn't be professional."

"That's not much of a reason."

"It is for me."

"You're sure?"

Holly paused, hesitating. Her voice trembled. "Very."

"I'm sorry. I thought we could be friends."

"That would also not be very professional."

"No. I suppose it wouldn't. But there are times to break the boundaries. This is one of them."

"You're mistaken," she said.

"We could discuss it over a drink."

"I couldn't do that." Holly tensed, suddenly aware of how alone she was. She felt open, vulnerable.

"Did you like the drawing?" he asked.

"Yes. It's very good. You're very talented."

"I had to do it from memory. I'd like the chance to do one in person, if you'd pose for me."

"I'm sorry. I couldn't do that either."

"I'm sorrier," he said. "Not my lucky day, is it?"

"What will you do now?" she ventured.

"Go back to work. I have to earn a living. I saw an old tavern in Springfield. It has a large barn. I'm going to restore it the way it was a hundred and fifty years ago, then turn it into a B and B."

"Sounds like a very good idea."

"I'm glad there's one you like."

Holly said nothing. The silence grew. She knew she had to hang up, but something prevented her. When he finally spoke, his voice was lower and more intimate.

"I feel very close to you, Holly. I think you know that. Your friendship is important to me. It isn't easy saying good-bye. Friends, then?"

"I'm sorry."

"Well. Almost friends, then?"

"All right. Almost friends."

"I have a feeling we'll be seeing each other one day. I hope it will be very soon."

The phone clicked off.

Holly's hands were shaking. How had he gotten her number? She felt a blade of fear pass through her like a sudden chill.

She tried to put the thought out of her mind. But the house felt suddenly cold, dark, and empty around her. She rose, went to the thermostat, and raised the temperature. Then she crossed the living room and checked the lock on the front door. She put on the alarm. Then she went upstairs, undressed, and stepped into the shower.

The water calmed her. It was reasonable for him to call. After all, she was responsible for his release. It was only rational for him to thank her. She had nothing to be afraid of. Besides, he was living somewhere far away. She shook her head and wondered what Clara would think when she told her.

Twenty minutes later she was under the coverlet and fast asleep.

The cell phone was still clutched in his hand as he stared up at her windows from his position, parked in the spongy darkness of her complex at the end of the cul-de-sac just opposite her house. The area was illuminated by two high arching streetlights that filled the darkness with a soft amber glow.

The air was crisp. The trees were still shedding their foliage, but the brilliant orange and purples of the last few weeks were fading. Leaves filled the edges of the asphalt roadways that curved through the complex, blowing across the well-tended lawns.

He had driven there at dusk and made a leisurely tour of the meandering roadways that serpentined through the complex. He took stock of the houses and the carefully pruned vegetation. It was a peaceful, almost idyllic setting, safe, serene, and secure.

From where he sat he could see her windows. He watched as the lights went off downstairs, then were lit on the second story which he assumed was where her bedroom was located. He sketched the interior design in his mind, tracing the pattern she would travel from kitchen, to hallway, then upstairs to one of the two bedrooms. He saw her shadow cross the window as she entered the bathroom and imagined her showering. He conjured the soft contour of her naked body, picturing the shape of her hips and the upward curve of her naked breasts, the fibrous tips of her nipples and the seductive slope of her belly.

He was a hunter, and she was now his prey.

Her coy refusals on the phone earlier had only whetted his appetite. He sensed her desire behind the words, caught the rapid intake of her breath and the clipped way she answered. They were all indications of the level of emotion she was experiencing. He sensed her confusion and understood the conflict she was experiencing. He knew how to raise the level of her inner voices until she would be unable to refuse their pleading. It would take time, but he had that now. She had provided it, and it was only just that she receive the fruits of her labors.

Still, it would not be easy. She was as elusive as an antelope. To trap his prey he would need skill and patience.

He had both.

There was to be no mercy this time.

Holly could see that from the rigid look in their faces as they sat staring up at her from their places around the classroom.

"What about pedophile priests?" Otto had just asked from his seat in the corner. "What do we do with them?"

"What we would do with any pedophile. Investigate the complaint. Then prosecute. And if they're found guilty, we imprison them," Holly responded.

"Yeah. And afterwards?" Otto asked.

"That depends. Let's go back to the definition," Holly stated, holding up her red-jacketed copy of the *Diagnostic and Sta-*

tistical Manual of Mental Disorders, which was considered the bible of her profession. "The *DSM* says that a pedophile is someone who seeks sexual gratification with children as a repeatedly preferred or exclusive method of achieving sexual excitement. With that as a given, there are a variety of factors involved, celibacy being one of them, along with the idea that having sex with women is evil. This often inhibited priests from having a healthy heterosexual involvement and refocused their interest on young boys."

"So, something can be done?" he asked.

"With intense therapy and follow-up, it's possible their tendencies could be controlled," she answered.

"Yeah." A voice piped up from the rear. "But doesn't the *DSM* say that pedophilia is incurable?"

She turned to the speaker, a dark-haired young man in a leather motorcycle jacket who was the class gadfly.

"Yes. That's what it says. However, if you read it carefully, that judgment only applies to pedophiles who molest prepubescent boys. And not even totally in those cases. A sexual fixation on adolescents can be overcome through intensive therapy plus pretty rigorous, and I mean rigorous, supervision and follow-up."

"But that hadn't been the case, was it? I mean, with the church. The abusive priests were returned to other parishes and continued to abuse kids."

"True. But many of the old mistakes have been corrected. We hope."

"Tell that to the kids who were abused," he said.

Holly nodded. "Before the recent scandals, most priests were sent to special treatment centers where therapists often certified them as capable of returning to their jobs under certain conditions, usually that they not be allowed to be involved with children. When they did request strict guidelines for follow-up, they were usually ignored. The church was complicit in that it believed that once a child abuser repented and showed contrition, he should be forgiven. And once forgiven, he could be returned to work with young children. In that way, the therapy itself was abused. And the abusers continued their abuse."

"So essentially, the therapy failed," the young man stated with a triumphant smirk.

"Not exactly," Holly continued. "By the end of the eighties, most experts had come to the conclusion that pedophilia was incurable. But there was a general agreement about how to minimize any possible relapses. First and most important, the offender had to acknowledge his deviance and the egregious consequences of his behavior, which is possibly the most difficult aspect of the treatment. I can attest to that. Most offenders do not believe that what they have done is in any way wrong. One of the worst pedophiles in the church, for instance, actually established a Web site advertising the benefits of sexual relationships between men and young boys."

"He should be hung," another voice exclaimed. Holly ignored the remark.

"So what exactly is the treatment?" Otto asked.

Holly held up the *DSM*. "Once there is a breakthrough and the deviant acknowledges his behavior, the most effective treatments are aimed at restraining both the pedophiles' access to children and his ability to hide, to rationalize, and to deny his actions. Then he or she is given libido-inhibiting treatments, along with diagnostic devices like the penile plethysmograph that measures sexual arousal—a sort of sexual lie detector. To this is added twelve-step therapy. The best way, of course, is when all of this is mandated by a court. Pedophiles must know that those who are treating them are obligated to consult with law enforcement. They have to know they will be held accountable for their actions and face imprisonment if they act out."

"Great," the young man in the leather jacket said. "So we give them all this stuff, the therapy and the peter-meter and the rest of the yadayada, and what happens when they do it all over again?"

"That was the subject of the paper I assigned."

"Yeah, sure."

"Which I'm assuming you didn't read?"

"Why read something meaningless?"

"So you don't believe any of what I described will work?" Holly asked.

"Not a chance."

"Then what is your solution?" Holly asked, knowing what his answer would be.

"Me? I'd lock them up for life."

"Regardlesss of the time served for a specific crime?"

"Regardless."

Holly stared at him as a feeling of defeat washed over her.

"How many of you feel the same way?" she asked.

There was a moment of hesitation, then hands began going up all around the room. Only two of the students refused to join the others—a belligerent young man with a shaved head who had sat slouched in his seat and said nothing the entire time, and a matronly woman named Evelyn, a white haired grandmother going for her degree. Even Alicia and Davida, the two she thought were her staunchest allies, had joined hands with the others.

Holly counted the result and wrote it on the green board behind her. Then she picked up her papers and walked out of the room.

The flowers were waiting when she returned home that evening.

They stood in a vase on the front step, wrapped in cellophane, an explosion of colors and shapes: lilies, gladiolas, white roses, delphiniums.

There was no card, yet she knew who they were from almost as soon as she saw them.

She felt charged with sudden excitement, a strange completely alien fluttering of her heart. She unlocked the door and carried them inside, tossing off her coat and heading for the kitchen.

She had just finished placing them on the dining table when the doorbell rang.

She knew who it was.

For an instant she did not know what to do. She felt a sense of panic, mixed with intensifying fear. She could not let him in, but neither could she allow him to remain standing outside. She would have to explain it to him again, the way she had on the phone and establish the necessary boundaries. She had to.

The buzzer rang insistently, snapping her out of her trance. She went to the door and opened it expectantly.

The man facing her was not Briscoe.

He was someone she had never seen before. A sense of relief flooded her, along with a sickening feeling of disappointment.

"Dr. Alexander?" he said hopefully.

"Yes?"

The man was tall, with sandy hair and regular features. He was dressed in a dark blue suit and carried an attaché case. He looked like someone who sold insurance or foreclosed on your mortgage.

"My name is Karl Anderson. I'm Carolyn Anderson's brother. I was just informed that you were evaluating Briscoe for early release."

"I can't discuss that with you, I'm sorry," Holly said, stepping back with her hand firmly gripping the knob.

"I don't think you've seen all the evidence."

"Mr. Anderson, I understand why you're doing this and I sympathize, but I can't help you. Briscoe has already been granted a provisional release."

"If it's provisional, it could be revoked. Isn't that true?"

"Yes" she said, trying not to show her impatience. "But that's highly unlikely."

"I'm only asking for an hour of your time."

"I can't. It's not possible. Besides it's no longer in my hands."

"Would you at least take a look at this?" He held up a plastic-covered binder.

Holly began closing the door. "Mr. Anderson, please don't put me in this position. I know she was your sister . . ."

"This has nothing to do with my sister." His tone hardened. "These are affidavits from three other women he did the same things to. The only difference is, they're still alive."

15

The house was in a cul-de-sac filled with similar houses, all of them typical suburban town houses pretty much like her own. It had taken an hour to drive there, a trip during which Holly had remained silent.

Earlier, Karl Anderson had sat quietly in her kitchen nursing a Coke as she read through the material he had given her. When she was through, Holly had looked up at him and said, "I'll need to speak to each of these women." Her voice was a hollow whisper.

Difficult as it was, Holly had managed to slow down her thoughts during the drive, forcing her mind to remain a blank. She wanted no premature judgments, not until she had a chance to come face-to-face with each of the women whose names were on the affidavits she had been shown.

Her first instinct had been to refuse to read the material. A sharp inner voice scolded her for even admitting him to her house. She had seen the evidence and the therapist's notes and had made her decision accordingly. Then why was she sitting beside him as they sped toward some unknown variable that could only cause her further torment and lead who knows where? The question gnawed at her as they drove.

Karl eased the car into the driveway and went around to

get the door, but Holly was already outside. They moved together in silence toward the front door, which opened before they could ring the bell.

The woman who opened it was a pleasant-faced blonde in her mid-thirties. She wore an old-fashioned lace-edged white blouse beneath a black velvet vest and an ample red plaid skirt. She was attractive, but at least forty pounds overweight. She seemed nervous and smiled hesitantly as they entered. There was something artificial, almost wooden in her manner, together with her overly made-up face and starched lace cuffs.

"Elaine McNeil," Karl said, introducing them as they stepped into the living room. "This is Dr. Alexander."

"Nice to meet you," Elaine said.

An ornately carved grandfather clock stood in the entry beside an old-fashioned coatrack. The house was furnished in imitation Victorian antiques, and overly heated. Karl had made the call to Elaine from Holly's kitchen, a call Holly was still not sure she should have allowed.

Holly took a seat on the tufted red silk couch as Karl sat on a leather chair opposite.

"Would you like some coffee?" Elaine asked nervously.

Holly shook her head, and Karl made a negative gesture. Elaine took a seat on the ornate wood-carved settee beside the fireplace, tucking her skirt under her plump knees and sitting forward expectantly.

"Briscoe has convinced Dr. Alexander that Carolyn cooperated," Karl stated abruptly.

Elaine nodded. "Yes. He's very good, isn't he?" she said, nervously flipping back a lock of her lacquered hair. "He makes you feel so special, so unique. By the time you begin to understand, it's too late."

"Understand what, exactly?" Holly asked, instantly regretting the edge of aggression in her voice.

Elaine smiled knowingly. "At first, I didn't know exactly. Not fully. I was too obsessed with him. He was so attractive and so incredibly *there*. The way so many men aren't. There were so many times I felt that he could read my mind."

Her expression changed suddenly, darkening as her eyes became more expressive.

"Then I began to realize that what really excited him wasn't the sex we were having, though that was so total, so over-powering. It was seeing how far he could go, how much he could make me do. I keep reliving it over and over. It's like an uncontrollable waking dream."

Elaine looked up, and her eyes seemed to beg for Holly's understanding.

"Tell us what happened," Karl said.

Holly could see how difficult this was for her. She almost felt like interceding and telling the young woman that she was under no obligation to speak. But she held back; some-how she had to know.

"Go on," he said. It was the tone of an attorney to a wit-ness. "Tell us what happened. Tell us what he did."

Elaine lowered her eyes. When she began to speak, her voice was a low, almost emotionless monotone, unspooling in Holly's mind like a moving piece of film.

Elaine was naked in the darkness, trembling excitedly as they made love.

The area was illuminated by a single glowing lamp stand-ing in the corner. Her pale skin glowed as the light played over her thighs and across her heavy breasts.

Her arms were raised above her head, her wrists clasped by leather manacles connected by a single chain fastened loosely to a hook on the edge of the table behind her.

He lay between her opened thighs, moving back and forth inside her as they twisted rhythmically on the surface of the table he had covered with leather padding. Waves of plea-sure rolled over her, so intense they were almost blinding. She twisted her legs to clasp his torso as if she wanted to draw him deeper inside. She cried out periodically, but her sounds were constricted by a tight leather collar that he controlled by a thong he held wrapped tightly around his right hand, tightening it each time she climaxed.

The sensation was both terrifying and compelling. She

had cooperated initially, as he brought her to new planes of feeling. Her climaxes were electrifying. He seemed to reach new depths inside her. She began having multiple orgasms so intense that she blacked out. The blackouts only lasted for an instant, but she could not breathe easily and asked him to stop. He tried to calm her, telling her they were almost there, whispering for her to trust him, that he would not hurt her. His lips were at her ear, urging her to relax and accept it. To just relax and let it happen. But she was too frightened.

The more she resisted, the tighter the collar became. She began struggling. Her fingers clawed at him. She was fighting to breathe. Fighting for life. But he would not stop or listen. His penetration became deeper and more insistent. She tried to scream, but no sound came from her throat. His eyes were fixed on hers. The pupils were hard, glittering, opal-like in the darkness. Eyes that were empty of passion, as cold as a bird of prey as it watches its victim struggling to escape.

That was when she knew she was going to die.

She felt her eyes roll up and froth begin bubbling from her lips. Then blood burst from her constricted throat.

Something snapped.

Air flooded into her lungs, and she could breathe.

She realized the clip on the collar had broken. She swung her hands down and struck him.

His eyes widened in surprise as she brought her knee up hard against his groin.

He cried out in pain as she brought both hands down hard against his face, hearing the snap of bone as the heavy leather bracelets struck bone. She sprang from his grip as he rolled away, and she was free.

She broke away from the table and rushed through the door. She tore out of the house. Everything passed before her in a blur of motion. She felt only her bare feet striking the dirt road. Then she was running, her skin lashed by brambles. She sensed him behind her, calling for her to stop. Somehow she reached the road and saw the lights of a car piercing the darkness as it came toward her . . .

* * *

Elaine paused and became silent. Holly sat back.

The room seemed drained of oxygen. Karl sat motion-less, his eyes fixed on Holly.

"I got to the road," Elaine continued, her voice quavering. "A man and his wife picked me up. Otherwise, I know he would have killed me."

"Did he contact you afterward?" Holly asked.

Elaine nodded. "He claimed that he went for help, but I didn't believe him."

"You're sure it wasn't an accident?"

"It was no accident."

"Why did you let him do it to you?"

"To prove that I loved him." Her shoulders began to shake and her eyes filled with tears. "He made me say the same thing over and over."

"What thing?" Holly asked softly.

"That I belonged to him. That I would give him every-thing. Everything I had to give."

Elaine paused, unable to stop shaking.

"I'm sorry," she said, staring at Holly with an agonized expression. "It comes back so vividly. I keep reliving it again and again. I can't get it out of my dreams."

Holly felt an overwhelming wave of pity. She wanted to take the young woman in her arms, but she forced herself to turn away.

To Karl she said, "Why didn't she testify?" She could see the anger building in his eyes.

"She wanted to," he said tersely. "But the DA wouldn't allow it. It would have compromised the prosecution."

"Why?"

"Because Briscoe had filmed the two of them having sex. He made it appear that everything happened with her con-sent. That she asked for it."

"Did you?" Holly asked, turning back to Elaine.

Her eyes lowered. "Yes. He made me ask him. It seemed to excite him when I did."

"Show her what else excited him."

Elaine waited a moment, then she unbuttoned her vest and stripped it off. She began unbuttoning her blouse. She peeled the lacy material from her body, exposing her white bra, then turned around with her back facing them. She unhooked her bra, exposing her back.

Holly stared at the expanse of white skin.

Elaine's entire back had been tattooed.

Starlings. Six of them. Their wings outstretched. Caught in a twisting web.

Holly felt her stomach constrict. She felt suddenly sick.

"Thank you," she said quietly.

Elaine picked up her blouse and stepped out of the room without turning around.

Holly returned her gaze to Karl. "You said there were three. What about the other two? Why didn't they come forward?"

"Their families were socially prominent. They didn't want a media carnival. He counted on that. He's very clever about who he selects for his victims."

"But neither of them died," Holly said, then regretted it as Karl's face changed expression. She could read the pain in his eyes.

"No, none of them died," he stated bitterly. "Only Carolyn. He was working up to it with Elaine, but I think his nerve failed. He didn't make the same mistake twice."

Elaine stepped inside the room. She had gotten back into her clothing and regained her composure. She faced Holly with an agonized expression.

Holly was silent for several moments as she tried to weigh what she had heard. Then she turned back to Karl.

"Why didn't the other two file charges at the time? They weren't children, were they?"

Karl looked at her, then opened the folder on his lap and turned it toward Holly.

Holly started.

Steel fingers gripped her heart. She was looking at the pictures of two fourteen-year-old girls.

The campus was windswept as the afternoon turned blustery. Leaves blew up in waves of grit. Students hurried between the buildings, laughing as the wind caught their clothing.

It was a pretty campus filled with wide lawns and brick colonial buildings, all centered around a white-spired, eighteenth-century clapboard church.

Holly waited for the bell signaling the end of classes. She had gone to the registrar and copied the young woman's program. As the students poured out of their classrooms, she checked their faces against the photograph Karl had given her.

Holly recognized Norma Keene immediately as she came through the doors, part of an eagerly chattering group of sophomores. Holly stepped toward the attractive young woman, introduced herself, and asked to speak to her for a moment.

"What is this about?" Norma asked.

"Jason Briscoe."

The look on Norma's face was itself a confirmation.

Fortunately, the cafeteria was almost deserted. Holly chose a table in the far corner and both women carried their coffee containers over to it and took seats across from each other. The ebullience that had been on the young student's face when Holly approached her had been exchanged for a darker, more subdued demeanor.

"I'm sorry," Holly began. "I know how this must make you feel, but I have been involved in recommending Briscoe's early release and I need some corroboration. It would be in strictest confidence. No one will ever know. You don't have to sign anything, and you won't be called upon to testify or give a deposition or a statement of any kind. I'd just like you to look at this."

Holly opened her briefcase, took out Elaine's affidavit,

and slid it across the table. "I have to know if anything like this ever happened to you."

Norma bent her head and began reading. Holly sipped her coffee and watched as the young woman examined the pages. When she was finished she looked up at Holly and slid the affidavit back toward her.

"Is there any way you could help me?" Holly asked quietly.

The girl was silent.

"Can you either confirm or deny what you've just read?" Holly continued.

The young student looked at Holly. Her eyes were expressionless as she slowly unbuttoned her sweater and drew it down, turning slightly so Holly could see.

The skin of her right shoulder was tattooed: a small blue starling imprisoned in the dark strands of a web.

Karl Anderson's office was in the upper tier of a two-story suburban shopping mall.

He was an attorney with a real-estate practice and no partners. It was dark by the time Holly got back from the campus. She found parking in front of his building and took the elevator to the second floor.

The door was locked, and Holly had to press the buzzer. It took a moment for Karl to open it and admit her to a spacious suite of offices, decorated with rows of law books and metal shelves filled with client files. There was a reception area, two desks for legal assistants, and a conference room. But none of the employees was in evidence.

Karl led her back toward his office and let her precede him inside.

A young woman was seated on the expensive-looking red leather couch decorated with brass studs.

Holly recognized the young woman from her photograph, but there had been a complete transformation in her appearance. The innocent-looking teenager in the picture Karl had shown her had morphed into a black-clad goth, complete with pierced eyebrows, black lipstick, purple hair, and tongue jewelry that glinted in the light when she opened her mouth to speak.

"Holly, this is Lisa," Karl said as he went behind his massive oak desk.

Holly smiled a hello as she took an armchair.

"Holly just came from seeing Norma," Karl continued.

Lisa made a noncommittal gesture. "We don't see each other much anymore," she said casually, eyeing Holly with a wary gaze. "You a cop?"

"No. I'm a psychologist. I work at the Brandywine Center for Sexual Offenders."

"He didn't rape us. It wasn't like that."

"What exactly was it like?" Holly asked pointedly.

Lisa twisted around in her seat, drawing a pack of cigarettes out of her huge black leather bag. She tucked one leg under her, exposing her slim thighs covered in black net stockings. She lit up using a big old-fashioned metal lighter, and exhaled, sending a wave of smoke toward the ceiling.

"I don't know. It was more like an S and M thing."

"How did you get involved with him?"

"It was Norma's idea." She exhaled. "She got us involved. She wanted to be an architect then, so we heard about this old reconstruction and we drove over to see it. Briscoe was there, working on it, and that's how it happened."

"Both of you had sex with him?" Holly questioned.

Lisa nodded. "Sometimes together and sometimes separately. He liked having us both at the same time."

"Did you get tattooed?"

Lisa smiled. "Sure."

"Can you show me?"

Lisa nodded and placed her cigarette in the large, heavy crystal ashtray on the table beside her. She rose and stripped off her dress.

Holly glanced at Karl, whose eyes were fixed on the young girl, his lips pursed in an unforgiving line.

Lisa stood before them naked from the waist up, clad only in her net stockings. She was tattooed all across her left arm and shoulder. A large dragon crawled over her left breast, its teeth closing over her prominent brown nipple. A snake traveled across her belly and disappeared below her navel.

She turned and bent to allow Holly a look at the place where the skin was a different color, barely visible within the mass of images. She could see the outline of a web and within it the faint shape of a small bird.

"His was first," she said simply. "It's kind of covered up. A bird in a web. Norma got the same one."

"What's that?" Holly asked pointing to the ridge of scar tissue along her spine.

"That's where he burned me."

Holly sat erect. "Burned you? What do you mean?"

"Like I said, we were into this S and M thing. That was part of it. He burned us. Sometimes with wax. Then other stuff."

"What else did he do?"

Lisa grinned. "You really want to see?" Holly read the desire to shock in her eyes.

Holly nodded, trying to conceal her trepidation.

Lisa gripped the sides of her leotard and drew it down. She opened her thighs.

Her pubis was shaved, the labia pierced with a tiny silver ring.

"He did that to you?"

She looked at Holly with a sidelong glance. She was in no hurry to cover herself.

"You can get dressed now," Karl said curtly.

Reluctantly, Lisa drew up her stockings, then slipped back into her dress. She plopped back down and took her cigarette out of the ashtray.

"Was it done against your will?" Holly asked.

Lisa shrugged, raising her eyebrows.

"Not exactly. I mean, we were both into it. It kind of turned us on. Not the burning or the real pain stuff. He liked tying us up, then hanging us from the ceiling, things like that. It was very Japanese. He had these Japanese books that showed all these girls being tied up and suspended from hooks in the ceiling. It was sort of cool."

"You enjoyed it?" Holly asked.

Lisa's lips tightened and she shook her head. "I liked it sometimes, but it was pretty painful. I think he got off on that."

"On what?"

"Hurting us. Giving us pain."

Holly paused. Lisa lowered her gaze. She seemed subdued, lost somewhere within herself.

"Why did it stop?" Holly asked.

Lisa shrugged. "I don't know. It just did. We got into other things."

"He just let you go?" Holly asked.

Lisa nodded. "He knew we were under age. He never pushed it. It only happened when we wanted it, when we contacted him."

"Then you initiated the sex?" Holly questioned.

Lisa nodded. "We thought we were really into something cool. Something no one else was into. That's why we went. I don't like to think about it much. I was going to have the tattoo removed. But I haven't. Not yet."

"But you will?"

Lisa looked up at her and nodded. And for an instant Holly saw the innocence she had seen in the photograph return to the young girl's eyes.

Construction was always a problem, but this time it was going with incredible smoothness. Partially, it was a result of the contractor he had hired. The rest was due to his incredible good luck. The property was in very good shape. Most of the original structure was sound. If his luck continued and the weather held, he could open a few weeks before Thanksgiving. So far so good. The rain that marked the early months of fall had sloughed off, giving the area a bountiful harvest of cool sunny days, perfect for working outdoors. A new roof had been essential and had gone on without a hitch.

Even the legalities had gone with incredible smoothness. The normal escrow period had been waived by the small local bank, which saw his project as a precursor to the development of the tourist industry in the area. His attorney had wrapped up the deal while he was still in his final days at Brandywine. His first act of freedom upon being released from maximum security was to drive to the bank and sign the final papers giving him ownership. The estate was considered a white elephant by the heirs of the previous owner, a retired gentleman farmer who had purchased it decades before and died well into his nineties. The heirs were spread across the country and wanted no part of the property. They had been more than eager to sell. Briscoe considered the purchase price a bargain.

The second thing he had done was to change his appearance. He had grown a fashionable-looking beard and dyed his hair so that the striking white wings on either side of his head were no longer visible. His hair was cut shorter as well, in the local suburban manner. His name too, was different. He was now known, locally, as Richard Maitland.

Things had happened so quickly that all the time and attention he would have lavished on other, more pleasurable pursuits was now absorbed in the finishing and decoration. Art and décor were particular passions of his. He loved beautiful objects and spent long hours over their collection. Collecting beautiful objects was also good business, as it drew the wealthy, who could afford the prices of an exclusive retreat far from the well-traveled tourist areas frequented by the fannypack white-sneaker set. Each object in the inn had been personally chosen by him, and placed in its particular nook and lit by baby spots to achieve the maximum effect. He used both antiques and reproductions; he was not a snob. For him, an object's beauty and craftsmanship counted above its age or provenance. Even in choosing the staff, he considered poise and appearance over prior experience.

Even there his luck had been remarkable. Ads in the local newspapers drew a remarkable collection of pretty blond girls and handsome young men with regular features and brilliant smiles. It had been difficult to choose. In the end, he picked half a dozen attractive young people and had been about to call the winning candidates when a young woman entered the office of the motel where he had been holding the interviews and made her way toward him.

The woman was Carolyn.

He remained still as she approached. His eyes were fixed on her. Her skin was perfect. Her hair was blond, seemingly the same silky shimmering tresses he had once held against his skin. Her eyes were blue, the transparent blue of the winter sky. She had the same long-legged body and supple waist. She smiled as he rose to greet her. He was smiling but still half in shock.

But of course it wasn't Carolyn. Her name was Laura Bergen. She was nineteen and she had come about the ad.

"I'm a student in Lancaster Community College. I work part time as a waitress and I'd like more hours to fill in my work schedule."

"What are you studying?" he asked.

"Pre-med. I want to be a vet. I love animals."

"You live with your parents?"

She shook her head. "I never knew my parents. I was brought up in foster homes. Right now, I live alone. I used to have a roommate, but she decided to join the Air Force. I'm sort of looking. But I like living by myself."

"No boyfriends?"

"Not at the moment," she answered, without reddening. Her eyes met his and held for a moment, almost magnetically.

"Why not?" he asked.

"Oh, you know how it is with young guys. They're so possessive. It gets too complicated. I need to concentrate on my studies."

"What kind of work were you looking for?"

"Anything, really. I can type. Work a computer. Handle a register. Wait tables. I don't mind what I do," she said.

"I think I'd mind."

She smiled and lowered her eyes.

"But I think we could find something to suit you," he continued, leaning forward so that his eyes were fixed on hers. "Something the two of us will be happy with."

She left ten minutes later, after giving him the number where she could be reached. He sat without moving, his eyes fixed somewhere distant. His pulse was raised and he felt a strange sense of displacement, as if he were somewhere else, somewhere far away and distant in time—in the garden of a villa, staring out at the green-covered hills, waiting for the young woman he had just met to reappear and complete his fantasy.

16

It was dark when Holly pulled into the visitors' parking lot at the rear of the state police barracks.

Five minutes later she was facing a heavyset desk sergeant who pointed her to an office along a green fluorescent-lit corridor.

Holly opened the glass door and looked around. Several detectives sat at their desks, while others conversed in different parts of the large room. Holly recognized Deputy Inspector Dan Shepard's lean figure and serious expression and felt a surge of reassurance.

He was checking through a file drawer as Holly entered. He turned as she closed the door and the look on his face betrayed both surprise and pleasure at seeing her.

"Well, hello there, Doctor," he said warmly.

"Can I speak to you in private?"

"Sure. This way."

She followed him to an office on the other side of the room and had to endure appraising glances from several of the men seated behind their desks, and one or two of the women.

Shepard took papers off a chair and gestured for her to sit as he circled behind her to close the door, then took a seat on the other side of his cluttered desk.

"To what do I owe the pleasure?' he asked, swiveling to face her.

"I wanted to see you about the Briscoe case. I recommended him for provisional release."

"I know. What's the problem?"

Holly hesitated, feeling a surge of anxiety. "I'd like to see the police report and the investigator's notes."

His eyebrows rose. "Why? None of that was admissible at trial."

"Maybe not. But I'd like to see them anyway."

"It's a little late for that, isn't it? I mean, the man's free, isn't he? And on your say-so."

Holly nodded. "Yes. I know."

"Then why?"

Shepard stared at her, surprised by the agony imprinted on Holly's features and the unmistakable look of anguish in her eyes.

"I think I may have made a mistake."

The building was shrouded in mist.

It was an old icehouse dating from the early years of the last century. A little beyond, Holly could make out the outline of an abandoned iron foundry, a moldering red brick hulk.

It stood two stories tall, surmounting a rocky escarpment above a narrow band of raging white water. Two rows of darkened windows with high narrow arches looked out over the surrounding woods, offering Holly images of silent eyes filled with despair.

Shepard had driven her there in his car, a journey that took over an hour along the winding back roads of the rural county where Briscoe had been tried. They had to slow down to find the narrow opening in the trees that shielded the thin band of gravel road that led to the foundry. The road was a series of sharp tortuous curves twisting down the steep hillside until it broadened into a wide access, below which the foundry stood. Now, she and Shepard were parked on the edge of the access a little above the foundry, seated in Shepard's black four-door sedan.

He turned to her and nodded toward the foundry. "This is the place where Carolyn was murdered."

Holly followed his gaze. The starkness of the landscape sent a shiver along her spine. Wild pines held to the rocks with clawlike roots as the water raged and frothed between narrow jagged stone embankments. Above them the mountains rose, steep and ascending. The trees were packed close together, in tight, almost claustrophobic, formations.

"What was it?" Holly asked, nodding toward the structure.

"It used to be an iron foundry. Briscoe leased it. He specialized in turning old hulks like these into hotels, offices, and B and Bs. He made a pretty good living at it. He was going to gut this building and turn it into upscale condos."

"I can't imagine anyone living here. It's so harsh."

"Maybe. But you'd be surprised what people buy. It's private. Maybe that was the selling point. Want to have a look-see?"

Holly hesitated, feeling a little queasy, but she nodded a yes.

They had no trouble getting inside.

The interior was dark and moldy, a maze of boxlike rooms rustling with tiny creatures who scattered when they entered and proceeded along a narrow, oppressive corridor.

Light speared through chinks in the walls, allowing them to see ahead in the confining space. Holly's pulse was racing. She felt strangled somehow, unable to breathe.

Cold air slapped her face.

She sucked in a deep breath, and her tension evaporated. They were through the corridor and facing a large open area under a huge dome spanned by a narrow iron catwalk. Above them was a giant skylight, a massive web of interlocking panes of glass.

"Something, isn't it?" Shepard said.

"Wild."

He smiled. "This way."

He led her across the ancient catwalk that spanned the dark open space below. It swayed and shifted under their weight, and Holly gripped the handrail.

"Don't worry. It'll hold us. That's the hearth down there," he said, pointing below them. "Where they smelted the ore."

Holly looked into the darkness. She was able to make out the shape of a large open furnace half filled with murky water, a dark gloomy pit. There was something chilling about it, and Holly drew her eyes away.

Shepard offered his hand. Holly took it as they stepped off the catwalk and he led her through another oppressive passage with several turns. He pushed open a door and led her into a darkened room. Above them was another skylight whose panes had been blackened with paint hanging in peeling strips. Several old couches were scattered around a large chrome-edged table. Heavy drapes hung from the walls.

"This is where he played his little games," the detective said. Turning to face her, his eyes focused on the ceiling.

Holly looked up. A gleaming metal hook was fixed into the transverse beam above.

"There was a harness hanging from the chain. We took it down and kept it for evidence."

He crossed the creaking floor and opened the door at the far end, gesturing for her to come.

Holly followed him through, emerging onto a rusty iron platform extending over the surging water below.

Shepard stood against the railing and pointed to a dark place between several fallen trees that formed an inlet in the raging current.

"That's where they found Carolyn's body. He placed it between those two trees. Of course, it was winter then and the stream was frozen. That's why they called him the Ice-Man."

* * *

Forty minutes later, Shepard pulled around a curve that took them off the rural highway and onto a narrow, two-lane, rural blacktop.

They had left the foundry and continued along the back roads through a series of narrow valleys filled with dairy farms. Shepard said little as they drove, as if what he had shown her had to be digested before they could speak.

He turned off onto a dirt road bordered by fields and a tangled neglected orchard, continuing for a few minutes more, until they drove onto what had once been a lawn bordering a gray two-story farmhouse faced with splintered wooden siding. The windows were boarded up. The front porch was littered with dead leaves and piled with brush. The house looked decayed, almost dessicated, like the skull of a dead animal.

"This is the old Briscoe house," Shepard said. "Where he was raised. It's still his property, but I think we can have a look-see, even without a warrant."

They got out of the car and walked toward the house, side by side on the uneven flag stones. "How long have you been working at the prison?" Shepard asked casually.

"Almost six years."

"Tough job."

"It has its moments."

"I'll bet. How does your current . . . involvement feel about your working there? I mean, it is dangerous."

"I don't have that problem," Holly responded, keeping her eyes straight ahead.

He glanced at her curiously. "Does that mean you don't have a current relationship or you don't have the problem?"

"All of the above."

Shepard smiled as he unlocked the front door with a key he fished out of his pocket, and they stepped inside.

The rooms were small, dark, and claustrophobic. The windows were plastered with grime. The walls were peeling, and exposed crumbling plaster lathing. The house had the feeling of having been abused.

They stepped into the kitchen, which was empty of appliances. Pipes protruded from the walls like the stumps of amputated wrists.

Holly reached out and opened a closet. A faded gingham apron hung on a hook inside, worn and threadbare from countless washings.

"What were his grandparents like?" She asked quietly.

"Pretty weird, from what I gather. His grandfather had quite a reputation. Story goes he used to trap stray cats, pick them up by the tail, and beat their brains out against the side of the house. Apparently, he forced the boy to watch. There may have been worse, but no one can prove it."

"By worse, you mean abuse?"

Shepard shrugged.

"Didn't Briscoe have a psychiatric examination?" Holly queried.

"They made the attempt, but he was pretty resistant. He never mentioned anything about his childhood."

He halted and looked at her. "There's something I want you to see."

They climbed the crumbling stairs to the second story. Three doorways looked out onto the landing. Shepard gestured toward the one in the middle.

"That was his room."

He led the way into a narrow room with a single window. Holly took a step inside, shivering against the sudden chill that seemed to envelop her.

The room was bare of furniture. There was something oppressive about the chamber, something twisted. The air seemed to hold a warning, the cry of a child that could not find an escape.

Shepard took out a small black flashlight from his pocket and opened the room's only closet. He knelt and removed a panel, exposing a chamber under the eaves.

A windowless darkness.

"Apparently, Briscoe used to hide in here when he was a kid so the old man couldn't find him."

Holly knelt beside him as he flashed the light inside. The air was sour, almost rancid. It stank of mold and of fear.

Only a small section of wallpaper still remained, hanging limply in the farthest corner.

"Take a look," Shepard said, holding the light on the remnant.

The paper was faded and dark, but the pattern was still visible.

It was a cluster of small birds. Their wings raised as if they were about to fly.

Over them, scrawled in crayon, was a madly twisting pattern of intersecting lines, trapping the birds in a prison from which there was no escape.

17

Ted was seated alone at the long cafeteria table, methodically gnawing his way through an oblong hero sandwich, when Holly came through the doors and headed his way.

He barely glanced up as she took the seat opposite, opened her manila folder, and laid three affidavits out in front of him.

"I'm eating here," he said through a huge mouthful.

"This is important."

"Christ! What?"

"Affidavits from three victims who didn't testify at Briscoe's trial."

"What are they supposed to prove?"

"That Briscoe used the same method of sexual enslavement on others beside Carolyn. And that in one case, he actually attempted murder."

"Proving what?"

"Proving Briscoe murdered Carolyn Anderson in cold blood. I'm revising my report. I want you to rescind his release."

"Great." He put down his hero and squinted up at her. "Only you're a day late and a dollar short."

"What do you mean?" she asked, feeling a sudden alarm. "His release was probationary."

"Not anymore," he said, reaching for a large manila envelope on the table beside him. He drew out a handful of papers and slid a printout over to her. "This came in yesterday morning."

"What is it?" Holly asked.

"Copy of a court order. His lawyers motioned the court and got a copy of your report. They used it to get the appellate court to take a second look at his case. The appellate court overruled the lower court judge. They said the therapist's notes were admissible and the ruling to suppress them was in error. They ordered a new trial."

"They're granting him a new trial?" Holly repeated numbly.

"Right. Only they got a brand-new DA down there who didn't think there was enough evidence to try him in the first place, never mind re-try him. He dropped the case. So, for all intents and purposes, your friend Briscoe is now a free man."

Holly stared at the printout, but she could not focus on the words. They seemed to swim in front of her.

He was a killer.

He was free.

And she was responsible.

A wave of nausea rose through her. She gripped the edge of the table. Her hands were shaking.

"He's a sociopath," she said, forcing the words to come. "He'll kill again."

Ted brought his gaze to hers.

"You should have thought of that before you got emotionally involved. Face it, Holly. You fucked up, major league."

Clara was waiting in the doorway as Holly drove up. Her face had the same look of concern it had worn since receiving Holly's call almost an hour before.

Clara said nothing as she stepped aside and allowed Holly to enter her spacious two-story home. Holly continued into the kitchen, where the aroma of freshly brewed coffee filled the room. A plate of muffins sat on the table, flanked by two porcelain mugs.

Holly tossed her coat over a chair and sat down. Clara went to the coffee machine and poured them each a cup. Clara was a coffee aficionado and her refrigerator was filled with plastic containers neatly lettered with the name of the various kinds of beans they contained. She usually announced the kind when she poured, but this time she said nothing. She took the chair opposite Holly, pushing the plate of muffins toward her friend.

Holly shook her head in refusal. "What I really need is a drink."

"You got it, sister."

Clara rose, went to one of the walnut cabinets that lined the room, and drew out a bottle of twelve-year-old single malt scotch. She placed two heavy crystal glasses on the counter, filled them with ice, and poured them each a generous libation.

Holly sipped her drink immediately, without waiting for the ice to melt. Clara warmed hers between her palms and waited with her accustomed patience.

"I screwed up, big time," Holly said finally.

"With Beth?" Clara questioned.

Holly shook her head. "With Briscoe."

Clara's eyebrows rose. She nodded to herself as if confirming a long-held suspicion.

"God. You had sex with him?"

"Nothing like that," Holly said with a look of distaste.

"That's a relief."

"It's worse. He's guilty, and I'm responsible for setting him free."

Clara sat back, her eyes intently focused on Holly.

"What do you mean, guilty? How do you know?"

"Carolyn's brother came to see me."

"Carolyn Anderson?" Clara questioned. "You mean the one he killed? The woman in the ice?"

Holly nodded. "Her brother introduced me to three other women. All of them were intimate with Briscoe. Two of them were only teenagers at the time. Only fourteen years old. He used them all exactly the same way he used Carolyn. The only difference is that he didn't kill them. He was working up to that."

"You're sure it wasn't an accident, like he said?"

"No. It was no accident. It was deliberate and planned. The others were a dress rehearsal. Unless there are other women we don't know about."

"But why? What drove him?"

Holly looked at her wearily. "I'm not completely sure. But I have an idea. This may seem completely crazy, but I think it was a way of possessing the mother who abandoned him, and purging himself of the fear he had as a child, the terror he experienced at the hands of a sadistic grandfather."

"You just lost me."

"I told you it would sound crazy, but I believe he inflicted hurt on his victims to replicate the way he was hurt. Sex with them was not for pleasure. It was a form of torture, a way of avenging himself on his mother for abandoning him to such a horrific existence."

"Okay, but murder?"

"Psychically, killing Carolyn should have been a form of release. A catharsis that would free him from his need to replicate the experience. Only it didn't work. The need would come back. It would have become a compulsion. He's forced to reproduce the same act again and again. It's the only way he believes he can free himself, but it enslaves him at the same time."

"Wow. That's quite a trip. Are we talking about a serial killer?"

"Very possibly."

"And you believed him."

"Yes. I believed him. He's lied to me about everything.

Everything he told me was a way of manipulating me. And I fell for it."

Holly clenched her fists and bit her lip, trying to ease the agony burrowing into her guts.

"Jesus, Holly. You're only human."

Holly shook her head sharply. "I was a fool. I committed the unpardonable error. I needed something and I thought I could get it from him."

"What?"

"I don't know. Some kind of connection? Or a need to trust. Somehow he found out about my past. Guessed or was told, I suppose. I don't know." Holly paused and looked up at Clara. Her eyes were filled with anguish. "Maybe I thought somehow that this was something I could make right. Some way of making up for what my father did. Instead of all the broken, smashed-up shit in my life."

Tears welled up in her eyes. She fought the urge to cry, but her body betrayed her.

A look of sympathy crossed Clara's face.

"I'm so sorry, Holly. Is there anything I can do?"

"No one can do anything. My report helped set him free. The appellate court used it to re-examine his case."

"What are you gong to do?"

Holly stared straight ahead. Her voice was low, still quavering with emotion.

"Everything I can. I've got to find a way to put him back inside. A way to keep him from hurting anyone ever again."

"How?"

"I don't know."

"It may be impossible."

"Maybe. But I've got to try. There's no one else."

"The police?"

"No one."

Clara stared at her, witnessing the despair in Holly's eyes. It was the look of someone who needed forgiveness, but Clara knew the only one who could forgive Holly was herself.

* * *

The apartment was a small one-bedroom with a tiny kitchen and dining area, and a living room with a bay window that looked out over the little town's main street. Yet, it had a certain charm, with its wide-planked wooden floors, lead-paned windows, and decorative moldings. It even had a small tile and brick fireplace in which a compressed paper log was merrily blazing.

Briscoe was seated on the couch, a lumpily upholstered affair draped in a loose chintz covering. In his hand he swirled a very robust zinfandel from Chile he had made sure to bring with him, as he knew whatever wine his hostess would serve would be some inferior cut-rate selection. He watched her now as she occupied herself in the tiny kitchen with the final touches to the meal she had prepared and whose aroma now filled the room. In spite of the magazines she had generously scattered across the wooden coffee table for his amusement, it was impossible to keep his eyes off her even with the profusion of animal life she kept inside the apartment.

Laura was a rescuer. She had accumulated several misfit kittens, three grown cats with missing ears, a mongrel with one eye that barked incessantly until she fed it a pig's ear, and several birds, all of whom had been wounded in one way or another. She had introduced him to all of them by name, and he had smiled and bowed as each was presented to him. Forcing away the deluge of memories . . .

His grandfather, trapping feral cats . . . opening the cages and forcing the boy to watch as he lifted each animal by its tail and swung it high over his head . . .

He lifted the glass, draining the rest of the wine. Then he picked up the bottle and poured himself another glass and one for her in the graceful long-stemmed crystal glasses he had brought her as a gift. She had exclaimed over them in delight. She had only small tumblers in which to serve wine.

Watching her was a source of visual pleasure. Laura seemed totally unconscious of her own innate grace. He had been observing her for several weeks since hiring her as a hostess/waitress/cashier; all three functions she performed to perfection. He had held back, not wanting to push the obvious attraction between them, an attraction that had been evident from the moment they'd met in the lobby of the motel where he had been interviewing candidates for employment.

Since then, she had appeared every other day, eyes bright and sparkling, to take up whichever assignment he chose to give her. Their conversations were laced with laughter and innuendo of the sort between a professor and an attractive student, just skirting the edge of danger and involvement, but the magnetism between them could not be avoided. Nor did Briscoe wish to avoid it. But he did not hurry. He allowed time to do its work, allowing the attraction to build and to percolate until it would reach its inevitable conclusion.

So it was with no surprise that he accepted the envelope she had handed him when she was last at the inn. Inside was a handwritten invitation to dinner at her place on Friday evening. He pocketed the note, but had said nothing other than to instruct her in some details of her work assignment. He made no other concession to their intimacy. He saw the hurt in her eyes but made no move to assuage it. When she has about to leave for the evening, he nodded for her to enter his office, where he smiled and told her he would love to come to dinner. Her expression broke into light and magic.

"Dinner's ready," she said, turning to smile at him. She took off her apron, revealing a black close-fitting jersey mini that clung to her streamlined figure and accented the smoothness of her well-developed thighs.

He rose and went to the table, taking the place she had set with linen napkins and mismatched pieces of antique Victorian hotel silver, a touch he found both tasteful and charming. She waited breathlessly as he tasted the cannelloni and when he pronounced it excellent, she grinned unabashedly.

"So, tell me," he said. "What do you know about your parents?"

She looked up, and her expression changed. "Not very much. Only their names. They were only kids. My mother was sixteen. My father was only eighteen when they put me up for adoption."

"Do you want to know more? There are ways to find out."

She nodded emphatically. "What kind?"

"Services that exist to track them down. I'd like to help, if you want me to."

"I don't think I could afford it. Not now."

"You won't have to. I'll take care of it."

She looked up at him and their eyes met. "I'd appreciate that very much. You're very kind. But why do you want to help me?"

"Because I like you," he said. He smiled and reached for his glass. "And I want you to like me."

She looked at him, then lowered her eyes.

Later, when they were seated side by side on the couch and she was serving him coffee, accompanied by music from her stereo, he reached over and took her hand.

"You have beautiful hands, Laura. They belong on a piano or a harp."

"I never had lessons," she said.

"That's too bad. I'd like to teach you."

She reddened and lowered her cup to the table.

"You're so different from people around here."

"Really? How?"

"The things you know. The way you speak. Everything."

"I don't speak that way to everyone."

She was silent. She raised her eyes to his.

His eyes held hers, as his fingers closed around the nape of her long slender neck. They rested there, without pressure, until her eyes closed and her lips rose to meet his. He felt himself stir. The passion he had been holding in check for so long now rose and surged through him.

It had been five years. He would no longer have to wait.

*   *   *

The letter was waiting on the carpet just inside her door.

Holly parked and hurried inside through the incessant downpour, huddled inside her raincoat. The weather had turned colder now, with icy winds and spells of chilling rain that turned into hail. Weeks had passed since her meeting with Shepard. Though the detective was trying to be helpful and they had exchanged numerous phone calls, he had basically come up empty. Briscoe seemed to have completely disappeared. There was no trace of him anywhere, locally or nationally. Shepard explained that there was no way for the police to hold Briscoe, even if they wanted to. The chances were good that he was no longer in their jurisdiction. Briscoe could be anywhere. Knowing this drove the nail deeper into Holly's being. It was as if a nerve had exploded in her spine, producing pain for which there was no relief.

Holly came through the door covered in droplets that sprinkled the letters and Christmas catalogues that arrived that day.

Holly scooped them up and piled them on the dining room table as she slipped off her coat and hung it over the kitchen door so it would dry without wrinkling in her overcrowded hall closet.

She usually ignored the mail when she first got home, preferring to go over it later, after she completed whatever chores she had assigned herself for that day, and which were enumerated on a pad on the kitchen counter beside the phone. She picked up her phone. The normal dial tone indicated that there were no messages. Holly started upstairs, but something about one of the envelopes stopped her.

It was large, square and heavy, and the paper expensive and formal. Holly was not expecting any formal invitations, and at first, thought it must be a sales promotion. She chose a small knife from the wooden block that held her cutlery and slit the envelope along the spine.

She extracted the invitation. The lettering was raised and in a flowing script.

You are cordially invited to the opening of Sheffield Place, an authentically restored colonial bed and breakfast.

It was only when Holly's eye had drifted to the location printed in smaller lettering beneath that she remembered. And with that memory blazing in her mind, she fully understood what she was reading.

The farm he had talked about buying . . . the restoration . . . the invitation was from Jason Briscoe.

Arc lights cut through the mist as the block of ice was raised above the surface of the pond, revealing the body of the woman locked inside.

The arm of the crane swung around, bringing the block closer. Light shone on the woman's pale shimmering body. On her perfectly preserved nakedness and the pale blue tint of her skin.

A group of men stood on the edge of the pond. Their eyes were fixed on the block as it swung toward them. They could see the woman's hand thrust above the block expressing a final desperation, a final attempt to cling to life.

The light washed over the exterior of the cube, bringing the woman into total focus. They could see the shape of her thighs and the round curve of her belly, the triangle beneath, and the twin curves of her breasts.

For the first time they could see her face.

The woman in the ice was Holly . . .

Holly sat straight up, jolting out of her nightmare with such suddenness that her head swam. She lay back on the pillows for a moment as the dizziness passed.

Her heart was pounding. She was breathing hard and felt moisture on her skin. She threw off the covers, rose, and headed unsteadily for the bathroom.

It took her a moment to find the switch. She put on the light, blinking as the sudden brightness hurt her eyes. Her fingers wrapped around the edge of the porcelain sink as she slowly raised her head and stared at herself in the mirror.

Her hair was awry, and her lips were swollen. She was still shaking. But her gaze was level as she met her reflection in the mirror.

It was not the same gaze that had been reflected back to her earlier. There was no fear in her eyes, only an icy look of determination.

The indecisiveness had gone. Something had hardened in her eyes, a sense of resolution that had not been visible before, locked into place like the steel bolt of a carbine.

Her course was set. Whatever she now did, there would be no going back.

18

The valley was a tourist's dream.

White steeples rose above clusters of pine and maple, with picturesque hamlets clustered along the two-lane highway that wound across the sprawling landscape of red barns and white silos painted with bold hex signs.

Holly had no trouble finding the inn.

It was located on a lovely stretch of road, adjacent to a field enclosed by white fences where several tawny horses grazed.

It was a crisp November day. Bright sun reflected off the windshields of the double line of cars filling the parking lot and lining the roadway on either side. Holly had to make a U-turn and come back before she found a wide enough parking space between two massive, gleaming Suburbans.

It was a car salesman's dream. SUVs were everywhere, one larger than the other, parked fender against fender all over the grass, brightly shining badges of local prosperity.

There was an overlay of newness about the place in spite of its obvious age. Paint shone everywhere. New white siding and black shutters gave it a formal air. The landscaping looked as if it had been hurried into place in order to meet the opening deadline. Several plantings were still in their boxes along the side of the house, along with piles of dark brown earth and gravel.

A chattering, upmarket, wine-drinking crowd filled the main rooms and overflowed onto the front lawn. Several children roamed the area, dodging and shouting among the adults, who seemed oblivious to their presence. The women were conservatively outfitted by Talbots and Anne Klein. The men wore Ralph Lauren, mock images of British gentry.

Holly skirted the front and made her way along the side of the large two-story structure, glancing up at the line of gables that projected from the roof.

She was only steps from the side door when she halted in her tracks. She felt the breath catch in her throat.

A woman came through the door. An apparition.

Light haloed her helmet of blond hair and illuminated her pretty face. Holly felt her heart stop.

She had come face to face with the woman in the ice.

The vision lasted only an instant.

It was not Carolyn, but an exact replica. Her hair was arranged the same way as Carolyn's. She even wore the same kind of skin-tight, lacy black silk dress and laced leather boots that Carolyn had worn.

The young woman was smiling at her.

She held a tray of canapes in her hands and made a gesture of offering. Holly remained rooted, almost transfixed.

"Would you care for something?"

Holly shook her head in refusal and the young woman smiled, turned her head, and moved on.

Holly shook herself free of the spell and followed the young woman at a distance until she finished her turn around the backyard and headed back inside.

Holly stepped through the side door and trailed her through a corridor that led into the service area at the rear of the house.

She paused as the young woman entered the kitchen and put her tray down on a large table cluttered with containers of aluminum foil. She began refilling the tray from one of the containers when a pair of hands slipped around her waist and she was pulled close up against someone whose face Holly could not see. His hands moved over her intimately, cupping her breasts.

The young woman squirmed against the intruder, but was not unhappy at being caressed.

"Stop it," she cried. "I'm working."

He released her and reached for a canape, but she slapped his hand.

"These are for the guests. You'll get yours later," she said provocatively as she picked up the tray and headed back out through the door at the far end of the room. She turned in the doorway and offered her admirer a smile as she went through.

Holly stepped back as the intruder stepped into view.

His back was to her as he lifted a piece of foil covering one of the containers. He took out a spare rib and brought it to his mouth just as Holly stepped into the room behind him.

"Did you think you'd get away with it?" she said evenly.

Briscoe turned, his eyes filling with surprise.

"Holly," he said, smiling. "So you got my invitation. I'm so glad you could come."

He looked as if he had stepped off the cover of *Town and Country*. He was dressed in a green corduroy jacket and a striped tie. His hair had been styled so that it feathered above his ears. Gone were the two white wings. He wore a closely trimmed beard. His face was smoothly tanned, emphasizing his striking good looks.

He tossed the rib into a trashcan, wiped his fingers on a napkin, and raised his hands in welcome.

But her words halted him.

"You lied to me. Everything you told me was a deliberate lie."

"That's not true."

"Not true? You never told me about Elaine McNeil, did you?" Holly said sharply, trying to control the anger rising in her chest.

He stared at her as his smile faded. His eyes went cold.

"I thought you were more astute. Elaine is an unfortunate neurotic who will say anything to get attention."

"Norma and Lisa. Did they want attention too?"

His eyes narrowed.

"I see you've been talking to Carolyn's brother."

"Who I've been talking to doesn't matter."

"What does?"

"Only the truth."

"The truth?" A smile played across his lips. "Oh yes. Like the little girls of Salem? Was that a case of the truth, or was it merely mass hysteria? I'm surprised you weren't able to see through that."

"The little girls of Salem didn't have tattoos."

"Everyone has a tattoo these days. Don't they, Holly?"

"You used me," she said sharply. "My recommendation got you released."

"And I'll always be grateful." He took a step toward her.

She stepped away, but the wall was at her back. She turned toward the door, but he extended his arm, blocking her path. His wolf's eyes were fixed on her. They were the eyes of a predator, and for the first time she suddenly felt afraid.

"Don't blame yourself, Holly," he said as his voice dropped intimately. "You needed to believe in my innocence. You needed to trust me. Don't be ashamed of that. We all have our needs."

"You murdered Carolyn." Her voice was a rasp.

"Murdered?" he responded, quizzically. "Carolyn was doomed to unhappiness. I merely helped her end her suffering."

She tried to move, but his eyes held her there.

"I'm a free man because of you, Holly. I will be eternally grateful. It's a shame we can't be friends. There was something very special between us. I think we both know that. Something beyond whether I was guilty or not."

His glance penetrated her being, stirring something she had thought was long buried. She felt as if she were suffocating. She wanted to run. To free herself. But she could not move. Her legs felt leaden. His eyes were hypnotic. If he touched her she would not have been able to cry out.

He leaned closer. Her vision swam as she felt his breath warm against her face. His pupils were black hypnotic dots.

"Something we both wanted but were forced to forgo because of the circumstances and your stubbornness. But there's no reason to deny ourselves now. I want you, Holly. You know that. Just as I know how much you want me. How much you want me to touch you."

His hand rose. His fingers touched her throat. She stiffened, but was unable lift her arms, unable to remove his hand from her body.

She watched as the tips of his fingers descended to cover her breast. She felt the pressure of his hand, the heaviness of his fingers enclosing her flesh. She felt her nipples stiffen and a luxurious lethargy encapsulate her. She realized she was wet. His eyes held hers. His lips formed an almost mocking smile. He moved close, his lips only inches from her own.

"No!" she cried, turning her head sharply.

Revulsion speared through her. She stiffened and pulled away.

"There was nothing special between us," she said, emphasizing each word. "Nothing except your psychosis."

His eyes went cold. He released her and stepped back as his lips curled into a chilling smile.

"Poor Holly. So desperately needy. So unable to satisfy her wants."

"With you?" she said. "Bullshit!"

"Excuse me!" A woman's voice called out. "Everyone's waiting for you to make a toast."

Briscoe turned. The same young woman was standing in the doorway across the room, a tray of champagne glasses in her hands. Her face held a look of hurt.

"Be right there," Briscoe said, turning away. "Laura, this is Dr. Alexander."

The young woman remained unsmiling.

He turned back to Holly. "Beautiful, isn't she?"

Holly was silent.

"Dr. Alexander is an old friend," he said, his eyes locking with hers. "We were just catching up on old times." He turned away. "Now, if you will excuse us, I have to rejoin my guests. Please feel free to look around. Remember, you're always welcome."

He crossed the room and took the young woman's arm as they stepped out of the kitchen. He did not look back.

"I saw him," Holly said, speaking quickly into her cell phone. She was in her car in the parking lot. Most of the guests were in back, swarming around the buffet tables.

"So, it was him," Clara responded, her voice on the other end furry with static. "What happened? Did you speak to him?"

"Yes, I spoke to him."

"God. You've got guts. What did you say?"

"I told him I knew he murdered Carolyn."

"Did he respond?"

"He said she was doomed to unhappiness, and he helped her end her suffering."

"Hell! He is one sick bastard. I wish you'd been wearing a wire. What else happened?"

Holly hesitated. "He put his hands on me."

Clara was silent, but Holly heard an intake of breath.

"I felt paralyzed," Holly continued. "I felt as if I were being hypnotized, as if he were controlling my body. It only lasted a few seconds. But I felt as if he had some kind of power over me."

"That's not good."

Holly laughed. The sound was hollow. "No. Not good at all. But don't worry. It won't happen again."

"Let's hope not."

"That's not all. He's got his claws into a young girl. She works there as a waitress. He introduced me to her. Her name is Laura. And she's the spitting image of Carolyn, the woman in the ice. Same face, same body, same haircut. Even the color of her hair is the same. It's obvious he's having an affair with her."

"How do you know?"

"I walked in on them. His hands were all over her."

"What are you going to do?"

"I don't know, exactly.

"You've got to warn her."

"At this stage, it might not do any good. She probably wouldn't believe anything I tell her."

"And if she becomes his next victim?"

Holly paused as that horrific possibility washed over her.

"I'm going to do everything I can to prevent it."

Laura was not hard to follow.

Holly had waited for her, parked on a crossroad, in the shade of a stand of oaks. She watched as the young woman left the inn just after sunset, driving away in a small blue two-door Honda.

After Briscoe left to make his toast, Holly had remained in the kitchen, torn between the desire to run and the need to shout out what he was to every one of the people gathered there. She was surprised to hear people calling him Richard, and then realized that he was probably wise to have changed his name. In the end, she realized that she would be considered some kind of lunatic if she buttonholed people and told them the truth. The timing was all wrong. It would have to wait. In disgust, she left the room, headed for her car, and called Clara.

Now, she drove behind Laura as the young woman's car wove back and forth along the winding road bisecting the narrow valley. Laura liked to drive fast, and Holly had to keep her foot on the pedal just to keep up with her.

Traffic was light, making it easy for Holly to keep the

Honda in view. It was only when they crested the ridge and left the valley that the road widened and traffic increased, making it more difficult to keep track of the blue sedan.

They entered a busy interchange, and for a moment Holly thought she had lost her in the cross-traffic, but the Honda reappeared just ahead, and Holly followed her as she drove off at the next exit, continuing along a service road and into the parking lot of a large suburban mall.

Holly cruised by slowly as the girl parked her car. She found a spot in the adjoining lane and waited until Laura walked past her before getting out of her own car and trailing the young woman inside.

The mall was not crowded. Laura slowed as she walked past several windows, eyeing the merchandise, then headed for one of the escalators. Holly waited until she was halfway up before she followed.

Laura got off the escalator on the next level and continued along the next tier until she entered a women's clothing store.

Holly waited outside, watching through the window as Laura meandered among the racks. The store was almost empty, giving Holly a clear view inside as Laura selected one outfit, then several others. Laura looked around, then started for the dressing rooms.

Holly slipped inside, took a dress off the rack, and began moving in the same direction.

The dressing room was uncrowded. There were no doors. Each cubicle was protected by a flimsy cloth curtain. All of them were empty except one.

Holly stood to one side, holding the dress against her body and pretending to view herself in the floor-to-ceiling mirror. The curtain was not totally drawn across the opening, and Holly could see through the narrow gap. She saw Laura's naked back and the side of one of her full breasts as she bent to slip off her jeans. Under them she wore only a narrow black thong.

Holly drew back the curtain.

Startled, Laura looked up.

Carolyn was facing her. Her face pressed against the ice.

Laura grabbed for the jersey she had placed on a hook in the wall, a movement that revealed her left shoulder to Holly's burning gaze.

On it was a dark blue tattoo. A bird caught in the swirling motion of a web.

19

The file was abruptly closed.

The thick fingers of Keith Maddox, the Springfield County District Attorney, spread themselves across the dark green folder like a small octopus.

Holly faced the chinless expanse of his carefully shaved face across the lacquered sheen of his polished mahogany desk.

The room was in semidarkness, lit by the warm glow of late afternoon sunlight. Maddox asked his guests to excuse the darkness, explaining that the fluorescents bothered his eyes. He was a short, stout man in a charcoal pinstriped suit with a small, carefully trimmed mustache over thin colorless lips. He wore a pale blue double-breasted pin-striped shirt with a white collar and cuffs and an expensive yellow silk tie. His cuff links were massive gold emblems of the presidential seal. The magnificence of his outfit contrasted with the shapeless brown tweed jacket and dark green cord pants worn by Dan Shepard, who sat across from Holly at the edge of the imposing Victorian desk dominating the center of the DA's office.

A look of distress crossed Maddox's face as he slammed his plump hand down over the file.

"I shouldn't even be reading this," he said. "Legally, Briscoe isn't a sexual predator. And even if he were, the statute permits me to act only if he is imminent danger of harming an identifiable individual. We have no evidence of that."

"Her name is Laura Bergen," Holly said sharply, trying to conceal the intense dislike she had taken to Maddox from the moment he had shaken her hand with only the tips of his fingers, as if she were offering him contaminated meat.

"And just who is Laura Bergen?"

"She's a waitress at his B and B. I believe she's going to be his next victim."

"On what evidence?" Maddox threw back at her testily. "Not on what we have here. The man's opened a business, for goodness' sakes. He's employing people. People who need jobs. That's not a crime."

"Ted Bundy was a Young Republican with a steady girlfriend and a law degree. That didn't prevent him from breaking into college dorms and killing innocent young women."

Maddox leaned back in his chair and pursed his narrow lips. "I see. So, now you're equating Briscoe with Bundy. I would consider that quite a stretch."

"Would you? I believe he has the same sociopathic disorder."

"Well. That's a reach, isn't it?" Maddox commented, turning his discounting gaze toward Shepard. But he did not receive the affirmation he was looking for.

Holly sat forward, bunching her fists just below Maddox's line of sight. "You're the DA. Are you just going to sit there and let it happen?"

"Am I supposed to prosecute him because some girl went out and got herself a tattoo?" Maddox asked. "She's probably got a safety pin through her belly button. And a bead in her tongue."

Holly started to speak, but Maddox halted her with a quick upraised motion of his palm.

"As far as the law is concerned, Briscoe is a respectable citizen. If he finds out about what you're trying to do, he could sue the pants off us. Am I right, lieutenant?"

"You're the lawyer," Shepard said curtly.

"Is that all you're concerned about, a law suit?" Holly said.

Maddox looked at her for a moment before he spoke.

"Why is this so important to you?"

Holly paused for an instant. "I was responsible for evaluating him. I recommended him for early release. He's free because of me."

"So you feel you made a mistake?" he said, smiling.

"Yes. I made a mistake." Holly looked away, unable to meet his mocking gaze.

"How did that happen?"

'I didn't have all the information. Material that was not admitted at his trial. I was introduced to it after I had made my recommendation. His lawyers used my evaluation to get the appellate court to order a new trial."

"Which they did."

Holly nodded. "Only the DA down there wouldn't prosecute."

"Really? Why not?"

"He said there wasn't enough evidence."

"But you want me to prosecute. On the same lack of evidence?"

Holly was silent.

"We release offenders every day. Why is this man so special?" Maddox continued.

Holly raised her eyes to meet his. "Because I believe Briscoe is a sexual predator. I also believe he suffers from a recurring compulsion, which means he's compelled to repeat his actions. It's only a matter of time before he acts out. He's killed once. He'll kill again. And very soon. Do you want another victim on your conscience?"

"Not on my conscience," Maddox said briskly, turning in his chair. "Perhaps on yours."

Holly rose to her feet, her eyes blazing. "If you're not interested, maybe I should make a copy of his diagnosis and drop it off at the local paper, along with a transcript of our conversation. Thanks for your time. I know you must be a very busy man."

Holly gathered up her file, stuffed it in her attaché case, grabbed her coat, and strode out the door.

She was halfway down the marble lined corridor when Shepard's voice echoed behind her.

"Just a minute, Holly!"

She turned to face him. "What is it?" she snapped abruptly.

"I'd like to help."

"Like you did in there? No thanks!" She turned away, then halted abruptly. "Shit!"

She turned back around. "Okay. What?"

"Look. Like it or not, Maddox is right. I tried to tell you that. There's nothing he or I can do. Not legally. But there are other ways."

"What ways?" she demanded.

"Get this Laura person to petition the court for a restraining order. At least that will put it on the record and keep him away from her."

Holly looked at him in disbelief.

"I work with serial rapists. Do you think any one of them was ever stopped by a restraining order?"

"No, but at least he'll know he's being scrutinized. That the law has been notified."

"It won't work."

"Holly, you can't go outside the law."

"I'll do whatever I have to," she said. "Legally or otherwise."

She started away when his hand caught her sleeve.

"Holly. Be careful. Think before you do something you'll regret."

"I've already done something I regret. Tell me how to fix it. Tell me how to put him back in the bottle, where he belongs."

Shepard faced her in silence.

Holly turned and started down the long marble corridor. His eyes remained fixed on her diminishing figure as she reached the exit and disappeared into the darkening gloom outside.

"Who was that woman?"

"Which woman?"

"The woman at the opening."

"There were a lot of women at the opening."

"You said her name was Doctor Alexander, or something like that."

"Ah. Yes. Doctor Alexander."

"You're not going to tell who she is?"

"I didn't say that."

"She's someone special. I could see that. Were you in love with her?"

"No. I wasn't in love with her. We were very close. But was she someone special? Yes. She was. Very special."

"How special?"

"That's not for you to know, little sparrow."

"Don't call me that. I hate when you call me that."

"I thought you loved birds."

"I do. But I'm not a bird."

"You have one tattooed on your shoulder."

"Because you wanted me to. You said it made me special. Does Doctor Alexander have a tattoo on her shoulder, too?"

"What if she did? Are you jealous?"

"Of her? Don't be ridiculous. Of course I'm not jealous."

"Good. Then let's talk about something else."

"Yes, I am jealous. Who is she?"

"She helped me out of a very tight spot once, a long, long, time ago. She was my guardian angel. Just like you."

"You're just saying that."

"No. I mean it. You're helping me lot more than she ever did."

"I don't believe you. How?"

"You're my mystery woman. My secret savior."

"Because I let you do everything you want?"

"Not everything."

"I won't do that. I don't like it."

"Even if it's important to me."

"It's wrong."

"Not if we both enjoy it."

"I don't. I told you I don't."

"You haven't given it a chance. You've just got to let go. You've just got to trust me."

"I trust you. I just don't want to do that."

"I thought you loved me."

"I do. I do love you."

"Then why won't you trust me?"

"I don't know. I just think it's wrong."

"Let me show you how. Let's try again. You'll see. You'll thank me."

"Not now. Not tonight. I just want to make love the regular way."

"But it's better the other way. So much deeper and more intense than doing it the ordinary way."

"What if something happens?"

"Nothing's going to happen. Not while I'm with you. You'll always be safe as long as I'm here. I'll always protect you."

"I don't know. I'm frightened. Where are you going?"

"It's late. I've got a full day tomorrow."

"But you always stay over. Don't go."

"Another night. When you feel less afraid."

"All right. I'll try again. Just don't leave me."

"Of course, I won't leave you. I'm never going to leave you. You belong to me forever."

It was just after seven, but it was already dark. Holly could see splinters of amber light through the plate-glass window from the streetlight on the corner. The store was located in a small three-story office building that dated from 1934, which was the number set in brick in the cornice at the top of the building. There was a health-food store next door. The store on the other side was unoccupied.

She sat on a wooden folding chair set before a long Formica table on which were piled stacks of mimeos and newsletters. A copier rested on a table at the far end. Boxes of paper were stacked alongside it. Posters were tacked up on the walls, advertisements for MADD and Megan's Law. The room had all the charm of a political campaign headquarters for a losing candidate. But charm was not the reason for its existence, only the grit and determination of the two or more score of women who organized and supported it with all the determination of their mothering instincts.

Three of those women now faced her across the dark expanse of the paper-laden table. Two of them were in their mid-thirties. The third was still in her twenties.

"We understand what you're saying," the first woman said. She was a heavy-set brunette with a prominent bosom, Mediterranean features, and dark, fiery eyes. "But we can't just take your word for it. We have to have some kind of proof before we go out and plaster the county with his picture. We could get sued."

Holly nodded. She understood, but it was impossible. "What you're asking is a breach of professional ethics as well as the rules of confidentiality I have to follow. I need you to understand that."

The first woman's mouth turned down. The woman beside her, a Celtic blonde with pale blue eyes, glared at her with suspicion and impatience. They had made it plainly understood when they arrived that they had given up precious time with their husbands and children to come down here to speak to Holly, strictly at the behest of Dan Shepard, with whom they had a special relationship. Only the younger woman looked sympathetic.

"We wouldn't have to use your name, or tell anyone where we got the information," the younger woman said. "But we can't just ask people to act on our say-so. We've got a responsibility to the membership. You've got to understand that."

"I understand," Holly responded. "But you've got to understand my position as well."

The first woman leaned forward, placing her hands flat on the table. "Let's cut this bullshit confidentiality crap. Helen's daughter was raped when she was eleven years old. Moire's kid was nine. My son was six when he was kidnapped and molested. That's the reason we're here. What's yours?"

"I've told you," Holly said. "To keep a killer from killing again."

"Fine!" The first woman continued. "If you want a philosophical debate so you can sleep at night, you came to the wrong place. We're here for one thing, to save the life of one innocent girl or boy, man or woman, regardless of their age." The other women both nodded.

"But we got to have some proof," she went on. "Psychologist or not, doctor, we can't just do it on your okay or because Shepard vouched for you. You can either give us what we need to satisfy our membership, or you can get up and walk out of here the same way you walked in."

Holly looked at the determination in their faces, and her lips tightened. She glanced down at her hands clasped so tightly the knuckles had turned white. She had gone before the tribunal, had argued her case, and she had lost. With a sigh, she reached down and drew the attaché case to the top of the table.

She laid it on the surface, unclasped the latches, and opened the lid. She reached inside, drew out the dark green folder, and handed it across to the three Furies seated opposite her.

19

The night was unseasonably cold for the beginning of November. It brought with it a dark premonition of winter. The fields glistened beneath a sheen of moonlight, filled with the stubble of corn stalks and the scattered remains of broken pumpkins discarded by the harvest.

In spite of the chill, the mall blazed with a false promise of holiday cheerfulness and the promise of Christmas soon to come. Despite the bright lights that lit up its façade, to Briscoe it had the appearance of a medieval fortress rising windowless and stark against the blackness of a starless night, a fortress entered through gated portals protected by the dark gaze of uniformed security.

Briscoe parked his van and approached one of the half-dozen plate-glass doors that secured the entrance. Shoppers had to file through an airport metal detector shaped like an inverted U.

Briscoe passed through the detector without incident, he went past the vacant eyes of the security guards, and headed toward the elevators. His eyes passed over the store windows glittering with merchandise. They made no impression on him. His mind remained focused on the problem that had absorbed him all day.

It had been several days since he had last seen Laura. She had not reported for work, her phone rang continuously, without her picking up and the messages he left had gone unanswered.

Where was she?

He had visited the community college and even embarrassed himself by peeking into her classrooms. Time came for work, but she failed to show up. In the last few weeks she had become the most important preoccupation of his days, even more important than the grand opening of the inn. As much as he disliked to admit it to himself, he needed her. Being with her was a kind of addiction. It had been the same with Carolyn. Need and desire, mixed together with feelings of revulsion and even of hatred. Feelings he found difficult to comprehend, but that were as real to him as breathing. As real and as necessary, which was why he had to find her.

Minutes later he had been transported to the food court on the third level where she worked part time as a waitress, a job she refused to give up, even when he offered to make up the difference in her salary. It was as if she didn't really trust him and wanted to have something else to fall back on. She wasn't quite as easy and as malleable as he had first thought. She was still resisting in spite of all the protestations of love she offered him.

He would have to break her will, as he had broken Carolyn's and the others'. She and he would have to become one before he introduced her to the final ecstasy . . .

His thought was interrupted by several rude girls who shuffled by. One of them brushed against him and laughed. He stifled his anger and continued past the brand-name shops. To him, the mall and its culture of consumerism was an anathema, a place where the masses went to amuse themselves. He was drawn there by something else besides the hunger for acquisition displayed on most of the faces around him, something that excited his emotions and tightened the muscles of his abdomen into a drumlike tautness.

The overpowering need to possess her . . . to have her offer herself fully and completely . . . and to want to give him everything . . .

He skirted the open eating area surrounded by kiosks offering a variety of exotic foods, along with the more pedestrian pizza and deli. A scattering of shoppers sat idly at the tables, but it was well past the normal eating hour, and some of the booths were already getting ready to close.

He headed toward the polished chrome diner located at the far end of the court, inset with red leather booths imitating the pseudo-deco style of the nineteen fifties.

A glance through the window revealed that the place was almost deserted, except for a single patron who rose from the counter as Briscoe entered. He held the door open as the man exited without acknowledging the courtesy.

Briscoe stepped inside and looked around at the unattended counter, smiling to himself at the anticipation of seeing the young woman who he knew would be alone inside the kitchen, getting ready to close.

He started toward the double doors when Laura pushed through them dressed in her white waitress uniform with its mock paper nurse's cap and apron, a red handkerchief in her breast pocket.

His lips formed a smile as he stepped toward her.

"Laura."

She glanced up at him and froze.

She faltered and looked away. Her eyes barely took him in.

In them, he could read her fear.

He took another step toward her, then halted as she recoiled.

"What's the matter, Laura?" he asked with concern.

"Nothing."

"Tell me what's wrong."

"I can't." She spoke through compressed lips.

His eyes narrowed suspiciously.

"What's going on?"

"Nothing."

"Then where have you been? Why haven't you answered my messages?"

"I was busy. I had exams."

"What exams?"

She was silent.

"Did anyone say something to you about me?"

She shook her head quickly, but he could see she was lying.

"Please go," she whispered. "I can't see you anymore."

"Why?"

Her eyes rose to meet his. "You know why."

"No, Laura. I want you to tell me."

The girl was silent, speechless.

"Tell me," he said forcefully, taking a step toward her.

He heard a noise and turned just as Holly stepped through the double doors behind her.

"Go ahead, Laura. Tell him."

Briscoe's eyes hardened.

"What did she tell you, Laura?" he asked.

"The truth," Holly said evenly.

Briscoe's expression changed. "No. Not the truth," he said harshly. "Whatever she told you is a lie."

He stepped forward and raised his hand, but Laura jerked backward as if his touch itself could somehow harm her.

"Laura, listen to me."

Laura turned to him. Her eyes were filled with loathing.

"I saw pictures of that woman. She even had the same tattoo."

Her hand went to her shoulder and began rubbing, as if she wanted to tear the skin off.

"I never want to see you again. I hate you! You're a murderer!"

She was holding something in her hand, a yellow piece of paper. She placed it on the counter, then she turned and hurried back into the kitchen. The doors swung closed behind her.

Briscoe's eyes followed her for a moment, then shifted to focus on the piece of paper on the counter in front of him.

The words were in large black lettering. Below was a small indistinct photograph.

BEWARE!
KILLER ON THE LOOSE IN OUR COUNTY.
HE HAS KILLED ONCE, AND WILL KILL AGAIN.

The photograph came into focus. The picture was of *him!*

He looked up, facing Holly. The muscles of his cheeks twitched, but his voice was low and controlled.

"You shouldn't have done this, Holly. You made a serious mistake."

"I know," she said fiercely. "And I'm paying for it."

His eyes remained on hers for what seemed like an eternity. They were the eyes of a predator, emotionless and cunning, lit with a cold intensity that sent a chill of foreboding spearing through her. Still, Holly refused to turn away.

"You've hurt me, Holly," he said softly. "You've hurt me very deeply."

His lips curved into a pale smile. He turned and walked out. The door swung closed behind him.

Holly watched as he crossed the food court and headed for the escalator. Then she turned away and went back inside to where the young woman was standing, her hands gripping the steel edge of the sink. She was shaking uncontrollably. When she looked up, Holly could see the fear in her eyes.

"What will he do?" she said through clenched lips.

"I don't know," Holly responded. "But whatever he tries, I won't let him hurt you."

Holly stood beside her for a moment, knowing that whatever she said would offer little comfort. Then she took the young woman in her arms.

* * *

She had been taken from him . . .

Briscoe walked as if he were in a trance. *He was marked now . . . marked like a beast . . .*

His eyes were unseeing. His face was a mask. His mind was filled with a single shining image, reflecting light like the surface of an egg.

The image of light splintering beneath the door of the closet where he lay hidden. The sound of his grandfather's boots resounding on the boards of the floor outside, hunting for him, coming for him . . .

His feet seemed guided by an unseen guard dog, steering him past the tables of the food court and drawing him toward the opening ahead, where the escalators plunged three levels down into swirling darkness. He paused there, at the top of the tier, his head swimming with vertigo. He felt caught, trapped by the sensation of being drawn down, of falling helplessly into the pit.

Something began penetrating his dream state. Someone was shouting.

It was only an annoying prick of sound at first, until it grew louder and louder and snapped him suddenly back into consciousness.

It's him! The guy on TV. The guy who killed that girl. The girl in the ice!

He heard the words, but for an instant they did not connect. He looked over at where the sound was coming from and saw a young man of nineteen or so in a leather jacket, standing at the railing and pointing at him. His other hand was upraised. In it, he held a yellow slip of paper.

Briscoe turned.

A group of young men were standing on the other side of the atrium, all of them staring at him. They were listening to the young man in the leather jacket, but their eyes were clouded with a lack of understanding.

Briscoe became alert.

He continued calmly toward the escalator, nothing about him suggesting haste or panic.

The first boy was still shouting.

"Stop him! Don't let him get away!"

The boy was moving now, heading toward him, waving his arms and pointing, trying to get the other boys to understand.

Just as Briscoe reached the escalator, they began to move.

He started down quickly, slipping past the other passengers and shoving some of them out of the way.

He turned his head.

The boys were swarming onto the escalator behind him.

He stepped off and ducked away. The escalators were staggered. He had to traverse part of the level to get to the next one.

He slipped past racks of women's clothing and dodged onto the next escalator. One more and he would be on the main level, able to reach the exit and safety.

The boys were shouting. Pointing. Warning others who he was. Their shouts echoed behind him like the roar of an incoming wave.

People were turning around, their eyes widening in alarm.

Briscoe knew he must not panic. He must appear normal, not as if he were being chased. He walked swiftly, but he could feel panic spreading in waves around him. He was now their quarry. The enemy in their midst. The infection they must eradicate.

The boys were on the second level, shouting and coming toward him.

"Stop that guy! Don't let him get away!"

He reached the next escalator and headed down, increasing his pace. It was crowded with shoppers. He struggled past them, shoving people out of the way. People yelled at him in annoyance, but he kept moving, hurrying down quickly through the press of resisting bodies.

His pursuers were at the top of the second escalator. The boy in the leather jacket was their leader. He jumped onto the chrome runway between the two moving stairs and scrambled down, followed by the others.

Briscoe shoved past the last of the shoppers. He was on the main level now, but his pursuers were sliding off the escalator, only several yards behind. He could no longer play at normalcy. He began to run.

Two young men were swarming behind him. One held something in his hand that looked like a piece of pipe.

"Get the son of a bitch!"

He looked up and saw three of them directly ahead.

He did not understand how they could have cut him off, but he turned and dodged into the transverse corridor only a few yards away. The exit doors were only forty feet ahead, looming just beyond an information kiosk.

He raced for them, realizing too late that the doors were chained shut. A sign proclaimed that the exit was closed for security reasons.

He was trapped.

Briscoe turned as the boys came toward him, closing in on either side.

He lowered his head and darted between them as the nearest grabbed for him.

Briscoe gripped the boy's hand and twisted, hearing the bone snap. The boy howled, dropping to his knees, his eyes wide with shock.

A second caught his arm. Briscoe half turned and swung, fist clenched, feeling the sharp impact of cartilage under his knuckles. The boy fell away as he turned.

He took a step toward freedom when they were upon him.

Hands grabbed his coat, fingers tore at his face. Fists slammed into his back. He tried to protect himself, holding one arm over his face while he lashed out with the other.

His fingers locked around a windpipe, gripped hard and flung the boy's body to the floor. But he tripped over the boy's prostrate form, and both of them were suddenly rolling on the ground.

Boots thudded into his shoulder and the back of his head. Something hard struck him across the back of his neck. His vision clouded. Shards of pain dug deep in his flesh.

He raised his arms to protect his face, taking another blow to the head before strong hands reached in and pulled the boys off.

Dark blue uniforms blurred in his vision as he was hauled away. Faces flashed past, staring at him with horror as the security guards rushed him along. Mouths were contorted with hate. Someone spat in his face. A woman's sharp talons lashed out and tore a piece of skin from his cheek. His ears were filled with a deafening roar as the guards half dragged him to the exit.

A police cruiser was outside, lights flashing. Two officers came toward him, pushing people out of the way. Quick words were exchanged with the security guards; then the officers flanked him on either side and led him out through a mass of grotesque faces. Voices echoed around him. Shouting obscenities. Calling him a rapist and a murderer. Screaming for his blood.

They hurried him into the back of the cruiser. His face was bleeding. He tried to speak, but his lip was cut. His mouth was filled with blood. Distorted faces filled the windows. All other sound was erased as his ears filled with the howl of the mob. The car rocked back and forth as fists pounded on the roof and windows.

The patrol car surged slowly, then gained speed, pulling away between parallel rows of parked cars, then onto the highway beyond.

He was safe . . .

Briscoe rested his head on the back of the seat as they drove, sucking in air. He tasted blood in his mouth. Jagged edges of pain cut into his back and whipsawed the side of his head. He felt his ribs to see if they were broken, but when he touched his side he felt a sharp sliver of agony and drew his hand away.

One of the officers spoke into his radio, but Briscoe could not make out what he was saying. The other asked him if he wanted to go to the hospital. Briscoe shook his head in refusal. Better not go back for his car, one of the officers warned.

He'd be better off getting it in the morning. Briscoe nodded in agreement. The officer asked where he wanted to be dropped off. Briscoe gave them the address.

His eyes burned. His head swam. Lights flashed as they sped through the darkness. The skin of his hands was raw and bleeding. One of the officers handed him a large gauze bandage. He blotted the blood from his hands and lip.

He leaned back for a few minutes, closing his eyes and seeking the comfort of darkness, but his mind could not rid itself of the image of the yellow slip of paper and what it contained. When he opened his eyes again his vision cleared, and he recognized a landmark. They were near. A few moments more and he would be home.

They were slowing down. Tires crunched over gravel as they rode onto the shoulder. He leaned forward and tried to look through the windshield.

Something was wrong.

The sky was alive, filled with a bright orange glare.

They stopped and he opened the door, stepped out, and staggered forward as the officers tried to stop him. A sound broke involuntarily from his throat, the cry of a wounded animal.

His inn was on fire.

People stood on the side of the road watching the blaze. He rushed away from the two officers, hurrying toward the inferno.

A local cop stood beside his patrol car, watching as flames consumed the structure.

"Hold on!" he shouted, blocking Briscoe's way.

"That's my place." Briscoe shouted. "Where the hell is the fire department?"

The cop regarded him for a moment, then leaned back against the fender. "Right over there." He pointed.

Briscoe turned to look.

Two yellow engines belonging to the local volunteer association stood a little way down the road, but no hoses had been deployed. None of the gleaming equipment had even been taken off the truck.

"Why aren't they doing anything?" Briscoe shouted.

"Don't know," the cop said. "Why don't you go over and ask them?"

Briscoe took a step toward the fire engines, then halted.

Firefighters stood in a line facing him. He could read the message in their eyes.

His lip curled into a sneer. His eyes were cold dots of contempt.

He turned and watched as the flames ate what was left of his inn, chewing on the antiques he had collected, the pictures he had carefully hung on the walls, the objects of brass and porcelain he had so meticulously arranged, destroying the beauty of his design. Cinders leaped from the blaze, sizzling like fireworks as they rose into the darkness, then arched toward the ground. The old timbers groaned, then crumbled. Two of the dormers came crashing to the ground as the bystanders cheered.

Briscoe turned and walked away. He made his way down the road, past the emergency vehicles, a solitary figure disappearing into the darkness.

The phone rang just as Holly was about to step into a warm bath.

She had settled Laura into the guest bedroom which had, until recently, been Beth's. At first, the young woman had resisted, defiantly proclaiming that she was not going to do anything that might disturb the normal equilibrium of her life. But under Holly's prodding, she had finally given in and agreed to stay for a few days until they could find her a safe place to stay. She was asleep now, tucked beneath the coverlet, one hand raised protectively and formed into a fist. Looking in on her, Holly smiled. At least subconsciously, she was fighting to protect herself.

The ringing persisted.

Holly ignored it at first, but the caller was insistent.

Holly stared at the tub, craving its warmth and the pungent smell of the bath salts she had sprinkled over the steaming water. Instead, she stepped into her bedroom and picked up the receiver.

"Yes?"

There was silence.

"Who is this?" she asked insistently.

"Hello, Doctor."

The voice was hoarse, unrecognizable for an instant. Then she knew.

It was Briscoe.

"I can't be with you just now, Holly. But don't worry. We'll be together very soon."

There was a click, and the phone went dead.

Holly tensed. Her expression went slack as the fear rose in her eyes. Her head swam for an instant as the future opened in front of her like an abyss.

The cabin sat on a rise surrounded by thick growths of pine. It was made of varnished logs.

Set back from the narrow asphalt back road that meandered between forested bluffs, it was reached by a long dirt lane between closely growing pine.

It was to this isolated location that Pierson had come to begin his new existence.

He had been out back that evening, gathering wood for a fire in the large stone fireplace that dominated the living room. The cabin actually was larger than it appeared. It had three back rooms besides the living area and the large country-style kitchen.

He made one or two trips and filled the woodpile outside the back door. Satisfied, he came inside out of the frosty air and began his preparations for dinner. He opened several cans of tomato sauce and started water boiling in a large stainless pot for the box of farfalle he had taken from the larder. Then he turned on the television.

He listened with half an ear to the news anchor, who was droning on about some items of local interest, when he looked up for an instant and saw the face on the screen.

His eyes were instantly riveted. His heart began pounding as the anchor related how a disturbance had occurred in a local mall earlier that evening. A mob, led by a group of teenage boys, had assaulted a local builder who was suspected of being a sexual predator. The builder was a recently released inmate named Jason Briscoe, known as the Ice-Man, who had been convicted of the murder of a young woman in eastern Pennsylvania five years ago. In addition, the bed and breakfast recently opened by Briscoe had been destroyed that very evening by a fire of mysterious origin. Anonymous flyers had been recently circulated, identifying Briscoe and warning residents to beware of his presence in the county.

Pierson's throat had closed. He could barely breathe. He sat down on one of the kitchen chairs and felt a rapid surge of emotion rising in his chest. His heart was hammering. He felt helpless, unable to move.

There was a roaring in his ears, so it took several seconds for him to realize that someone was using his metal knocker and was pounding on his front door.

Pierson rose and stumbled to the door, trying to clear his head.

He had no idea who it could be. He had never met any of his neighbors. Some serviceman, he thought, delivering propane or there to check his phone line. He wracked his memory for details of some appointment he had forgotten, but nothing came. That was why the shock was so profound when he opened the door and stared into the face of the man standing outside. The man whose face he had just seen on his television screen.

Impossible.

But he was there. Standing in the darkness outside. His face was bruised, but he was still smiling.

"Hello, Frank," he said softly. "Does that invitation still stand?"

Pierson was trembling. Unable to speak, he only nodded before stepping aside to allow his guest to step into his home.

20

Thanksgiving now descended upon them.

Pumpkins were everywhere, decorating stores and malls and scattered in various patches where children and their parents wandered, selecting suitable fruits to carve up for pies. Holly even took Laura to look for one, watching as the young woman chose a huge orange oval with the delight of a child. They brought it home and had fun together preparing it for baking. Laura was an excellent cook and loved making her special dishes for Holly. She had mastered the art of northern Italian cooking and prepared sauces and pasta with finesse. She used a knife like a sous-chef, slicing onions and shallots with blinding speed. Holly winced as Laura held the razor-sharp blade only millimeters from her fingers. Laura even demonstrated her technique for preparing pasta *al dente* —a skill Holly had never been able to master—by taking a strand from the still-boiling pot of pasta and twanging it like a guitar string. It was perfect every time. Holly marveled at her abilities in the kitchen, while Laura only laughed and told her how easy it really was. "Not for me," Holly said firmly, more than a little envious of her young guest's prodigious talent.

Laura was proving to be a welcome houseguest. Unlike Beth, she was quiet, efficient, and loved to do housework, which she claimed diverted her from darker thoughts. But she was impatient to find her own apartment and resume a normal existence.

Holly enjoyed her presence, and they went out to dinner and shopping together. They bought new clothes for Laura, especially lingerie. Laura could not abide wearing anything that Briscoe had touched. This she confided to Holly when they were inside a shop in one of the malls she liked to wander through.

"I can't wear those clothes anymore. None of the things he bought me, or the things I wore when I was with him. I can't even stand to look at them," she said as a shiver went through her.

"I understand. I know the feeling," Holly responded. She felt total empathy for the young woman. There but for the grace of God, . . . she whispered to herself when Laura had stepped into the fitting room. But these excursions were not without tension and some risk, though she never mentioned this to Laura. She didn't have to. They shared the knowledge that he was out there somewhere, perhaps even watching them from a distance, waiting to get to Laura alone. This fear haunted Holly's nights and filled her days with anxiety. Knowing that Laura was alone in her house, defenseless and vulnerable, kept Holly on a knife-edge of tension.

She kept in touch during the day, making countless phone calls at first, then allowing them to diminish as the days passed without incident. Laura kept bravely insisting that she was fine and that nothing was wrong, but Holly could hear the fear in her voice.

"I'm okay. Really. I appreciate your calling, but I have my cell, and if anything looks suspicious or out of the ordinary, I'll be on the phone to you."

"Or you'll call 911." Holly was insistent.

"Or I'll call 911," Laura echoed.

At Holly's insistence, Laura took an informal leave from her classes at the community college. She called in sick to her job at the diner. She remained in the house during the day, watching television and reading so she could keep up with her studies. She was anxious about not missing anything important, and Holly made a trip to see her professors who were more than glad to include material for her to read and several exams for her to take.

Holly knew Laura couldn't be cooped up forever, but it disturbed her when she found out that Laura had left the house on her own and walked around the complex or had taken an even longer stroll over to a local shopping area. But there was little Holly could do to stop her. She didn't want Laura to feel imprisoned.

"You can't keep her locked up," Clara said repeatedly, and Holly knew she was right. But it did nothing to ease the constant tension she felt. The best moment of the day was when she parked in her drive and hurried to the front door to find it opened just before she got there and Laura standing in the doorway, smiling at her.

For a moment, it gave Holly the illusion that her sister had returned. The fact that Laura was staying in Beth's room, sleeping in her bed, and even wearing a few things Beth had left behind in the closet only reinforced the impression. It was difficult for her to admit to herself, but in many ways Laura was the sister she had always wanted, the warm, positive presence she craved but had never known. It stung that Beth could not provide what she needed and that Holly was getting it from someone who would soon leave to take up her own existence. Of course, they could still be friends, but it would not be the same. This period of enforced closeness, though necessary, would come to an end, Holly knew. But she faced it with regret. She knew she must not allow herself to get too close to Laura emotionally, but it was difficult to enforce her own edict. Their parting, when it came, would be painful, but it could not be helped.

Clara understood her dilemma without Holly having to say a word.

"You'll miss her when she goes, won't you?" Clara said one day when they were taking a short coffee break.

Holly nodded. She was unable to put her feeling into words. Clara placed her hand on Holly's shoulder reassuringly.

At the end of the first week, Laura indicated that she wanted the tattoo on her shoulder removed. This was done by a dermatologist Holly had once visited. The operation left only a small scar to mark where the tattoo had been. It immediately lifted Laura's spirits and released some of her fear, though there were many evenings when she descended into depression.

"How could I have felt anything for him?" she asked, tears running down her face. "He isn't human."

"He knew how to manipulate you. But you mustn't blame yourself. Then he'll have won."

"How?"

"He'll still have some power over you."

"I know you're right. But he seemed so kind. He was helping me locate my real parents. How is it possible he could have done those things?" She looked up at Holly. Her eyes were filled with anguish.

Holly was silent.

"I gave him my body," Laura said with a tortured expression. "I did things with him . . . sexually. Things I never would have done with anyone else." She let her voice trail off, her eyes filled with tears.

"I understand." Holly's hand covered Laura's, who gripped hers tightly. There was nothing Holly could say or do to ease her memories.

"Why did I allow him such power over me?"

"You didn't know where it would lead."

"I should have suspected something. Something should have warned me."

"You weren't the only one it happened to. You're not alone. He knows how to get to women. He understands our weaknesses, our need for love."

"But why did they . . . all of us, give in like that, why?"

"I don't know. I suppose there is an explanation. But part of it is unexplainable."

In spite of all the analysis she had experienced, it was a question Holly found impossible to answer. Each woman's situation was unique. But whatever those differences, he had found a similar pattern in their needs and exploited them. Holly knew that all too well. She had almost succumbed herself.

The more immediate issue was what to do with Laura's hair. The problem was solved by the imaginative beautician Holly used. By dyeing it dark brown and styling it differently, Laura no longer resembled Carolyn. The new hairstyle excited her. Laura was restless and eager to begin work again. She wanted to be independent and earn her own way. Holly admired her tenacity, but was still fearful of Briscoe's presence.

At Holly's suggestion, Laura quit her old job at the diner and went to work at Beth's old place. The restaurant needed help and hired her instantly. Holly spent several tense evenings while she waited to pick up Laura after work. Miraculously, there were no incidents.

Briscoe seemed to have dropped completely out of sight. There had been no contact since the last phone call. No one had seen or heard from him. At least, that was the word from Shepard. But it failed to make Holly less afraid.

The detective had called several times, and while Holly was not exactly ducking him, she was dreading the eventual moment when she knew he would ask her out again.

"We've tried locating him," Shepard said. "But no luck so far. He seems to have disappeared. His place has been boarded up. I questioned the carpenters who did the job, but they were acting under orders from Briscoe's attorney, and he won't tell me anything. He keeps claiming lawyer-client privilege. The truth is, we have no reason to make any inquiries."

"Then why are you doing it?"

"You tell me. I'm still waiting for you to accept my dinner invitation."

Holly hesitated. What prevented her from saying yes? She knew she was attracted to him, but part of her was still too frightened to begin a relationship again. That meant trust, and she was not ready to incorporate that word into her emotional vocabulary, especially not after what had transpired between her and Briscoe. She had allowed herself to believe, and she was paying the price. She felt off balance and slightly afraid, as if what she had allowed to happen between herself and Briscoe was a failing that could somehow be repeated.

She felt as if she had been touched by something evil that was now affecting everything she did and would affect everyone she came in contact with. She knew she must not allow her thoughts to wander into that darkness, but she could not help herself. She would need some therapy before she allowed herself to open up like that again, but she was too busy to fit it into her schedule. She was like so many members of her profession, too involved with their patients to get the help they often needed for themselves. She scolded herself for this failure, but did not make the necessary appointment, putting it off until after the first of the year.

She was thankful for one thing. Clara had not yet gotten wind of the detective's continued interest. If she had, she would have made Holly's life a living hell. Days at work were stressful enough without Clara's constant entreaties to her to open up and give the guy a chance.

Unlike the rest of the world, Holly did not look forward to the coming season. The holidays were always difficult. Inmates became restless and depressed. Medications had to be reevaluated and dosages often increased. Group sessions sometimes became violent. Grudges developed and festered. Some inmates had to be isolated out of fear they might act out murderously, and there was always the danger of suicide.

Holly's schedule was already overcrowded, which only added to the misery. Several new admits had swelled her caseload to the limit and beyond. Ted, of course, was unsympathetic. When she complained of being overloaded, his response was always the same.

"You're the best," he would say with a malevolent grin. "Who else could I give them to?"

Holly knew this was Ted's way of punishing her. The Briscoe situation was never brought up, though Holly knew it lay just below the surface. Though it was perceived by most people on staff as just another failure of the legal system, Ted took Briscoe's release personally. Holly had provided the means to that end. It was a transgression that would not be forgiven. Holly knew that. It was Ted's way. He seldom forgave, and he never forgot.

Now he had something else to rake her over the coals with. She had decided to recommend Calvin Washington for early release.

When she presented it to him, Ted raised his eyes and stared at her as if she were out of her mind.

"This guy attacked you, remember?"

Holly nodded. "He was distraught because I had given him a less than positive evaluation."

"Which got his release turned down."

"I know. But I think what happened may actually have helped him. The self-control he exhibited was awesome. It was a therapeutic breakthrough."

"Oh man," Ted exclaimed. "And what if he's not ready, and you only think he is? What if this is another disaster waiting to happen, like Briscoe or Ulman? Remember Ulman? You can't come to me and say, I fucked up. Not this time."

"Both of those cases were different. I never recommended

Ulman. The system released him, not me. Briscoe was my mistake; I admit it. But only because I didn't have all the facts. If I'd had them, I never would have recommended his release. Never."

"You mean you two didn't have some kind of thing going?" Ted asked with a malicious grin.

Holly felt blood rush to her face.

"That's unfair, and you know it."

"That's not an answer."

"No. We had nothing going between us," she said sternly. "Other than my initial belief in his innocence. I went to bat for him because I thought he had been convicted for something he didn't do."

"No, itsy-bitsy bit of counter-transference ever entered the picture?" he said, his grin widening.

"If it did, it never played a part in my reasoning. I made my recommendation strictly on clinical grounds. Now, what about Calvin?"

Ted looked at her. "Submit your evaluation, and I'll consider it."

"Thank you." She turned to leave.

"Hold on. Speaking of taking chances, what about Pierson? I haven't seen any follow-up on him."

"It's on its way," she said as she hurried out of Ted's office.

Her stomach tightened. Not only had she fabricated when she denied any emotional involvement with Briscoe, but her follow-up visit to see Frank Pierson was now thirty days overdue. She had purposely kept away to allow him to make his adjustments to his new environment. She did not want to play mother hen and stifle his ability to do things for himself. He had her beeper number in case of an emergency, but so far he had not used it. Her only contact with him in all that time was a single phone call. His voice had been filled with excitement, and she had never heard him happier.

"I love it here," he said cheerfully when she asked how things were going. "It's quiet and calm. No one bothers me. I have perfect freedom."

"You're getting along with the neighbors?" she asked.

"What neighbors? I don't see anyone."

"No one?"

"Well. There is someone." His voice dropped to almost a whisper.

"Tell me."

"I can't. It's kind of a secret."

"Oh. It's that kind of someone," Holly said in a teasing tone.

"Well. In a way."

"But you won't tell me?"

She heard his hesitation. "No. I can't. Not yet."

"Is it someone local, someone you met there?"

"No."

"Then it's someone you knew before? From where?"

There was a stifled silence. She sensed that he was on the verge of telling her, but something prevented him.

"All I can say is that it would surprise you if you knew. And that's all I can say."

He would say nothing after that. Holly knew better than to pursue the subject, and broke off with the promise that she would be seeing him soon. And now she would have to keep her promise.

Night brought a chilling silence over the nearby woods. It was the only thing Pierson hated about the cabin. There were so few neighbors, none he knew or could speak to. Not that he really wanted to. This was about as far as he wanted to venture for the time being, far from the places of desire and temptation. He had even refused his brother's offer of a computer. The Internet had been the reason for his incarceration in the first place. He wanted no repetition of that possibility, or of the chance he might be sent back. Prison had been a devastating horror, except for the man now sharing his cabin.

The thought of him being so near sent a shiver along his spine. His physical presence was enough to quicken Pierson's breathing. Since his appearance, they had spent almost every day together, except for the hours when his guest got into his car and disappeared. Pierson never asked where he went. He knew better than that. There was a closed-off area of his guest's personality where he knew it was wise not to trespass. So he asked no questions, waiting for his housemate to reappear. Often he returned with groceries, but most of the time he said nothing about where he had gone. Or said nothing, period. He was anything but talkative. Other than that first night, they never mentioned what had happened to bring him there.

The thing he seemed to like best was the woods. He mentioned having grown up in an area like this, remote and deeply wooded. The one time Pierson had been invited to go along, he came to realize how good a woodsman his houseguest really was. He knew how to follow a trail, and knew exactly where he was merely from the position of the sun. They had hiked for miles in the thickest part of the forest, but they never got lost.

In a way, Pierson was grateful for the time his guest spent away. Being in such close proximity was incredibly difficult. His adoration of his housemate was impossible to keep completely under control. His eyes followed his every movement. They never touched physically, but once or twice their eyes met and held. But he was too afraid to attach a meaning to whatever he saw in the other man's glance. Was it desire, or something else? Whatever it meant, he dared not hope. Prison forced men to make sexual accommodations they would not ordinarily make on the outside. They formed long-term relationships, even marriages. Many even returned to prison just to satisfy these desires. Whatever his guest's need, he knew he would satisfy it. Sometimes his own desire became so overwhelming that when his guest had gone, he would enter his room and lie down on his bed, inhaling the scent of his body on the still-warm sheets.

Now, he stood by the stove, preparing dinner and listening to the sound of the shower. When his guest emerged, he would finish setting the table. His thoughts lost their focus. All he could think about was his body under the rushing water.

He heard the bathroom door open.

"Come in here," the voice inside commanded.

Pierson put down the large wooden spoon with which he had been stirring the stew and stepped toward the door. His heartbeat was audible to himself as he pushed it open and stepped inside.

Briscoe stood in the bathroom. He was naked except for the large bath towel he held around his body as he continued to dry himself.

"I was making dinner," Pierson said. He could not take his eyes off the other man's form, the square shoulders and well-defined musculature. The deep cuts of his abs. He felt weak suddenly, aware that the man in front of him could snap his neck with a twist of his powerful wrists.

"Come here."

Pierson came closer. Briscoe's eyes paralyzed him. They seemed to pierce him to his core. His hands were trembling. He felt weak suddenly, as if he were going to black out. He stopped in the middle of the room and looked away. On the bed beside him was something he failed to recognize. It was a kind of leather harness connected to a rope at whose end was a large gleaming metal hook.

Briscoe was looking at him. His lips formed a chilling smile.

"Get undressed."

Pierson felt as if he were entering a dream. He unbuttoned his shirt and stripped it off, then unfastened his belt and let his jeans slide down his thighs. His legs were shaking, but he could not draw his eyes away.

Briscoe tossed away the towel.

Pierson gasped. His heart hammered. Calmly and deliberately, almost as if he were in a trance, he slowly dropped to his knees.

21

The apartment was lovely.

Airy, bright, and freshly painted, it was situated in an older development only half a mile from Holly's complex, on a cul-de-sac off a pretty, tree-lined road. The rent was reasonable for the location, though it meant Laura would have to work two extra shifts, but she didn't seem to mind and dismissed the added workload as no problem. She still attended community college two nights a week, but had decided to cut back on her classes next semester until she fully adjusted to her new environment. Holly had helped bring over her things, but Laura was less interested in her possessions than in the menagerie she had accumulated. She had farmed them out during the weeks she spent at Holly's. Now they were hers again. What concerned her most was how her animals would adjust to their new quarters, leaving Holly to take care of more mundane matters, like connecting the phone, electricity, and water.

In that way she was like very much like Beth, whose communications were astonishingly brief and delivered mostly over the answering machine or voice mail at the office.

"Hi. I'm great. Work's great. The house is terrific. My new friends are terrific. And yes, my dear inquisitive sister, I am attending AA regularly, which is where I base my social life. Don't panic. No boys. Not yet. I'm still being good. Just me, my Big Sam's five-gallon jar of Vaseline, and my miraculous, never-lets-you-down, 560-horsepower vibrator. Thank god for Edison. He invented it, didn't he? I know he invented everything else."

In spite of the flippancy, Holly was glad to get the messages. But her own calls generally went unanswered, except when Beth needed a few extra bucks.

Clara shook her head in disgust.

"You're some trip. You finally got rid of your sister. Now you've got this new kid to worry about."

"It's only temporary," Holly replied. "She knows how to take care of herself."

"I'll bet," Clara commented sarcastically.

"She rolled right over for Briscoe, didn't she?"

Holly was silent.

"The police don't think he'll reappear. Not with his face plastered all over the county. It's too dangerous for him."

"Isn't that how he operates? Putting himself in danger, I mean? He seems to enjoy it."

"I don't know. You could be right. But all his victims were willing. They were all women who fell under his spell. With Laura, the spell's been broken. I don't think he'll go near her again."

"I hope you're right. Of course, there is someone else he could come after."

"Like who?"

Clara looked at her and her eyes narrowed. "Like you."

"That's crazy," Holly said as she turned away and stepped through the door into her office, unable to prevent his words from re-echoing in her mind as they had every day since his phone call.

"*I can't be with you just now, Holly. But don't worry. We'll be together very soon.*"

* * *

Holly had intended to leave the prison right after lunch so that she would arrive at Pierson's place in daylight, but that had not happened.

She got caught up in a series of phone calls, which gave her a late start. Then Ted appeared, demanding she fill in the details of some last-minute reports he had to get out before year's end. The stream of paperwork seemed unendurable. She finally finished, but everything caused her to be so late that when she finally approached the exit on the turnpike, it was in almost total darkness.

It irritated her that Ted was making such a thing over her failure to visit Pierson. She had talked with Pierson several times over the phone and had come away gratified. He seemed to be adjusting nicely to life on the outside, although he still had not ventured very far from his home base. Still, that was normal for someone just released from incarceration.

She made a right and continued along the long winding secondary road through deeply forested country. Tall stands of pine towered on either side, making it seem as if she were driving through a long, deep tunnel. She had driven only fifteen minutes when rain began falling. She hated driving on a strange road in the dark, especially when it was raining. Fortunately, there was almost no traffic.

She turned on the wipers as she passed widely separated cabins. Few had lights. Some were set almost right on the road. Others were set back from it in grassy settings scattered with the skeletal remains of farm machinery and the rusting hulks of old cars. There was a tumbledown market, a one-pump gas station that rented videos and DVDs, an agraco-op, and not much else. The area had the hard-times look of rural poverty.

She felt a twinge of anxiety and glanced down at the clock on the dash. It was late. Laura's shift would be over. She would be heading off to class. Holly wanted to be home when Laura called after returning from college. They had made that a nightly ritual. Holly wouldn't be able to sleep if she didn't get the call indicating that Laura was home and safe. Tonight, Laura had agreed to stop by after class for a late-night supper. Holly wanted to be home first so she could prepare, but that now looked impossible. She had wanted to make a salad and a stir-fry of fresh vegetables and tofu, a favorite of Laura's. She would just have to stop at the local deli and pick up some precooked items and reheat them.

Holly looked away from the road to check a familiar landmark, a decaying old barn standing hulk like at the side of the crossroad. By allowing her attention to wander, she had almost missed the turnoff. She slowed and backed up, then made a wide turn onto the narrow road.

The cabin was not hard to find.

A yellow mailbox marked the beginning of the dirt track that led to Pierson's isolated house. The road was slick, with rain filling depressions and puddles with a yellowish foam. She plowed through without stopping, shooting an ochre spray all over the hood and the sides of the windows. She had to turn on the wipers full blast just to see.

Trees closed in on either side as she drove. Some were dead, and their bare, twisted branches reached out like the arms of old crones. She was finally able to glimpse the cabin through the closely growing trunks. A yellow light was on outside the front door, throwing a cheerful glow into the rain-speckled darkness.

She pulled up in front, gathered her tape recorder and briefcase, and then stepped out into the chilly atmosphere. She smiled as she saw the elaborate fall decorations surrounding the front door, multicolored leaves wreathing various fruits of the season. It was like Pierson to add such a homey touch, even though no one was around to see it.

She knocked once. There was no response, so she knocked again.

"Frank. It's me. Dr. Alexander," she called. Still no answer. She raised her voice.

"Frank?"

She placed her hand on the knob. It turned, and the door opened.

The cabin was in darkness. The interior was still, and the air motionless, overheated and oppressive.

She took a step inside and raised her voice. "Frank. Hello."

She felt a pang of annoyance. The appointment had been made the week before, confirmed and reconfirmed. Though she had not spoken to him in several days, Holly expected him to remember. After all, he had little else to occupy him. He was not yet ready to venture into the world to find companionship or a job. He preferred being out here by himself, where no one would know who he was or where he had been. A self-inflicted form of isolation, and perhaps even punishment.

So where could he have gone?

Holly took another step and stumbled into a piece of furniture.

"Shit," she cursed softly. There was a square of light ahead. She continued toward the kitchen and the source of the illumination. She realized that the refrigerator door was ajar.

Holly felt her first stab of apprehension. Leaving the refrigerator door open was not like Frank. He was neat to the point of obsession.

She went toward the door and glanced inside.

It was empty except for a single block of ice. Vapor rose from the block, misting the interior.

Holly stared at it, then brought the tips of her fingers to the block and wiped away the mist.

There was something inside.

She blinked and, for an instant, failed to understand what she was seeing. Then she froze in horror.

Locked inside the ice was human flesh.

A severed penis and testicles, gleaming unnaturally in the rays of refracted light.

Holly cried out and reeled backwards as the rush of the

gag reflex convulsed her. The sink was behind her. She turned and vomited.

It took only moments, yet it felt like an eternity as she coughed, spitting out streams of acidic fluid. The spasm finally subsided, allowing her to take several deep breaths.

She heard a noise and turned. The refrigerator door had swung wide, filling the room with rays of bright metallic light.

That was when she saw him.

Pierson was seated at the table. He was naked. His sickly white skin gleamed unnaturally in the uneven light. His body was rigid, held in place by a cord wound around his neck and connected to the chair he was seated on. His eyes were open, the pupils staring into nowhere. There was a large basin on the floor between his legs, overflowing with an inky liquid.

Blood.

Holly remained immobile. The world had come apart. Her head felt light, her mind somehow disconnected from her feelings. She viewed the body impersonally as if she were standing at a distance. She could feel her heart beating and sensed the tension in her muscles. Her chest heaved as she struggled for breath.

A board creaked, and the world suddenly came back together.

Someone was inside.

She was instantly alert.

"Who's there?" she called out through her constricted throat.

Silence.

"Stay where you are. The police have been alerted. They are on their way."

No sound or movement. Nothing.

Perhaps she had imagined it? No! Every instinct screamed that someone was there, inside the cabin with her.

The killer.

Holly moved quickly. She started back into the living

room, heading for the front door. She gripped her keys in her hand and fled into darkness and thickly falling rain.

She pulled open the car door and slipped inside, inserted the key, and turned it in the lock. She heard a clicking sound, and her heart froze. Frantically, she turned it again. Nothing but a series of clicks. The battery was either dead or had been disconnected.

Quickly, she dug into her bag, which she had left on the passenger seat, searching for her cell phone.

It was not there.

She bit her lips, struggling against the immobilizing terror that now gripped her limbs.

She had to get out of there. Now.

She threw open the door and headed back down the dirt road between the towering ingrown rows of pine on either side. The wind was rising, splattering her face with freezing rain.

Her heart was pounding wildly. Naked branches were locked in eerie patterns around her as her soles scuttled on the gravel. Dark trunks loomed ahead, branches creaking and snapping in the wind.

Where was she going?

She was disoriented in the darkness. The road she had come on, and that she thought was straight, now forked directly ahead. Which way?

She heard the snap of brush underfoot, and the heavy tread of boots on dry twigs. She turned to look.

Something was moving in the tree line behind her.

He was there. Coming for her.

Panicked, she rushed forward, impulsively taking the fork to the right. Leaves crackled. The boots were gaining on her, thudding in her ears.

She began to run. She had only gone several yards when the dirt track abruptly ended, disappearing into a deeply forested glade.

Thorns tore at her jacket and slashed her skin. She was

caught in the brambles. The image of the trapped bird instantly filled her mind, wings beating futilely as it tried to escape.

She fought the desire to scream. Instead, she brought up her arms to protect her face. Lowering her head, she crashed through the entanglement. Arms flailing, she cleared a path.

An instant later she was free.

She started forward, then tripped and stumbled headlong, falling on her knees in the soft, wet earth. She fought for breath, staring desperately around her. Silvery trunks rose ahead, blocking out the sky. It was almost impossible to see in the gloom, yet there appeared to be a kind of path ahead. It was very narrow, the kind of trail made by deer.

She struggled to her feet and started forward, following the path, feeling her way between the rough, closely growing trunks.

Brush crackled behind her. She heard feet driving through dead leaves, the heavy tread of thick-soled boots.

She began to run.

The beating in her temples had stopped, replaced by a strange, icy calm, then a burning sense of dread as disparate thoughts connected in her head. Pierson telling her about Briscoe and the feelings he had for him. It was Pierson who must have told Briscoe about her, giving him the ammunition he had used to manipulate her.

Bits of Pierson's last conversation rechoed in her mind.

Someone was there with him . . . someone who would surprise her . . . someone he had met before . . .

It was Briscoe who had killed him. He was there in the trees behind her.

Coming for her.

Rage rose in her chest.

She was not that bird. She would not be his victim.

She sensed movement behind her and wheeled around to face him. Her voice was a shrieking howl of defiance.

"You bastard! You murdering son of a bitch!"

But there was no one, only the wind and the darkness and the rain slashing whiplike against her face.

Holly turned and began to run, hands out in front of her as she struggled between the narrow trunks of pine. Her shoes slid on the wet ground, slipping on layers of pine needles.

The earth rose steeply just ahead and she struggled to overcome the rise, bending to grab at the exposed roots as she pulled herself forward. She was out of breath. Her pulse was racing. But she managed to reach the crest.

She headed downslope as the trees abruptly thinned. Then she was running as the slope suddenly released her. She tried to brake her motion, grabbing at young saplings until there was nothing left to grab and she was deposited on the slick wet surface of the county road.

She stumbled to a halt. Her legs were wobbly. She could hardly stand. She struggled forward, finally regaining her balance, and looked up.

Headlights appeared through the mist.

Holly stood in the center of the road and waved her arms. Miraculously, the pickup came to a stop. She mumbled something to the thin-faced driver in an old plaid coat who opened the door. Somehow she found the strength to climb inside.

He had become the hunter.

That was how it had always been, as a boy with his grandfather, tracking deer in deep snow, or hidden in a blind, awaiting the low beating wings of geese, or the sudden spring of a jackrabbit.

He had learned not to move, not to breathe, to respect his prey even as he tracked it, closed in on it, and raised his rifle for the kill.

They would rest in a culvert, the two of them pressed together against the cold, the old man's breath warm against his neck, his heavy body stretched out behind him, the acrid reek of alcohol tinging the icy air. The old man took his pleasure brutally, making the boy cry out in pain.

Now nothing would interfere with his own. He had located his prey only days before, sniffed out its new lair, and discovered where it had gone to ground. Now, he was on its track, sensing the animal's fear in the air as he closed in behind it with the exhilarating knowledge that very soon it would be his.

But not yet.

He had learned that there were other pleasures besides the immediacy of the kill. The pleasure that came in prolonging the awaited death so that both hunter and prey engaged in their final dance. Nothing must be rushed. The final climax had to be sustained and savored, or there was no point to the game.

Anyone could kill. To prolong it slowly was an art.

22

Laura was not a reckless person.

She had followed Holly's directions to the letter and left class just after nine. By nine-twenty she was pulling into the cul-de-sac at home and parking her car in the spot in front of her house. She intended to make a quick stop home to drop off her things and change. Then she was due at Holly's for a late bite.

She had her house key in her hand before she opened the door. Her cell phone was gripped tightly in her other hand, her thumb beside the button that would signal 911. She looked around carefully. The street was quiet. Nothing was moving. The rain that had fallen earlier had stopped. The asphalt glittered with tiny jewels of moisture. She pushed open the car door and started out, slamming it behind her. She headed directly toward her door and reached it quickly, inserted the key, and was inside with the door locked within the space of three deep breaths. "I hope you're proud of me," she said aloud.

She dropped her books on the small table beside the door before she turned on the lamp next to it. The room filled with a warm amber glow.

"So where is everybody?" she said. "Are you guys all asleep?"

Normally there was a rush of furry bodies there to greet her expectantly before she poured snacks into the line of plates on the floor in the kitchen where they were fed.

"What's the matter, don't you guys want a nosh?"

Still no sound. No movement. No flutter of wings from the bird cages, no barking.

Mystified, she crossed the rug toward her bedroom.

"You all hiding?"

She stepped inside, flicked on the light, and her eyes widened in terror.

They were all on the bed together. Their paws outstretched. Ears pointed. Eyes open and staring up at her.

The tiny birds were in their claws.

She screamed, turning to run. When her heart jumped out of her chest, she reeled backwards, her back up against the door.

He was there, standing in the doorway, directly in front of her. Smiling. His hypnotic gray eyes fixed on her like twin lasers.

"What's the matter, Laura? Didn't you think we'd ever see each other again?"

He stood in front of her in the shadowy stillness, unmoving, his eyes fixed on her.

She froze. Her mind refused to accept his presence. Refused to believe he was there. Then something inside her revolted and she shouted, "No!" She would not be his prisoner.

She bolted, turning and running for the door. She grabbed the knob, but it refused to turn in her hand. The door was bolted. She spun around and rushed to the window. She grabbed the metal handles, but the window refused to rise. Her fingers fumbled with the lock, but they could not move it.

Trapped, she turned to face him. He still had not moved. When he spoke his voice was a whisper.

"Why are you running away from me, Laura?"

His eyes held hers. His gray wolf's eyes, framed by the dark wings of his hair. The look in them was dark, electric.

She could not look away. She felt as if her mind would explode. She stared at him, torn by her desire to run, to escape, but held there by a force she could not explain. A heaviness had enveloped her being, a weight that felt as if bars of lead had been attached to her body, making it impossible to run, to move.

He took a step toward her.

"Don't you realize you belong to me, Laura? You'll always be mine."

She raised her arms. Her body began to writhe. Her hands twisted together above her head, trying to keep him away. But she was trapped. Just like the bird in the tattoo.

Helpless, she began to wail.

It was still raining as they carried Pierson's body out of the cabin, enclosed in a black vinyl bag that the two white-clad technicians loaded into the coroner's van.

Shepard followed the body out, then walked over to where Holly was standing, wrapped in her raincoat, her throat encased in a muffler. The rain had slackened, but the temperature was nearly at freezing.

Shepard opened the door of his big Suburban van and waited until she got inside. The motor was running and the heater was on, warming her hands and her frozen cheeks. He got in beside her, looking at her for a moment before he spoke. Holly found it difficult to meet his gaze.

"If Briscoe was here, no one around here saw him. There are no prints inside, and the rain did a good job of washing away any footprints outside the house. Whoever it was who stalked you didn't leave a trace. Besides, why would he come after someone like Pierson?"

"I'm not sure."

"Did they know each other in prison?"

"Yes. Pierson thought he was in love with Briscoe."

Shepard was silent, considering the information. "Okay, suppose he was. That still doesn't give us a motive. I thought Briscoe only liked women. Is there any reason for us to believe otherwise?"

"I don't know. He craves control over his victims. I don't think their sex is a factor."

"So you think he'd make love to a man?"

"Love has nothing to do with it. It's all about power and powerlessness. Sex just adds to the mix. It's the vehicle through which he achieves his goal."

Shepard didn't look convinced.

"Consider this," he began. "We've got a recently released inmate in this jurisdiction who most people believe is an undesirable sexual deviant. A mob almost kills him and burns down his inn. Now a second inmate, this time a convicted pedophile, is murdered in the same jurisdiction. What this points to is a kind of hate crime, much more than any possible connection to Briscoe, especially with the lack of any evidence to point us in that direction."

"That's sounds logical, but I know it was him."

"Come on, Holly. Give me a break. I need more than your feelings."

"When we last spoke over the phone, Pierson said there was somebody here with him. Somebody who would surprise me."

"But he didn't say who?"

Holly shook her head. "He wanted to keep it a secret."

"Then we can't name Briscoe. Not directly. Why do you think it was him?"

"I think he's going after everyone I love or had any feelings for."

"Why?"

"Revenge. For taking Laura away from him and for what happened to his inn. I think he knows I had something to do with it."

"How could he?"

"I met with those women. They released those flyers."

"Then why isn't he coming after me? I put you in contact with them."

"He doesn't know that. Besides, you're not the focus of his fantasies. I'm worried about Laura and my sister."

"He's not going to go near them. Especially not your sister. Not when he knows you've been in touch with us. He's not that crazy."

"You don't know him."

"Do you?"

"I'm finding out."

"If it will make any difference, I'll put in a call to the troopers over where your sister is, to be on the lookout. Only, we have to remember that he's John Q. Citizen now. We could question him about Pierson, but other than that, we'd have nothing to hold him on. In the meantime, we'll keep looking."

Holly said nothing. Her stomach tightened. They would not find him. Nor would they find fingerprints or any other evidence that might link him to Pierson's murder. Holly knew that for a certainty.

His words haunted her, echoing repeatedly in her head.

Don't worry Holly. We'll be together very soon.

She stared into the darkness. Her mind was still numb from the horror she had witnessed.

She stared at the interlaced branches of the trees. Stripped of their foliage they too seemed defenseless, as naked and alone as she now was.

23

Shepard insisted on driving Holly to a local restaurant, where he bought her a cup of steaming coffee. She needed it. She felt frozen, both her body and her soul.

They sat in a booth in the back. Thankfully, the place was almost empty. It took a few moments before Holly noticed her surroundings. The place was a typical Formica-topped lunchroom, with a scattering of wooden tables and a long, almost empty, counter, as cheerless as it was efficient. The food was basic. Paper napkins, burgers, and BLTs. Shepard ordered one of each, but Holly wasn't hungry.

He was looking at her with a look she couldn't fathom.

"What is it?" she asked.

"This is a hell of a way to get you on a date."

"Is that what you think this is?"

"Just wondering why you've been avoiding me."

"I haven't. I've been busy with Laura. And work. I have a lot of year-end paperwork to clear up."

"So do I. But it doesn't stop me from having a steak for dinner. You're not a vegan or something like that, are you, and did I just make a major faux pas?"

"No. I'm not a vegan, or something like that. I even eat meat once in a while."

He smiled.

"I know how you're feeling."

"I don't think you do."

"My wife was killed during a carjacking four years ago."

She looked at him. The expression in his eyes surprised her. She could read the pain in them and realized just how guarded he had been.

"I'm sorry." She didn't know what else to say. "Do you have any children?"

"A boy. He's eight."

"It must be tough, bringing him up by yourself."

"It is sometimes. He's a pretty hardy little kid. My mother helps. But basically, it's just the two of us. I'd like you to meet him one day. I think you'd like him."

Holly looked away.

"This isn't a good time for me," she said. "I'd like you to give me a little time."

"I understand. Take all the time you need. I just like knowing that one day I'll be looking at you over a tablecloth, with a candle between us."

His eyes met hers with a steady gaze. She looked back at him and forced herself to smile.

"I've got to go. I'm expecting Laura for a late dinner."

"Will you be okay? I could drive you. And someone will drive your car back home."

"No, it's all right. I'm fine now."

"Sure?"

"Very. But thanks. I appreciate your concern."

"I'm there if you need me. So, try to need me."

Her mind felt frozen on the way home, empty of thought. The police had re-connected her battery, but a loose cable did not convince them that someone else had been there, stalking her. If she had the radio on she did not remember what she heard. She made a quick stop at the deli. It was only after she parked and let herself in that she realized that her house was empty.

She called out Laura's name, but there was no response. Laura was always punctual. She never forgot a date.

She called Laura's cell phone, but there was no response. The message was forwarded to her voice mail. It was possible she had stopped back at her own house to feed her pets. But still, Holly thought, she should have been here. Holly held herself back. Laura could have gone shopping, she could have worked overtime. She could have gone to one of the malls she liked. Holly resisted the urge to call the restaurant where Laura worked. It was dinner hour, and they were in the frantic mode. They would be in no mood to find where Laura had gotten to and when she had left. It would only get Laura in trouble with the owner. She glanced again at the clock, then transferred the deli items from aluminum to plastic and placed them in the microwave. She cut up vegetables and rinsed them in the colander. She assembled the usual condiments, set the table, and put out the wineglasses. There was no point opening the wine until Laura got there.

After thirty excruciating minutes in which the phone failed to ring, Holly got back into her car, drove the ten minutes to the cul-de-sac where Laura now lived, and breathed a sigh of relief as she pulled up. Laura's car was parked in her space in front. And a light was on inside. Laura must have gotten home late and made a quick stop to feed her pets.

Holly raised her umbrella and crossed the little walkway to the house. She used the key Laura had given her to open the door, and stepped inside.

"Laura?" she called. No one answered. Holly was gripped by a sinking feeling, a premonition. She went from room to room, calling Laura's name. She stopped at the bathroom door and knocked, but there was no answer. The door was unlocked. No one was inside. All of Laura's cosmetics and her bath preparations were lined up in perfect order. The bathtub gleamed. Holly felt a slight dizziness. It was pouring out, so she would not have gone for a walk.

Then where was she? And where were her animals?

Holly started for the door when she heard something. There was a noise coming from upstairs. She gripped the banister, then began ascending the staircase.

She heard it distinctly, a faint kind of vibrating, like a child tapping on a drum.

Holly stepped onto the landing. The noise became louder, more insistent. It seemed to be coming from Laura's bedroom. Holly felt an unfamiliar tug of anticipation. An off center feeling that something was wrong. She grabbed the knob and flung open the door.

The room was unlit. The drumming stopped. She had trouble seeing for an instant, and paused in the doorway, wondering if she had imagined the noise. She reached for the light switch when something flew at her out of the darkness.

She cried out as it struck her, then shot away into the corner.

Holly shivered with revulsion, then moved quickly, flipping on the switch.

For an instant she saw nothing. But something was inside the room with her, something alive. The air trembled with its presence. She was unable to make it out, not at first. Not until it rose and struck the wall before falling behind the bed. Holly wasn't sure, but it seemed to resemble some kind of gigantic moth.

But it was not a moth. Nor was it like any creature Holly had ever seen.

Then what was it?

Holly went closer, taking several cautious steps toward the bed. She jerked back as the creature rose again, then dropped onto the flowered coverlet, twitching and writhing like a mouse inside a sock.

No, not a sock. It was a hair net. And something was inside. But before she could determine what it was, it rose, wavering and trembling as it fluttered along the ceiling.

Then she understood.

Inside the netting was a small feathered creature.

A starling caught within a web.

Her stomach clenched as if someone had struck her with an ax.

It was a sign. His message to her.

And as the sickening feeling welled up inside, she knew that Laura was lost to her forever.

The hall was filled with the usual suspects. Beth eyed the gathering with a feeling of warmth. The group formed the nucleus of the new circle of friends she had made since coming to town. They met every Tuesday night at the Kiwanis, a typical cross section of the community. There were two car salesmen, a nurse, a hairstylist, a mechanic, an electrician, a lawyer. The list went on. Not only were they her support group, but they were providing her with the social contacts needed to survive in a small close-knit community. She appreciated their acceptance of her, which was mostly due to her sponsor.

Helen was a middle-aged widow with white hair who worked as a receptionist for a local pediatrician. She had two children and four grandchildren. She had been battling a lifelong problem with alcohol and had been sober for almost nineteen years. Ironically, Helen had not been drinking the night she drove her husband home from Thanksgiving dinner with her family, but the other driver had been. He barreled into them, doing over ninety on the scenic winding two-lane blacktop that criss-crossed the rolling hills of the county. Her husband was killed instantly. Helen and her children had survived, and she became a mainstay of the local AA group. She had taken to Beth almost from the beginning.

Helen tolerated no nonsense. She was unrelenting, a specialist in the administration of tough love. Why Beth had responded to her so readily was still a mystery. Helen was smart in the ways of addicts and knew every twist and wriggle they employed. The usual feelings of rebellion that arose in Beth in the presence of a personality like Helen's was curiously absent this time. Of course, there was no sibling rivalry in her relationship with Helen, no history of antagonism and resentment. Perhaps it was the mother thing, or maybe she was just growing up.

Helen was already setting out the coffee cups and filling the urn when Beth entered. Beth fell in beside her, opening the box of cookies she had brought for the meeting. Helen smiled at her and rested a plump hand on Beth's arm.

"How was work?" she asked.

"Busy," Beth responded. "I had to threaten Cosmos with a cleaver so I could get here early. He wanted me to work a double."

Helen nodded. She was used to stories about the tyrannical owner of the diner where Beth worked.

"How was your day?" Beth asked.

Helen made a deprecating gesture. "Dr. Bradley is a gem. A wimp, but a gem. Do you know what the expression *sans bolla* means? No balls."

"Are you kidding? Both have been missing from my life for the last six months." The two women laughed.

"Well, he's useless when it comes to fighting the HMOs. Every day is another battle that starts all over again. And I don't like to lose."

Beth nodded sympathetically as Helen sliced the coffee cake she had brought and set it out on a glass platter beside Beth's plate of cookies.

"I think we may have a new admit," Helen said slyly. "And this one's cute for a change."

"That would be a miracle."

"Take a look for yourself."

Helen turned her head, and Beth followed her gaze to the front of the hall where people were taking seats for the meeting that was about to begin.

There was somebody new. But she could only see the

back of his head as he settled himself in a seat in the rear. Beth smiled to herself. Whatever he looked like, as long as he was under eighty and not in a wheelchair, Helen would think he was cute. Helen loved to flirt.

"We'd better get going," Helen whispered.

Beth allowed Helen to lead the way into the dimly lit hall. They headed down the aisle, took their usual seats together, and bowed their heads as the meeting began with the usual prayer.

Beth settled in her seat. She was tired. It had been a grueling weekend. There had been a county fair, an antique auction and several church bazaars, all of which brought both locals and tourists to the town center. The diner had been filled to overflowing with demanding customers who came in unceasing numbers. There had been no break. Her limbs felt leaden and her eyes wanted to close, but she tried to remain alert for Helen's sake as the meeting went through its usual preliminaries. Whatever curiosity she might have had about the newcomer was drowned by her fatigue. She must have dozed off for a moment, because when her eyes opened, Helen was turned around in her seat staring at the man who had just risen to speak, her eyes sparkling with interest as she reached over and squeezed Beth's hand to get her attention. Beth fought her indifference and edged around in her seat.

The new guy was introducing himself. Helen had been right this time. He was cute.

He looked over at the faces turning towards him and for a brief instant his eyes met hers. Beth smiled to herself. Maybe things were looking up.

PART TWO

PART TWO

24

Christmas.

The holiday Holly dreaded most was almost upon them. Its arrival was imminent. An arrival that caused deepening depression in the inmates, which in turn sparked their aggression, which in turn led to hostility and sometimes bloodshed. And once, Holly remembered with a shudder, even murder, when an inmate stabbed another through the eye with a needle-sharp shank concealed in the hollowed-out heel of his boot.

Along with pressure from Ted to complete the avalanche of paperwork that usually accompanied year's end, there was the continuing agony involving the mystery of Laura's disappearance.

Where had Laura gone?

The police had been over the house thoroughly. There had been no sign of forced entry, no sign of anything out of the ordinary, other than the slew of dead birds murdered by Laura's quartet of predatory felines. The cats had also disappeared. There were no strange prints. Only the puzzle of the tiny blue starling trapped in the hair net, which the police merely shrugged their shoulders at.

After all, Laura was an animal rescuer. All the wildlife

they found in her apartment was proof of her avocation. The bird was just another foundling she had carried home and most likely nursed back to health. How it got into a hair net was of little interest. Holly's insistence that it was Briscoe's trademark, they considered a little far-fetched.

There was very little evidence pointing to him since Briscoe had not been seen in the area since the night of the fire at his inn. The police listened as she related his involvement with Laura, but they were not totally convinced. He had hired her to work at the inn, that was true, but other than that there seemed to have been little contact between them. The police had circulated photographs, but no one seemed to have seen them together other than at the inn. They had never been seen at any of the local restaurants, bars, or other places of leisure. His name was placed in Laura's file, but other than that he was not considered a suspect.

Only Shepard seemed intrigued by Holly's supposition, but Holly could not figure out whether it was because of his detective's instinct or his personal interest in her. In any case, that interest seemed to have waned. Perhaps there was too much professional detritus between them now. First Ulman, then Pierson, and now Laura. Plus all the stuff about Briscoe in between. There seemed little breathing room for a personal relationship.

"Go ask him out," Clara said. But Holly found that impossible. It was another opportunity she had let slip through her clumsy fingers.

Added to her failure was Holly's guilt over Beth. She had had only minimal contact with her sister since Pierson's death. They had exchanged a few phone calls during the two months since Holly had last seen her sister, and that was about it. Beth seemed to be doing okay. The good news was that she had found a competent sponsor, someone who was keeping her under a tight rein; that is, if her sister's phone calls were to be believed. At least there were no men, who were usually the cause of Beth's frequent downfalls. Thankfully, the program permitted no romance for at least a year.

Holly felt happy for Beth, though her stomach tensed each time the phone rang. Every time she heard Beth's voice, she braced for the worst. Often these little peaks of gladness in her sister's life were followed by a disastrous plunge into depression, followed by a renewal of her addiction. Thankfully, that had not happened. Not yet, anyway.

Holly had planned to have Christmas dinner with Clara and her family, something she had done for the last few years. The rest of her time off she wanted to spend at home in the vain hope that Laura might reappear or at least make contact.

Beth's invitation was her first surprise. A card had come decorated with red berries, inviting her to Beth's home for Christmas. There would be a small gathering of her new friends and someone special she wanted Holly to meet—Helen probably, her new sponsor. So, of course, Holly had accepted after making her apologies to Clara, who shook her head at the announcement. Clara did not predict any happy result coming from Holly's continued relationship with her sister.

Now, it was Christmas Eve, and Holly was in the middle of wrapping the present she had bought for Beth—a pair of aquamarine earrings that matched the ring Holly had once given her. The only gift, Beth claimed, that she had ever really liked.

There had been a surprise phone call from Beth earlier that morning, reminding Holly that she would be expecting her around six, though the party would start around seven. Holly assured her that she would not be late.

Holly was buoyed by the eagerness in Beth's voice. She could not remember when her younger sister sounded so positive about life.

Holly checked off her list.

There were the usual last-minute items to complete before the long holiday. Holly hurried through them, goaded by Clara, who kept urging her on and pointing to her watch. Everyone was gathering at Charley's before they separated for the long holiday weekend. It was a function Holly would have to attend, but first there was a final late afternoon group session.

It turned out to be a major breakthrough.

They were only half an hour into the session when Kroll began shaking uncontrollably. His fingers gripped the edge of his chair. His eyes were set like twin bolts of metal, staring deep into memory. Spit dripped from the edge of his mouth. His lips were trembling.

"What the fuck is with you?" Reyes questioned.

Kroll remained silent as every eye in the room focused on him.

Holly started to intervene, then checked herself, sensing something dramatic was about to occur.

He began in a choking rasp. Spitting out the words as if they were poisoned.

I was eight. Maybe nine. What the fuck's the difference? They took me up on the roof. There were maybe nine or ten of them. Big boys. A kind of a gang. They dragged me to the edge and said they would throw me off. I was so fucking scared, I shit myself. Then they pulled down my pants and grabbed my dick. One of them had a knife and said he'd cut it off. He put the blade against my dick and nicked me. I started screaming, but they held my head so I could see the blood. I was screaming and crying. I said I'd do anything. Then they bent me over and fucked me. All of them. One after the other. It hurt so fucking bad. I felt like I was being ripped apart. I saw the blood on my thighs, but I was too scared to cry. Then they shoved their dicks in my mouth and I had to lick them clean. They made me blow them and I had to swallow their come. They came for me every day after that. I had to go up on the roof with them. With anyone who wanted it, day or night, any time, all the time, until we finally moved away.

When I fucked all those girls, when I dragged them away, beat them and fucked them, I was doing it back to them, to those scumbags who made me do it when I was a kid, hurting them the way they hurt me. I didn't start out wanting to hurt those women. But I couldn't help myself. I did it to them like those motherfuckers did it to me.

Kroll went silent. His eyes were distant, glazed. He could not stop shaking.

The room was silent.

"It's okay," Reyes said softly. "We've all been there. We've all been fucked one way or another. Go ahead. Let it go."

Kroll shoved himself out of the chair, falling hard on his knees, then doubling over, with his face almost touching the floor and his fists clenched above his head. The scream came first, the shattering sound of withheld agony. His body shook violently, until the violence became a wail and the tears finally flowed.

It was Reyes who dropped to his knees beside him. He put his arms around Kroll and held him until the sobbing subsided.

Holly stood, ending the session and the group filed out quietly. Their eyes were filled with their own remembered agony. Only Kroll and Reyes remained, still holding each other, until Reyes finally rose and left the room, leaving Holly with the dubious task of finding consolation for a sin that could not be undone or forgiven.

Holly had intended to leave the facility by four, but there was something waiting for her when she re-entered her office. It was a heavy manila envelope, a present to her from the United States post office. She knew what it was before she opened it. She took a seat at her desk and stared at the creased and dirty envelope, deciding whether to open it or leave it for after the holidays. But that was something she could not do.

The envelope was addressed to her but it contained all of Laura's mail, all the mail collected since the last delivery before she disappeared. Holly felt a screw of tension. The package probably contained nothing of value, but what if it provided a clue, some evidence of Laura's whereabouts? She could not miss that chance.

Holly poured the contents onto the desk. There were no bills. Those had been paid long ago. It was junk mail mostly. Dozens of offers for credit cards, auto loans, and refinancing. Even offers to meet eligible singles, which brought a pang of bitterness to Holly's throat.

There was a single letter.

It was addressed to Laura personally and came from a firm called The Peterson Agency with an address in Cleveland Holly did not recognize. She took out a box of tissues, covering her own hands as she carefully eased open the envelope. This was the method Shepard had taught her so as to leave any fingerprints or other identifying matter intact. Inside was a single sheet of letter sized paper. Holly brought it closer to the light.

It was addressed to Ms. Laura Bergen.

> *Dear Ms. Bergen,*
> *In regard to your recent inquiry, we have reason to believe that we may have located one of your parents.*

Holly gasped and dropped the letter. Her throat closed, and she could not read further. She pushed her chair back so as not to allow her tears to fall on the single sheet of paper in the center of her desk.

It was it was closer to five when Holly drove away from the starkness of the prison and entered Charley's armed with a bag full of gifts.

Clara and her coworkers had already gathered at the bar and greeted Holly with shouts of welcome, kisses, and warm hugs.

"What's the matter?" Clara whispered. "Are you okay?"

"I'm fine," Holly answered, smiling. "No. I'm not fine. A letter came for Laura."

"What did it say?"

"That they might have located one of her parents."

"Oh Jesus." Clara said. "Hell. I'm sorry. I know how that must make you feel."

"Yeah," Holly said.

"You need a drink."

Before Clara could order one, Ted handed her a martini and Holly handed him his present, to which he pretended the usual surprise.

"I'm impressed," he said trying to bite back a grin.

"Why?" Holly said. "Don't you think you deserve it? For all the support and help you've given me this year."

"Ouch," Ted winced. "You want me to give it back?"

"Don't be silly. I was making a joke."

"Many a truth is said in jest, as my old mother used to say," Ted remarked. "If I've been a bastard, it's because I need you. I don't want to lose you, Holly. Even though."

"I'm a major pain in the ass?"

Ted grinned.

"That's not going to happen," Holly continued. "I'm not going anywhere."

Ted shrugged. "The chances you've been taking are turning my hair white."

"What chances? I've been a very good girl."

"Yeah. For about a week. That thing that happened to Briscoe, his inn burning down. I know you had nothing to do with it because if you had and his lawyers had gotten into it, we'd be in on hell of a lot of trouble right now. You know that?"

Holly was silent. She took a sip of her martini.

"Funny, I'm not hearing you protest your innocence."

"You know how I feel about the Briscoe case."

"I know you want him back in prison. Maybe we all do. But that's beside the point. We're all professionals here. We roll with the punches. He was released, and that's that. Case closed."

"Pierson is dead and a beautiful young woman is missing," Holly said. "I think he's behind both."

"But not the police. Not until they have enough evidence to make a case. Until then, whatever you believe is pure supposition. As far as this institution is concerned, he no longer exists."

"Are you giving me a warning, Ted?"

"If you want to consider it a warning, I won't contradict you."

"Officially?"

Ted forced a smile. "Not in writing, if that's what you mean. You've got a terrific record, Holly. I feel I helped create it. I don't want to see it destroyed."

An arm slipped around her waist. "Hey! What's going on here? It's Christmas, remember?"

Holly looked up into Henry's broadly smiling countenance.

"You and I are supposed to have a few drinks and sneak off together. Everyone's expecting it. And I don't want to be the one to disappoint them."

"Neither do I," Holly said. "Let's sneak."

"Now you getting the idea, woman."

Holly bounced her hip against his, and they did a bump-and-grind together.

"Well, is it true?" Clara commented, shoving Henry up against the bar.

"Is what true?"

"What they say about big black men?"

"Hey little momma," Henry laughed. "Let's you and me go somewhere and work it out."

Henry slipped his arms around both women and they boogied down the bar, to the hoots and applause of the rest of the group, leaving Ted holding his present and taking a long, hard swallow of his single-malt scotch.

Holly doled out the rest of her largesse and received gifts in return, surrounded by a laughing joking crowd, until Clara took her by the arm, removed the still unsipped drink from her grasp, and steered her toward the exit with a firm admonition.

"Hey. What are you doing with my drink?" Holly cried, trying to regain her glass.

"You're driving, remember? One's enough."

"Yes, mother. Just one more sip."

Clara put the glass on the bar behind her. "You're going to be late for Beth's party."

"I'll make it. It doesn't start until seven."

"Don't forget the holiday traffic," Clara warned easing Holly into her coat: There were more kisses and hugs—including one from Henry that lifted and spun her around the floor—before she was at the door with Clara a step behind, warning her to drive carefully. "You know the roads this time of year."

"Yes, mother. I promise," Holly said as she swept Clara into a warm embrace.

"And if there's a problem, any kind of problem, you know where you can always come," Clara whispered in parting. "There's plenty of food. And you're always welcome."

"Thank you," Holly said. "I love you. Merry Christmas."

Clara kissed her. Holly returned the kiss, smiled and stepped through the door into the cold forty-degree weather. It was dark and damp outside. The trees were stripped of foliage, their naked branches stark against the night, glistening with moisture.

She crossed the wet parking lot, clutching the gifts she had received against her body. She fished for her keys in her bag, but it was dark and she struggled to find them. Her hand finally closed around them, but when she drew them out, they slipped from her fingers. Lurching for them, she lost half the presents, sending them scattering across the asphalt.

"Fuck!" she exclaimed as she knelt, searching for the keys. But they were nowhere. She began feeling under the car.

"Looking for these?"

Startled, Holly looked up.

Ron Cutler

A face loomed out of the darkness beside her, and her heart froze.

"Calvin," she gasped. She stared at the enormous jagged scar that disfigured his cheek, then at his menacing, hulking frame.

She rose to face him. Her heart was pounding. Her eyes darted toward the door to Charley's across the expanse of black asphalt. But it was too far to run. She realized no one would hear her if she screamed.

She met his gaze, but his eyes were opaque pools of reflected light. Unreadable.

"What are you doing here, Calvin?" she asked softly. Her pulse thundered in her ears as her mind flashed back to the terror she had felt when he trapped her in the copy room, threatening to cut her and make her bleed.

"I wanted to give you this."

Something came at her out of the darkness. Silver sheened, it glittered in the reflected light of the amber lamps starkly illuminating the parking lot.

A knife.

Holly reacted instantly, jumping back against the chassis, her hands held defensively in front of her.

"I ain't gonna hurt you," he said calmly, as Holly realized that what she was looking at was not a knife, but something wrapped in silver paper and tied with a green velvet bow.

"It's a present."

"Thank you," she stammered, flushing with embarrassment as she reached out and took it from him.

"I'm sorry. It's so dark out here. I got scared."

"My fault. I should have told you I was coming," he said in the same low tone. "Just so you know, I've been workin'. And I'm clean. I've even been seein' my kids. I just wanted to say Merry Christmas and thanks for what you done for me." He paused, then continued in a halting tone. "I never had a chance to say I was sorry for what I done that time."

Holly could not speak. She struggled for a response.

"I'm glad, Calvin, very glad," she said softly. "You earned your freedom. Merry Christmas. And if you need anything."

He made a negative gesture; then he stooped and began gathering up her spilled presents. He rose and held them toward her. She took them from him and placed them on the backseat of the car.

She turned, wanting to thank him, but he had already walked off into the gloom.

Holly stared at the silver object in her hand. The gesture moved her. Perhaps there was some hope after all. She realized that her eyes were wet. The tears were for Laura and Pierson and all the other forlorn inmates she tried to reach, locked in their isolated cubicles of desperation. For all of them and all of their victims.

And also for herself.

25

Clara had been right; the traffic was as miserable as the weather.

It was also the season of accidents. Troopers were all over the interstate. Signal flares blocked off lanes and yellow towlights flashed far down the turgid, sluggishly moving stream. Holly avoided looking at the mayhem as she passed. She hated rubberneckers, who only made the traveling worse as they slowed to look at each fender-bender and tied up the advancing lanes even more.

It took almost an hour just to reach Beth's exit, and another half an hour along the curving country road, where she was stuck behind a knot of slowly creeping drivers, before she finally reached the outskirts of the small town where Beth now lived.

It was a town that had seen better days. There was something forlorn about the landscape of tattered thrift shops and moldy-looking stores selling marked-down merchandise. Beth had described it as charming. Holly supposed the place had a certain kind of appeal, depending on your point of view, but was one Holly failed to see. There was a throwback to the sixties atmosphere of failed hippiedom, a time warp magnified by the sudden appearance of several youths wearing bell bottoms and hair to their shoulders who crossed the street in front of her. Beth despised the prosperous upwardly mobile suburbs. It was obvious that this place suited her, though Holly could not help feeling that it was a kind of backward slap at her. Holly had always been the striver who had given their parents pleasure because of her successes, while Beth preferred playing the role of the inefficient underachiever, doing her best to hide her intelligence and capability beneath a never ending cloud of self-pity and depression.

Holly remembered to make a left just past the firehouse and drove slowly through silent residential streets filled with old frame houses, many of which were decorated for the season with multicolored lights and outlandish displays. She found the familiar intersection, and several blocks later she finally turned into Beth's quiet, tree-lined street.

Multicolored Christmas lights were strung across Beth's front porch, adding to the illumination that came from inside. Beside the electric lights, there was a lit candle burning in every window. Cars were lined up on each side of the street, forcing her to find a spot almost at the next corner.

She opened her trunk, took out a shopping bag filled with presents, and started back along the street. The evening had turned colder and she felt the sting of tiny ice crystals on her face that signaled the possibility of snow.

A huge wreath covered the front door, which was flanked with wooden nutcrackers festooned with spirals of crepe paper. Holly smiled to herself at Beth's excesses. But that was just like her. She had always gone overboard. Too much was never enough for her younger sister.

Holly tried the door, which opened to the warm smell of a roasting turkey. She expected music, but strangely there was none. Beth loved rock played at high decibel levels. Instead, the interior was silent, almost hushed. There was candlelight everywhere. Tinsel and pine boughs lined the banister and covered the hall table. Holly put her presents down beside a heap of other gifts filling the hallway and started inside.

She passed the door to the kitchen. The table was heaped

with food waiting to be consumed. A huge bird filled a serving tray. Side dishes were crowded beside it. Turnips, sweet potatoes, carrots. Holly felt pangs of hunger and realized she had not had lunch. She was tempted to scoop up something, but instead took a step toward the living room, which was crowded with people. All of their backs were to her as they concentrated on something at the far end of the room.

Holly realized she was over a half hour late, but at least she would not miss this event, whatever it turned out to be. Something was going on, but it was difficult to see. She edged along the wall and rose on tiptoe.

A gray-haired man in a suit stood in front of the fireplace holding a leather-covered book. He was facing a couple whose backs were to her.

He was intoning something Holly could barely hear, until he suddenly raised his voice.

"Under the laws of the State of Pennsylvania, I now pronounce you man and wife."

The couple leaned toward each other and kissed. Then they turned to face the warmth and applause of the gathering.

Holly took in their features and her mind went blank.

It was as if the neurons in her brain had been suddenly severed and her mind was unable to process the images conveyed to it. Then, with the abrupt suddenness of a car crash, the image in front of her and the thoughts that translated it came together and gave it meaning.

The bride was her sister, Beth.

The man she had just married was Jason Briscoe.

Time stopped as she stared at the couple.

She could not speak as her features reflected the immense horror of what she had just witnessed. Mouths moved, people applauded, but she heard nothing. Her being was enveloped in shock and silence.

The room began to spin.

She could no longer breathe. She stumbled, reaching out to keep from falling.

Her hand made contact with something.

Wings beat against her fingers. It was a small caged bird.

A starling! Like the bird in the tattoo. The creature trapped in the net at Laura's.

Holly stared at it in horror, then turned and rushed for the doorway to the bathroom just a few steps away.

She slammed it shut behind her and turned the lock. She turned on the tap and scooped freezing water into her mouth with her hand. She was afraid to touch the glass.

He might have drunk from it.

A feeling of revulsion overcame her. Her hands were shaking uncontrollably. She gripped both sides of the porcelain sink to steady herself and stop the tremors.

She looked up and faced her ashen image in the mirror. Her temples were pounding. It took several seconds for her to realize that someone was knocking on the door.

Beth's voice penetrated the thin panel. "Holly? Is that you in there?"

Holly stared into the mirror, staring into the hollows of her eyes.

"Holly. Are you all right?" Beth's voice called.

She let go and steadied herself. Her fingers were trembling, but she managed to unlock the door.

Beth was standing outside. She was smiling. Radiant.

"I'm sorry. We waited as long as we could, but the judge had to get home."

This could not be happening.

Holly forced the words out. "You didn't tell me."

"I know. We wanted to keep it a surprise. We met at AA. Isn't that something? Just two months ago. Besides, Jason wouldn't let me tell you. He wanted to see the look on your face."

"Beth," Holly began. "He's . . ."

Beth's face clouded. "I know all about him, Holly. I know he was in prison, and I know why. And what you did to get him free. Your belief in his innocence. We owe all this to you."

Holly was unable to respond.

"Nothing like the holidays for bringing families together, is there, Holly?" Briscoe said, as his arm slid around Beth's waist.

The words struck Holly like a blow.

Holly stared at him. Her head was still spinning.

"The world is a lonely place, Holly," he said evenly. "We all need someone. Your turn will come. We both pray for that."

Holly turned to Beth. "We have to talk," she said urgently.

Beth smiled. "Of course. We'll have plenty of time. You're staying with us in the guest bedroom. Now come in and meet our friends. All the people I told you about. I especially want you to meet Helen."

Holly felt her knees go. She reached out to touch her sister, then withdrew her hand. "I can't. I'm sorry. I have to go."

She turned and rushed headlong toward the door.

Beth's voice trailed after her. "Holly. What's wrong? Where are you going?"

But Holly was already outside. The slap of icy air momentarily revived her. Her head still spun, but now she could breathe. Her shoes clattered on the uneven flagstone sidewalk. She reached the car and pulled open the door. Presents tumbled out. She knelt to retrieve them. When she rose Briscoe was facing her.

"I told you we'd be together very soon, didn't I, Holly?" he said smiling. "You see I kept my word."

Blood flushed her skin, anger bursting like water released from a dam.

"If you hurt her."

"Hurt her? Why would I hurt her? I care about Beth, almost as much as I care about you."

His smile widened. Holly could not draw her eyes from the cold menace she read in his eyes.

She was unable to speak. She bolted, tearing open the door and sliding behind the wheel, then pulling the door shut and turning the key.

She pulled away, a cloud of dead leaves, like a ship's wake, flying up behind her.

Briscoe remained on the sidewalk watching her go. He was no longer smiling. His eyes were fixed on the red scar of her taillights as they disappeared into the gloom.

In those eyes was the glitter of triumph.

She drove blindly, unseeing.

The road was a shimmering smear in her vision. For a blinding instant she fought the urge to drive straight ahead into something, to end her existence in an explosion of flaming gasoline.

She passed through one stop sign after another, then a red signal and another yellow warning light before she found the strength to slow down. Her hands gripped the wheel so hard it was only when she slowed that she felt the pain in her fingers. She eased her hold and pulled over to the curb.

Her brain was aflame. Her lungs felt as if they were on fire. Her mind was whirling. She had to slow down and think. Her first instinct was to flee, to run, to find shelter somewhere, anywhere. But something prevented it. Laura's image was fixed in her mind, then Pierson's. Briscoe had destroyed them both, erased their beings as he had erased the woman in the ice. He would erase Beth's the same insidious way, so that no one would find it out, and her death would go unnoticed. She would become another statistic, like Pierson and Laura, killed by an unknown hand without the possibility of knowing who did it. The marriage would mean nothing. In fact, it would offer him some kind of cover. How or why she had no idea, not yet. But she knew there was no mistake about his purpose. What he had done he had done not to destroy Beth, but to destroy her.

What he had done was a form of torture, something he had devised to create excruciating pain. She felt it now, in her temples and throughout her entire being. It was as if she had just found out the news of her sister's death. The pain could not be more. He knew this. He had crafted it that way. It was all a part of his plan. He was diabolical, an evil that had to be stopped. Whatever she had done before had been ineffectual and idiotic. It may even had led to Laura's death. She had tried to stop him in some logically moral way, to put him back in prison where he belonged. That had been a mistake. She knew the error of that now. There was only one way to stop him. She had to eradicate him forever, just as he had eradicated his victims. No matter what the cost.

But first she had to save her sister.

She put the car back into gear and eased back into the dark empty street. There was only one place now she could go.

26

The motel stood on the edge of town, its yellow neon sign cheerlessly advertising a vacancy.

The room was functional. Chintz curtains and matching bedspread made a futile attempt to add some charm. There was a small desk and chair, and the omnipresent TV set on a small brown dresser. A single window faced the parking lot in front. There were no other cars. Yellow stripes separated each slot, added to the feeling of desolation. A seventeen-year-old boy stood behind the counter as she registered. He handed her the room key with a smirk on his pimply face.

Holly's first action upon entering the room was to call Clara.

"He's got her!" she cried. She had tried to remain calm, but the words burst out without her being able to control them.

"Holly, slowly. Who is he, and who has he got?"

Holly took a deep breath. "Briscoe. He's got Beth."

"What are you talking about? How?"

"They're married."

"Married? How is that possible?"

"I don't know exactly. They met at AA. Somehow he managed to locate where she was and sucker her into a relationship. And get her to marry him."

"Oh Jesus. Why?"

"He wants to destroy me, Clara. For what I did to him, or for the relationship he wanted and didn't have. God knows what his reasons are. His mind is completely twisted."

"God, Holly. I don't know what to say. What are you going to do?"

"I don't know yet. Stay here. Talk to her. Make her understand."

Clara was silent.

"Holly. It's not going to be that easy. She must love him, or think she does."

"That's impossible. You know what he is."

"It's more than possible. Every one of his victims thought she was in love with him, until . . ." Clara's voice trailed off.

Holly was silent, trying not to visualize the unimaginable.

"Are you sure you want to stay there?" Clara questioned. "Maybe you ought to come here. Figure things out when you're less emotional."

"No. I can't leave. Not now."

"Whatever you say. Just know I'm here if you need me."

"I know. Clara, thanks."

"For what?"

"Just for being there."

There was a long pause.

"Holly, I don't know what you're thinking of doing, but if I were in your place I'd be thinking of doing a lot of things maybe you shouldn't be thinking of doing. Do you understand me?"

"Yes."

"So before you do anything, anything you might not have thought through clearly, I want you to call me and discuss it with me. No judgments. We'll just talk it over. Okay? Promise me you'll do that."

"Sure, Clara. I will. Promise. But don't worry, I'm not there yet."

"Baby, you are giving me one major worry."

"I'm sorry. Just bear with me for a while, okay?"

"You know I will."

Holly could not sit still.

She paced the narrow area between the door and the bed, went to the phone repeatedly, started to dial, then gave up the attempt. Perhaps Clara was right. Nothing she could say to Beth would mean anything, not while Briscoe was there. She would have to wait until she could see Beth alone.

She sat on the edge of the bed, her eyes fixed somewhere distant, battling the waves of feeling that now warred within her. She felt lost suddenly, as if she were at sea, drifting in an empty boat at the mercy of every buffeting current. She cried out several times, unaware of what she said. Then she wept. Strangely, tears would not come, only waves of deep, aching anguish that twisted and convulsed her.

Then emptiness.

She felt barren of every emotion and feeling. She was dead inside, a void filled only with a dry, aching nothingness.

All of this was her fault. The pleasure she had taken in facing down the establishment, wanting to be right, proving that they were wrong. Why? So she could rectify a wrong committed by her father decades ago, in a different time and space. What meaning did that have now? None whatsoever; her work only served to satisfy her own sense of pride and ego. And at what cost? It was she who had loosed this horror on the world when he was safely incarcerated, beyond the possibility of harming the innocent.

It was she who had released him.

She became aware of the pain only gradually. Her eyes refocused, and she stared down at her hands. Her fingers were knotted into fists, the nails digging deep into the flesh of her palms. And with the pain came a deep upwelling thrust of knowing.

She was now the helpless creature inside the web.

He had enclosed her there. Imprisoned her. Stripped her of everything she held close. First Pierson, then Laura, and now Beth, the one person in the world she truly, deeply loved.

And with this knowledge came a chiseled, granite-edged sense of purpose, a rage like that she had felt when she was alone in the woods.

She would not be that helpless creature. She would not allow him to trap her inside the evil he had created.

She had failed Beth once, failed her as a child when, suffused with pride in her own accomplishments, she had allowed her sister to slip into failure and self-doubt. She would not fail her again.

They brought Briscoe to the barracks in an unmarked police cruiser. Finding him had been almost embarrassingly easy. His name had appeared in the real-estate section of the newspaper in an article reporting his purchase of an old Victorian on Mulberry Street, which he intended to convert into an upscale bed and breakfast. The article had been seen by a sharp-eyed policewoman, who brought it to Shepard's attention. The article pointed out that the purchase was being seen as a possible precursor to the revival of the dormant tourist industry and had already caused a small stir in the area, kindling the hope of jobs and renewed prosperity.

He was brought to Shepard's office and installed in the chair in front of the lieutenant's desk. He sat there patiently, awaiting his interrogator. There was a playful smile on his lips as he sat there alone in the room, watching the detectives in the large area outside. He acted as if he expected the delay, knowing it was a tactic calculated to make him sweat.

From his position across the detective's room, Shepard was able to observe him through the glass walls of his office. Briscoe's features were impassive. His face bore the look of a man who had been through similar ordeals many times before. He almost seemed to welcome it.

Shepard opened the door and entered, taking a seat behind his desk and looking up at the man opposite.

"I'm Lieutenant Dan Shepard. We brought you in because we'd like to ask you some questions. You're not accused of anything. This is strictly voluntary."

Briscoe's lips curved in a disbelieving smile. "Okay, shoot."

"Were you acquainted with a former inmate at Brandywine named Pierson?"

"He was the library clerk. He brought us things to read."

"He was released shortly after you left."

"Is that a fact?" Briscoe's eyebrows arched in surprise.

"You didn't know that?" Shepard questioned.

"Why should I?"

"You never went to see him after his release?"

"Why would I want to do that? I barely knew the guy."

"Where did you go after the fire destroyed your inn?"

"I went looking for another location."

"Where?"

"All over. Pennsylvania. New Jersey. Parts of Ohio."

"Is there any way you can prove where you went? Hotel bills? Credit card receipts? Rental car?"

"I slept in a trailer. I paid cash for gas."

"Can anyone vouch for your whereabouts?"

"I met with several real-estate brokers. I can give you their names."

"You never visited Pierson? Never slept at his cabin?"

"I don't even know where his cabin is. Why don't you ask him? I'm sure he'll tell you I was never there."

"Pierson is dead. He was murdered."

"Was he?" Briscoe said. "That's too bad."

"You didn't read about it, or see it on the news?"

"I told you. I was traveling."

"You're not very concerned, considering that he was your information pipeline."

"Not even close. I barely spoke to the guy."

"You don't seem very sorry that he's dead."

"He was a pedophile. They don't tend to live very long. It goes with the territory."

Shepard's eyes met Briscoe's in an unwavering stare. Playing eye games was not Shepard's style, but he sensed Briscoe was toying with him.

"Did you know a woman named Laura Bergen?"

"Sure. She worked for me."

"She was more than an employee, wasn't she?"

"I don't know what you mean."

"You didn't have a relationship with her?"

"It's what happens when you work with someone. You form a relationship."

"I mean, outside of work."

"Outside of work? No."

"We have statements from witnesses that indicate otherwise."

"What witnesses? My sister-in-law?"

"We'll produce them when the time comes."

"Well, they're mistaken," he said evenly. "We may have met once or twice outside of work. She was trying to locate her parents. I gave her some advice."

"That's all?" Shepard said. "You two weren't intimate. Sexually?"

Briscoe smiled. "There were possibilities that could have been explored if my place hadn't burned down, but we all miss our chances, don't we, Lieutenant?"

"Answer the question. Were you intimate sexually?"

"No. Unfortunately."

"Unfortunately?"

"She was a very beautiful girl."

"Why did you say, was?"

"Just a figure of speech."

"She's missing. Did you know that?"

"No. But I haven't been back in the area."

"You don't look surprised."

"Why should I be? Lots of girls her age go missing. Just turn on the news."

"You don't seem very concerned."

"Why should I be? She didn't have any family. She probably went off with someone. Girls her age tend to do those things. They don't leave notes explaining why."

"They don't usually leave everything they own behind."

Briscoe shrugged. His eye brows were raised. "Nineteen." He said with a smile. "An unpredictable age."

Shepard leaned forward. His eyes were pinpricks. "I think you know where she is."

"Do you?"

"Just like I know you visited Pierson. And murdered him."

Briscoe's smile widened. "Maybe I murdered everyone. That would clean up all your unsolved files, wouldn't it, Lieutenant? But then what would you do with all your free time?"

Shepard's tone was direct. "I think you murdered Carolyn Anderson."

"So do a lot of people," Briscoe said.

"I also know about the other women you played your little games with."

Briscoe shrugged. "Is this the part where I ask for my lawyer?"

Shepard stared at him. He realized the futility of going further.

"You can go."

Briscoe smiled and rose. "Thank you for an entertaining afternoon. Anything I can do to help, you just have to ask."

Briscoe opened the door and crossed the room. He nodded to the two uniforms who brought him and went through the exit doors.

Shepard's mouth twisted in frustration. It had been a waste of time. He had been outplayed. He felt as if he were in a chess tournament and had just lost his rook and his bishop. He was lucky to still have his queen.

27

It was a brilliant hard-edged winter day. The morning was dry, cold, and clear. Rays of sun glittered on the snowbanks like facets of polished granite. The hamlet was huddled within its sheltering wall of mountains. Smoke rose from chimneys along the quiet curving streets. The cough of an engine occasionally broke the stillness as a lonely vehicle rumbled along the rutted byways. One or two people braved the cold to walk their dogs; the hoarse barking carried for blocks. All this Holly could see from where she was parked lower down across the street from Beth's house.

Earlier she had made a call from her cell phone, speaking to Clara, who was back at work at the prison. Holly asked her to tell Ted she was taking several personal days. Then she made a request that was outside Clara's jurisdiction but that she knew Clara would not deny her.

"You sure you know what you're doing?" Clara asked.

"It's what I have to do."

Clara's response was a strained silence. But she did not say no.

* * *

Briscoe left the house at noon.

He turned up his collar against the wind, waved to a neighbor walking his dog across the street, then got into a dark blue Suburban and drove away, leaving a wake of cold gray exhaust. His handsome motionless features filled Holly with revulsion. It was like looking at the bust of an emperor or a king who had done horrendous things to his people but whose face registered no emotion other than vanity.

When the Suburban pulled around the corner, Holly left her car and headed toward the house.

It took several rings for Beth to appear at the door. Her expression was anything but cordial.

"What do you want?" she asked coldly as she stood in the half-opened doorway.

"Beth. I have to talk to you," Holly said urgently. "Please. Let me in."

Beth stepped back, allowing Holly to enter. She led the way into the kitchen filled with stacked dishes and platters from the previous evening.

"Why did you leave?" Beth asked. "You made me look like an idiot in front of my friends. It was really insulting."

"I had to. There are things about him you don't know."

Holly could see the blood rise in her sister's face.

"Don't do this, Holly!" she said testily. "I know everything there is to know."

"Will you at least listen?"

"To what? More shrink stuff? It's all bullshit!"

Holly lowered her tone and took a step closer. "I know you think you're in love with him. But he's chosen you for a reason."

Beth jerked back sharply. Her eyes blazed.

"He chose me because he loves me. That's why he chose me!"

Holly knew the danger. The ground upon which she was about to tread was as thin as winter frost. But she had no choice. There was no longer a way back.

"No," she said firmly. "Not because he loves you. Because

you're open and vulnerable. Like all his other victims. That's why it was so easy for him to take you in. To make you believe what he wanted you to believe."

Beth turned away sharply. "Stop this!" she shouted. "You wanted me to find someone, remember? Someone to love and make a life with. I found him, and now you want to take him away. What do you want me to do? Go back into rehab, is that it? So I can come crawling back to you like one of those crippled birds you used to find and fix up when we were kids."

"No, Beth." Holly shuddered at the analogy. "That's not what I want. I never did. I only want you to be whole and happy."

Beth turned to face her. Her eyes had hardened. "I'm a woman, Holly. I'm not a little girl anymore. I can make my own decisions. I have to live my own life."

Holly extended her hands to her.

"I know that," she pleaded. "I understand. But he deceived me, too, that's why I recommended his release."

"Bullshit! He was innocent and you know it. He was railroaded by a scumbag prosecutor who knew just how to bullshit that small-town jury."

"That's what I thought too. But it's more complicated than that."

"What's complicated? Because he liked to screw? So do I. That's what brought us together."

"Beth, you've got to listen."

"No!" Beth shouted. "No more! I must be crazy. You do this to me every time. I don't even know why I asked you to come. Even my sponsor thought it was a bad idea. I thought you wanted me to be happy. But you just want to control me like you always have. As long as I'm the failure and you get to shine, you're happy. You can't stand it that this time I got the brass ring and your marriage failed."

"You're wrong, Beth. That's not it at all. It's got nothing to do with my marriage. It's got everything to do with him and what he's done. The women he's turned into victims."

Beth's voice dropped, becoming hard and even. "I want you to go."

"Beth, please. I can't go. You've got to listen to me."

"Don't you get it? I'm through listening to you."

Beth shoved past her, turning in the doorway. Her eyes were on fire. "Get out, before I have to call someone."

Holly realized she had lost. "All right, Beth. I'll go. But I won't go far. Not until you hear what I have to say."

Holly left the house as Beth slammed the door behind her. The sound echoed in the quiet street with chilling finality.

28

Holly sat on the bed in the motel room, brushing her hair, wearing the heavy winter robe she had brought. The movement helped ease the coil of tension and frustration now wound tightly inside her.

The drive back from Beth's had not worked to calm her. The streets became a blur as she ignored the stop signs. Her ears were filled with Beth's unyielding tone and the sound of her voice as she demanded that Holly leave. She was facing an immovable wall, and she no longer knew what to do.

Philip had objected the first time Beth needed her help. "You've got to let her crash and burn," he'd said off-handedly. "She's got to hit bottom first; otherwise you'll just be going through a revolving door." Holly felt abandoned by his attitude, though Philip's father had been an alcoholic and she supposed in some way he knew, perhaps better than she, what the right course of action should be. But they were at the period in their marriage when all they seemed to do was fight, so whatever he said, she would stubbornly do the opposite. Besides, she was the professional. This was her field of expertise not his. Her professional pride was involved, along with the desperate need to save her sister by whatever means possible. She would seek the approved course of action, which was to find a good rehab program and get Beth into it as quickly as possible.

It had not been easy. If Holly was stubborn, Beth was even more so. She dug in her heels and refused to budge. She was living in a squalid one-room apartment in a run-down tenement in New York's East Village whose barred windows looked out on a filthy backyard strewn with garbage and tiny multicolored ampules of crack. The area was a slum, inhabited by stumbling winos and emaciated, hollowed-eyed junkies.

Holly was afraid every time she drove there, but she would not let up. Beth was nineteen and involved with a wasted, sunken-cheeked musician of fifty, though Holly never knew him to play any instrument other than a heroin needle. The apartment was a mess of dirty laundry and unwashed utensils, though when and what Beth actually ate was a mystery. She had lost forty pounds and seemed to live on air. Fortunately, Beth had not reached her lover's level of addiction. Holly had been giving Beth money to live on. The arrangement was meant to be temporary, but Beth never seemed to hold a job for more than a week. Though she knew Beth hated her for it, the money was Holly's only real hold over her sister, the only power she actually had.

She and Philip argued continuously over it. He wanted her to cut Beth off completely, but that was something Holly would never do. The outcome was too terrible to contemplate. The idea of her sister selling her body or stealing to support her habit sent shivers of horror through her. The East Village streets were filled with women who had traveled that path, their eyes as dead as their spirits.

"You won't learn," Philip said. "You're an enabler. You'll let her drag you down with her. You'll even let her screw up our marriage."

Holly resisted, but secretly she knew he was right. Not about their marriage—there were many more pressing issues that were still unresolved—but Holly knew Beth enjoyed the power she held over her sister, the power to exacerbate Holly's guilt and manipulate her emotions. But Holly did not have the power to resist, as she did not have it now.

In the end, Holly had prevailed. Beth went into rehab, and the musician faded into history. It was the beginning of a whole series of incarcerations. Every time her sister failed at a job or a relationship, the pattern would recur: addiction to some kind of drug, either chemical or alcohol, followed by Holly's intervention and a trip to a rehab. It would happen again, she knew. Only this time the trip might end in Beth's death.

Impulsively, Holly reached for the phone, dialed for an outside line, and punched in the numbers. The answering machine picked up after four rings, and Beth's voice came over the line.

"This is Beth. I can't come to the phone right now. Please leave a message."

Holly hesitated an instant before she spoke, emotion filling her voice.

"Beth. I don't want to hurt you. If you feel anything for me, and I know you do, please don't reject me. I care about you very deeply. I'm here, at the motel. Please, Beth. Call me." She left the number.

She hung up, sitting upright and reflecting for several moments on what she had said.

Then she rose and went into the bathroom. She turned on the shower and waited for the water to get warm.

It took only a few moments for the room to fill with steam from the hot water, and the mirrors to fog. Holly slipped out of her robe and stepped into the tiled cubicle, allowing the stream of warmth to comfort her.

The solitary figure stood motionless in the darkness outside, his eyes fixed on the square of light that came from Holly's bathroom.

He stood alone in the sharp cold of that December evening, watching with the patient eyes of a hunter. Waiting for her as he had waited outside the windows of other women, on other nights far colder than this. Yet he was not cold. If anything, his skin burned with the heat of anticipation.

He liked the night. He was invisible in the darkness, able to see what others could not. He had learned to move silently while a young child, slipping through the open window of his own room and crossing the roof without making a sound to escape to the trees and woods without his grandparents' knowledge.

What he had done in those woods was a secret no one had ever discovered. He had tracked animals back to their dens, scooping up their helpless offspring and bringing them back to his room, where he invented ways to prolong their suffering. Older, he slipped across the fields in summer to spy on his neighbors, climbing trees or trellises and lying silently just outside their open windows, watching them as they moved inside the warm interiors, removed their clothing, lay on top of their women, or furtively hid their valuables. He was the secret watcher, the master of all their secrets. The tracker who would not be denied his prey.

A shadow flickered across the light. He raised his eyes.

Holly's shape was silhouetted in the window. She was naked, her arms raised as she combed her wet hair. She turned from side to side, revealing the curving, upward shape of her breasts.

The light went out an instant later, returning the area to darkness.

Briscoe remained unmoving, testing himself in the bitter cold. The way he had done as a child. Knowing that very soon he would have what he wanted.

The knocking woke Holly.

She struggled out of sleep and into her robe, and went to the door of the motel room.

"Yes?" She called out sharply.

"FedEx for you," the voice responded.

"Okay."

She unfastened the latch and opened the door. Light streamed inside. She recognized the clerk. He was the same boy who had checked her in two days before, the same leering smirk on his pimply face.

He handed her the multicolored envelope, and she murmured a thank-you. He remained in the doorway, staring at her with an insolent expression. She shut and relocked the door, then went to the small desk and turned on the brass lamp standing on its dimly gleaming surface. She tore off the seal and removed the contents. Clara had come through as Holly knew she would.

In her hands she held Briscoe's file.

29

Beth's diner was set back from the road on a small knoll. Cars were parked on all sides of the shinning aluminum exterior designed to evoke nostalgia for an era of war, sacrifice, and the simple pleasures of a jukebox, a Coke, and a burger. There were booths with red-leather seats and white piping around the edges, and chrome stools along a chrome-edged counter over which hung the tail of a P-40 painted with an American flag. Pictures on the wall showed pilots in leather helmets and goggles, with white scarves and sheepskin collars. A leather bomber jacket with insignia from the Eighth Air Force was framed in plexiglass. The waitresses wore starched white aprons and matching caps with big red handkerchiefs in the top pockets of their blouses, chewed bubble gum, and called every customer honey.

Beth arrived for her shift a little before eight and parked her black pickup at the far end of the lot before hurrying out, dressed in a white uniform and apron under her open winter coat. She struggled to attach the white paper hat to her hair with bobby pins. When she looked up, Holly was facing her.

"Oh shit! What are you doing here?" she cried in a hurried voice, trying to go around her sister, who persisted in blocking her way.

"I've got something to show you."

"And I've got to get to work!" Beth snapped.

"Not until you see this."

The terrier look was in her sister's eyes, causing Beth to halt in hapless frustration. "Okay. What is it?"

"Your husband's file."

Beth jerked back, holding up her hand defensively.

"You want to destroy him? Is that it? He was ready to forgive you. His inn was wrecked because of you."

"He told you that?"

"No. I figured it out. But even so, he wanted you at our wedding."

Holly advanced a step, holding out the file. "You've got to read this."

Beth raised her voice. "Keep away from us. We don't want your poison."

She tried to go around, but Holly prevented her.

"Beth, you've got to understand."

Beth's face twisted with rage. "Oh, I understand all right. I have someone now. Someone who loves me. I don't have to get my rocks off cock-teasing a prisoner."

Holly's eyes widened with anger. Her hand rose with lightning quickness, striking Beth across the face with a sudden, sharp blow that sent her reeling. She lost her balance for an instant then regained her footing.

Holly felt instant regret. "I'm sorry," she said softly. "I didn't mean it. Please forgive me."

"Go to hell!"

"Beth! Please."

"Get away from me, you bitch!"

Holly stepped toward her sister. "Beth. I'm begging you. I don't care if you never want to see me again, but you've got to read this and hear what I have to say. He's a killer, Beth. It's your life I'm talking about."

"My life is none of your business. Stay out of it." Her eyes were fierce. "If you don't get out of here and stop bothering me, I'll call the police."

Holly hesitated, then stepped out of the way. Beth hurriedly brushed past her. In a moment, she had climbed the stairs and gone through the glass door.

Holly stood watching her, still clutching the file. A feeling of finality washed through her. She had gambled and lost. She became aware that a group of people had just gotten out of their car and were staring at her. She closed the file, turned, and walked away.

"I'm sorry, Holly. I can't arrest someone for his sexual fantasies."

Shepard stared at her from across his desk.

Holly had appeared in his office just before noon, demanding an immediate interview from a bewildered and irate desk officer. Only Shepard's intervention saved her from being escorted out by two uniformed officers.

"What about these?" she demanded, placing the affidavits from Elaine and the two girls she had brought with her on the desk in front of him. "They show they're more than fantasies."

Shepard picked them up, scanned them with a patient expression, then laid them down again. He did not mention that he had seen them when she had shown them to the District Attorney. "They don't prove anything. They weren't even admissible at his trial."

"We don't know how many other crimes he's responsible for."

"What crimes are those?"

"Frank Pierson. We both know Briscoe murdered him."

"We don't know that. It's only a guess," Shepard said. "Officially, no one knows who killed Pierson. The case is still open."

"You know how to close it."

Shepard stared at her, then leaned forward in his chair. "Look, Holly," he began in a patient tone. "Pierson was a convicted child molester. He had to register under Megan's Law. He had to inform us of every move he made. He was limited to a specific locale. He had to wear a monitoring bracelet and attend counseling sessions. There were plenty of people who knew where he was and who he was. People who might have wanted to do him harm. You saw the FBI report. Besides, Briscoe wasn't even in the state at the time."

"Did you question him?"

"Yes. We questioned him. He had an alibi."

"He's lying. I know he went to stay with Pierson right after his inn was burned to the ground."

"Why? Did Pierson tell you that?"

"Not in so many words."

"Then how do you know?"

"Because I knew him. He had fallen in love with Briscoe in prison."

"Come on, Holly. We've been over this before. Inmates all get crushes."

"This wasn't a crush. Briscoe was the first grown male he ever felt anything for. It was a milestone for him. When we last spoke, he intimated something."

"Intimated?"

"I know it's not evidence. But I got the feeling that he was excited emotionally, like a high school kid who just got the date of his dreams for the prom, and I think it was because Briscoe had contacted him."

"But he didn't spell it out, did he?"

"No. It's a feeling."

"What am I supposed to do with that?"

"And Laura? What about her?"

"We questioned him about her. He disclaimed any knowledge. He said she was just a girl who worked for him, that's all."

"Who he just happened to have tattooed with the same design as the one on all his other victims?"

"It's still not enough. We'd need more evidence than a tattoo. A tattoo no one else has seen except you."

"And the dermatologist who removed it and the tattoo artist. Someone had to have tattooed her."

"Maybe it was Briscoe. He's an artist of sorts, isn't he?"

"You're right. I hadn't thought of that. Why can't you at least place him under surveillance?" It was less a question than an agonized plea.

"If he were a convicted sex offender, I could. But he was released without prejudice. His conviction was overturned. I have no reason to order surveillance."

"Then you won't help me?"

Shepard stared at her. "To do what, exactly?"

"Save my sister's life, or can't you understand that? You know what kind of monster he is!"

Shepard looked at her for a moment before he spoke.

"I didn't recommend his release, Holly. You did."

She stared at him. Her eyes were stung. He knew he had made a mistake, but there was no other way to make her understand.

"Holly, listen to me. This is my community. Do you think I want someone like Briscoe living here? But I have to work within the law. This department cannot handle any more lawsuits, especially based on an unauthorized investigation where there is no proof of wrongdoing. Marrying your sister is not a crime."

Holly leaned over and gathered the papers back into her file. "You have no idea of the lawsuit you'll be facing if anything happens to her."

She scooped up the file, turned on her heel, and walked out.

30

Holly started back to where she had parked her car: on a snow-swept street decorated with forlorn images of a fast-fading holiday.

Her mind seemed unable to contain a single thought other than the smallest and most mundane needs of her ordinary existence. It was as if she were standing in a burning building but could think of nothing but the shopping list of items she would purchase from the nearest Thrifty.

This thought almost made her laugh, but joy was no longer part of her vocabulary. Dimly, she realized that her unconscious was doing its job. By blocking the incessant throbbing knowledge of impending disaster, it was keeping her sane and forcing her to find a way to survive.

It was already dark when she arrived at the store. Amber lights threw blurry haloes against the gloom, like some out-of-focus computer game.

The next half hour seemed to pass in a blur. She selected the items she needed in the almost empty emporium, wheeling her cart like a zombie as she traversed the deserted aisles. She offered her items to the single checker on duty, paid for them then left the store and returned the way she had come. The mall was deserted. The knowledge that people were at home celebrating and enjoying their families made her feel even more forlorn. She no longer had a family. She wanted home and her bed, even it was in a motel.

When she stepped off the elevator at the lower level, she realized that she had forgotten exactly where she had parked her car. Facing her was a maze of concrete columns painted with numbers that failed to register. She continued into the darkness, searching for her car. It was cold, the chill of a tomb. Her heels echoed in the vast deserted space like the forlorn beat of a drum sounding a retreat. She was halfway along the desolate floor when she heard footsteps behind her.

She turned to look, but no one was there.

She walked on. The footsteps continued, keeping pace with hers. Again, she halted and turned. But there was no one.

Irritated, she started down the aisle as the footsteps echoed, almost mimicking her movements. It was then she realized how alone she was. Alone and in a dangerous place. Panicked suddenly, she increased her pace. So did the person following her.

Her heart began beating wildly, echoing the terror she had felt in the woods the night she had run from the house where Pierson had been murdered.

And with crushing suddenness, she instinctually knew *Briscoe* was there, just behind her in the darkness.

"Stop, you son of a bitch!"

She was shouting into the empty air. No one was there.

Not a sound now, only her excited breathing in the stillness.

She turned and began to walk.

The footsteps started again, keeping pace with hers, sounding like thunderclaps on the concrete floor.

She continued along the tier, heading further into the dim tunnels of concrete. The air was so cold it was hard to breathe. Clouds of vapor issued from her chilled lips.

She reached into her pocket and found her keys. They were her only weapon. Anger flashed in her eyes as her fist closed around them. The despair that had ravaged her for so many hours had been replaced with rage and the deep, consuming desire to hurt. She would fight him with anything she had. Even kill him if she had to.

She halted, unable to go on, drawing the keys from her pocket and holding them like tiny daggers. She waited for him to come.

But no one came. Only the wind and the eerie, almost palpable silence.

Her eyes swept the area.

There, miraculously facing her, was her car.

She hurried over to it and inserted the key, pulling open the door and sliding behind the wheel. She locked the doors, turned on the ignition, and pulled out, scanning right and left as she drove along the series of descending ramps. But there was no one, only the dark silhouettes of parked cars huddled like mourners in the gloom.

An attendant took her ticket. The gate lifted, and she sped off into the freezing night.

The yellow motel sign blinked its message of a vacancy on its neon signpost. She had come to depend on it as a guide in the darkness and a hated marker of her despair.

No cars were parked in front of the other rooms, but a single vehicle stood parked in front of her door.

Shepard opened the door and stepped out of his car, waiting to greet her when she nosed the car into the space beside his.

"Hi," he said cheerily.

"What are you doing here?" she asked. She was glad to see him, but her tone was unwelcoming, a reminder of her frustration the last time they had been together.

"I was waiting for you." He nodded toward the package she took out of the car. "What's in there?"

"Just a little nitro and a detonator," she responded, holding it out for inspection. "Anything else, officer?"

"How about some dinner?" he said with a crooked smile.

They drove to a small roadside restaurant that specialized in steaks and seafood. They were seated at a corner table across from the woodburning fireplace, where a cheerful blaze illuminated the tinsel decorations. There were only two other couples seated in the room, both of them fortunately just out of earshot. Holly consumed a scotch and was surprised at just how hungry she was. She was conscious of Shepard's eyes on her as she devoured the broiled scallops she had ordered after eating a huge bowl of steaming chowder.

After the table was cleared and dessert ordered, Shepard looked up at her and smiled.

"Thanks. I enjoyed this," she said.

"You didn't have any Christmas dinner, did you?"

"Two Big Macs."

"I'm sorry. I didn't mean to be so hard on you before."

"I deserved it."

"For what it's worth, my feeling is that Briscoe won't do anything to harm your sister, not now that you've raised the alarm."

Holly looked up at him with a keen gaze. "You're wrong," she said sharply. "He has to. It's his compulsion. A need he can't control."

"Even with us watching him?"

"That doesn't matter. It actually increases his desire."

"Desire?"

"Yes. It's very sexual. In fact, it actually replaces sex. Healthy sex, I mean."

"I thought everything he did was connected to sex."

"It seems that way. But it's not."

"Explain that. I'm just a dumb flatfoot."

"That sounds like a line from a movie."

"Bogart, maybe. Or George Raft. I'm a big fan of Turner Classics."

"So am I."

"See, we do have something in common after all. I mean,

besides two murders and a disappearance. I've known romances that survived on a lot less than that. But continue."

Holly paused for a moment.

"All right. Pay attention; there will be a short quiz afterward."

Shepard smiled as Holly went on. "You see, the desire he feels is not connected to the actual act of sex itself. He uses sex to entrap and envelop his victim. But what he's really after is power over them. The power he feels then mirrors the powerlessness he felt when he was a child. Is that any clearer?"

"How do you know what he felt as a child? We don't know very much about that part of his life."

"We don't have to. You showed me where he lived and where he hid when his grandfather came looking for him."

"Okay. So he hid in a closet. Lots of kids do."

"They don't draw pictures of birds being trapped in a web."

"And what does that prove?"

"A lot. I think it gives us a clue to his inner life as a child. The birds are as helpless as he felt himself to be. The web signified the oppression he felt as a child and sums up all of his feelings of powerlessness. All children are powerless, but they don't necessarily feel oppressed by it unless that feeling is accompanied by a sadistic presence. More than likely, he was not only oppressed but also probably sexually abused. I think it's the key to his personality. And why he keeps repeating the same pattern in the tattoos."

"Did he ever mention being abused?"

"No. I shouldn't be talking about this. It breaks the rules of confidentiality."

"Okay. Then don't."

Holly looked up at him, and their eyes met. "He spoke of his grandparents as kindly, almost benevolent people. That's a complete contradiction of what we know, isn't it?"

Shepard nodded. "I think so. Have you warned your sister about him?"

Holly's lip tightened. "She refuses to listen. She thinks

I'm trying to take something away from her. Besides, she believes that she's in love with him."

"Why do you say believes?'

"Because I've been in situations like this before with her."

"Explain that."

"Yes, officer."

"I didn't mean it that way."

"I know," Holly smiled. "What I mean is, Beth likes to yank my chain. I think this whole thing with Briscoe is a good way for her to do it. What better way to get under my skin than to get involved with someone I treated and who just came out of prison? It sums up her whole rebellion ethos."

"She sounds like a little girl who hasn't really grown up yet."

"In many ways she is."

His eyes darkened. "How long before you think he'll act?"

"I don't know. But it will be soon. The wedding was a setup to entice me here. Now that I'm here, he won't wait long."

"To hurt her, you mean?"

"Possibly."

"Is there some way you can get her away from him?"

"I don't think so. But I think she's safe for the moment."

"Why?"

"Because she's not the real victim."

He looked at her and his forehead knotted. "Then who is?

Holly paused and brought her eyes to his. "I am."

His eyes remained on hers. "You think he wants you?"

She nodded. "I know he does. That's why he went after Beth."

"You're sure about that?"

"Very sure. He's only using Beth to get to me."

"Then why doesn't he just go after you?"

"Too easy. He wants to prolong my agony. He considers himself an artist. Torture is his form of art. All of this—Pierson, Laura, marrying Beth, using my concern for her to keep me here—all of it is a form of control, a way of exerting power over me. And he doesn't want it to be quick. He likes to draw out his pleasure for as long as possible. We saw that with Carolyn."

"Christ, this is confusing," Shepard said.

"Only because you haven't worked with the breed," she said quietly. "It started in the prison. Only I didn't realize it then. He knew things about me. Or found them out. Maybe Pierson helped him, I don't know. But he wanted more than just getting me to write a favorable report."

"You're sure?"

"He contacted me afterward. He wanted to take it further, claiming there was something special between us. A kind of bond."

"Was there?"

"Of course not. I told him it was nonsense."

"It wouldn't be the first time, as I'm sure you're aware."

"No. But not in this case. And not with this woman."

"But if it's the compulsion you say it is, then why didn't he continue pursuing you?"

Holly was silent for a moment. "I'm not sure. I think he was going to, but then he found Laura and somehow she tied into his relationship with Carolyn. They were very similar, both physically and otherwise. She was malleable, where I wasn't. She was willing to enter into a sexual relationship, even have herself tattooed. I was difficult and resistant. That doesn't fit his MO."

"Then why now?"

"Why?" Holly repeated thoughtfully. "Because I hurt him. When I got Laura away from him, I destroyed his control fantasy. He believes I was also responsible for destroying his inn. His other work of art."

Shepard leaned back, his eyes were focused narrowly. "What do you intend to do?"

Holly waited a moment before she answered. "I don't know exactly. But I can't leave here. Not until I can find a way to convince Beth that she's in danger."

"What about your job?"

"I'll work something out. This is more important."

"Holly. Be careful. He's got a lot of people around here feeling that he's been victimized."

"That's how he operates," she said firmly. "I've been there. I know."

Shepard's brow furrowed. "You know, I can't do anything, not unless I have a reason."

"Then I'll find you one."

Their eyes met. There was no wavering in them. Her jaw was set.

"Just be careful," he said softly. "I don't want anything happening to you."

She lowered her gaze, as her eyes focused somewhere in the distance. "It already has."

Helen wasn't that hard to locate.

All Holly had to do was find a church and contact the local AA from the notice on the community bulletin board. The person she spoke to put her in contact with Beth's sponsor, after clearing it with the sponsor first.

Things got harder after that.

Helen's voice on the phone was anything but cordial, especially after Holly identified herself and asked if was possible for them to meet. An icy pause developed until Helen grudgingly said yes. Holly said she would go anywhere and offered to drive to Helen's home, but the other woman said she would rather meet on neutral ground and mentioned a local coffee house just a little way out of town.

They met the following afternoon. The place was easy enough to find. It was a converted old farmhouse just off the road that sold fake antiques, frilly country aprons, stuffed dolls, scented candles, and soaps, along with a collection of kitschy items tourists could take back home with them. They also served a startling assortment of herbal teas in a small cozy area in the rear overlooking patchy snow-covered fields.

Helen was seated at a small oak table. She was the only customer. Holly smiled as she made her way over, but Helen did not return the expression. She was an overweight, blowsy-looking woman in her mid-fifties dressed in layers of wool and gingham. She had grayish hair that she wore in a bun behind her head, fixed with an assortment of decorative pins and tortoise shell combs from which curling wisps escaped, surrounding her chapped cheeks. She eyed Holly with hostility as Holly took the seat opposite. A steaming pot of tea was already on the table.

"I ordered tea," she said as her eyes met Holly's almost defiantly. "Unless you want coffee. They have a pretty good selection."

"Tea's fine."

Helen nodded and lifted the pot, filling both her and Holly's mugs. She added three natural packets of sugar, and milk to hers. Holly took one Sweet 'n Low. A silence developed as they each stirred their cups.

"We would have met the other day if you'd stayed around," Helen said. "But I understand you left kind of quickly."

"Do you know why?"

Helen nodded. "Beth said something about you and Jason not getting on."

"It's a little more than that," Holly said. "Did she tell you anything about him?"

"Some," Helen answered. "Getting married was not supposed to be in the program for each of them. We don't recommend even seeing anyone for at least a year. But it happened so fast, no one had a chance to say anything. Of course I did. But Beth was determined."

"Does that mean you're no longer her sponsor?"

"No. Of course not. We're committed to our people, no matter what."

Holly nodded. "I'll come to the point. What Beth did or why she did it is not important now. What is, is the fact that she is in serious danger."

"Danger of what?" Helen asked.

"Losing her life."

The other woman stared at her skeptically.

"Okay. I know Jason did time for a crime he didn't commit. I checked it out independently of what Beth told me. The law released him with no prejudice. I think he deserves a second chance, don't you?"

"What if I told you that he was actually guilty of the crime he was accused of committing? And that he was released because of me. Because of the report I wrote helping to exonerate him."

"I don't understand. You helped free him, and now you're accusing him?"

"Because I discovered other evidence after I wrote my report."

"Look, all this is very interesting, but I'm not a cop. What's it got to do with me?"

"You're Beth's sponsor. You have influence over her. You could warn her. She won't listen to me."

"From what she told me about your relationship, I wouldn't blame her."

"What do you mean?"

"Beth doesn't see you as a real sister, just as someone she happens to be related to. You helped her over the years, but you never took the time to understand her, or make a real friend out of her. You were too busy with your own career, your marriage, or whatever."

"I've always been there for her."

"Sure. But not in the way she needed." Helen shifted in her chair, her eyes rose to meet Holly's. "I'm not even sure I should be here. Beth might consider it a betrayal. And frankly, I wouldn't blame her, the way you acted at the wedding, humiliating her in front of her friends."

"I was stunned by what happened. My first instinct was fear. Fear of what might happen to her."

"So you ran away. Sure, it wasn't Beth you were afraid for, but yourself?"

"This isn't getting us anywhere. Beth's husband has killed before and is capable of killing again. I believe she is in mortal danger. And I need your help if we're going to save her."

"I don't think you need anybody's help," Helen said. "I just think you're looking for someone to do the dirty work for you. And frankly, it ain't gonna be this little Indian."

Holly looked at her. "That's your final word?"

"You could say that."

"Would you be willing to look at the record?"

"The record you compiled? I don't think so."

"Why not?"

"It would complicate my relationship with Beth, and I won't risk that."

"So you won't help me?"

"I'm afraid not."

"All right. Thanks for your time." Holly reached for the check but Helen's hand was already on it.

"It's my treat."

Holly rose and threaded her way between the aisles. Her eyes were fixed straight ahead. Whatever she had to do now, she would have to do all by herself.

31

Bright sun, blue sky and a crisp breezy 32 degrees with a wind chill of 28, so the radio announced.

Holly shivered behind the wheel, watching the front entrance of the lumberyard where Briscoe had disappeared almost 30 minutes before.

She had been tracking him since just after nine, when he stepped out of the house he shared with Beth and began a series of errands around town where he made stops at the local hardware store, a plumbing supplier, and a convenience store.

She had trailed him at a discreet distance and was almost sure she had not been seen. But she could not be positive. It was a small town, and traffic was anything but heavy.

What exactly was she doing?

The thought gnawed at her as she watched and waited. What did she think she was going to accomplish? But she couldn't just sit in the motel room; that was impossible. She had to do something to force his hand, or cause him slip up somehow. Or was she just being stupid?

The truth was that she couldn't help herself. She persisted, dogging his tracks as he made his way from one building supplier to the next, parking on a side street or in an alley and trying to look innocuous. This time she was parked across from the rambling lumberyard on the edge of town. Her car was between two pickup trucks on the muddy, deeply rutted shoulder of the dirt road, backed up against towering piles of stacked wood. She was fair game for every carpenter and mill worker who ambled by, almost all of whom offered her a smile or a wink. So much for deep cover.

Disconcerted, Holly glanced in the mirror. What the men were reacting to mystified her. She was dressed in a bulky brown shearling coat and wore a red beret and dark glasses to protect her eyes against the glare. Her lips were chapped. She wore no makeup, and her face looked pale from lack of sleep. There were dark patches under her eyes. A heavy sweater protected her, and she wore long blue silk underwear beneath that, but the cold still penetrated to her bones. She could not risk keeping the engine on for fear of the car overheating. There was nothing she could do but pound her feet on the floor, check her watch, and wait. After twenty minutes, she was beginning to feel like a block of ice herself.

Mercifully, Briscoe strode out of the yard five minutes later and got into his black mud-spattered pickup. He pulled out and made a wide U-turn, heading in the opposite direction. She ducked as he passed her, but his eyes never turned toward her. The glare off her windshield would have made it impossible for him to see her even if he had.

Holly forced herself to wait, then repeated the same pattern. Remaining a full stoplight's distance behind, she followed him out of town.

She maintained a discreet separation as they headed east, allowing several other vehicles to slip between them. She did not want to get too close and risk being seen. She began to feel like a character in a movie, only there was no director to yell "cut." Tension began twisting in her gut. What if he had already spotted her and was leading her on a fool's journey to nowhere?

They were on a winding two-lane road that ribboned between pine-covered mountains on either side. She lost sight of him each time the road dipped or curved, and was forced to speed up to avoid losing him. The sun was a sheet of bright metal, fracturing light across the snow-flecked windshield. She squinted, trying to locate him as the brightness momentarily blinded her. When she could see again, she realized that he had disappeared. Holly gripped the wheel, trying to control her anxiety, but when she rounded the next curve he was still there, nearly a quarter of a mile ahead.

They had gone several miles when his pickup slowed behind a lumbering yellow panel truck. They cruised like that for a mile or so until Briscoe pulled out suddenly, slipping across the double white line forbidding him to pass and disappearing around the slow-moving vehicle.

Holly accelerated as the road sharply curved, but they had entered a series of double s-curves, and there was no way she could pass. When the road straightened again, the yellow truck was still ahead of her but she couldn't see if Briscoe was anywhere in front of it.

Her fingers tightened on the wheel as the double line broke into segments permitting her to pass. She pulled out and accelerated, passing one car, then another, as the road curved around a sharp bend.

Holly pressed down on the pedal, pulling toward the lumbering truck ahead, when a Klaxon shattered the air. She jumped as the sound filled her ears. A massive, gleaming 18-wheeler was sweeping around the curve, heading right toward her.

Holly cut back sharply as the chrome-sheathed big rig barreled by, nosing her vehicle safely back behind the lumbering yellow truck.

Her heart was still pounding as they rounded the next curve, but she edged out and glanced across. The way ahead was clear.

She cut the wheel in the other direction, hit the pedal, and swept around the yellow truck in a sharply accelerating burst of power. But when she pulled back into the lane, the road ahead was empty.

Briscoe was gone.

Holly scanned the distance ahead. The road was straight, rippling toward the intersecting mountains for several miles in front of her. The needle pointed toward eighty. The road rose, then dipped, then rose again. When it crested, the next rise she caught sight of the pickup a quarter of a mile ahead, just turning off into the trees.

Holly inhaled sharply and slowed down, following the battered strand of asphalt as it drew her on to where Briscoe had disappeared. She glanced over sharply as she passed a narrow dirt road barely marked by a mud-splattered sign. Pine rose thickly on either side, blocking the sun and casting inkblot shadows across the road.

She knew this place.

She went by quickly, speeding up, then turning off at the next siding. She waited impatiently for traffic to thin before she cut across the road, her tires squealing, and headed back the way she had come.

She checked the rearview before she cut across the highway and drove on to the muddy track, slowing to a crawl as her Volvo bounced across the frost-hardened ruts.

She steered carefully, following the narrow, treacherous dirt track as it descended along the steep downturning slope.

This was where Shepard had once taken her. To the old steel mill alongside the river that Briscoe had once owned. The frightening red brick pile, with its double line of narrow arched windows staring across the bleakly eroded banks, where Shepard had pointed out the metal hook fixed in the ceiling from which Briscoe had suspended his victims.

The place where they had found the woman in the ice.

Trees hemmed her in, and at first she could make out nothing as the road turned and dipped. It was barely wide enough for a single vehicle. The trunks grew so thick they made visibility impossible. The sun had disappeared. The area was in deep inky shadow. Then the road curved sharply and the trunks abruptly thinned. Through them she could make out the old foundry and its moldering red brick walls, but she could not see the pickup. It could have been parked around the side or

be somewhere inside. There was also the possibility that
there was another way out and he had led her here as a per-
verse kind of joke.

Or was there another reason?

For the first time the reality that she was in danger began
to enter her mind. Had she been so fixated on Beth that she
failed to think enough about protecting herself? She dismissed the panic. He had come back here for a reason. She
had to discover what it was.

She put the car into reverse and crawled back the way she
came. When she reached the highway, she swerved around
and drove back in the direction of town until the road widened
and she could pull over onto the shoulder.

She took the tire iron and a flashlight out of the trunk,
locked the car, and started back on foot. Clouds now blocked
the sun. The sky had turned a gunmetal gray. It was getting
colder.

As she hurried down the steeply descending track, snow
began falling in large, widely spaced flakes. Trees hemmed
her in on both sides. The sky was darkening. Mud sucked at
her boots on the damp ground, but she stuck to the middle,
where it was drier. Five minutes later she was at the place
where the trees thinned and she could see the foundry dead
ahead.

The path opened out on a broad level area. The foundry
stood opposite, rising two stories to a rust-scarred metal roof.
There was no sign of the pickup, only newly imprinted tracks
scarring the mud. Facing her was the same slatted opening
Shepard had taken her through, cut into the crumbling façade
like a missing tooth.

She pulled the door open and stepped inside, immediately assaulted by the odor of rot and decay. She tightened
her grip on the tire iron and headed into the maze, flashing the
light and trying to remember the way she and Shepard had
gone. The light picked out the maw of open doorways. Her
boots felt their way along the spongy floorboards. The splin-

tered panels groaned under her feet. Light filtered through slits in the boarded-up windows like elongated candle flames.

She continued along the main corridor until she heard a sound.

She stopped suddenly, all her senses quickening.

Something was creaking just beyond the door ahead.

She hesitated, fighting the urge to run, and stepped toward it. She placed her hand on the rotting wood and felt a shudder of apprehension. A premonition of what she might find on the other side.

A woman, her arms locked above her head. Swinging helplessly from the chain.

She pushed the door open and stepped through.

She was on a large wooden platform. Wind clawed at her face with icy talons. Her vision blurred—as something suddenly swung toward her.

She jerked backward, the tire iron raised defensively, as her eyes cleared.

A chain hung from a metal hook attached to a joist in the open framework above her. Leather manacles hung from the end of the chain. They were open like gaping twin jaws.

She felt dizzy and reached for the railing beside her. The stream roared below. The railing shook under her hand, and she took a step backward. She glanced down and jerked back in terror.

There was a woman in the water below.

She was partially visible beneath the thin sheet of ice that covered the portion of still water alongside the foundation. She was naked. Her head was shaved. Her eyes stared up at Holly. They were a brilliant shade of blue.

A scream escaped Holly's throat.

"Laura!"

Holly turned and ran back through the darkness inside. Her head was throbbing. Her mind hammered with a single thought.

He had murdered Laura.

She was at the door, feeling for the latch. It was stuck, refusing to open. She fought with the latch. She felt trapped. The walls seemed to be closing in on her. She had to get out.

Suddenly, the door sprang open and she threw herself forward, just as two arms locked around her, holding her in a viselike grip.

She screamed. Struggling. Fighting to get away.

"Holly! Stop it. It's me!"

She looked up into Shepard's startled features.

"What's wrong?"

She fought to get out the words. "There's someone in the stream. Under the ice. It's Laura!"

An instant later, they were charging back though the darkness. Shepard burst onto the platform a step ahead of her.

"Down there!" she pointed, leaning halfway over the railing.

They both stared down into the icy water.

But the woman was gone.

There was nothing below but the racing torrent.

They could not see the figure hidden in the trees opposite, across the rushing stream. He watched as they scanned the surface of the water, then headed back inside. He moved quickly then, animal-like, a dark shape within the maze of intersecting branches. The brambles were thick and provided perfect cover as he headed upstream to where he knew he could cross in safety without being seen. He broke cover and darted back across the bridge of jutting rocks to regain the bank on the other side, where he had parked the pickup partway up along the dirt road that continued back behind the foundry.

He circled around the old structure, heading up along the steep bank, then disappeared in the deep woods, where he waited until the two figures emerged through the rotting plank door, crossed the muddy flat, and began their ascent back up along the twisting dirt road leading to the highway above.

They would be back, he knew. The policeman anyway. He would return to look for the body the woman claimed to have seen. But they would find nothing. What he had hidden he had hidden well. This was his territory, and they were strangers. They would see only what he wanted them to see.

He waited several more minutes, giving them time to find their way back up the road before he slipped back to where he had left his vehicle. He opened the door and got inside. They would not hear the engine, nor the sound of his tires on the muddy ruts as he accelerated, driving his truck along the dirt track that circled behind the foundry and into the woods and met up with the old logging road that cut between the mountains. That would take him back to the main highway ten miles closer to town.

He would get there early and await her return. He would wait until the policeman followed her back and left her alone in the motel room. Then he would act.

32

Holly's hands cupped a thermos filled with hot coffee. She was in the front seat of Shepard's car, still shivering, though he had wrapped a blanket around her just before he hurried back to search farther downstream.

Her mind was in torment as she sipped the comforting liquid.

What had she really seen? Was it Laura or someone else? And if so, who?

Only one thing consoled her. She knew it was not Beth.

She looked up, watching as Shepard's lanky form reappeared through the trees. He walked with the sure grace of an athlete, which somehow reassured her.

He opened the door and slid behind the wheel. "Nothing downstream," he said. "Nothing on either bank. At least that I could see."

"I saw it. Her. I know I did."

"Are you sure it was a woman? It might have been something else."

"Like what?" She felt her ire rise at his tone of disbelief.

"I don't know. Sometimes when we're excited, a log can look like a person."

"I saw a woman. Not a log."

"Okay. A dummy maybe. Something rigged to look like a woman."

"Maybe I'm the dummy," she said calmly. "Is that what you're saying?"

"Come on, Holly. I'm on your side, but you've been in a highly agitated state since you got here. Maybe you didn't exactly see what you thought you saw."

"I know what I saw." She hated her harsh tone and regretted it as soon as the words left her mouth. She turned away, staring out the window.

"You could be right," she said after a moment's pause. "He knew I was following him. It could have been his little joke. Another way of torturing me." She turned and looked at him. "You were following me, weren't you?"

He looked at her for a moment. There was a look in his eyes she could not quite read.

"Yeah," he said softly. " I suppose I was."

"Why?" she asked firmly.

"I guess I wanted to see you didn't get into any more trouble. But that seems to be a pretty impossible thing to do."

His eyes crinkled and in spite of herself, she began to laugh. It was the first time since she could remember.

They returned to the motel in separate cars. Holly pulled in first as Shepard drew into the space alongside her. He got out of the car as she locked her door and came around to her side.

"I'll walk you in," he said in the firm, decisive manner she both liked and found irritating. She did not want to be protected. Or did she? Perhaps that was all she really wanted now. Someone to step into her life and make all the terror dissolve and the horror disappear. It was a wish she knew would not be granted.

"Thanks, but I'll be fine. Good night," she said, starting inside. She paused at the door, turned to face him, and said, "Thanks."

"Wait a minute," he said, stopping her. "Look. Sorry if I made you feel as if I didn't believe you back there."

She glanced up at him. His eyes were warm and gentle. They had a calming effect.

"It's not you. It's me." She spoke in a different tone, hearing the sudden burst of anguish in her voice. "This is all my fault."

"No. Not your fault. We both know whose fault it is."

He reached up and touched her face, then drew his finger away so she could see the wet stain on the tip, which was when she became aware that tears were coursing down her cheeks.

Shepard made the coffee.

He brought it over from the minibar to where Holly was sitting on the small chintz covered love seat beside the desk.

She had closed the blinds when they entered, as much to cut the final glare of sunlight as the prying eyes of the pimply desk clerk. Only the lamp on the end table was on, and Holly welcomed the late-afternoon darkness that masked her swollen eyes.

She knew she looked a wreck, but she hadn't the strength to do anything about it. She took the mug of black, steaming liquid, shaking her head when he offered the artificial sweetener and the Coffee-mate she hated for its viscous taste, but there was nothing else. She had neglected to buy a container of milk when she was out shopping. He took the chair opposite, his coffee mug enclosed within both hands, and looked up at her with a look of patient kindness.

"You look worried," she said, glancing away nervously as his eyes fixed on hers.

"I guess I am. Are you going to be all right?"

She didn't answer at first. "I don't know," she whispered. "I don't know what to do anymore. I love my sister more than anything else in this world, and now she as much as hates me."

Her shoulders began shaking. She felt the tears spilling down her face. She clutched her arms against her chest as waves of anguish broke over her.

"I'm sorry. I don't know why I'm crying."

"Sure you do."

He put his cup on the desk and knelt beside her.

"It's all right. Just let it go."

She felt his arms come around her and lost herself in the comforting warmth of his body and his soapy, woodsy smell. She drew back an instant later, aware that her forehead was resting against his chest. She inhaled deeply, then pulled away, but the contact remained, something pulsing but still uncertain that now enveloped them.

"I'm okay," she whispered. "Sorry."

"Nothing to be sorry about. You're human, remember."

"I'll try to remember that, doctor," she said, forcing a smile.

Their eyes met and held. The irritation she had felt earlier was gone. She wanted his warmth and the promise of protectiveness in his gaze. His hand touched her face. But she glanced away.

"I'm sorry. I'm just so tired."

"No problem. You'll be okay?"

She nodded as he rose and reached for his coat. She followed him to the door. He put his hand on the knob but she halted him, placing her hand over his.

"I know you've been sticking your neck out and I appreciate it," she said gently. "I really do. And for following me today."

"I'm here if you need me."

"Thanks, Dan. For everything."

He leaned toward her and their lips met, tentatively, then with greater force. He drew her against him and she gave herself up to the kiss, letting go in a dizzying vertigo that made her head swim. His hands moved over her as she pressed against the hardness of his body. His scent enveloped her. She lost herself in the sensation.

His beeper sounded with jarring suddenness.

"Christ. I'm sorry," he said as they separated. "Professional hazard. Can I use your phone?"

"Of course."

He went to the desk and began dialing as she returned to the couch and sat down. Her hands were trembling. Her body felt vibrant, alive.

"Shepard here," he said into the receiver. His eyes were still leveled on hers. She could not draw her gaze away.

He listened for several seconds, then said, "Got it," and put down the phone.

His expression changed as he took the seat beside her on the couch and took her hand. His eyes fixed on hers.

"I sent faxes to all the local dealers who specialize in S and M gear. One just responded. Looks like Briscoe placed an order."

The digital dial flashed 10:30 in tiny green numerals.

Holly glanced at it with irritation. Shepard had returned to his office two hours earlier. She had hoped for his call, but the phone had not rung.

She paced the room, unable to keep her attention on the TV for more than three or four minutes at a time. She sprang up every few moments, trying to find something to distract herself with. At 9:30, she decided to wash her hair. She forced herself to remain under the stinging needles of the hot shower and somehow got through the mind-numbing ritual of shampoo and conditioning.

Twenty minutes later Holly was in her robe, standing in the bathroom drying her hair with the blow-dryer, one eye impatiently glued on the unmoving clock.

Why hadn't he called?

Irritation ground through her, feeling like bits of sandpaper just under her skin, but she fought off the sensation. He was her ally, not her enemy. There had to be a reason for the delay. His words re-echoed in her head. He would track down the information, and then he would call her. She knew it might take some time, but she could not control her impatience.

She wanted him to return and take her in his arms. She wanted to make love to him and lose herself again in his embrace. She still resonated with the sensation of his kiss and the feel of his hands as they moved over her body. She wanted him deep inside her. It had been so long, and she was not ashamed to admit her need.

She allowed the noise of the dryer to obliterate her thoughts. In a strange way, it provided a kind of solace, a space in which her mind could remain empty. A place where the terror could not intrude.

She tossed her head from side to side as she worked the dryer, watching herself in the mirror. Her face looked wan, scrubbed of all expression. She made a grimace to spite her looks, then turned off the machine, wrapped the cord around the still-warm mechanism, and placed it on the shelf above the sink. She turned out the light and stepped back inside the darkened motel room, lit by the single lamp beside the bed.

The TV was still on. An outlandish-looking commentator from CNN was relating the financial news in an almost comical British accent. Holly started for the couch when she sensed a sudden movement behind her.

Startled, she wheeled around, just as her wrist was seized in a viselike grip and her arm was drawn up painfully behind her. She cried out as her assailant drew her hard against him. His breath came sharp in her ear.

"Did you enjoy your drive?"

The voice was unmistakable.

It was Briscoe.

Holly struggled, turning, trying to rake his face with her nails. "You son of a bitch!" she cried sharply.

She kicked, striking his knee. He released her suddenly. She glimpsed agony imprinted on his face an instant before she bolted for the door.

She never reached it.

His fingers gripped her arm, halting her in midstride and slamming her hard against the wall.

He slammed her again, harder, knocking her breathless. Her head spun as he flung her down on the couch. In an instant, he was upon her, pinning her down with his heavy, muscular body.

She tried to scream, but his hand cupped her jaw, forcing it shut. She rose, trying to free herself, but his elbow struck her hard across the cheek and she blacked out.

She awoke an instant later, still struggling, but he had locked both her wrists behind her. His knee was between her legs, separating her thighs. His other hand reached into her robe, moving over her naked belly as she twisted against him.

She arched, trying to escape, her mouth open in a silent scream, aware of what he was about to do. But he was too strong.

She was as helpless as the other women he had used, as defenseless as the victims she had heard her inmates describe.

His fingers pushed between her legs, separating her thighs and gripping the mound of her sex. She writhed helplessly, trying to twist away, trying to bite, to rip his flesh. But he was always just out of reach.

His fingers tightened forcefully, insinuating themselves between the yielding lips of her sex. He was opening her, entering her, touching her deep inside.

She felt a wave of nausea and cried out, but her mouth was pressed against the pillows, muffling any sound.

His breath was hot against her ear. "See how easy it would be," he whispered. "To put my cock inside you."

His tongue licked her neck as she shivered with revulsion.

"What's the matter? Not interested? You should be flattered. And here I've been so faithful to your little sister. She's so hot and you're so cold. You could learn a lot from her about being a woman."

His fingers dug deeper, injecting themselves painfully. She twisted her neck, trying to rise, but he shifted his weight, forcing her face deeper into the pillows. She gasped for breath, still fighting him with all of her hatred.

"So wet. So warm. So open and wanting," he whispered. "And so available, weren't we? Just an hour or two ago. When we would have spread our legs wide and fucked the brains out of our sexy policeman. What a shame he had to leave. Poor Holly. Poor, frustrated, horny little Holly. Hasn't been laid for a century and a half."

"You scum!" she spat, choking for breath as her nails stabbed at his eyes.

He jerked back defensively. His fingers relaxed around her wrists, allowing her to free one arm.

He drew her against him as she brought her nails to his face. Then his fingers clamped over her wrist.

"Go ahead. It's what you want, isn't it?"

He gripped her wrist and raked her nails down along the side of his face, gouging the flesh of his cheek and tracking strands of blood.

He locked both her wrists with one hand, then drew the other hand to her face and rubbed the blood on his fingers into her lips.

"They say, once you've had a taste, you can never go back."

She struggled against the thick, almost sweet sensation, trying to twist her head away, but he gripped her jaw, forcing her to look at him.

She spit at him, and as he drew back, she shot her head, forward striking him in the cheek with her forehead.

The impact stunned her. His hand gripped her hair and snapped her head back against the wooden arm of the couch. Pain shattered her skull. Her head swam. Colors flooded her vision like a madly spinning kaleidoscope.

He ripped off the tie of her robe and before she could summon the strength to resist, he had tied her hands behind her. He pulled open her robe, exposing her completely. She tried to turn away, but he pulled her to him.

"I won't hurt you, Holly. I only want to give you pleasure."

His eyes examined her with clinical thoroughness, as if she were something he wanted to buy. His hands hovered over her body, his fingers moving over her as if he were playing an instrument: touching her breasts, her thighs, her belly, and the texture covering her mound. His hand slid beneath her, separating her cheeks and burrowing between them. It was as if he wanted to leave his mark on her, to imprint her with his touch.

He leaned closer, and his lips touched her ear, his words a hot whisper against her flesh.

"Do you see how easy it would be? All you have to do is let go. Just let go."

She closed her eyes, trying to separate herself from what he was doing, to keep it from reaching her.

His fingers touched her throat.

Her eyes opened. His lips descended to mesh with hers. She struggled against his kiss as his fingers tightened over her windpipe.

She twisted against him, fighting for air. Her throat was on fire. She struggled for breath as terror tightened around her like cords of ice.

As Carolyn had struggled before he ended her existence. Before he slipped her into the cold, into the freezing ice that congealed around her warm, once living flesh. Into the cold and dark, forever.

Abruptly, he released her.

She coughed, gasping for air as oxygen flooded back into her searing lungs.

"Want to kill me, don't you, Holly?" He said softly. "Well, guess what? I'm going to give you that experience. It's going to be my parting gift to you."

He rose. Standing in front of her, his eyes glittering unnaturally. The marks on his face were distinct snakelike tracks, still running blood. His lips formed a cold sardonic smile.

"Until next time," he whispered against her ear.

He reached down and pulled the tie, releasing her hands. Then he stepped away into the darkness. A moment later she heard the door as it slammed shut, leaving her shivering and alone in the darkness.

33

A bored, thin-lipped technician took samples of skin from under Holly's nails as Shepard watched from the doorway of the glass-walled cubicle.

"So, what's up?"

Shepard turned to face Detective Sergeant DeMarco, who had just stepped to his side.

DeMarco was a balding, pugnacious figure in a blue sweater and baggy cords. He was a recent transplant from the NYPD and had all the abrasive edges to prove it.

"We're taking skin samples. If they match, I'm going to charge him with assault and attempted rape."

"Any bruising? Tearing of the skin? Trauma to the vagina?" DeMarco asked casually.

"No. Her wrists look like they've been tied. That's what she claimed."

"But no outside corroboration?"

Shepard shook his head.

"What time did she report it?"

"10:30 or so."

"Then you have a problem."

Demarco offered Shepard the pink copy of the police report in his hand.

"Briscoe came in about ten. Said she attacked him when he got out of his car."

"Briscoe says *she* attacked *him*?" Shepard said. His tone was incredulous.

"Yep. And he's got a witness."

The witness's name was Shandy.

He lived a few doors down from Beth. He was in his early seventies, small, sharp eyed, and crusty. Shepard eyed him with a dubious expression as DeMarco asked him to repeat what he had told the investigating officer.

He tightened his lips with resignation and repeated his story in an emotionless monotone.

"I was walking my dog, like I always do, when I seen a woman come out of the bushes. You know, like she was waiting for him. She tore up his face good, it looked like."

"What did she look like?" Shepard asked.

"Youngish. Thirty or so."

"What was she wearing?"

"Tannish coat. One of those sheepskin things. And a red cap. A beret."

"A beret? You're sure of that?"

"Sure. I had one just like it, years ago. Black, not red. Not as wide, though. You'd be surprised how they keep your head warm."

"Could you point her out if you saw her again?" Demarco demanded.

Shandy hesitated, then shrugged. "I'll give it a try."

Holly stood against the back wall of the lineup. The wall behind her was marked with white lines indicating height. She stood under bright fluorescent lights flanked by three other women she had never seen before, all dressed in street clothing. She wore her shearling coat and her red beret.

Shepard stood beside the witness in the darkened room as

DeMarco leaned against the wall opposite, peering through the one-way glass, a crumpled piece of paper in his hand. His eyes were filled with doubt.

"That's her," the witness said, pointing to Holly. "The third from the left."

"You're sure?" Shepard asked sharply.

The man hesitated. "Well, it was dark, and I was across the street. But she looks like the woman I saw. Same height and all. Same coat and red hat. Beret. I told you, I had one."

"You never saw her before?" DeMarco asked.

"Nope." The man responded. "Never."

"Okay. Thanks," DeMarco said as he opened the door, gesturing for the witness to step out. "We'll call you."

"I can go?" the man asked hopefully.

"You need a ride?" DeMarco asked.

The man shook his head. "My daughter's outside."

DeMarco nodded, and the man quickly exited.

"So what do you think?" DeMarco asked.

"I'm not sure," Shepard answered. "He's seventy-something. He could have a sight problem."

"Hey, he could be fucking demented. Only thing is, Briscoe's lawyer's been burning up the line. Claims there's a lot more between her and Briscoe than she's telling. I got his number, if you're interested," DeMarco stated, offering the rolled-up paper in his fist.

Shepard looked at him, then extended his hand.

Holly sat alone in Shepard's office, holding a Styrofoam cup filled with black, tasteless coffee.

She took an occasional sip and allowed the warmth to pass through her. She felt steadier since coming to the station, but her hands were still trembling.

She had endured the physical examination and the humiliating questions about what he had done, and how far he had penetrated her with his fingers, and where else on her body he had touched her. The questioner had been a female detective who never smiled and whose face betrayed zero emotion in an attempt at total impartiality. After that, Holly had been taken to the lineup to which she had submitted voluntarily after Shepard had asked if she would mind allowing herself to be viewed by a potential witness.

That was twenty-five minutes ago. Now she felt exhausted and wanted to go home. Only two other detectives were at work at that hour, having a conversation across the empty room. Occasionally their laughter penetrated the thin walls of Shepard's office. It was laughter that failed to cheer her.

She looked up and observed Shepard through the glass partition as he crossed the large desk-filled room outside and came toward her with his attractive, straight-shouldered walk. His face was grim. But seeing him brought her a sudden blanketing feeling of warmth.

Shepard opened the door and stepped inside. His eyes failed to meet hers.

He entered quickly, moving to the chair behind his desk. He slumped into his seat and glanced up at Holly with a pointed expression.

"What's the matter?" she asked.

Shepard leaned forward. The look on his face was serious. "This is going to be tough. I'd like you to remain calm until you hear everything I have to say."

"What is it?"

"Briscoe is claiming you assaulted him."

"That's crazy," she said, feeling sudden anger.

"He's got a witness."

"That's impossible."

"It was dark and the witness was across the street, but he identified you."

"That was why you asked me to stand a lineup?" she said incredulously. "I thought the witness was someone who might have seen him leave the motel."

"Sorry. But we had to. Apparently, no one at the motel saw anything."

"How did he identify me? Was it my face? My clothing?"

"You know I can't disclose that."

Holly leaned forward intently. "Beth has a coat just like mine. I bought it for her two years ago. You can buy a red beret anywhere. They could have worked it out together to give him an alibi."

"I called the diner. Beth's been at work all evening. I'm sorry, Holly. But he's pressing charges."

She stared at him as the door opened and a stocky uniformed policewoman stepped inside, her eyes fixed directly on Holly.

She was finger printed, each finger rolled separately on a glass-topped cabinet and imprinted on a white card. Then she was walked to a cubicle surrounded by floodlights and asked to hold a number against her chest as a policewoman took three pictures, one full face and two in profile.

She was driven to the county court, a granite building where she was unloaded from the police cruiser and escorted inside through the battered entrance reserved for those entangled with the system. The place was harshly lit and had the rank smell of despair. She waited her turn on a bench filled with dead-eyed hookers and various miscreants of both sexes, most of whom were in handcuffs. She had at least been spared that, thanks to Dan Shepard who, besides seeing that she was not put in manacles, offered her his office for the night rather than a bunk in the tank, where she would be locked up pending her plea. The other alternative was the long drive to the county facility, where she could still receive justice from a dispassionate night court judge.

When she was finally called, she pleaded not guilty to first-degree criminal assault. The judge ordered her released on bail of two thousand dollars and set a date for her arraignment. She paid her bail with her credit card, avoiding the two oily-looking bail bondsmen who scurried to her side. She was warned when to appear, or the bail would be forfeited and a warrant issued.

She nodded that she understood, but she felt as if she'd

been injected with novocaine. Her entire body was numb. She left the courtroom and started out of the facility, heading along the stark, green-walled corridor toward the glass exit doors, when Shepard came around a corner to intercept her.

She tried to dodge him, but he blocked her way.

"Wait a second. Where are you going?" he demanded.

"When I know, I'll fax you," she said in a bloodless tone, brushing by him with a cold expression.

"Holly. Wait," he said, turning to stop her as she went by.

"Please get out of my way."

"Listen to me."

"I said, get out of my way!"

"I'm trying to help you."

"How?" Her voice rose in anger. "By taking my measurements for an orange jumper? Now, please, I want to get the hell out of here!"

He stepped aside and watched her disappear through the heavy glass doors into the chilling darkness outside.

She drove through the darkened streets of the town, unable to think, unable even to formulate a plan.

Her head was still reeling from what had just happened, the chilling indignity of what she had been put through. The cynical faces of the police and the impassive court functionaries. The ineffective numbness of the bureaucracy. The stomach-grinding knowledge that she was now considered a perp with a court date and no witnesses to back her up, or testimony to confirm her ordeal. The outrage of knowing that the world would consider her guilty.

Worse was the disrupted connection between her and Shepard that felt as if someone had yanked all her wiring out of the walls. True, their intimacy was only in the fledgling stage, but she had craved it, and now it was gone, as much her fault as the circumstances. She knew he was only doing his job, but she could not forgive him for it. In the space of one night, they had gone from potential lovers to adversaries.

The sky was lightening. It was almost morning. Clara would

just be getting up and getting ready for work. She pulled over, took out her cell phone, and dialed her friend's number. Clara answered in two rings.

"What's going on, Holly?" Clara said, her voice still hoarse from sleep.

"How did you know it was me?" Holly asked.

"You're on my musical ring. Trouble. Trouble here in River City."

"That's not very funny. Not this morning."

"Why? What happened?"

"He broke in last night and almost raped me. When I reported it, he accused me of assaulting him and produced a witness to back him up."

"That's completely nuts."

"No. It's part of his strategy. I know he got Beth to pretend she was me and fool the witness into thinking I did it."

"Oh god, Holly. That's awful. Is there anything I can do?"

"I have a court date. I'll need a lawyer. Do you know anyone out here?"

"I'll find somebody. Somebody good. Actually, I think I know just the guy. I'll call him and have him contact you at your motel. You're still staying there?"

"I have to. I can't abandon Beth. Not now."

"Even after what you think she's done?"

Holly sighed. "She's under his spell. And she's angry at me for trying to break them up. She thinks I had a thing for him, and that I'm jealous."

"Knowing Beth, that's par for the course."

"Thanks, Clara. Sorry for waking you."

"I was just getting up, anyway. What do you want me to tell Ted?"

"Just that I'll call him."

"Okay. I'll get back to you about the lawyer."

Holly put down the phone. She started up and pulled into the empty street just as the street lights went off. A mist obscured the buildings, shrouding the town in a soft glow and giving it a mysterious, almost poetic aura that obscured the reality of dirt and decay. Holly felt ravenous suddenly. What she needed was the comfort of a stack of pancakes and a cup of real coffee.

The only place open was Beth's diner. She felt her stomach cramp as she pulled in and got out of the car. She climbed the steps to the entrance and peered inside. If Beth was inside she would pass and go back to the motel. But Beth was not inside. Holly went through the entrance and took a booth at the far end. A handful of people sat at the counter, but most of the booths were empty. Eyes followed her as she was seated and when she looked up, they were still on her. She read hostility in their looks. But how was that possible? She was a virtual stranger in their midst.

She studied the menu, then waited, checking her watch. The waitress seemed to be ignoring her. A customer stood up, a young man in worn jeans and a hunter's jacket. He turned and stared in Holly's direction. She met his contemptuous gaze, then looked away. His look was a challenge. He tossed some change on the counter, then sauntered down the aisle toward her. When he was parallel to her booth, he paused and offered her a hard, probing stare.

"Can I help you?" Holly asked.

"No. But you can help yourself right out of here. That would sure as hell help the rest of us."

He continued past her and went out the door, holding it open long enough for the cold air to penetrate. Holly shivered, trying to find meaning in what he had said. When she looked up, the other patrons who had been staring at her slowly looked away. Their eyes were filled with the same burning contempt.

"Excuse me, miss," Holly said in a loud tone. The waitress kept her back to her. "I said, excuse me."

The young woman finally turned around, one hand on her outthrust hip. She was an overweight platinum blonde with sallow skin. The hair color and her skin were not a match.

"I'd like to order," Holly said.

"Kitchen's closed."

"The sign says you're open all night."

"Yeah, well, the cook went home sick."

It was obvious that she was lying. The still-steaming food in front of the people at the counter proved it. Was it because of Beth, she wondered? Had she spread the story of Holly's misdeeds all over town? Or was it something else?

"My sister works here," Holly stated

"Yeah, well she ain't workin' here tonight."

"Can I please speak to the manager?"

"He ain't here either. There's just little ole me, I guess. And I sure ain't gonna cook you shit."

Snickers and giggles accompanied this pronouncement.

Holly skin was blazing. She folded the menu and rose, then went out the way she came in. Her eyes swept the counter, shooting dots of anger at those glances that rose to meet hers. She had faced down rapists and murderers. These were no match for her.

She was so distracted that she almost drove past the motel. She made an illegal U-turn and pulled into the parking lot. "Oh god," she said aloud. All she needed now was a ticket. Fortunately, no policeman materialized.

She had just opened the car door and stepped out when a man's coarse voice boomed toward her.

"Hey, bitch! Get your ass out of town! We don't want you here!"

A beer can flew through the darkness, bounced on the asphalt, and struck her bumper before clattering away.

She jumped back reflexively just as an engine roared and tires squealed.

Holly turned, catching sight of a black pickup on huge mag wheels as it peeled away down the side street.

She remained rooted for a moment, her mind seeking some way of reacting to this new assault.

She looked up and saw the obnoxious clerk in the motel office. He stood at the window watching her. His eyes were blank of emotion, pitiless and indifferent.

She realized that she had now become the enemy, someone who might destroy some meager chance of future employment in a town desperate for work of any kind. Briscoe represented that hope; his new inn would provide employment for those who built it and staffed it, and would become a magnet for a new surge of tourism that would revitalize the area. All of it was a slim hope, but a hope nevertheless, and she was the now the enemy of that hope. Holly turned away, unlocked her room door, and hurried inside.

The phone was ringing.

Holly slammed the door shut and tore the receiver off the hook.

"Yes!" she shouted irately, expecting Shepard's voice with some new summons for her to return to the establishment of the law.

"Holly?" the familiar voice said. "It's Ted."

"Oh, sorry," she responded, sitting on the edge of the bed and trying to control her rapid breathing.

"Is everything all right? You sound winded."

"No. I'm fine."

"Don't you ever check your messages? I've been calling for the last two days."

"Messages?" she said incredulous. "No. I didn't get any."

The desk clerk's face jumped into her mind, with its cynical stare and sardonic grin.

"Ted. I'm glad you called. I'm having a problem. I'm going to need some more time off."

"*You're* having a problem? Briscoe lodged a complaint against you with the licensing board, which puts it squarely right up my butt."

"Ted. Listen to me."

"No. You listen. Your license has been suspended pending a full investigation. That means you're suspended from the facility until further notice without pay or benefits. Those are the regs, and it's my job to inform you. Nothing personal. Is that understood?"

Holly got to her feet, suppressing her urge to scream at him. "Yes, Ted. I understand. Thanks for all your help and support."

She banged the phone down, shouting, "Fuck you! You stupid ungrateful asshole!"

She sat back down, eyes fixed on the blank wall beside the bed.

Now she was friendless, jobless. And about to face criminal charges.

She felt a sudden weariness, as if all of her strength had evaporated. She lay facedown on the pillow. She did not reach for the box of tissues on the night table, but allowed the tears to come, to run unchecked down her face and into the flowered coverlet.

She must have drifted off, because when she opened her eyes she became aware that someone was knocking at the door.

She sat up quickly, ripping several tissues from the box and drying her eyes.

"Yes," she called out. "Just a minute."

She glanced at herself quickly in the mirror over the dresser, tightened her expression, and went to the door.

"Who is it?" she asked cautiously.

"It's Dan."

She hesitated, then opened the door.

Shepard was standing outside, silhouetted against the glow of light from the street lamp.

"Can I come in?"

"What's the matter?" she said as she stepped back to admit him. "My mug shot out of focus?"

He looked at her sideways as she closed the door.

"You're angry. I understand. Just understand none of this is intentional. It's just procedure."

"Procedure," Holly exploded. "Bad enough I'm facing a charge of felonious assault. But that son of a bitch got the board to suspend me. I could lose my license. Not to mention salary and benefits, which have just been cut off."

"Sorry," he said softly. "I didn't know."

"So now I'm the perp. Isn't that wonderful?" Her eyes were blazing. "Do you know what just happened? Someone threw a beer can at me. Called me a bitch, and told me to get the hell out of town and leave Briscoe alone. Is that a joke or what?"

He stepped toward her, placing his hand on her arm. "Holly. You've got to calm down."

"Calm down?" she echoed, her voice ragged with emotion. "He almost raped me, right here, on this couch, less than twelve hours ago. And I'm the one who had to make bail."

"I know how you feel."

"No. You can't." She turned away, her back toward him. "I have to face the realization that the woman who pretended to attack him was my own sister."

"You really believe that?"

"It had to be either Beth, or someone else he put up to it. What else could it be? Beth must hate me to do something like that. Or do you believe I actually assaulted him?"

"I didn't say that."

"No!" she said, turning to face him. "You haven't said anything."

"I'm in your corner, Holly."

"Sure you are. But you're also a cop."

"I care about you, Holly." His voice was earnest. "I care about you very much. I know that's not very important to you right now. But it happens to be important to me."

She looked up at him and her expression softened.

"You're wrong. It's very important. Especially now."

"Maybe when things get a little calmer, we could go somewhere and get your mind clear of this."

"How can I do that when I know what he's capable of?"

"Yes, but you know how careful he is, how methodical. He's made it a legal matter, so he knows we're watching. Beth is going to be okay. The situation will work its way out. You have no criminal record or any history of domestic violence. His witness is an old man who saw what was happening from a distance and really isn't capable of making a facial identification. All he saw was a woman in a brown coat and a red beret. The judge is bound to dismiss. You've just got to trust me a little."

"Don't say that word, please," she said, becoming suddenly agitated.

"Do you want me to go?"

She looked at him, hesitating.

"No," she said, her expression softening. "I don't want you to go."

He reached for her hand. She let him take it and lead her over to the bed. They sat together side by side. Then he put his hand under her chin and turned her head toward him. Their eyes met and held.

"You know how much I want you," he said.

He kissed her softly, not pressuring her, but allowing her to come to him. She responded, her hands spread on his chest. She felt his urgency and the pulse of desire in her breast that rose to meet it, but something held her back. She turned away.

"I'm sorry," she said, unwilling to face him. "I just can't do this. Not now."

"I understand. Just relax and let me hold you."

She met his gaze. His eyes were steady and warm, beacons of hope she needed so desperately.

They lay on the bed together and he put his arms around her.

"Just close your eyes," he whispered. "I won't leave you alone."

She closed her eyes and clung to his warmth as tentacles of exhaustion wrapped themselves around her. In a moment she was asleep.

Shepard held her close, his arms locked securely around her. His eyes were open, staring into the distance, filled with apprehension and uncertainty.

34

The county courthouse was a gray granite pile, decorated with Ionic pillars and built like most facilities of the law Holly was used to.

She had served the law, prowling the corridors, a young and idealistic DA, eager to secure justice. But justice was an elusive spirit, difficult to capture and fond of evasion. She thought she had left that life when she got her degree in psychology, but her job at the prison brought her in regular contact with the intricacies of the legal system, so she was no stranger to the dry, dispassionate exchange of plea and counterplea, including, now, her own.

Her attorney was a wrinkled little man in a black bow tie and worn tweed suit whose hooded eyes resembled those of an owl. He carried a bulging worn leather briefcase and a newspaper folded under his arm. He did the crossword in ink. Their brief phone conversations consisted of ahs and ums, and I understand, and a final "Don't worry, we'll handle it." None of it was very reassuring, and Holly had lost several nights' sleep before she had to finally make her appearance.

He had been recommended by one of Clara's many and savvy political connections. His name was Arthur Greenwald, and he seemed to be on close acquaintance with all the bailiffs, clerks, and even the judge herself, a diet-thin middle-aged woman with streaked blond hair who wore her narrow Benjamin Franklin glasses on the edge of her short, wide nose and whose sharp upward glances from the mass of paper piled on the bench before her were meant to both intimidate and reassure, depending on who stood in front of her. Although which look was meant for her, Holly could not quite determine.

"We were lucky," Greenwald said as they came out of the courtroom along the scuffed green linoleum corridor.

"Lucky?" Holly echoed in a hollow tone. "How?"

"We got the bail dismissed. So you can appear on your own recognizance. Personally, I don't think they've got much of a case."

"Great," Holly responded coolly. "So what now?"

"Briscoe's obtained a restraining order, so you can't go near him or your sister. My advice is to leave town for a while and let this thing die."

"He almost raped me," Holly countered. "What about that?"

Greenwald kept his eyes straight ahead as he spoke. "To make it stick we need corroboration. Right now, we have none. Only your accusation. We have no sperm deposit. No DNA. No nothing."

Holly read serious doubt in his expression. She tightened her lips and set her eyes straight ahead as they approached the grimy glass door leading to the outside and a welcome dose of fresh air.

"So what's the lucky part?" she asked, pushing through the door.

"You're free," he countered.

"Free," she echoed bitterly.

Holly wondered in what sense of the term he could possibly mean it.

* * *

The outsized corner lot embraced a turreted Victorian mansion whose history went back well over a hundred years. It had a wealth of gingerbread decoration, a wraparound porch, and massive cornices of filigree. The windows were various colors of stained glass. The house was surrounded by scaffolding on which several orange-helmeted carpenters worked with deliberate skill.

Shepard watched them from where he was parked on the hilly rise above the decrepit green and white manse in a street of equally ancient houses, all of which were in the same dilapidated condition tourists mistook for charm. His keen eyes were fixed on the area with a policeman's patient gaze.

He had been there for almost an hour, waiting until Briscoe's black pickup pulled past the huge rusting Dumpster that had been set alongside the curb directly in front of the structure. Briscoe made a wide turn and parked halfway up the cluttered driveway.

Shepard waited until Briscoe stepped out of the pickup and disappeared down the alley alongside the house. Then he opened his door, stepped out of the car, and approached the work site. He went past the Dumpster and turned into the alley, his shoes crunching on the layer of gravel.

Briscoe stood alone in the rear yard. The area was cluttered with construction materials. He was examining a large blueprint draped over a makeshift carpenter's table fashioned of odd-sized planks and supported by two sawhorses. He looked up when Shepard approached, and his eyes narrowed. The markings on his face were healing, but they were still red and very visible.

"What can I do for you?" Briscoe asked.

"I'm looking into the assault charges against Dr. Alexander."

"You want to know why I'm pressing charges against my sister-in-law? That should be pretty obvious after this," he said, gesturing toward his scarred face.

"You want to tell me how it happened?"

"I filled out a complaint. It's all in there. Or haven't you read it?"

"It's seldom as clear as that. Especially in cases of domestic violence."

Briscoe looked at him, and his lip curled sardonically.

"There's plenty of violence, but nothing domestic about this situation."

"Care to explain that?" Shepard asked.

"My sister-in-law entered our house once, for about five minutes on the day we were married. She's never been back. Doesn't that tell you anything?"

"Do you want her back?"

"I can't allow her to terrorize my wife. And I can't have the same situation here like the one that developed last time, over in Springfield."

"Meaning?"

"A valuable property worth a great deal of money and that took a great deal of effort to create was destroyed. I think you know why that happened."

"Are you saying Dr. Alexander was responsible for that?"

"Directly or indirectly. It doesn't matter. She instigated it. She was trying to overturn my release."

"Why do you think something like that would happen again?"

"She was my therapist in Brandywine. She evaluated me for early release."

"How is that relevant?"

Briscoe regarded Shepard with a patient look. "Do you know what transference is, Lieutenant?"

Shepard looked at him, and his brow furrowed.

"Vaguely. You tell me."

"It's part of the therapist-patient relationship. It happens when the patient transfers feelings and emotions to the therapist. Sometimes love, sometimes hate. It works both ways."

"Go on."

"In my case, I think the reverse happened."

"You mean she transferred her feelings to you?"

Briscoe nodded. "That's how I see it."

"Okay. What kind of feelings?"

Briscoe shrugged. "You tell me. She's been alone a long time."

"So this has nothing to do with your guilt or innocence. She just has the hots for you. Is that it?"

Briscoe smiled to himself. He reached into his pocket and took out a small, flat, black cassette that he offered to the lieutenant.

"Listen to it," he said with a shallow smile. "Then you tell me."

Holly heard defeat in Clara's voice as soon as she picked up the phone.

"Oh honey," she said. "What trouble you are in."

"That sounds like a spiritual. Are you going to start singing?"

Clara laughed. "Holly, I do love you. I really do. If nothing else, you got some set of *ganules*."

"Thanks for the compliment. Considering castration is one of our options, I wonder what you're telling me."

"I don't know what to tell you. I tried talking to Ted, but he wouldn't listen. He said it's out of his hands, that he's only following the regulations, the twit. I called my contacts in Harrisburg, but they told me there was nothing they could do, not at this stage. You've got to fight this thing. Once the court case is in progress, then they might be able to do something about getting it dismissed."

"That's great. Only what do I do about Beth?"

"Holly. She made her bed."

"No, Clara. He made it for her. That's what no one wants to understand. It's all part of some diabolical plan. I still haven't figured it out yet."

There was a pause. "Holly, listen. You're starting to sound like Mrs. Paranoia. Like one of those conspiracy nuts. You'll be running around the courthouse next, clutching your papers to your chest and buttonholing everyone who comes in so you can tell them your latest theory."

"Thanks. I didn't realize I was that bad."

"Not yet. But you're getting there."

"So what do I do, Clara? Sit at home and prepare my defense, while he finds a way to eliminate my sister, like he did with Laura and with Pierson and who knows how many others?"

"You're in a tough spot, I know. I don't mean to minimize it. But I don't know what good you're doing out there. It's only getting you into more trouble. Why don't you come back home? You can stay with me."

"Thanks, Clara. But I can't leave. Not yet. Not while I know she could be in danger." Holly heard the raw edge in her voice.

"I understand how you feel. I really do. If it were one of my kids, I'd probably do the same thing. But it's you being in danger I most worry about. Especially after what happened. He could come at you again. You'd be just as vulnerable. Then who'd be there to protect you?"

"Thanks for that. It makes me feel a little saner."

"All I can tell you is to slow down and think. Don't do anything you'll regret."

Holly laughed. "It's a little late for that."

"Oh, Jesus. What are you planning now?"

"Planning? Oh, not much."

"Holly, come back." There was an urgency in Clara's voice Holly had never heard before. All of the usual flippancy was gone. "Come home. You can stay with me for as long as you like. We'll figure a way out of this."

"I wish I could, Clara. I really do. I'm about at the end of my tether here. Everyone in town hates me. They think I'm persecuting him, and that somehow I'll take away their jobs. But I have to stay. I can't abandon Beth. Not now. I just can't."

"What do you want me to do?"

"I don't know. Just hold up the net when I come flying off the roof."

"Holly, you've got to stop tangling with him. He's too dangerous. You've got to pull back. For everyone's sake, before it's too late."

Holly was silent. Clara was right. It was good advice, but it had come too late. What she had to do now was beyond her power to control.

35

Darkness fell early.

It was bitter cold. A chilling wind drove debris along the gutters like a madwoman with a broom.

Holly sat low in her car, watching as the streetlights came on, dotting the darkness with amber halos and providing pale illumination through the closely thatched branches of the ancient oaks.

Her focus was not exclusively on Beth's house, which stood dark and silent diagonally opposite. She was also focused on the other houses that lined both sides of the street. Cars came and went through the early dinner hour, then tapered off to an occasional lumbering vehicle. There were few pedestrians. An occasional dog walker, but no one else.

By eight-thirty, the street was silent and deserted.

She had bundled up well, but now her fingers and her feet, were frozen, and she had to bang them on the floor of the car to keep her circulation going. Her nose felt like an icicle. She hunched her shoulders and grabbed the door handle.

It was time.

Holly crossed the street and moved toward the side of Beth's house. She walked slowly, keeping low as she went along the alleyway between Beth's house and the one adjoining. Beth's windows were dark, but there were lights on in the neighbors' and she could hear the raucous sound of the TV.

Holly slipped into the backyard. It was dark. There were no lights on in back.

She slid her mittened hand along the chill, ice-covered slickness of the aluminum siding until she found the back door. Her hand closed over the knob. It turned, and to her surprise, the door opened.

Holly had been prepared to jimmy the lock. She carried a screwdriver and a metal pick in her pocket, having purchased them in the local hardware store several hours before, braving the look of ill will she got from the cashier. Living alone had forced her to master several skills, among them how to open a car door with a hanger, and how to pick a lock.

She had learned both techniques from various inmates who provided detailed lessons on their criminal activities. Holly always took comprehensive notes. There were certain advantages to working at a prison.

Holly relaxed a bit at not having to apply her knowledge in the freezing atmosphere. Entering the house provided instant relief. The heat was on, and she felt an immediate rush of warmth on her skin.

She closed the door and started inside. The house was silent except for the erratic purr of the refrigerator. She knew the house well from her previous excursions. She had helped Beth paint some of it.

She went past the living room to the hall closet and eased the door open.

She took out the small black flashlight she had also purchased and turned it on. It provided a surprisingly bright circle of light. The closet was crammed with clothing. Holly pushed them aside and almost immediately found what she was looking for. Facing her was Beth's brown shearling coat. An exact match for the one Holly had on.

Holly reached inside. Shoved into the sleeve was a red

beret, one identical to Holly's. It was same outfit the police had asked her to wear at the lineup. Her surmise had been correct. Beth had been the culprit. She felt little elation at the discovery, only the sour distaste of betrayal. She gathered the coat in her arms and closed the door, starting back the way she came.

Using the flashlight to guide her, she moved quickly toward the back door. She was almost there when something halted her, glimmering in the edge of her peripheral vision.

She could see it through the open door of the master bedroom. A large rectangular object lay on the bed.

Holly flashed the light on the bed, revealing a large black box covered with a shiny lacquer finish, the kind sold in fancy specialty stores. It even had some kind of gold logo on the top, a rearing lion. Holly's brow furrowed. No, this was not Beth's style at all.

Holly stepped inside the room and went over to the bed. She reached down and lifted the top off the box.

She raised the layer of tissue paper exposing the garments inside. They were some kind of apparel. But for an instant, seeing them only in the narrow circle of illumination from the flashlight, she was puzzled as to what they were. She had assumed they might be some kind of fancy European lingerie, but she was mistaken. They were totally unknown to her. She reached down and lifted the first one out. It weighed more than she thought and was ribbed with flexible seams and lined with small metal eyes and heavy black lacing. It took her another moment to understand what she was looking at. Then she realized it was a black leather corset fitted with a double row of laces. She put it down on the bed and went back to the box. Two pair of cushioned leather manacles and a close-fitting leather hood were inside. Next to them was a shining plastic ball connected to two slender leather straps—a gag.

Holly recoiled just as Beth's voice pierced the stillness.

"What the fuck are you doing here?"

Holly jumped back, startled as the light suddenly came on.

"I asked you a question."

Holly turned to face Beth's angry countenance. In her sister's hand was a silver-plated 38-caliber revolver pointed directly at her.

"Going to shoot me?" Holly asked calmly.

"I heard someone come in. I didn't know it was you."

"Where did you get that?" Holly gestured at the weapon.

"My husband got it for me. For protection when he's not here."

"What'll protect you when he is?"

"Fuck you!" Beth exclaimed. "Now I asked you, what the hell are you doing here?"

"You know what I'm doing here. Your husband broke into my motel room and almost raped me. Are you aware of that?"

"Get out! I mean it. We have a court order against you."

Holly started toward her. Her eyes were fierce.

"I'm not going anywhere. You helped him fool that witness." She held up the coat and beret. "You wore these. The coat and the beret. Tell me the truth!"

Beth backed up a step, but still kept the gun raised. A look of pure joy crossed her face.

"You're jealous, aren't you? Finally jealous of me. The emotionally crippled little sister you always had to protect."

Holly stared at the triumphant expression on her sister's face and all the anger suddenly drained out of her.

"Oh god, Beth. Don't you see what he's doing to us? Don't you understand anything? Do you think you met him by accident? Are you that blind? That naive?"

Beth's expression changed, anger distorting her features. "I won't listen! Go away. Get out!"

"All right." Holly said. "Don't listen to me. At least, look at the statements of the other women he's tormented. Or are you too afraid to find out the truth and realize that I'm not the one who's been lying?"

Beth hesitated. Holly could read the confusion in her eyes. She reached out over the gun and touched her sister's arm.

"Just give me a chance to prove it to you. That's all I'm asking. Then I'll go away and leave you alone. If that's what you want."

"Leave me alone," Beth said in a strangled tone.

Beth shook off her hand and hurriedly started past her as Holly followed.

"He's a murderer, Beth. He tortures women. Mutilates them. Two of his victims were only fourteen. It starts with that stuff in there. He uses it to gain control of you sexually. To break you down and get you to submit to whatever he wants. Then he'll mark you. Just like he did with the others. A bird trapped inside a web. Only the bird is you, Beth. And you can't escape. After that, no one will be able to save you."

"I don't want to hear any more," Beth shouted. "Get out! Leave us alone."

But Holly would not stop. She felt as if she were standing at the edge of a precipice in a howling gale. It was as if her sister were about to go over the edge and her life was held by the power in Holly's aching fingers as she clutched at Beth's wind-whipped clothing.

"You're afraid what I said is true, aren't you?" she cried desperately. "Aren't you? Admit it!"

"Get the fuck out of here," Beth cried, but her tone was lower. Some of her anger seemed to have ebbed. The fierceness in her eyes was less pronounced.

"He's using you, Beth. Using you to get to me."

Instantly, Holly regretted her mistake as the ire returned to Beth's face.

"It's always about you, isn't it?"

"No, Beth. It's about both of us."

"You're crazy!" she shouted. "Stop persecuting us, you stupid, freaky bitch!"

Beth turned away suddenly, her face pressed against the door, her eyes filled with tears. The gun hung uselessly from her fingers.

"It's always about you. Never about me. Never about what I want, or what I need."

"No, Beth. This is not about me. I only want to protect you. That's why I stayed; that's why I'm here. You're the most important thing in the world to me. You know that. I've proven it to you a hundred times. You know you can trust me."

Beth turned to face her. Her eyes were ice.

"Do I?"

When Beth spoke, her words chopped through Holly like the steel blade of an ax.

"Jason is the one person I've been able to trust in my entire life. The only one who really cares about me. About me!"

"I care about you," Holly whispered. "I always have."

"The hell you do! You can't have him, so you want to take him away from me. Only I won't let you. Stay the hell out of my life! I never want to see you again!"

"You don't mean that, Beth." Holly said, reaching out for her.

Beth smacked her hand away. She turned and started away as Holly tried to stop her.

"Wait, Beth! Please!" Holly cried desperately as her hand gripped Beth's blouse. But Beth would not stop. The seam tore as the material gave way in her hand.

Holly stared at her sister. And her eyes widened with horror.

On Beth's shoulder was a tattoo.

A tiny blue starling, trapped in a web.

"Oh god, Beth!" Holly cried out. "He's marked you!"

Briscoe's voice came like a whipcrack out of the darkness.

"Leave her alone!"

Holly turned.

He was there. Standing in the doorway, his cold gray eyes fixed on her like a bird of prey.

"She broke in," Beth said as she rushed to him. "I found her in our bedroom."

"Don't worry. She can't hurt you anymore," he said and put his arm around Beth. Then he looked up at Holly. His eyes were calm, pitiless. "You need help, Holly. You're out of control."

Holly met his gaze. "You won't get away with it. The police know all about this."

"You're right," he shrugged. "They know the only one who can harm us is you. Officer, she's in here."

He moved aside as two officers stepped into the house, impersonal in their dark blue uniforms.

Beth looked at them, her voice on the edge of hysteria.

"She won't leave us alone! She won't stop persecuting us!" She turned to face Holly, her eyes wide and filled with anger. "I hate you! I hate you!"

One of the officers started toward Holly.

"Come with us, please. Or we'll have to handcuff you."

"I'll come," Holly said calmly, holding Beth's coat close to her body.

"She's holding our property," Briscoe said.

"Does that belong to you?" one officer asked.

"No. But it's evidence," Holly uttered firmly.

"I'm sorry," the officer said. "Not without a warrant." He took the coat from her and handed it over to Briscoe.

The other officer took her by the arm and guided her out of the house. In the doorway she halted, turning back to face Briscoe.

"You won't get away with it," she said with quiet reassurance. "Not this time."

He looked at Holly and his lips formed a chilling smile as the officers escorted her outside.

36

Holly sat alone in the rear of the police cruiser.

Her heart still pounded from the effect of what she had seen tattooed on Beth's shoulder.

The bird was Beth . . . the two were one . . . and now Beth was lost to her forever . . .

These realizations drove away all other thoughts so completely that she was almost unaware of arriving at the state police barracks or of the officers leading her from the car into the building until they were a few feet from Dan Shepard's office.

He stood outside as the officers guided Holly toward him.

"It's okay. I'll take it from here," he said as they turned to go. Shepard was indifferent to the knowing stares of the other officers as he led her inside and sat her on the couch opposite his desk. He drew the blinds so that they were cut off from the peering eyes outside.

"He's had her tattooed," she said when Shepard settled himself into the chair beside her.

"What were you doing there, Holly?" he asked quietly.

"I went there to find Beth's coat. The shearling coat I bought her. That's why the witness thought it was me. I found it in her closet. She even had the same red beret I've been wearing. Ask the officers. They saw it."

"But you broke in. You violated the restraining order."

"The coat's in there. Send one of your men to get it. You'll see."

He looked at her, and his brow furrowed.

"I can't. Not without a warrant."

"Then get one."

"I'd need probable cause. And her having a similar coat isn't going to convince a judge to give me one."

She looked up at him, and her eyes were questioning. "Didn't you hear me? He had her tattooed. Don't you understand what that means?"

"I do. But the fact still remains that you violated a court order."

"Are you going to arrest me?" she said as her throat tightened. "Because if you're not, then I'm leaving."

She started to rise when he raised his hand, stopping her. His eyes projected a severity she had never seen before. The intimacy between them earlier no longer seemed to exist. She felt as if she were a teenager again and had just been brought down to see the school principal.

"I need you to be straight with me, Holly. Can you do that?"

"Yes."

"Were you jealous of Beth's relationship with Briscoe?"

She stared at him as if he had just struck her. "Jealous? What are you talking about?"

"This," he said. Leaning back he touched the play button of the tape recorder on his desk.

There was a burst of static, then Holly's voice echoed in the room.

"Please don't reject me. You know how I feel about you. Why are you doing this to me? I love you."

He snapped it off.

"Where did you get that?"

"It was on Briscoe's answering machine," he said flatly, facing her with a probing gaze.

"It's a lie! I never said that to him. I was speaking to Beth."

"Then how did it get on his machine?" He asked calmly.

"I left a message for Beth, on her answering machine. He must have doctored the tape."

He looked at her, his eyes intense. "Are you in love with him, Holly?"

Holly felt her head swim. This could not be happening. "You must be crazy to ask me that."

"But you were attracted to him?"

Holly stared at him, confusion in her eyes.

"Yes. Once, maybe. I don't know. I was confused. I thought he might be innocent and that he had been railroaded. I felt sorry for him, I guess. Maybe it was more than that. My father had sent men up he knew were innocent, men he labeled as sex offenders but who weren't. I couldn't allow that to happen again. Perhaps I let my emotions run a little wild under the circumstances. But whatever it was, it lasted for only for a moment. Before I found out what he really was."

"He used the word transference. He said it worked both ways. Does it?"

"Yes, it can. But that doesn't mean it happened. It's only in his head. He only thinks it did."

"So you weren't in love with him?"

"I don't know, exactly."

"Then you were?"

"Is that what you want to believe?"

"Give me a way to draw a different conclusion."

She saw the disbelief in his eyes and anger rose in her. "Either arrest me or let me get the hell out of here."

He hesitated, his glance still locked on her. She could see the decision forming in his eyes.

"I'll let you go, but on one condition. That you leave town and agree to let us handle things from here on out."

"And if I can't do that?"

"It's not an option. Not after tonight. The restraining order applies to this entire area."

"This is bullshit," she said sharply. "He's manipulating you. The same way he manipulated Beth and all the others. You, of all people, should understand that."

"He's not manipulating me. But you have to understand. He's made friends here, provided jobs in this community. Jobs people need. People here think he got a raw deal and that he deserves a fresh start. They see you as a threat. I want you to go for your own protection."

"So I just pick up and get the hell out. Just leave my sister alone with him with everything I know he's capable of."

"You don't have a choice. If you're not out of here by ten o'clock, I'll have to place you under arrest for violating the restraining order."

She met his implacable gaze.

"Thanks. Thanks a lot for everything."

She rose and left without looking back.

Beth sat huddled at the kitchen table. A single light was on above the sink, casting long, disquieting shadows across the room. She didn't like the dark; she had never liked it. She had always kept a light on when she slept. But she was too weary to get up and put on the kitchen light.

The house was quiet. Only the bird fluttering in its cage interrupted the silence. The shearling coat lay where it had been flung, across a kitchen chair, one empty arm dangling. She had no strength to pick it up. All of her energy had been drained during the scene with Holly. Her back ached, and there was a tremor in her fingers. The gun lay on the table in front of her, alien and cold, gleaming like a surgical instrument beneath the stark light from above. It had seemed so right when he had given it to her. But she had held it at her own sister.

She felt like a child again, about to be scolded.

She rose and picked up the weapon, intending to return it

to its place inside the top drawer of her bureau. The rip in her sleeve annoyed her, and she glanced at it in the hallway mirror, seeing the reflection of the blue tattoo. For an instant it looked almost surreal, as if the bird, dark blue and gleaming, was about to take flight and rise from her shoulder. But that could not happen. It was imprisoned, the way she felt she was.

Why had everything changed so suddenly?

At first she had blamed it all on Holly, on her remaining there and persecuting them. Everyone agreed, especially after the way she had behaved at the wedding. But she knew that they were wrong. Nothing was the way it seemed.

It was Jason.

Something had changed between them. It happened as soon as Holly arrived. He seemed distant somehow. A watchfulness had come over him, a strange alertness. His eyes looked like those of a hawk about to swoop down on its prey.

What was his prey?

The thought nagged at her sharply, but almost as soon as she thought it, she tried to dismiss it. Why was she thinking this way? He was her husband. He belonged to her. Or did he? Was her sister right? Was all this a sham, and had he only married her to get back at Holly in some incredibly weird way? The thought had been torturing her every since Holly arrived. As hard as she tried to dismiss them, her sister's words had driven nails of anxiety deep into her skin.

She stepped into the bedroom and stared down at the objects on the bed.

He said he had bought them especially for her. They had played little tie-up games in bed, but they had never gone this far. Not manacles and a gag. She had seen them before on various Web sites and in certain magazines, but she had never been interested in that kind of thing. Talking about it in bed with him had been a kind of game. She had not been serious. But obviously he had.

She shuddered suddenly. Something in her rebelled against the thought of putting the things on. When the packages came she had been thrilled. But when he insisted that she open them, what she found inside had only chilled her. It seemed to confirm something Holly had said. What exactly, she could not remember. There had been too many words between them, too much anger.

What they had done—what he had asked her to do that night in the street outside—had been wrong. She was angry then, but now she realized they had gone too far. Holly was under arrest and facing a criminal charge. She had never intended that. He had told her it was the only way for them to get a restraining order, so she had gone along with it. She had not realized what would happen later. She had to go to the police and tell them the truth. She knew that. She would tell him. But the thought of facing him and telling him that she would made her pause. She realized that she was trembling. With a strange, eerie suddenness she understood for the first time that she was afraid . . . afraid of the man she had married.

"You don't look happy."

She jumped as his voice broke the silence.

"You frightened me."

He was smiling as he stepped into the darkened room. "I'm supposed to frighten you. It's part of my charm. Give me the gun."

She handed it to him. He opened the drawer and laid it inside.

"Where were you?"

"Out and about."

She recognized the look in his eyes. The distant eeriness that frightened her.

"Give me your hand."

"Why?"

"You'll see."

She raised her hand toward him. He gripped it firmly and began twisting off her ring.

"What are you doing?"

"You won't want this anymore."

"But I do."

"Why would you want anything she gave you?"

"I don't know." She felt confused suddenly. "She's still my sister."

"What exactly does that mean?"

Beth struggled to say the words.

"What we did that night. In the street. When I pretended to attack you, so we could fool the old man."

"What about it?"

"It was wrong. We have to tell the police."

"She has to be punished for what she did."

"Not by me," Beth said firmly.

"Then I'll have to do it."

The look in his eyes terrified her.

"Just do what I say and you'll be fine."

"I won't," she whispered.

His smile widened. "To honor and obey, remember?"

"Not like that. We went too far. She doesn't deserve what happened."

"I think she does."

She felt pressure and looked down as he twisted the ring. "You're hurting me."

"That's the idea."

He locked her hand in his powerful fingers and twisted the ring off. She cried out in pain and fell backward onto the bed. He put the ring in his pocket and moved closer, shoving his legs between hers, widening them.

"Get undressed. I want to see you in your new outfit."

"I don't like it. I don't want to wear it."

His expression clouded. "I'm not asking."

"Screw you!" she exclaimed and started to rise. The slap came with a suddenness that shook her. It was the first time he had ever struck her. She stared at him in shock and surprise.

"I said, get undressed."

Rage inflamed her.

"And I said, screw you."

She pushed up from the bed and started out of the room when his hand flew across her face. This time he had doubled his fist. The blow sent her reeling. She struck the wall and blacked out for an instant.

"Now strip."

"I won't! You hit me, you bastard," she cried in outrage. "You hit me! No one lays a hand on me. No one!"

Her face was flaming. She raised her fists and charged at him. He sidestepped. His hands were quick, seizing her just above the elbows, causing twin jolts of pain that paralyzed her arms. She cried as he twisted them behind her, wrapping her wrists with a strip of leather he grabbed from inside the box.

"What are you doing? Stop it, you shit!" she shouted as he threw her down on the bed.

"We'll have to fix that mouth of yours," he said. His smile held no warmth.

"Let me go, or I'll scream."

"We'll just have to fix that, won't we?"

He gripped her beneath the jaw as she struggled against him. He forced her mouth open, filling it with the smooth round ball and quickly tying it around the back of her head with the leather ties. He stood over her as she lay beneath him, fighting against her bonds. He looked down and his eyes fixed on her with cold dots of contempt.

"Well, little sister, if you won't undress yourself, I'll just have to do it for you."

It was a room she hated and never wanted to see again. The entire motel now filled her with revulsion. Just being inside made her skin crawl. She tried to avoid looking at the couch where he had assaulted her. She threw her things into her suitcase as quickly as possible, gathered up everything in the bathroom in one trip, and dumped the stuff into the bag.

For an instant, she thought of leaving everything behind, as if the fact that her things had been inside this vile cham-

ber had somehow poisoned them. But she recognized the ir-
rationality of the thought and dismissed it from her mind.
She zipped up her suitcase and carried it to the door, along
with her overnight bag. She could not face the stupid grin on
the desk clerk's face, so she left the key on the bed and the
door wide open as she went out.

She trundled her bags outside and flung them into the
trunk of her car, flashing a look of defiance at the faces staring out at her from behind the office window. She had no intention of signing her bill. They could charge her credit card.
She would never enter that smelly office again. Let them
come after her.

What consumed her now was rage. A deeply burning anger,
glowing like molten metal, boiled in her gut. She felt a reckless desire to do damage for what had been done to her. If
she had the means she might even have set the motel on fire.
Burned down the entire town. Why not? The thought of actually doing it brought her a sense of instant satisfaction.
The fire she imagined consuming the town and all of its horrendous inhabitants was akin to the fire raging deep inside
her. She had been played, betrayed, manhandled, and manipulated. Her body had been violated. Her emotions had been
torn to shreds. She had even undergone the oppressive grind-
stone of the law. She was sick to death of playing the victim.

She got behind the wheel and started up. Her skin was
burning, and she scarcely noticed her surroundings or the
chill of the icy night air. She started to pull out when she noticed the gleaming object hanging by a thread from the rear
view mirror. It took an instant for her to focus.

It was Beth's ring.

The ring she had given her.

Holly gripped it in her fingers, then snapped the thread.

She fought the impulse to open the window and fling it
into the darkness. Instead, she placed the ring in her pocket
and turned the wheel, exiting the almost empty parking lot
with a final defiant screech of her tires.

She pulled up to the first stoplight and waited as the light remained interminably red. A light that would not change. She looked down and noticed that her cell phone was blinking.

She picked up the receiver and punched the code for her voice mail. The phone rang twice and the recorded voice informed her that she had a message.

Beth's voice came over the line.

"Holly," she began in a tone of contriteness. "I'm sorry for what happened. I don't want you to worry about me. We're going away for a while to let all this blow over. Don't try to find me. You don't understand how I feel or how much I love him."

Beth paused. The next words seemed forced.

"I don't have a choice. I want to give him everything. Everything that I have to give. Everything. No matter what."

The line went dead.

Everything that I have to give . . .

The words resonated in her mind—they were the words spoken by all of his other victims.

"No, Beth!" Holly screamed. "Oh god, no!"

Breath seized up in her throat. Her vision went blank.

She fought to recover as the light now turned green. She hit the pedal and swerved in the middle of the intersection, almost hitting an oncoming car. She saw the startled look on the driver's face. She sped away as the other car's horn blared in anger.

She pulled over to the curb in the middle of the next block, stepped on the brake, and jerked to a stop.

Her hands gripped the wheel as she tried to keep herself from shaking. Her heart was hammering violently. She tried to slow her breathing, fighting for self-control.

You can't go to pieces now. You can't!

She closed her eyes and let her head slip forward against the wheel. She had no recollection of the next few seconds, only of her eyes popping open and the cold, clear realization of where she was.

She straightened, taking a deep breath, then another. She

wiped her eyes clear of moisture and pressed the button to open the window.

The night was clear. The air against her face was sharp. She shifted into drive, eased the car back into lane, and continued along Main Street. The avenue was almost deserted. There was no one on the sidewalks. The windows of the stores formed cheerless rectangles against the murky darkness.

Where was she going? What was she going to do?

She looked up and saw a dark blue sedan behind her in the rearview mirror. The two men inside wore the uniforms of the local police.

"Hi, guys," Holly said aloud. "Want to come along for the ride? No problem."

She passed the final stoplight and hit the accelerator, following the curving center stripe as it marked the long, sweeping curve leading out of town. The car behind stayed right on her tail. She passed the 40 mile an hour sign at 60, but she was not pulled over. They did not want to ticket her; they wanted her safely out of town.

Ten minutes later she reached the place where the county road met the state highway. Holly slowed at the yield sign and made the turn onto the highway. The car behind her slowed to a stop. They did not follow. The men inside watched her taillights disappear before they turned around and headed back into town.

Holly was doing 70. Traffic was light. Only a few cars were going in her direction, one or two big chrome-plated semis playing tag with each other as they sped up or dropped behind. She passed several exit signs, then slowed as she approached the next one, eyeing the signs for food and lodging. She signaled and drove onto the exit ramp, stopping at the light at the top of the rise.

There was a gas station on the intersecting road. She pulled in to the self-serve and checked her gauge. She got out, inserted her credit card, and topped off her tank, eyeing the road to see if she had been followed. Only one or two cars passed, their brights sweeping the area like floodlights. None of them stopped.

She got back inside and pulled out. She made an immediate left across the overpass, returning her back onto the highway, back the way she had come.

37

Holly spent a shivering half hour parked outside the diner, waiting until the shift broke, and suffering the tedium of cars pulling in and out. She kept an eye out for the blue sedan with the two uniformed policemen, but they failed to materialize. A police cruiser did approach, but the two officers parked and went in for their customary doughnut and coffee. Holly squeezed down in her seat, but they parked at the far end of the lot and never even noticed her.

A short time after they left, an icy rain began falling, embroidering surfaces of the parked cars and the chrome sides of the diner with delicate beads of moisture. The windows filled with frost, and her windshield constantly needed defogging.

A few minutes after ten, several waitresses streamed out, heading for their cars. Beth was not among them.

Holly moved quickly. She exited the car and climbed the concrete steps, entering the diner through the rear door. She passed through a corridor filled with brimming trash cans and shelves filled with tomato paste and canned lentils, then stepped into the steaming kitchen.

The cooks looked at her curiously as she crossed the over-heated room with its collection of hanging pots and wet aluminum surfaces, then pushed through the set of swinging doors into the dining room.

There were only a few patrons seated at the booths. A waitress stood behind the counter fixing her apron. She was a short redhead with overly rouged cheeks and thick ankles. Holly recognized her from her first visit. She looked up as Holly approached, and backed up defensively.

"You keep away now," she said, holding up her hands. "I'll get Steve. You ain't supposed to be in here."

Holly stopped in front of her. "I'm not going to cause a problem. I just want to know if Beth is still here."

The waitress pushed open the door to the diner. "Steve!" she shouted urgently.

An instant later, Steve appeared. He was dark haired and muscular, his chest hair curled above the collar of his T-shirt like a fringe of soiled lace. His expression was not friendly.

"You got to go. Now! Or I call the police," he said in a thick Greek accent.

"I'll go," Holly responded. "Just tell me where my sister is. I'm not going to hurt her, or you or anyone else. I'm on my way out of town and just wanted to say good-bye."

"She told me she got a restraining order, right? So you can't see her, right?"

"No. I can't go to her house. But I can see her when other people are around."

Her words were not strictly true, but they seemed to calm him. He looked at her and sniffed.

"Okay. It's none of my business. All I know is she took off for a week, maybe longer. She said she'd call to let me know when she is coming back. Now go. Please. We don't want trouble with nobody."

"Did she say where she was going?"

He shook his head. Holly turned to the waitress, who also gestured her lack of knowledge.

"Thanks. I really appreciate it," Holly said as she turned and went out the way she came in.

Steve followed her at a cautious distance as if she were

about to do something unpredictable and dangerous. He stood in the doorway as she got back into her car and pulled out of the parking lot. Then he slammed the door shut and turned the lock.

The trees along Beth's street shimmered with a coating of ice, offering crystal reflections in the reflected light of the amber lamps and reminding Holly of the light show her parents had taken them to every Christmas. She and Beth would sit in the back of the car holding each other's hand and be awed by the outrageous display of glittering images.

Be alive . . . please be alive . . .

She prayed as she approached.

The house was dark. No lights glowed in the windows. Even the outside light beside the door was unlit.

She parked across the street and walked to the front door. She tried the knob, but it was locked. Then she went back along the walkway toward the back, heading for the alley between the two houses.

She had her flashlight in her hand as she picked her way along the gravel path. The house next door was also devoid of light. No sound of the TV filled the air. The wind was bitter. It stung her lips and burned her cheeks.

This time the back door was locked.

Holly took the pick and screwdriver out of her pocket. She took off her mittens and tried to work it in the lock, but her hands were too cold. Her fingers refused to respond.

She put the tools down, took off her beret, and placed it against one of the panes of glass in the door. She used the butt end of the flashlight and brought her hand down hard. The glass splintered. Holly struck it again, and chinks of glass fell away. One of her inmates had taught her this trick. It had been his specialty, his way of gaining entry to the houses of the women he assaulted.

Cautiously, she introduced her hand, feeling for the knob, then the lock below. She turned the knob, and the door opened.

Holly stepped inside and closed the door behind her.

No lights were on. She stepped into the kitchen. The refrigerator hummed as her flashlight played across the surface of the appliances. Everything was in its place, neat and orderly. The cat's wicker basket was empty.

She crossed the kitchen and stepped into the hall. The bedroom door was open. Holly crossed the hall and stepped inside, shining her light in several directions.

The room was a mess. Clothes were scattered everywhere. The shiny black box she had seen earlier lay on the bed. It was empty.

Her stomach clenched, knowing what had been inside. She went to the dresser.

The top drawer was open. It was filled with lingerie. She could see the shape of the revolver underneath the silky garments. She pushed them aside and her hand closed over the shape of cold metal. She looked at it, pressing the latch to swing open the drum. It was filled with five bullets. She closed it and slipped it into her pocket.

She shined the light higher. Several photographs were lined up at the bottom of the mirror. All of them were snapshots of Beth in various locales. There was something familiar about the one in the center. Holly took it off the mirror and focused the beam of light. Beth was standing on the platform over the onrushing water. Behind her was the looming brick wall of the foundry. She could just make out the line of arched windows. Holly put the photo back on the mirror, then stepped out of the room.

She knew where they had gone. The trail had been marked, and all she had to do was follow it.

She retraced her steps back through the kitchen. A moment later she was back outside, head down as she hurried through the alley, her mind focused on a single thought: the knowledge that what was about to happen had already begun. And the terror of knowing that she might be too late.

* * *

Shepard was at the vending machine filling a Styrofoam cup with an oily, viscous liquid that only smelled like coffee when DeMarco stepped out of his office and called over to him.

"Hey, Shepard. Call for you."

Shepard waited until the machine finished filling his cup. Then he threaded his way back into his office through the room overcrowded with adjoining desks.

He picked up the receiver.

"Shepard."

"It's Steve. Steve from the diner."

"Oh yeah," he said, hearing the familiar accent. "What's up?"

"You said to call if there was any trouble."

"Right. What's happening?"

"That crazy lady was here. Beth's sister. She was asking for her."

Shepard was instantly alert.

"You mean tonight?"

"Sure tonight. Maybe thirty minutes ago."

Thirty minutes ago he had been reassured by two uniformed officers that Holly had been safely escorted out of town.

"What did you tell her?"

"Just that Beth went away."

"So, you told her a story?"

"No story. I tell her the truth."

"You mean, she actually did leave?"

"Like I said. Beth, she went away."

"When?"

"Tonight. She called to tell me."

"For how long?"

"I don't know. She said a week, maybe longer. She said she'd call me when she was coming back."

"Did she say where she was going?"

"No. She didn't tell me nothing. But she sounded kind of funny. Not like her usual self."

"Funny, like how?"

"Oh. Like she wasn't feeling too good or maybe like some-body was squeezing her arm. You know what I mean. Like she wasn't herself talking."

"Thanks. Thanks a lot."

Shepard hung up and his expression darkened. He grabbed his coat and hurried out, leaving the cup steaming on his desk.

38

Headlights leaped toward her as they rounded the curve ahead, momentarily blinding her.

Holly flicked off her brights and slowed as the other car rounded the curve and zoomed past without dimming its lights. Then night enveloped her again in its unfriendly grasp.

The rain that had started earlier had stopped, but the wind had not ceased. It blew with a howling intensity, sculpting the evergreens into unusual shapes, like a kid combing his hair against the grain. The road was slick and sheened with frost. Holly held the wheel firmly as she guided the car along the narrow two-lane strip. She steered by watching the stripe of white along the edge, and when that disappeared, she followed the center line. But both were in need of repainting, and when the road went to black she slowed down and followed her instincts.

The ribbon of asphalt wound and dipped through the narrow valleys bracketed by pines rising in densely packed phalanxes along the steep ridges on either side. Though she had traveled this road twice before, once with Shepard and once the day she saw Laura's body beneath the ice, night distorted her recollection. There had been quite a few cars on the road after she left town, but they quickly dwindled to one or two and then to none. Now there was only an occasional vehicle in the opposite lane whose lights offered some modicum of human contact in the chilling blackness.

She glanced at the green-lit numerals of the dashboard clock and realized that there had been nothing on the road for the last ten minutes. No lights. No one on either side of the road. No one except herself and the sighing wind.

She did not want to have a breakdown in this part of the country. Her car phone did not work here because of the mountains. Help would have to wait for morning, or the chance of a passing stranger. By that time she might freeze to death.

By that time Beth might be dead.

She slowed down, looking for the turnoff, trying to remember a marker, something to guide her, but there was nothing, only darkness and the densely packed pine trunks. She tensed, gripped by a sense of desperation. She was a player in a game that was not her own. A tiny chess piece being moved by a hand she could not see, a mind fixated on her doom. But she had to go on, no matter what. She had to save her sister and what was left of her own life.

She had to get to the foundry . . . but how would she find it in this darkness?

She watched as mile after mile ticked off on the odometer. The road continued its maddening gyrations, twisting and turning between the mountains like the tail of a child's kite caught in a gale.

Had she passed it, she wondered? *Please god, let me not have passed it*, she prayed. The road curved, then curved back. Her stomach began to churn. She knew she was lost. Helplessly lost. And so was Beth. She would never find her sister . . . never . . .

She rounded the next curve, and suddenly it was there, directly in front of her: the opening in the trees and the dirt road descending into darkness.

The foundry was just below.

She braked hard, hearing the screech of her tires on the gravel. She gripped the wheel and slowed to a stop, peering down the narrow dirt lane. It was empty of any vehicle, at least as far as she could see.

She pulled in close, easing her wheels off the road lest some passing car strike her vehicle. The gun on the seat beside her gleamed dully against the cushions. She picked it up, hefting its unaccustomed weight. She had fired a gun before, but only at a pistol range, an experience she had not found unpleasant. The memory gave her reassurance as she eased off the safety. She had enjoyed the feeling of power the gun gave her, along with the chilling knowledge of its potential to kill. But she knew there was a difference between hitting a target and actually aiming at a human being. Would she be capable of that?

Her stomach tightened as she opened the door and stepped into the dark, freezing air.

Shepard felt the broken glass under his feet an instant before his flashlight picked out the broken pane.

He slipped his hand through the opening, opened the back door, and stepped inside. His light swept the room as he crossed the kitchen and went into the hall. His arm brushed against something. It started to fall. He grabbed at it and held it upright. It was a birdcage, but there was no bird inside. The cage was empty.

He went into the living room. His light picked out the familiar domestic objects but recorded nothing amiss. He went back into the hall and pushed open the bedroom door.

The room was in complete disorder.

He stepped inside, feeling clothing under his feet. He stepped around the garments gingerly and went to the bureau. The top drawer was open. He flashed the light inside.

Lingerie had been pushed aside. He put his hand inside. There was a small, heavy object at the rear of the drawer. He pulled it out. It was a box of .38 cartridges. Bullets, but no gun.

He flashed his light, and his eyes took in the pictures on

the mirror. Snaps of Beth mostly. One was slightly out of place. He fixed his light on it. It was another photo of Beth. The locale was indistinct, yet somehow familiar. Where?

Thoughtfully, he turned and started out of the room, then paused, facing the kitchen. He stepped back inside and went to the refrigerator. He opened the door and scanned the interior. There was the usual assortment of foods. He picked up the container of milk and shook it. Full. People who went on trips usually dumped their milk. He stepped back and pulled open the door to the freezer.

He jerked back in surprise. The compartment glowed with an amber light. It was empty except for a single square of ice fitted between the middle shelves.

Imprisoned within it was a tiny feathered creature.

Its eyes were open. Its wings were extended at the instant of flight.

And then he remembered where the snapshot on the bureau had been taken.

Holly inched down along the gravel road. Her shoes slipped on the wet surface, and she had to slow down to feel for traction.

She held the gun in one gloved hand, the flashlight in the other, keeping the beam low. She knew the light might be seen, but she had no choice. There was no moon, and the road was too dark. Without the light she would have been completely blind.

It was extremely cold, even colder than it had been in town. Her breath hung vaporlike on the heavy air. The sky was black and starless. The wind had ceased, leaving an eerie unnatural stillness. She could hear her own footsteps crunching on the shimmering stones.

The pines beside her rose skyward in tight formations. Bunches of gleaming needles hung in close-cropped bunches from the twisted branches. Her heart was pounding. It filled her ears with the harsh beat of a muffled drum. She took several deep breaths, trying to steady herself, but the icy air seared her lungs.

The road dropped steeply. She followed the downward curve as it spiraled toward the stream below. She could hear the onrushing water growing louder as it raced through the gorge. Through the thinning branches, she could see white foam as the water snarled and galloped over the stones. She came around the final turn and the roof of the foundry came into view, gleaming dully in the reflected light of the rushing water below.

She stepped off the path into the screen of trees and the foundry appeared just as it had the time Shepard had taken her there. The blackened brick walls gave off the same forbidding aura. The double row of narrow windows still stared blindly into darkness. The stream ran alongside it like a shroud, the shimmering current gleaming like interwoven strands of hammered metal under whose sheen she had glimpsed Laura's upturned face.

She descended toward a littered yard filled with rotting sheds. Light glimmered on the railroad tracks curving behind the building and leading nowhere.

Beth's pickup was parked just outside the door.

Holly felt her pulse quicken, both with fear and the reassurance of knowing she had finally found them.

She moved toward the pickup quickly. A crow shrieked, startling her. She heard its flapping wings and saw its dark shape rising from the roof of a shed. She came closer scanning the interior of the pickup with the flashlight, but there was nothing inside. She slipped around to the other side just as tiny pellets of hail began to rattle along the chassis.

The hail came on suddenly, falling in sporadic clusters that rattled on the metal foundry roof like bags of released marbles. Holly bent her head and dodged toward the small slatted door cut into the wall ahead. It was the same door she had entered before, but there was no comfort in its familiarity.

She touched the weathered boards and pushed the door

open. The boards gave under her hand, swinging back on rusted hinges. She inhaled deeply and stepped inside.

A bone-chilling darkness swept over her, wrapping her in a mantle of icy dread.

She shivered, staring into the blackness as if it were a grave. Envisioning Carolyn suddenly, wrapped in her shroud of ice. She listened for some sound, some warning within, but heard only the wild scatter of hail on the metal roof, then the sharp pelting of wind-driven rain.

She clutched the pistol tighter in her hand. She held the gun low, away from her thigh, knowing that it could go off if she fell. She raised the flashlight, then jumped back suddenly as a drop of chilling rain struck her face.

She moved into the corridor, following the circle of wavering light and trying to remember how things looked in daylight. Her chest was tight with anticipation. Her breathing was constricted. The musty dampness assaulted her, the rotting dampness of a tomb.

In spite of the cold, her cheeks were burning. She had been afraid on the road, terrified that she would miss the turn. Something else now replaced her fear. Her rage had returned, and she could feel the palpability of her anger like something alive inside her chest.

She raised the gun. All her survival instincts were on full alert. Her finger was tight on the trigger as she moved deeper into the maze of twisting corridors.

Wind struck her face. The corridor petered to an end, leaving her in an drafty open space. She shined her light over the area. She was in a kind of anteroom from which several narrow corridors branched off on either side, funneling deeper into the darkened interior. She had not remembered this from her previous visit. She felt as if she were lost in a mine somewhere deep underground and felt a sudden pang of uncertainty.

Which way?

She hesitated, not knowing which corridor to choose, but knowing she must choose one. She shined the light straight ahead and crossed the floor, heading for the doorway opposite. She tightened her grip on the handle and started through.

She inched forward, uncertain of her footing. The rotting floorboards felt spongy under her soles. She raised the light, illuminating a turn dead ahead. She shuffled toward it, then edged around it into pitch blackness.

Her lips compressed as she felt her way. The pounding of her heart etched itself in her ears, almost erasing the sound of the stream outside. She followed the narrow beam of light as it crawled across the wall and higher over the beamed ceiling until it picked out the shape of a wooden door ahead. A pitted brass latch protruded from it halfway down.

She reached out, her hand closed over the latch, and she pulled. The latch creaked and the door slid open. She felt a sudden updraft of cold air against her face.

Facing her was a thin sliver of light, moving slightly, like the flame of a dying candle.

Holly moved toward it carefully, directing the beam, feeling her way along the floor with her feet. She took a step, then another. Her foot extended, felt ahead. Into nothing. She flashed the light down and realized her foot was extended over open space.

She drew back hurriedly.

Below was a sheer drop into darkness. She heard the sound of rushing water; then sound exploded in her ears.

A whirring of quickening energy, like a cable being wound around a whirling drum.

Startled, she drew back as something came flying up at her out of the water below.

Holly raised the light, choking back a scream.

An object dangled in front of her, swinging back and forth from a rusting chain. Water flowed off its gleaming white shape as if it had been encased in melting plastic.

She stared at it in horror.

It was a woman's body. She was naked. Her head and pubic area had been shaved. Her ankles were bound. Her face was masked. Her hands were manacled behind her back.

It looked so unreal at first Holly thought it had to be a mannequin.

But as it turned toward her she realized this was no mannequin. This was flesh and blood.

She reached out and pulled off the mask. Stupified, she stared into the woman's face with shock and disbelief.

The woman was Laura.

Her eyes were open, lifeless.

Holly reached out to touch the wall beside her. Nausea welled up in her throat. Her head swam. She felt faint and opened her hand to grip the wall, allowing the flashlight to slip from her fingers. It rolled away into the darkness.

The cable went taut. Gears whirred in reverse and the body dropped suddenly, falling out of sight, descending like a spinning orb of light until it was swallowed by the icy pit below.

Holly's head was throbbing. Claws of dread tightened around her chest. She felt weak, as if all her strength had been instantly drained from her. He had killed Laura, just as she knew he had. But the shock of seeing her body almost stilled Holly's heart.

A voice splintered the silence. A woman's voice, distant and faint, coming from somewhere behind her.

"No, please! You're hurting me! Stop! I can't breathe!"

The voice was almost a whisper, but Holly knew it belonged to Beth.

"Please, help me! Please god! Help me!"

Holly forced air into her constricted throat. She turned and raised her arm, feeling her way back along the corridor. Back the way she had come.

"I'm here, Beth!" she called into the darkness. "I'm coming."

"Oh god! Help me!"

Beth's voice was a cry of anguish.

"Where are you, Beth?" Holly responded. "Tell me where you are."

No answer.

Only silence.

The corridor came to an abrupt end. Holly stood in total darkness. She was back somewhere in the center of the maze whose shadowy paths opened on all sides around her. Beth's voice seemed to have come from one of the passageways. Or from all of them.

She had to choose an entrance, but which one?

Holly felt her way, moving past opening after opening. Then she stopped, hand outstretched, feeling for the opening beside her. She started inside, plunging into total darkness.

Her fingers felt along the slime-covered walls. Water leaked down in spreading rivulets, foaming in grimy puddles on the rotting floor. Her feet lost traction, sliding along the slippery, uneven planks. Water poured down through a hole in the roof, soaking her. Her foot struck something. She reached down and touched a metal rail. Narrow-gauge tracks bisected the passage. She felt the rush of icy air and heard the roar of the water below. She sensed an empty space, prayed, and took a long step over it. Thankfully, she landed safely on the other side.

She went on. The sound of her own breathing echoed back to her. The corridor seemed to go on and on forever. But she knew it had to end. Her ordeal continued for several more seconds, until her hands struck a wall in front of her. She had reached a turn. She edged around it and instead of darkness, her eyes were assaulted by the glare of blinding light.

She raised her hand to shield her vision.

The light spilled out of a brick archway just below. She was standing at the top of a long passageway that angled steeply beneath her feet. Holly leaned back, edging herself against the wall as she went down, one hand outstretched and holding the gun, the other upraised to shield her eyes.

"I'm glad you finally got here, Holly. We've been waiting."

Briscoe's voice resounded in the confined space, echoing painfully as if it were being broadcast through a loudspeaker.

Holly recoiled, squinting through her fingers, which were webbed with fractured splinters of blinding light.

She was able to make out his form. He was silhouetted directly in front of her, only twenty feet away. His voice filled her ears like a whisper in a tunnel.

"I knew you'd come. We were sure you'd figure out where we'd gone."

She felt off balance and raised the gun, gripping the weapon with both hands, trying to steady the barrel that wavered in front of her, concentrating with every fiber of her being to aim straight for his heart.

Beth's voice hammered breathlessly in her ears.

"Shoot him, Holly! Don't let him hurt me anymore."

"What are you waiting for, Holly? You want to kill me, don't you? Isn't that why you came? I told you I'd give that to you. That it would be my parting gift."

Holly's hands were shaking. Conflicting emotions clawed through her. He was right. She had come to kill him. Then why was she hesitating?

Why hadn't she pulled the trigger?

"You'd do anything to save your sister, wouldn't you, Holly? Even commit murder for her. I told her you would. She didn't believe me, but I said I'd prove it to her. I told you you'd do whatever it takes. So, what are you waiting for? Go ahead, shoot!"

Her vision swam. His image was moving in and out of focus as her mind reeled.

"You killed Laura," she gasped through her constricted throat.

"Poor, pathetic Laura," he responded. "Trying to protect her was so feeble, so unlike you. I expected much more of a challenge."

"And Pierson. Why did you kill him?"

"Why not? He deserved it. Someone would have eventually. I just got there first."

"What do you deserve?" she spat.

"Whatever I can get."

He deserved to die. He had to die. She had released him so he could murder again, and now she must see justice done.

"Then die!" she cried.

She stepped toward him and pulled the trigger.

At the shock of the exploding shell, her feet slid out from under her. She stumbled forward on the slippery surface as the gun jumped in her hand.

Shattering Briscoe into a thousand pieces, scattering him across the floor into hundreds of shards of broken matter.

Her mind recoiled. She felt reality splintering, as if she were staring into the broken lens of a kaleidoscope.

What she was seeing was not possible!

Her mind balked, refusing to accept the impossible.

Then, in an instant, she knew.

What she'd shot wasn't him, but his reflection.

She had been facing a mirror!

Magically, her vision cleared and she saw her sister.

Beth was there, facing her behind the rim of broken glass, her body illuminated by a stream of spidery light filtering down from the rusting skylight in the roof above.

She was naked except for the leather harness Holly had seen on the bed. Her head was shaved. A leather mask covered her eyes. Her mouth was filled with a plastic gag. Her arms were upraised. Leather cuffs surrounded her wrists, suspending her from a heavy chain fixed to a wooden beam above.

Holly realized that Beth could not have spoken. It must have been a recording. With horrific suddenness, Holly realized what had just happened.

If she hadn't tripped on the slippery planks, she would not have misfired. Her bullets would have gone directly through the mirror and killed her sister. That had been his intention. His final demonic act of revenge. To have her kill Beth, the one person in the world she loved and needed to protect.

The knowledge of what she had almost done caused her breath to freeze in her throat. She no longer felt rage, only desperation.

"You wanted me to kill her," she shouted. "To kill my own sister!"

There was no answer. Only her own voice echoing back to her. Then silence.

"Hold on, Beth!" Holly cried. "I'm coming!"

She started toward her sister, halting suddenly as freezing air moved into her face. She extended her arm. There was nothing in front of her.

It was almost impossible to see in the murk, but there was just enough light coming from the broken glass skylight above her for Holly to make out the dim outline of the area.

Beth was suspended from a beam that crossed above the open hearth where Shepard had told her iron had once been smelted. A circular walkway surrounded the pit. Bridging it was a rusting metal catwalk that arched spiderlike across the hearth below. Crossing this flimsy pathway, she realized, was the only way she could reach her sister. She had crossed it once with the detective, but the experience had sickened her. She felt it could give way at any second. But she no longer had a choice.

Holly tightened her grip on the trigger and stepped onto the catwalk, which trembled and shook under her feet. Bits of rotting wood and rusting metal showered down into the pit below.

Holly reached out for the handrail and looked down. The hearth was directly beneath her, a circular brick oven filled with murky water, gaping like an open mouth. She felt an instant of vertigo, but shook it off.

She inched forward on the quaking walkway, one hand on the fragile railing, the other still gripping the pistol. Her eyes peered into the dimness, struggling to see.

Something moved in front of her.

Holly tensed, sucking in breath and raising the gun warily. The object was moving back and forth. She inched closer until she realized it was only a strand of knotted rope dangling from the skylight above, and used to open and close the panes and allow for ventilation. The panes themselves were fractured like cakes of shattered ice.

Holly exhaled and inched forward. Beth was just ahead, only a few yards away, her body twisting back and forth slowly on the creaking links of chain. Holly would be able to reach her and pull her to safety, though the catwalk she was on was anything but safe. She prayed it would hold them as it had once held her and Shepard.

"I'm here, Beth! I'm coming. Just hold on."

Beth was trying to speak, but her mouth was blocked by the gag. Holly could hear the sound but could not understand her sister's vocal plea, though it sounded like a desperate cry for help.

She moved quickly as the metal trembled beneath her feet. The catwalk felt like a brittle skeleton that might shatter into pieces at the slightest shock.

She leaned over the railing and extended her arm, reaching out to Beth just a few feet away. He fingers touched her sister's face, sliding around to untie the mask. She flung it away into the darkness.

Beth was facing her. Sounds erupted from her throat. Her eyes were wide. Too late, Holly realized the sounds were screaming a warning.

Something flew at her out of the darkness like a swooping bat, wrapping itself snakelike around her neck and jerking her backward against the railing.

She lost her balance and felt herself going over. She reached out to grasp the handrail. The gun flew out of her hand and clattered along the catwalk.

Holly gasped for breath as the thong tightened. Both hands reached up to grasp it, to stop it from strangling her.

Suddenly he was there, behind her, his body pressed against hers.

His hands gripped each end of the braided leather, drawing it tighter around her windpipe. His body pinned her against the metal railing.

His breath came hot against her ear.

"Why fight me, Holly? I know what you want. What we both want. A way out of the loneliness. Of being afraid all the time. All you've got to do is let go."

"You murdering filth!" she cried through her burning lungs. "You wanted me to kill my own sister!"

"That's right, Holly. You're going to kill Beth. Just like everyone expects. Poor deranged Holly. So jealous, she couldn't stand her sister having the man she so desperately wanted, so she followed us and wound up committing murder."

"Wanting you?" she spat. "You disgusting, deranged son of a bitch."

He laughed.

"That's quite a mouthful."

The thong tightened, squeezing her throat closed. She tried to shout, but she could no longer speak. His lips were at her ear, but the sound seemed to come from somewhere far away.

"We're not so different, you and I. You wanted to kill me, didn't you? You came here for that. You felt the excitement when you pulled the trigger, you know you did. That wild explosion inside. The sense of freedom from everything that ever held you back. There's nothing like it, is there, Holly? You should thank me for letting you experience it. Did you come? I always do."

Holly twisted her head and spat directly into his face.

He drew down hard on the thong. The pain bit deep. She felt her throat contract, the cartilage snap. Her head swam. She felt herself dropping, falling into the darkness. Into the sweetness of oblivion.

The pressure eased. Her eyes opened. She could breathe again.

His breath entered her ear. "How does it feel? Being so

close to the edge. Just like Carolyn. And the others. In a minute, you'll understand. You'll feel everything she felt."

He shifted his position, his powerful thighs pressed tight against hers, drawing her closer against his belly. She felt the hardness of his sex against her buttocks. He held the thong with one hand as the other slid across her belly, moving lower, between her thighs.

"You belong to me now, little girl," he hissed in a strange new voice, one she had never heard. "You can hide, but I'll always find you."

It was his grandfather's voice, she realized. He wanted to enter her the way he had been entered, the way he had entered Carolyn. To end her life at the moment of his climax.

He was breathing hard. His skin was hot. His fingers gripped her. Holly stopped struggling, allowing his hand to possess her.

Her hand reached out, searching desperately in the fetid air.

The end of the knotted rope was dangling in front of her, just out of reach, only inches away.

"Come with me, Holly," he whispered. "Let me take you where I know you want to go."

His hand reached lower, sliding under the edge of her woolen skirt. His fingers slid up her thigh, probing beneath the edge of her panties. He caressed her sex, separating the lips and entering her with his fingers.

She forced a moan and leaned forward, as if to accommodate him. She felt his fingers penetrate deep inside her.

"That's the way," he uttered softly, moving slowly, insistently against her. "Go there with me, Holly. We can go there together. Just you and me. The way it should have been."

He eased up slightly, allowing her more air. She filled her lungs as she felt his hand reaching down behind her to unzip his fly. She heard the grating sound of the zipper in the stillness. In a moment he would be inside her.

Her fingers extended. Reaching. Groping. Just one more inch.

He pushed her skirt above her hips. She felt his sex against her leg as he bent her forward and separated her thighs with his knee.

"It's good, isn't it, Holly? Tell me how good it is."

"Yes," she gasped.

"Tell me you want to give me everything. Everything you have to give. Tell me."

"Everything," she whispered. "Everything I have to give."

The tips of her fingers touched the knot. But it slipped away.

His flesh probed against her.

"Yes" he cried. "Now!"

Her hand closed around the rope.

With all of her strength, she pulled it down.

For an instant, the rusted hinges resisted, tightened by the cold.

Then they gave way.

Her ears filled with the sound of tearing metal as the skylight came crashing down on top of them, exploding glass in all directions.

The frame struck Briscoe on the forehead, opening a huge gash above his eyes. His warm blood spurted across her cheek.

He cried out, dropping to his knees, clutching his eyes, and releasing his hold on her.

Holly fell sideways. Her knees struck the catwalk painfully. Her body almost fell through the opening, but she gripped the railing, trying to scramble away. She started to crawl.

Briscoe reached out and pulled the end of the thong.

The leather tightened around her neck, jerking her backward. Her body struck the floor; broken glass lacerated her skin.

She turned and looked up. He was crawling toward her. His face was covered with blood.

She turned quickly. The gun gleamed dully on the grating only a few feet away.

Holly dove for it.

She grabbed the handle and turned onto her back, bringing the barrel up toward him. But he was too quick. He sprang toward her. His body covered hers as his hand closed around her wrist, shoving her back down against the metal grating.

His finger slid over the guard, covering the trigger. His voice was a hoarse croak in her ear.

"We mustn't forget Beth. She's been waiting so patiently."

He forced her arm over, swiveling it toward Beth, suspended from the chain just on the other side of the railing.

"It's up to us to end her suffering."

Holly fought, trying to move her arm, but he was too powerful. His finger tightened over hers painfully.

"All you have to do is squeeze," he whispered.

His arm tightened, bringing the gun up. The barrel was pointed directly at Beth.

She jerked the barrel up just as he pulled the trigger.

The gun exploded in her ears. But the bullet flew away into the darkness, missing Beth.

"If at first you don't succeed," he whispered.

She struggled, trying to twist away, using all of her strength, but he was too powerful, crushing her against the rusty metal grating.

She reached back, trying to tear at his eyes. Her fingers were slick with blood as they dug into his skin.

She felt his finger tighten inexorably. His body was half over hers, pressing her painfully into the metal floor of the catwalk. Her face was down against the rusting metal. His breath against her cheek was mingled with hers. She could not fight him any longer. Her strength was gone. In another instant he would force her to pull the trigger, ending Beth's life.

She would not be his victim.

She looked up desperately. In front of her something gleamed. She drew her hand away from his face and reached across the grating.

Her fingers closed over a shard of broken glass.

Her arm was now totally extended. He lifted his body slightly as he pointed the gun. The barrel faced Beth at point-blank range.

His finger began to squeeze.

She had to do it now!

With the last of her strength, Holly twisted around. The force of her action upset his aim. The gun leaped in her hand as he pulled the trigger.

Her arm jerked back and over, then plunged down.

The glass sliced deep, entering between the double fold of tendons at the nape of his neck.

He screamed as it cut into his flesh. He half rose, and Holly rolled away from under him. The gun slid off the cat-walk, dropping into darkness.

Holly watched breathlessly as he tried to rise, placing his hands flat on the grating. He lifted himself to his knees, as he reached out to grasp the railing, struggling as he drew himself to his feet directly above her.

Both arms reached back, trying to clutch at the dagger of glass protruding from the base of his skull.

He drew it out covered with blood.

He stared at it. His eyes bulged. His mouth opened and closed, but no sound came. His eyes locked with hers as he staggered back against the flimsy handrail, his gray wolf's eyes now holding the look of a frightened child.

Holly cried out at the instant the metal gave way. Rising on one arm halfway off the grating, her hand reached instinctively toward him.

His body hung there suspended in midair as the railings dropped away. He turned, his hand reaching out to her. Their fingers almost touched.

Then he fell.

Tumbling into the abyss below, into the maw of the great open pit.

Holly stared down transfixed, unable to draw her gaze

away as his body splashed into the foaming pool of freezing water.

He struggled against the current. His hands rose, gripping the edge, trying to pull himself out of the hearth. But the sides were slippery with ice.

He fell back, gasping for air, his fingers clutching aimlessly as he slipped beneath the sub-freezing water. Then he went under. For a moment there was nothing, only the swirl of tumultuous darkness surrounding him like a foaming cloud.

One hand shot up from the depths, fingers spread, grasping for life.

Then it sank, lost in the frothing blackness.

"Holly!"

Shepard's voice exploded in the gloom. Holly turned toward the sound.

"Don't move. Stay where you are."

Shepard was climbing toward her from below. He reached the catwalk and began approaching her gingerly as it swayed dangerously beneath his weight.

He knelt beside her. She raised her face to his. There was blood on her cheek. He wiped it away. His eyes were warm, and she felt her heart open. She reached out and he took her in his arms. She clung to him, allowing the terror to ease, her emotions to subside.

"Briscoe?"

"Down there." He followed her gaze below.

"We have to get Beth," she whispered, raising her arm.

His eyes widened in surprise at the sight of her sister, her skin gleaming in the darkness.

"I'll take care of it."

He rose and started toward her.

The rain had stopped.

Clouds were moving off to the north, propelled by the

gusting winds. The sky was clearing, but it was still extremely cold.

They walked, Beth between them, back up the steep dirt road, until they reached Shepard's car. He had gone back for a blanket, and they wrapped Beth in it before they started out. She was still in shock and allowed them to lead her. Both her shoulders were dislocated, and she cradled her arms against her in a makeshift sling Shepard had fashioned from the gauze bandages in his first-aid kit.

They eased her inside the car, and Holly got in beside her.

Shepard got behind the wheel and they pulled away, heading back toward town.

Beth laid her head against Holly's shoulder. Her eyes were open; she stared straight ahead. She had not spoken, not even when they removed the gag, but her hands held Holly's in an unbreakable grip.

Beth glanced up as Holly brushed the hair away from her face. Their eyes met and Beth's lips formed the pale outline of a smile.

The temperature was falling. Rain clouds had cleared off. The sky was bright with stars. The moon appeared, huge and overwhelming above the interlaced branches of the ancient oaks. Its light played across the foundry and filtered down through the broken skylight, down to the hearth below where Briscoe lay suspended in the viscous liquid.

His mouth was open, his head was thrust back. His hands were raised one above the other, fingers clutching in a last desperate attempt to reach the surface. His eyes were open, staring fixedly into the darkness as the water congealed around him. Crystals of ice surrounded him like a school of tiny fish, shimmering as they froze.

By morning his body would be preserved within a solid block of ice. Only his hands would be visible, rising above the surface like sculpted images on a headstone.

Birds sheltered beneath the foundry's old iron beams

waiting for the storm to end. Now they fluttered up through the opening where the skylight had been.

Their wings beat rhythmically as they ascended toward the moonlit sky. One after another they escaped into the freezing night, free to fly anywhere they chose.

Look for Ron Cutler's next thriller,
coming in 2005 from Pinnacle Books.

The road wound along the river which shone like burnished metal in the fading light. It was broken in places where the asphalt crumbled to dirt compacted by tire tracks and the deep knuckled tread of tractors. The area was still rural, unblemished by the developers' tracts edging into the eastern side of the county. They still farmed here, the gently undulating fields separated by thick patches of wooded land.

It was late in October, yet the man still walked here every day at this hour, a figure in a black windbreaker moving with a purposeful stride along the edge of the road. He walked alone, taking the path that led away from the small stone farm house he occupied by himself. The house was nestled secretively within a dark glade where the river ran shallow over sharp rocks creating a rapids of swirling water. It was almost invisible from the road, providing a unique kind of seclusion. The man did not mix with his neighbors, other than to pick up groceries at one of the local stores. His bland features and quiet demeanor did nothing to mark him out of the ordinary. His comings and goings were not remarked upon or discussed. And if anyone mentioned that someone had moved into the old Caldwell place it was usually greeted with an indifferent shrug.

The man was tall and lean. His hair was close cropped framing a long pale face and watery gray eyes protected by aviator glasses with wire rims and opaque lenses. He had the look of someone used to being in control, but he offered no clues to his occupation, spoke seldom, and rarely smiled. Other than his daily solitary walk, he seemed almost invisible.

But then there was the boy.

The man had first seen him through the window of the house as the boy stood in the stream casting his fly rod. Fishermen often came to fish the rapids that fronted the property, but except for an occasional glance he was almost unaware of their presence. The boy was different. There was a special grace to his movements as he performed an intricate ballet with rod and line. The man watched fascinated as the fine filament caught the light and touched down on the surface without leaving a scar or ripple. The boy was beautiful to look at. His blond hair glinted like a helmet, setting off his deep set blue eyes and classical features. He had the body of a dancer with long well shaped limbs and wide shoulders. He lived on the neighboring farm and came to the stream almost every day. When he failed to appear the man felt an ache inside, a deeply resonant surge of desire that plunged through him like a foaming tide.

The intensity of the feeling would not abate. It tormented him throughout the day and disturbed his sleep. He tried to pray, kneeling on the cold wooden floorboards of the old house, fingers clenched around the rosary, trying to resist the temptation that seemed to be devouring his soul. He went to the closet and stared at the surplice that was now forbidden to him, but he did not put it on. The thought of wearing it was now was much too painful. At night, he stripped naked and lashed his back with his leather belt, raising painful welts and lacerating the skin until his back became a bloody washboard. But desire throbbed through him even through the pain, a desire he could not resist.

It had been his companion throughout his life in spite of the shame and degradation it continually put him through, and led ultimately to his downfall. But the thought of the boy's smooth thighs and quivering belly drove him to distraction. He could not help himself. The feeling was beyond his control. And when the boy next appeared he left the house by the backdoor, circling back into the woods until he emerged on the road farther down, heading toward where the boy was positioned on the bank as if he happened on the scene by accident.

He stopped and waited, watching as the line went taut and the rod bent signaling a fish on line. The trout flew up from the water and rose, twisting in the air as it fought to break free. The boy was expert, teasing the line, allowing it to play out, then reeling it in. It took almost twenty minutes until he gaffed it and dropped it into his basket. The effort exhausted the boy and he dropped onto the bank almost at the man's feet.

The man knelt and asked if he could see the fish. The boy turned, seeing him for the first time and smiled. "Sure." He said, "Go ahead." The man could see the glint of pride in the boy's eyes, the eagerness to show off his trophy. And so his courtship began. Exchanging bits of conversation. Locating where the boy lived and where he went to school, what he wanted to study and what his interests were. Useful bits of information, like the bait the boy used on his hook, unaware that what he provided might be used to hook him. They met, but not every day. The man had to be careful. Extremely careful. Someone might be watching. But over the next few weeks, things had progressed to the point where he felt safe enough to invite the boy inside ostensibly to see the old house, something the boy was curious to do.

The man had left the study door ajar when he went into the kitchen to get them a drink. He had left certain books and pictures around for the boy to see. Images filled the internet screen. The boy's face flushed when he examined them. The man could see his eyes fill with excitement. He allowed the boy to sate himself before he stepped inside with the tray. The visit did not last long. He had offered the boy a nibble, a glimpse of pleasures to come. Now he had only to reel him in.

He had picked the moment with off-hand casualness. The boy had mentioned an old barn dating to the early Dutch settlement. The man expressed an eagerness to see it and the boy offered to act as a guide. It would be a perfect opportunity. He had rarely been disappointed.

The man continued along the road. The boy would be coming from his house taking the path that led into the wooded glen dividing their property. The man intended to meet him there.

The road curved ahead. A path trailed off to the left, wriggled between several oaks, then pointed directly into the dark stand of trees beyond.

It was only four o'clock but the sky had already begun to darken.

The trees closed in quickly, forming a murky canopy over head. The man quickened his pace. His heart was already beginning to hammer. He felt daggers of excitement deep in his gut.

There was a quiver of movement ahead and the man thought he saw the boy approaching. But it was only a shadow.

The trunks grew thick on this stretch of the path. The light had almost disappeared. He continued between the thick stands of brush, then halted abruptly.

Someone was on the path ahead.

For a instant his heart rose with anticipation. But it was not the boy.

The figure remained motionless, silhouetted by the light filtering from above.

The man took a step toward the stranger, then another. He had only to pass him and continue. The thought that it might be the boy's father suddenly assailed him, but he quickly dismissed it. Even if it were, he had done nothing wrong. He was just spooking himself. It was probably just another fisherman or even a hunter out scouting the woods, since deer season was almost upon them.

He purposely broke a branch underfoot, stepping on the dead leaves so as to warn the stranger of his approach. But the stranger did not move.

He was only two or three feet away when the stranger turned.

His face was in darkness. The man saw only his eyes, dark and intense, glittering like a cat's.

"Nice to see you, Father Mckay. Out for a walk?"

Those were the last words he remembered before he smelled the suffocating odor and the darkness closed around him like a shroud.

He opened his eyes.

He felt as if the were emerging from a dream. At first he could see nothing in the gloom. Then gradually consciousness returned. It was dark and cold and he was crouched painfully in a narrow iron cage. His wrists and ankles were bound in heavy iron bracelets that chaffed his skin. He was dressed in some kind of robe beneath which he was naked. The air was cold on his flesh. The material had an almost paper like consistency that did nothing to warm his body. He shivered with terror as his fingers gripped the metal bars. He felt a dizzying sense of fear that forced him to cry out with a bowel wrenching moan. The sound came back to him, reedy and thin, like a dying bird.

His movements caused the chains to rattle. He was gripped by the dizzying sensation that he was about to plunge into darkness. He could hear his heart beat, pulsing like a trip hammer. He closed his eyes and forced himself to pray but lost the sense of the words. *Our father, who art . . . Our father* . . . He fought the surges of panic that bruised across him like crashing waves, trying to steady himself, to remain still. Slowly, his heart began to regulate. The effort exhausted him. His lids closed like leaden weights.

He lost all sense of time, as he lapsed in and out of consciousness. There was only the darkness and the fear and the constant terror of falling into some abyss. Somewhere in the void came the sharp creak of metal on wood, then the cage began to move.

He was being lowered, slowly, moving down into the darkness. He was overcome by a sense of vertigo and felt as if he were being sucked down into a void.

Light began filling the chamber.

He gripped the iron bars staring at the stark stone walls surrounding him. He was in some kind of crudely built tower, a structure from another age, huge and imposing.

The cage came to rest on the stone floor. He tried to speak but no sound came from his lips. He felt dizzy and his fingers gripped the bars as he tried to keep from falling. He closed his eyes and when he opened them the room was filled with light.

Two huge yellow tapers were set in metal stands, their flames flickering like searching tongues. They were set on either side of a towering podium that resembled a pulpit or a seat of judgment.

He felt a strange chill, an in-rushing sense of doom as if he were about to be judged.

"Father Mckay," a voice called, the sound echoing ominously.

He looked up. A dark figure sat at the podium. His face was shrouded beneath a hood.

Startled, Mckay realized that the figure was dressed in the black robes of the Inquisition. Mckay glanced down. He was wearing the scarlet robe of the accused. His mind reeled. This was madness. Something out of a medieval nightmare.

The hooded figure leaned forward. "You are accused of violating your holy orders and, using the cloak of sanctity, you sodomized over sixty innocent young men and boys. Have you anything to say before this court passes judgment upon you?"

"No!" Mckay shouted, his voice was a rasp. "You have no right to judge me. Who are you?"

"I am he who has been given the power to avenge."

"That right belongs to God," Mckay said in desperation. "The law released me. The statute of limitations had run out on the charges against me."

"I am not bound by such statutes. I ask you again. Have you anything to say in your own behalf before sentence is passed upon you?"

"This is wrong. The law released me. I can only be judged by God."

"I am bound by the Cipher. My duty is to bring to judgment those who have not yet been punished or those who have evaded punishment."

Mckay stared at the dark figure above him. His knees were shaking. He gripped the bars as he searched for something that would save him. But his mind refused to function. There was nothing he could say. He had been stripped of his priesthood and sent into exile while his church sought to deal with the multitude of lawsuits that stemmed from his transgressions. He had been tried and convicted in a court of law, then miraculously freed because the appellate court decreed that the statute of limitations had run on his crimes. He had taken that as a sign that he was being forgiven.

"I ask only for forgiveness," he pleaded. "I have repented for my transgressions and done penance. I deserve a reprieve."

"You must answer for what you did. And what you were about to do. Which places you beyond repentance."

Words caught in Mckay's throat, almost choking him. He could no longer speak. *They knew what was in his heart.* He was doomed. There would be no reprieve.

He dropped to his knees. His body shook and he began to sob.

"Please God, save me," he whispered.

There was the rustle of parchment. Then the voice intoned. "As you did unto others, so shall it be done unto you. So it is written in the Cipher. May God have mercy on your soul."

Mckay rose. "Mercy!" he cried. "Please, God. Have mercy."

There was no one there. The figure had disappeared. The podium was empty.

Mckay's mind was in turmoil. Was this real or had he been dreaming it? Was this just some monstrous joke. He laughed aloud and shook his head, trying to clear his thoughts. There was a creak of wood on metal as the cage slowly turned. It made half a revolution which was when he saw it.

A thin rod of bronze stood in the center of the bare stone chamber, pointed and tipped, glowing white hot.

For an instant he did not understand, then the horror speared through him as the chains jerked taut and the cage rose high above the floor.

"Please God no!" he shouted. "Have mercy on me!"

He heard the creak of the wooden joist as it lifted the cage and swung him over the glowing shape. Then the sound of the joist as it lowered him, cog by cog. The bottom of the cage fell away. He was suspended over the glowing rod. He heard the chains snap taut as they spread his legs apart and felt the intense heat searing his skin.

He heard the scream as if it were outside him, as if it came from someone else.

It was the birds that alerted him.

Ravens. Black-winged, their beaks like tiny spears. Bound in a kind of frenzy.

They rose in alarm as the curate made his way toward the thickly growing trees at the far end of the compound that housed the bishop's residence for the archdiocese. It was still dark when the curate had been awakened by the racket. He hastily dressed and went to see what was the matter. There was a layer of ground fog that reduced visibility to only a few feet. He carried a flashlight and wore a heavy jacket against the morning chill. He saw more clearly as he crossed the barren yard and approached the stand of trees that formed a kind of park at the far end of the walled acreage. The birds had gathered around something in the center of a small clearing within the trees. He could make it out now. A figure stood motionless in the center of the clearing. He must have been feeding the birds for them to have been reacting that way. It might have been one of the young priests, of which there were several housed in the main residence.

The curate squinted, trying to make out his features through the thick fog. He was about to shout a greeting when the words caught in his throat. *Something was wrong. . . .*

He halted at the edge of the clearing, his hand opened and dropped the flashlight, his eyes bulged in horror.

The figure was facing him. He was naked. His skin was bled of color, startling white, like the bleached bones of an animal. His body was suspended on some kind of metal frame like a grotesque scarecrow, the arms spread in a mockery of a crucifix. It took an instant for the curate to realize that the body had been hacked into four separate pieces, the flesh suspended from hooks like a slaughtered cow. And another moment to see that the figure's head was impaled on a spit that bisected the body. His face had been punctured by the sharp beaks. Blood ran from the empty sockets where the birds had been feasting. The features were bloated almost beyond recognition.

But it was a face he knew.

Nailed to the creature's naked chest was a long curving square of vellum. On it was a list of names. Names the curate recognized from the profusion of court cases now besieging the arch diocese. The names of those who had been violated. The curate realized that what was left of the man who had violated them was hanging there in front of him.

He was staring at the dismembered remains of Father Aubrey Mckay.

The curate shrank back, unable to detach his eyes from the grotesque images now suffusing them. He felt a sickening wave of nausea, but he fought back the reflex and turned, running back through the trees the way he had come. Feet pounding the path as he cried out, trying to erase the terror that now filled his mind.

In a moment, the birds returned, cawing down from the trees until they covered the body with a cape of fluttering wings.

BOOK YOUR PLACE ON OUR WEBSITE AND MAKE THE READING CONNECTION!

We've created a customized website just for our very special readers, where you can get the inside scoop on everything that's going on with Zebra, Pinnacle and Kensington books.

When you come online, you'll have the exciting opportunity to:

- View covers of upcoming books
- Read sample chapters
- Learn about our future publishing schedule (listed by publication month *and author*)
- Find out when your favorite authors will be visiting a city near you
- Search for and order backlist books from our online catalog
- Check out author bios and background information
- Send e-mail to your favorite authors
- Meet the Kensington staff online
- Join us in weekly chats with authors, readers and other guests
- Get writing guidelines
- AND MUCH MORE!

**Visit our website at
http://www.kensingtonbooks.com**

More Books From Your Favorite Thriller Authors

More Nail-Biting Suspense From
Your Favorite Thriller Authors

More Thrilling Suspense From Your Favorite Thriller Authors